The Master Yeshua

the Undiscovered Gospel of Joseph

The Master Yeshua

the Undiscovered Gospel of Joseph

Joyce Luck

Winchester, UK
Washington, USA

First published by Roundfire Books, 2015
Roundfire Books is an imprint of John Hunt Publishing Ltd., Laurel House, Station Approach, Alresford, Hants, SO24 9JH, UK
office1@jhpbooks.net
www.johnhuntpublishing.com
www.roundfire-books.com

For distributor details and how to order please visit the 'Ordering' section on our website.

ISBN: 978 1 78279 974 0
Library of Congress Control Number: 2014956327

A CIP catalogue record for this book is available from the British Library.

Design: Stuart Davies

Printed and bound by CPI Group (UK) Ltd, Croydon, CR0 4YY, UK

Author's Note

This book is a work of fiction, narrated from the point of view of a man named Joseph, the nephew of Jesus, a Joseph writing in or around 75 CE who in no way has ever existed anywhere except in the author's imagination. I have conceived of Joseph as a former Essene and now an Ebionite (or the *Ebionim*), those Jews who followed the Way of Jesus as taught by James the Just, Jesus' brother and the first leader of the Jerusalem Church on Mount Zion. The Ebionites all but vanished into history after the early Church Fathers selected the theology of St. Paul to be orthodox and declared the Ebionites and other groups heretical. However, as I tell my literature students, even fiction can often reveal great truths. It is up to the reader to discover them.

Note on the Manuscript

For the sake of clarity, I have changed many words or names to their modern-day counterparts: for example, Anatolia becomes Turkey; or I have used a modern-day name as a synonym, e.g., Joseph will write "The Great Sea" but sometimes use "the Mediterranean," or he will say "school" most of the time instead of *bet sefer* or *yeshiva;* or he will use "bath" interchangeably with *mikveh,* and so on. For simplicity, I also have him writing "Jew" interchangeably with "Judean" or "Israelite" or "Hebrew"; and "Israel," "Judea," "Palestine," etc. for the same basic provincial territory; and "Qumran" instead of "Secacah." In the same vein, he will write "church" or "church-house," or "Bishop" or "deacon," although assuredly those words did not exist at the time. Likewise, I have also called months by the names with which most readers will be familiar (e.g., October, May, etc.) even though the Hebrew calendar is very different (*Rosh Hashanah*, the Jewish new year or the Feast of Trumpets, most often falls in September, and the names of the month are, obviously, different.) I have also deliberately avoided giving actual years because our modern calendar differs from the various calendars of the time period under consideration. The reader may count the years if he or she pleases. If so, I'm working from the scholarly assumption that the historical Jesus was born in about 6 BCE and died in about 30 CE, although many good arguments (some of which I have also adapted) place his death squarely in 33 CE (hence the "historic earthquake" on April 3rd, 33 CE, which geological evidence seems to support, although the actual dates necessitate a broader window of about 26-36 CE). Where there are errors, they are either intentional for the sake of narrative fiction, or they are a failure of my own scholarship and that of no one else.

The Disciples

James the Just, the brother of Yeshua and first head of the Jerusalem Church

Jude, the brother of Yeshua, who is called Thomas or *Didymus*, the twin

Philip*

Simon, called Peter or *Cephas*, "the rock"*

Simon Peter's brother Andrew*

Nathanael, whose parents were of that land called Nubia*

Judas Iscariot, the treasurer, son of a wealthy Jerusalem merchant, the betrayer

James, son of Zebedee, called *Thaddeus*, "my heart"

John, son of Zebedee, brother of James and called "the beloved"

Matthew, the tax collector

Simon, the ex-Sicarii called "the Zealot"

Bartholomew, the freed slave

Mary of Magdala, sister of Philip and who replaced Judas Iscariot

*originally followers of John the Baptizer

Prologue

I was at prayer. Then, the pounding of running feet and the frenzied shouts of men outside the church-house donated by Eleazar startled me. I rose, left the courtyard, hastening down the corridor, and emerged, blinking, into the hot street.

Simon Peter's son, Mark, was with me, and someone rushing past saw us. He stopped, grabbing Mark's arm, pulling at it, fear in his voice as he addressed me.

"Hurry, Joseph, the priests have James," he said.

By that, he meant my uncle. Panic throttled me. Mark swore an oath under his breath, and we both joined the crowd hurrying up the hill towards the Temple Mount.

Mark, as Peter's son, had had his own problems with the High Priest Ananus *ben* Ananus—another of the Annas family, that same family whose High Priest Caiphas had arranged the crucifixion of my uncle Yeshua—and Mark was about ten years older than I, but he doggedly kept pace with me, the younger man in my thirties, as we sprinted towards the Temple. The dust kicked up in front of us by others running clogged my nostrils and filled my mouth, so I pulled my *tallit* over my face to keep from choking.

The people were all gathered at the corner of the eastern wall of the Temple, calling up to the priests to stop. You must understand: my uncle James, called the Just, was loved by all, Jew and Yeshua-follower alike; he led our Jerusalem church-house, the Mother Church, and also spoke in many synagogues and was the holiest of men. He never broke the Laws of Moses; he counseled love and humility, kept very little for himself except for what he needed to live on and otherwise gave all his money to the poor, just as his brother, Yeshua, had taught us. He prayed so much that great calluses covered his knees. James had never spoken against the High Priest, except to say that the man was failing in his duty to the Law to not share the Temple tithes with the rabbis of Judea.

Now we could see from the street that the Temple guards had seized James and the priests were hurling epithets at him, some of them beating him about the head and on his body, demanding that he renounce the blasphemy of the false Messiah.

"Stop! Stop this madness!" The cries around us got louder as we saw the guards drag James close to the wall, a half-dozen priests and Ananus following closely.

"Do not interfere! He has blasphemed against God!" Ananus called down to the crowd. "You all know the punishment for this sin."

"He's entitled to a trial," growled Mark. He raised his voice. "Ananus, you know that the prefect must agree with your sentence."

"But he is not here, is he?" called down another priest, and it was true. The Roman prefect, Festus, had recently died, and the new prefect from Rome had not yet arrived to take his place. I gasped at this realization. There was no one in any official capacity to stop them.

"You must not do this thing!" I called up, but my cries, and those of the crowd, went unheeded.

James, who was nigh near to seventy at this time, was not resisting. I could see his lips moving in prayer, and then it was as if time slowed down, and the next few seconds seemed to take an interminable number of hours.

At Ananus' order, the guards lifted the aged James, and as the people below, including me, including Mark, shouted in anguish, the guards threw him over the wall. James tumbled, his cloak whipping about him, crying out a most horrible cry, and then his frail body hit the ground with a thud. Everyone gasped. James lay still at first, then began moaning. His right leg was twisted in a most abnormal way, and it was clear the bones of that leg had shattered.

We could all see James lying there, now writhing and crying out in pain, but we could not get to him easily, for the eastern wall of the Temple backed up against the drop-off to the Kidron Valley. Still, Mark and I, and some others, began making our way to him, slipping and sliding on the rocky slope. Mark lost his footing and I grabbed his arm before he could fall, although his knee went down and was slashed by the rocks and pebbles. Choking back tears, horrified by what we had just witnessed, we continued on.

Then the priests, seeing that James had not died from the fall, began hurling stones down from the Temple Mount onto him. Those evil men—the lot all misguided Sadducees—must have planned this sentence for James, just as the Annas family had planned Yeshua's, and had gathered a pile of rocks in advance for their wicked purpose. Some of the stones came deathly near to us the closer we got to my suffering uncle.

"If we hit one of you, we will not take responsibility!" called down Ananus; and Mark let loose a stream of oaths, promising revenge that I knew he would never take, because our Lord had forbidden it, but Mark, much like his father Simon Peter had been, was a man of great temper and often rashly loosened his lips to vent rage.

And then it happened. A large stone, well aimed, was dropped directly on top of James's head, crushing his skull.

His groans stopped, and he was still, blood forming a pool around him.

The priests turned and left the edge of the wall as a great wail went up from the crowd.

I finally reached my uncle's side and knelt next to him, lifting my eyes to heaven, weeping, keening a cry of grief that grew louder and louder until I thought my heart would burst.

"Why, God?"

* * *

James the Just, brother of the Lord, was buried in the Kidron Valley by us that very day, as the Law requires the dead must be buried before sunset. Mark, I, and some others carried his body down the slope into the valley, while others went to fetch a linen shroud to wrap his body in and water with which to wash and purify him. Still others dug a pit for the burial. A rabbi from one of the synagogues, a man named Samuel, who had much loved James and admired his wisdom—although Samuel did not view Yeshua as the Messiah but only as a prophet—came to bless the body. I, as James's nephew, also said a few words and prayed aloud to God, and inside my heart I prayed that James and Yeshua would reunite in heaven and continue in the afterworld in service to the Lord. We tenderly laid James into the ground with his head facing the Temple then filled in the grave with dirt. The gravesite was marked by a stone, and all those who were there vowed to take up a collection to purchase a small stele and carve the name of James into it to mark his burial site in a fashion more befitting someone of James's status.

What is not known is that a few nights later, Mark, I, and some other trusted members of the church-house returned well after sunset, about halfway through the moon's ascent into the heavens, as all in Jerusalem slept, to the site where James was buried. There is, of course, no Law that says a body cannot be moved after it is buried. And there was a tomb for the family of Yeshua, a tomb that had been kept secret ever since it was first hewn at the beginning of my uncle's ministry.

We placed James's body onto a stretcher, filled the burial pit back in, then tamped down the soil and kicked stones over all to make the grave appear undisturbed. (Eventually the promised headstone—or stele—was erected, and no one else was any the wiser that James no longer rested there.)

No, we carried James stealthily in the night several miles to the property of the family of Joseph of Arimathea, who had, along with the Essenes, paid to have a simple family tomb constructed for the family of Yeshua. At the beginning of Yeshua's ministry, since he was to be the Messiah, it had seemed only fitting to have such a tomb hewn into the rock, although it was very humble and small. The only decoration on the outside was carved over the entrance: a pyramid shape with a circle representing the sun. This was done to honor Yeshua as both Messiah and avatar of the Great Brotherhood, a body of mystics representing many lands and religions, to which Yeshua had belonged. He had taken his final initiation before his ministry in the Great Pyramid in Egypt—an honor bestowed upon only the most worthy of initiates.

When we rolled back the stone and brought James into the tomb, we laid him into one of the niches, or loculi. The custom was to let the body decompose, and return a year later to place the bones into a limestone box called an ossuary.

I paused a time as the others waited outside for me, for this was also my family tomb. In it were my grandfather Joseph, after whom I was named, the first to have been laid in, his bones dug up from his grave in Nazareth and moved to the tomb shortly after its construction. The next to go in was Yeshua himself, in secret, several nights after his crucifixion. I walked over to the ossuary in which laid his bones and rested my hand upon it for a moment, my head bowed in reverence.

"Uncle," I said, "James is now here with you, gathered also to the bones of his father."

My grandmother Mary was in the tomb, and my other uncle Joses, also my aunt and a cousin, and finally my own beloved wife, who had died of a sickness not long after giving birth to our only child and daughter, Rachel. It was then, and remains, my hope that one day my own bones will be placed into the ossuary with those of my wife. How I have longed to join her!

The remains of Mary of Magdala, although she was not a family member, rested additionally in this tomb, for she had no tomb when she returned to Jerusalem from her travels in Gaul, and it had seemed only right and fitting for her to be laid here with Yeshua, as she had been a beloved disciple and apostle.

Tears streaking my cheeks, I knelt and scratched with my knife the words "James, son of Joseph, brother of Yeshua" onto the side of the ossuary that would hold James's bones when we returned in a year. I then returned and looked upon my uncle's shrouded body.

"Bless you, James, and may we meet again in the Kingdom of Heaven," I said.

I left the tomb, and we all rolled the stone back into place. I did not know then that the next time I visited the tomb would be my last.

* * *

The death of my uncle James, now some thirteen years ago, was the catalyst sparking off all Israel's descent into utter chaos, when the people had finally had enough of the Romans and their puppet Herodian kings and enough of the Sadducee priests who colluded with them both, so the rebels—the Zealots and Sicarii—stepped up their actions after James's death, but to no avail. Rome merely further tightened its grip on us. The priesthood, for the most part, became even more corrupt and Ananus positively unbearable, even though the new prefect sent him to Herod Agrippa to depose him for what he had done to James, when the Pharisees complained of this illegal execution on the arrival of the prefect. Yet that was the only action he had taken, so the Annas family still controlled the Sanhedrin. Finally, some four years after James died, the entire province of Palestine—Galilee, Samaria, and Judea—erupted into full-fledged rebellion. During the worst of it, brother turned on brother, and within the walls of the Holy City itself, under siege by the Roman emperor's son Titus, rebel Jewish faction at last turned against rebel Jewish faction. Jews were killing Jews.

At first I had thought then, including even Simon, the last and youngest of Yeshua's brothers and who had taken over the head of the Mother Church to replace James as Bishop of Bishops, that finally, the prophesied End of Times had arrived, but that did not happen. No, despite our taking early victories, the Romans destroyed us, carrying away many Jews as slaves, burning Jerusalem, and throwing down the Temple. Titus stole the Temple treasury, the great golden Menorah, the table for the shewbread, and many other holy objects that to him were nothing but gold to be seized as booty.

Our beautiful Temple no longer stands, and only the pitiful western wall that had served as part of the foundation for the Temple platform itself remains.

Yeshua's prophecy that no stone would be left standing of the Temple, a prophecy he'd made some forty years before, has therefore now been fulfilled. All is destroyed, not just the Holy City, but even remote Qumran, where I was in my twenties as a brother of the Community of the *Yahad,* and so many held dear to me have now died or been martyred.

Why am I even alive?

I am approaching fifty, considered an aged man. I should be dead. In terrible moments of the blackest despair, I wish I were dead. Yet my uncle Simon still lives, and he is almost eighty, and he forges on, resolutely.

I suppose I have survived because I reside in Pella, in the Decapolis territory, which was to where Simon, we Ebionites, and about half of the Essene Brethren from Qumran fled when the rebellion broke out. We are all Followers of the Way, Jews who are followers of the Messiah Yeshua—and war is never the Way, as our Lord and Master instructed us.

And now I sit here, at this table banged together from scraps of wood scavenged from here and there, in the little church-house I oversee. I live here with my daughter, Rachel, who preaches most eloquently, and her husband, Daniel, who farms.

And I am thinking about something my uncle Yeshua once said to me when I was but a child of three, almost four, when most of the family and a crowd of followers came with him to Jerusalem to celebrate the Passover. I did not know then that Yeshua would be crucified just two days later.

Yeshua had said to me, squatting in front of me, reaching out to tousle my hair, then looking intently at me with his soft eyes, "One day, my nephew, you will set down my story the way it really happened."

Perhaps I have lived to fulfill these words as well. And then I can finally die.

Aleph: Birth and Early Life

Chapter One

I am Joseph *ben* Jude, my father the brother of our Master Yeshua, and, like his brother James the Just, one of Yeshua's disciples. As Yeshua's nephew, I am also of the one hundred and twenty. Having now determined to set down my uncle Yeshua's story, I've asked my daughter, Rachel, to procure for me many sheets of parchment made of goat skin—for it is a long tale—and to obtain for me several reed pens. The ink I have made myself out of charcoal, for much of my life I was a weaver of textiles, even though that is considered by most to be women's work, and ink is easier to make than the dyes I once created. I am proud of my occupation as weaver. In my earlier life I tended a few sheep that provided my wool, or I gathered flax, and I was well known as a maker of garments whose dyes held their color, including even the famous blue dye that no one can copy unless they know its secret; and when I was in Qumran in my twenties, I was weaver of the white linen robes worn there by the Brethren. After my sojourn in Qumran, I traveled the land to preach the Way of my uncle Yeshua, and I sold my textiles—garments, scarves, cloaks, prayer shawls, even mats—in the forums, or marketplaces, to earn my living. Truly, my aging hands are no longer nimble, so Rachel has learned spinning and weaving from me and now does most of that work; but, if I go slowly, certainly I can write. Now, I concede that my Greek is only passable. I am no great wielder of words as was Homer. But, I will use Greek since it is now the common written language. I would hire a scribe to take down my words, for that would be easier, but that seems to me a waste of coins better spent on the poor since I am perfectly capable of writing this narrative myself.

I will confess I'm also using Greek because I harbor a silent wish: if it is the will of God, may these words one day make their way to the Gentile converts brought to Yeshua by Paul, that self-appointed apostle. Paul, may peace be upon him, never knew Yeshua as did my family, and I have heard some letters of Paul's read aloud in church-houses as I sat there flinching at his words, so I must be clear: Paul did not have authority from either the Mother Church, or James, designated the First Bishop by Yeshua, to serve as an apostle. Paul was given permission by James to preach the Word and the Way to the Gentiles, but James never made him an apostle, and then Paul, sadly, strayed from the path. Even Simon Peter, as stubborn and suspicious as he was, had been willing at first to give Paul a chance, but he ultimately came to consider the man untrustworthy for his distortions and rejection of the Law, and Peter came to speak of Paul most bitterly. This was because Paul began adding his own interpretations and theology to what he'd been told of Yeshua's teachings, attaching his own meaning to Yeshua's spiritual Resurrection, and he began teaching that one could be saved through faith alone and not also through good works.

My uncle James and my father, Jude, tried to correct this misperception by sending letters of their own to the various churches, but I am not sure that their words have struck the mark. Therefore, the situation we, the Ebionites (it means "the poor men") find ourselves in at present lies heavy with irony: some Jews hate us because they think we believe, like the pagan converts, that Yeshua is a god, or the literal Son of God, yet we do not, for there is only *one* God, *one* Divine Presence; whereas the Gentile Yeshua followers, now called Christians, think we err, are too Jewish in following the Torah, and they believe we blaspheme by not calling Yeshua a god.

Aside from Paul's letters and a collection of Yeshua's sayings written by my father (he resembled Yeshua so much that he was given the nickname Thomas or *Didymus*, the twin), there are two recent books of which I am aware that tell the story of Yeshua, but they are incomplete, and the second one even makes up a miraculous birth story, added, no doubt, to appeal to the pagan

Romans. Their gods are always born in some astounding way, such as Athena being full-born from the head of Zeus: and these miracles are common not just among the Roman pagans—consider Krishna, one of the Hindu gods, said to be born of a virgin. God is great, and God is benevolent, but the Divine Presence assuredly does not break his own laws of nature for no good reason. It is also a custom to attribute works written by unknown persons to persons of authority, and the earliest of these books about Yeshua, Mark, was assuredly not written by my old friend, although he was a frequent companion of his father in his travels, so I can see why his name was chosen; and the other is said to have been written by Matthew, who could not have written it since Matthew the disciple is long dead, and the book only recently appeared. Otherwise, there is much in the two accounts that is true, but there is also much in the books that is missing, and some that is simply incorrect.

So, to set the story aright, I must begin with the beginning, and that is to explain how Yeshua came into this world as the prophesied Jewish Messiah, and as the avatar of the new Piscean Age representing the Great Brotherhood. By avatar, I mean a gifted human being so insightful into his own divine nature that it is not an exaggeration, or much of one, to call him a human emanation of the Divine Presence. There have been other avatars, but this narrative is concerned with Yeshua only: although, as you will see, Yeshua certainly studied the teachings of these others and was inspired by them.

By way of providing needed background, the first piece of information to know is that my uncle Yeshua, and all my family, was raised as an Essene. Our family—aunts, uncles, cousins, all of us—have been Nazarean Essenes for many generations. We Essenes believed Yeshua had been chosen by God even before he was born. Indeed, all the Great Brotherhood—of which the Essenes were participants—had long anticipated Yeshua's arrival. His coming was foreseen by many prophets, Isaiah and Daniel among them. Therefore most people, even the Romans, knew that a Jewish Messiah had been prophesied for many generations. Word had spread so that even the Persian Zoroaster had confirmed the coming birth of a great savior. Now, the Persians, like the Egyptians, are excellent astrologers, and they shared their knowledge freely with the Essenes in exchange for our wisdom. (Our contact with Gentiles, incidentally, was one of the many reasons the Pharisees and Sadducees disliked the Essenes, although we did not eat of the Gentiles' food or sit at table with them since that is forbidden.) But well before Yeshua's birth, from the Persian magi the Essenes knew of a rare sun, moon, and two-planet conjunction (Saturn and Jupiter) that would be occurring in the sign of Pisces, a conjunction said to herald the birth of a mighty king. At Qumran, the Essenes referred to this knowledge as the Messianic Star Prophecy. Also, according to the movement of constellations in the precession of the equinoxes, we were leaving the Age of Aries and entering into the Age of Pisces, the fish; and, since Rome had seized all Palestine—so our land, given to us by God, no longer belonged to us—the time seemed ripe for the promised Messiah to come.

In consequence, knowing the time was now at hand, the Essenes tasked themselves with finding a suitable husband and wife to be parents to the child who would be the Messiah. This sounds, perhaps, presumptuous, but the Essenes read Scripture carefully and meditate and speak with God, and we practice various arts of divination and reading signs, so we saw ourselves only as carrying out the will of the Lord. If it turned out the child was not the true Messiah, then the child would not be the Messiah. Truly, God knows all, and in this sense all things are predestined, but the gift of free will adds a variable to humankind's knowledge of the future, so that it is more correct to say that human beings are *potentialed*. We choose to act on our potential, or we do not.

The Essenes thus set out to create the circumstances in which

Yeshua might be helped to reach his full potential as Messiah. The Nazarene Essene community at Mt. Carmel was selected to do the primary work of nurturing and teaching the child, instead of the community at Qumran, because another prophecy stated that the Messiah would be of Nazareth in the Galilee, a land already seething with rebellious cutthroats and bandits who despised the Romans and hated their own poverty, although the child would be born in Bethlehem (being from the House of David). Mt. Carmel is but an easy day's walk from Nazareth. Indeed, from the hills above Nazareth, Mt. Carmel can be seen, with a most glorious view of the plain, which is lush and green and is the best farmland in all Israel.

Abiding in the village of Nazareth was a righteous Essene named Joseph, schooled at Mt. Carmel, and by trade an artisan or *tekton* (a contract builder—since most houses are built of stone, which is ample, whereas good wood is harder to come by, my grandfather Joseph worked mostly as a stonemason, although he did occasionally work in wood when larger projects weren't available, making doors or door frames or fashioning plows). My grandfather Joseph was widowed, his wife having died in childbirth. He had never married again, so he was childless. He was also of the House of David, and thus a son of Joseph would fulfill that portion of the Messianic prophecy. Joseph traveled to Qumran to be examined by the Essene Council of Elders, and they were satisfied Joseph had no self-serving agenda in being father to the Messiah and wished only to serve the Divine Will.

Choosing the mother of Yeshua was not as easy. Twelve Essene maidens, one to symbolically represent each of the twelve tribes of Israel, were selected to be taught and trained in the Mt. Carmel school, of whom Mary was one. Her mother, Ann, had dedicated her daughter to this work when Mary was just four years old. Now, all of the virgins were worthy for various reasons, but since Mary was ultimately the one chosen by a sign from God, the reader of these words will perhaps indulge me in a digression about my grandmother Mary.

She was a miracle herself! I will try to not wax rhapsodic, especially since I knew her best only when she was aged, but even then I could plainly see she was a beautiful spirit in a glorious vessel, like Sarah had been to Abraham. Even with a careworn face and streaks of gray in her hair, she remained—well, a vision of beauty. The very face of Love. Yet there was a determination about her as well, and a playful seriousness—I recall a time when we all lived in Capernaum, when I was a child, that I climbed a tree to retrieve a trapped kitten and froze in fear when I turned to come down and realized how high I had gone. My grandmother did not hesitate when she heard my panicked cries. She climbed that tree as nimbly as a cat herself, and, reaching me, began backing down the tree so I could follow her route; or if my foot would not reach, making a foothold for me with her own hands. Once her own feet were back on solid ground, she reached up, said, "Let go," lifted me, and set me down safely. "So, Joseph," she said, now that I and the kitten were rescued. "What do you think? Is it wise to risk your life to save another creature?"

"No, *Savta,*" I said.

She ruffled my hair. "How can you say that, when both you and your kitten have been rescued? God saves all those who do good in His name—even if your old grandmother is the one He sends to do His work."

It is a good lesson.

So, I imagine my grandmother as a young girl, and I picture her as fearless yet pretty, loving yet strong, all at the same time. I can see why, when Joseph and Mary reached Bethlehem for Mary to give birth, some men in the inn are said to have taunted him, the old man in his thirties, for having such a sweet young wife who embodied so many different qualities. Some of what they implied was outrageous—"What, did he offer to pay her dowry himself?" and "Seems as if a father has taken his own daughter as a wife" and things such as that—but Joseph ignored them. The Divine had smiled on him, and he knew it. We should all be so blessed.

I never met my grandfather—he died before I was born—but I think I would have loved him very much.

Back to Mary and how she was chosen of the twelve virgins.

All the maidens were schooled, protected, raised in purity, and were devout. The Nazarean Essenes prayed for guidance, then simply waited for God to make His choice. It happened on a normal morning when Mary was fourteen, as the maidens were climbing the temple steps at Mt. Carmel on the way to greet the sunrise for morning prayers. Let me hasten to explain that the temples at our schools and communities are not intended to be replacements for, nor modeled after, the Temple in Jerusalem. Our temples are places of worship, and though they do contain an altar, anyone may approach the altar, and we do not sacrifice animals. Essenes did not accept this ancient and barbarous practice. Instead, many burned incense upon the altar, especially sandalwood, which is said to open the body's centers and make one more receptive to God.

That morning, Mary happened to be the maiden leading the way. As she climbed the final step to the platform, a descending dove appeared and alighted on her shoulder. Stunned, Mary held still for a moment, waiting to see what the dove would do. It stayed, content to rest a short time, then moved closer to Mary's face and perched there, where it tarried for some minutes. This was a clear sign: the dove of Noah, the dove of peace; a white bird long revered even back to Egyptian times and the birth of the Great Brotherhood.

The Divine had chosen my grandmother Mary. Oh, what a blessed miracle! The dove stayed a while longer, then simply took flight. Mary fell to her knees and thanked and blessed the Lord, as did everyone who bore witness to the scene, including the eleven other virgins. The choice of Mary over the others made even more sense when one considers that, although through her father she was of the tribe of Levi, through her mother's father she was of the tribe of David. So Yeshua would be twice of the Davidian line, a true King of Kings.

And now I am tired. Writing these things down, and recollecting, then joining together all these scattered tidbits of information, is like painting with a very small brush, and my aged hands can do only so much at a time. I must ask Rachel to apply a soothing balm, and I will rest my eyes for a while. I do not know why I am all of a sudden adding a record of my own days to this narrative. I suppose these are the things one goes back to strike out before copying out the next scroll. I confess, I have never written my own book before. Until now, I have only copied out the words of others, and that was at Qumran, in the scriptorium.

But I did pause just now to look up, briefly, at my daughter Rachel, who arrived here with refreshment. She knows me so well—knows when I tire, keeps a careful watch on her old father. She pleases me very much, is learning my profession as I have said and also teaches others in the Church and is devout in our ways. Her husband, Daniel, loves her as well as I do, for I do not think it is possible for anyone to love her any more.

* * *

I have put down much information to take in and digest, to be sure; and for this I express sorrow; this knowledge has been kept secret among the mystics for so long that it flows from my mouth as if by rote and I forget that all the world has not heard these things. I pray I do not rush through things too quickly. But it is a glorious morning, and I am well rested, ready to continue the story.

Towards one of the last years of Herod the Great's life, Mary was wed to Joseph in the month of January. I regret I cannot be precise about the year and day because the Essene calendar (which is solar, based on the calendars of Enoch and Jubilees) differs from the regular Jewish calendar (which is solar-lunar, based on the Persian calendar adopted during the Babylonian Exile). This is why sometimes Passover and other Feast days fall on different days for the Essenes, as opposed to other Jewish groups—yet another of the many reasons the Sadducees and Pharisees disliked us. Mary was sixteen, a maiden, and after they wed, she and her husband commenced conjugal relations, as is natural. Shortly thereafter, Mary found herself with child.

No, an angel did not appear and inform my grandparents that Mary, a virgin, would conceive a child by the Holy Spirit descending upon her. Neither was she like Leda and impregnated by a swan. Nor was she like Isis, turned into a kite and impregnated by a false phallus attached to Osiris, whose dismembered body Isis had otherwise been able to collect back together. Yeshua was made in the normal way: and this is miracle enough, for do not miracles reside in everyday things? I have too often forgotten this myself, worn down by the cares of the day.

Now, to back up a little and explain a thing that was occurring simultaneously. Elizabeth, my cousin (thrice removed), was my grandmother Mary's cousin, albeit considerably older than Mary since Elizabeth was the daughter of Mary's great aunt; Elizabeth was also with child. There is one story circulating about Elizabeth that is incorrect: that she was raised in the Temple of Jerusalem. That idea is somewhat logical since she had married a priest, Zacharias, but Elizabeth herself was an Essene and "raised"—really, just raised and taught in our ways, in Ein Kerem, the same place where I took my schooling, which is four miles to the west of Jerusalem, in the hills. How, you may ask, is it that a Temple priest can marry an Essene, whom the priests hated?

Indulge an old man in another digression. Women are not officially Essenes. They are referred to as "associates." Or, this is how it was. I'm afraid I keep going back and forth between past and present when describing the Essenes. It's because I'm not sure what to call us anymore. Now the survivors are followers of Yeshua—well, at least most of us are; the last hold-outs not killed at Qumran went to Masada, where they perished—and many call us "Nazoreans" today. Or Ebionites, as I have written. And already followers of Yeshua are as diverse and different as the various sects of Jews.

Essene women are schooled, trained, study, and are members of the community just like any man except that they do not officially go through the initiations into the upper degrees—at least not so in Judea or Galilee. In Egypt, they do. I think this is simply out of respect for Jewish custom and also so that we don't call additional negative attention to ourselves. Jewish women, considered one step up from Gentiles, were not even allowed beyond the second court in the Temple in Jerusalem. So people would not understand women being initiated into the highest degrees and serving on the Council of Elders. And yet, their opinions, intuitions, visions, dreams, and insights are highly valued. We do not in practice consider them "lesser" than men. Yeshua was right when he later called all of this hypocritical, of course, by saying they are equal yet not allowing them to be formally initiated. I will say one thing: if it hadn't been for my grandmother Mary intervening in the family when Yeshua diverged from the expected path early in his ministry, Yeshua may very well have been rejected by even us as the Messiah. There was a brief time my uncles feared he had lost his mind. It was my grandmother's persuasion that put us onto Yeshua's new path.

I see I have strayed far, far away from the story. Well. Elizabeth and Zacharias bore a son late into Elizabeth's life. Since she was already beginning to cease her menses and as yet had been childless, the pregnancy was a surprise. Both she and Zacharias felt their prayers had been answered, so they dedicated their child to God. He could, of course, have been a priest in the Temple, and this was Zacharias' first thought when a healthy son was born. Elizabeth, however, had dreamed a dream in which an angel of the Lord indicated the child would have a higher purpose. As prophesied, a person was needed to herald the coming of the Messiah. The Essene High Council agreed, since Elizabeth was Mary's relative and Mary was by then already pregnant with Yeshua. It was quite perfect, actually. So Elizabeth and Zacharias—for a Temple priest, a humble man and a true servant of the Divine, a genuine Levite, not one of those who bribed the Romans or the Sadducees for his position—agreed to send their son to an Essene school—in this child's case, Qumran—and train him in this most special of missions. He is, of course, the man now known to us as John the Baptist, called the reincarnation of Elias.

Having referred to the angel, I should be wise—I do not wish to be misunderstood—and digress once again to write down an explanation of them. These beings are guardians and helpers. Scripture always has people falling down in fear at the sight of one, but that is not how the Essenes viewed angels. According to Scripture, Enoch took his place among the celestial beings as heaven's scribe, so like human beings they are servants of God, only closer to Him. They may appear in dreams or in the waking state as visions of light, mostly to convey messages. Often the communication is shrouded in mystery and it is left to the human being to interpret it. This, of course, is one way the Lord may intervene without removing free will. For although the Divine is all-knowing and all-powerful, thus making predestination a truth, as I have written, free will inserts a variable. We may choose as God does not will us to choose.

The Essenes believe that an angel is assigned to each incarnating human soul at birth, for guidance and protection; for special persons, they may indeed have more than one angel given to them. I suspect Yeshua had many. I believe my angel calls for help assisting me at times. I feel his presence at my right shoulder if I quiet my mind; and during times of trouble, I sense the others.

This is, again, difficult to explain to those uninitiated in the mysteries. Perhaps I sound like a rambling old man who has lost possession of his senses.

Nevertheless. This is the story of how Yeshua's parents were chosen, how his cousin John the Baptist was chosen, and how the Nazarean Essene community was charged with Yeshua's education. Now I must gather some old letters from my father and Uncle James and read over them. Then, in a few days, I will set down the story of Yeshua's birth and his flight into Egypt.

Chapter Two

For the first six months of my grandmother Mary's pregnancy, Joseph, by all accounts a rough man although pious—and by "rough," I mean his face and hands were burned by the sun, his beard ragged and graying, his hands gnarled from some of the knuckles having been smashed from dropped stones or other accidents in his work—Joseph cared tenderly for his young wife.

Mary told us later that she had teased him: "I am perfectly capable of fetching water from the well," but as she suffered bouts of nausea during her first three months, Joseph asked a neighboring Essene's wife if she would not help her, and she gladly did. However, no one but the Council of Elders at Qumran, the leaders at Mt. Carmel, our extended family, and a few others—as needed—at this time were told that Mary was carrying the Messiah and that Elizabeth, great with child, was carrying his herald.

When news reached my grandparents in Nazareth that Elizabeth had given birth to John, a healthy son, Mary and Joseph packed a few things, shut up the house, and traveled south to Jerusalem, to Ein Kerem, to be with the small Essene community there as Mary's own time approached in a few more months, and for Mary to assist her cousin with the babe. All of this had been prearranged.

There is a story that circulates in which Mary and Joseph traveled to Bethlehem when Mary was great with child, just days before Yeshua's birth, due to a census called by Caesar, which was said to require men to return to the cities and towns of their births. But this is false. Yeshua was already at least a dozen years old when this census took place. Besides, the Roman census takers were merely collecting information about families' land holdings and other property so that they would be able to calculate the taxes that caused so much hardship among the

Jewish people. Joseph was not required to go to Bethlehem for that—the census took place wherever one resided, for that is where one's property and goods are. No, the truth is, Mary and Joseph were already near Jerusalem, and when Mary's time approached, they took the short trip to Bethlehem, for Yeshua was to be born in a prepared Essene grotto there. This was done strictly to fulfill the prophecy of Micah, for did he not prophesy that out of Bethlehem would arise a great king, a king greater than David?

Let me pause to describe the typical Essene grottoes. These are caves, but they are in no way uncomfortable. Although the Essenes at Qumran isolated themselves by choice, others scattered about the land did not. And unlike the more apocalyptic Brethren at Qumran, many of whom were trained as soldiers in addition to being scribes—other Essenes would never raise a finger to harm any other person—customarily, not even animals did we eat, and as I have written, we certainly did not agree with sacrificing them. Essenes followed very seriously the principle of "care for your neighbor." It is better to suffer yourself than to abide the suffering of others. Hence, the Judean and Galilean countryside is spotted with grottoes where we stored medicines and herbs (the usual kinds, such as stinging nettle, rhamnus, bollata, willow bark, mallow, lavender, ginger, and so forth). For the superstitious who believed their illness was caused by a demon, we did have incantation bowls and would speak the ritual words, but this was more to help ease the mind of the afflicted, for as a general rule we believed—and the remainder of us still believe—demons are more maladies of spirit rather than genuine evil entities. (But to believe in them is to give them power.) We also made rooms available to weary travelers, to whom we offered food and gave rest. In every major city, there was what we called an "Essene gate" with nearby lodgings for the same purpose—to offer healing treatment, solace, rest, and to welcome visitors to the city. We even had an

Essene gate in that now-destroyed city of strife, Jerusalem.

Now, in the heat, the grottoes are cool and pleasant; in the cold, they remain warm and cozy when the fires are lit. They are also generally rather large. Part of the cave may be natural, but it is normally extended by further cutting into the rock and creating several rooms—not unlike the underground tombs hewn out of stone for the Pharaohs in Egypt. The surfaces of the rock walls are covered with a mud plaster throughout, and in some of the main rooms, the walls may be further painted over with various decorative scenes: but no idols. The floors of habitable rooms are laid with stones and sanded down or burnished, although storage rooms or upper rooms where animals are kept are usually part of the natural cave and have dirt floors. Ample light is provided by oil lamps that burn in carved-out niches in the walls, and ventilation is achieved by inner windows and doorways that connect rooms and by airshafts cut through the rock to the surface. I have not personally visited the grotto in which Yeshua was born, but I have been inside the one near Mt. Carmel on one occasion, and it was as comfortable, safe, and secure—perhaps even more so—than any house above ground.

And this comfortable place with its privacy is an additional reason the grotto just outside Bethlehem was chosen. Joseph knew well in advance which inn in the town to enter and to speak to the innkeeper, who was the Essene in charge of hospitality, his home near the Essene gate, and he anticipated Joseph's visit. This brother merely left the inn with Joseph and Mary following and led them to the prepared cave where the midwife was quickly summoned to assist, for, as it turned out, the baby was coming too soon.

The true wonder of this story is that Yeshua's birth did indeed coincide with the conjunction in the sky of the four heavenly bodies. It was as if Yeshua himself in the womb knew when to be birthed, because he was born a month early, in October—although this premature birth would later lead his enemies to accuse Mary of being with child before marrying Joseph, so they would call him the son of a fornicator. Some went so far as to say Joseph was not even his father but that Yeshua was the son of a Roman soldier—a Roman, one of the *Kittim*: such sacrilege! As it was, our nearby Brethren from Qumran and Ein Kerem, watching from the hills, had been able to track the stars and planets approaching each other in the nighttime sky over the course of that month. When they all converged as one, they say, the night was as lit up as the day, and the great star was visible even in the morning. Yeshua was born that very morning, thus fulfilling the Messianic Star Prophecy. If this was not a clear sign from the Divine of a holy birth, I do not know what else could be.

My uncle, Yeshua, the Messiah—Jesus the Christ—had been born.

* * *

After eight days, as is the Jewish custom and the Law, Yeshua was circumcised and given a name. The name Yeshua—a rather common Jewish name—was chosen because it means "savior" or "deliverer." When the days of Mary's purification were completed, she and Joseph took the babe to the Temple in Jerusalem as is also the Law, for it is written that every firstborn son that opens the womb shall be holy to the Lord. There, although as I have said, the Essenes did not approve of animal sacrifices, Joseph and Mary offered the two required pigeons, for the family was very poor in those days and could not provide a lamb. Also, pigeons are considered by many to be vermin. Indeed, upon the Temple (when it stood) there were golden spikes along the top walls and roof of the sanctuary to prevent birds from alighting and dropping their waste all over the place. Such a holy place, built to slaughter creatures of God in every way! Of course I am being ironic, and perhaps bitter as well, and for this I apologize. I will strike this last part out when I go back to recopy this narrative.

Anyway, Joseph, Mary, and Yeshua the babe then returned to the grotto where they were to tarry until Mary and the child were strong enough to return to Nazareth.

However, three members of the Great Brotherhood had been meanwhile making their way towards Judea, seeing in their own lands the heavenly bodies in the sky converging, and wishing to greet the new avatar. Actually there had been four, but the fourth met with some trouble and never arrived. This was the sage from the Far, Far East. The other three, a priest from Upper Egypt, a mage from Persia, and a Hindu priest from India, were to meet in Jerusalem and from thence travel to Qumran to find out the site of Yeshua's birth. As is customary when someone of status or means enters a new country, he goes to offer respect to the king to let it be known the visit represents no threat. So the three wise men bore gifts for Herod, who was in Jerusalem at the time for *Sukkot,* or the Feast of Tabernacles, and also gifts for the babe. What these men did not know—what none of us then knew—was the true extent of Herod's paranoia. Herod was practically on his deathbed from living a life of great luxury and overrich food and too much strong drink and was said to have some ghastly disease of running sores and itching all over his body, yet when the magus mentioned the birth of a new king, Herod overreacted. I write "overreact" because it was clear to all he was dying, so what threat could a child be to him? Of course, in hindsight, this should have been no surprise from Herod, that half-Jew-by-marriage-only usurper king who had slaughtered three of his own sons, his most favored wife, her brother, and their mother, all to protect his throne.

Herod rearranged his expression to one of benevolence, feigned interest in this new king and asked the men where the babe was, so that he, too, might go himself to pay homage. Of course they, at that time, did not know the exact location of the grotto, so they could not divulge this information, or else all may have been lost within that very week! Wise men, they also sensed Herod was a dishonest man and not to be trusted—neither he nor his remaining sons, his heirs. They paid Herod his homage as required and took their leave, promising to return to Herod's court to tell him where the Messiah was before departing Judea.

They traveled to Qumran, were told of the innkeeper in Bethlehem, to whence they traveled, and he led them to the grotto. The wise men gifted Yeshua with incense, among it the highly valued frankincense; and myrrh; and then added some gold on second thought, while giving a warning.

"You must depart here," they said. "Herod your king seeks to do the child harm."

This was enough for Joseph, who had been visited by an angel the night before in a dream and who had said the same thing.

Mary and Joseph gathered their scant belongings and made haste with the three men, who wished to leave Judea in secret to avoid Herod, to the Community of the *Yahad* at Qumran, which was where Joseph and Mary at first assumed they might hide—for Qumran is a desolate place, in the desert near to the Dead Sea, or the Sea of Salt. The Council of Elders there considered the issue very seriously, prayed on the matter, and consulted Scripture. There they found the answer. The prophet Hosea had given the words of God: "When Israel was a child, I loved him; and out of Egypt I called my son." Now, these words had always been taken to refer to Moses and the Exodus, "son" being the Hebrews, but if Yeshua was Moses reincarnated as an avatar, as some believed would be true of the Messiah, the prophecy could take on a deeper, richer meaning, for was it not also Akhenaten, Pharaoh of Egypt, land of many gods, who first conceptualized of God as *one* Divine Presence? Also, communities related to the Essenes, called the *Therapeutae*, were scattered all about Egypt, a land of great learning. Would it not be good for Yeshua to receive his earliest education there? The Egyptian priest offered to lead the family to his homeland.

It took another day or so for the community at Qumran to gather together provisions for the family's journey and to select a few other Brethren to accompany them for protection. The other two wise men departed in secret to their own lands, and Mary, Joseph, Yeshua, the priest, and the Brethren commenced the journey to Egypt one evening, after the sun had sunk well behind the horizon. They traveled under cover by night until they reached the border of Egypt, for this method of travel was safer for the child.

Chapter Three

The Judean desert is hot and stifling, but it is said the sands of Egypt can become so hot the soles of your feet would scorch should you take off your sandals. And then there are the sandstorms, or even just blowing sand thrown by the gentlest of breezes. Unless your face is covered, the sand gets into your eyes and can scratch them badly, for it is not a fine sand easily rinsed out with water, but a gritty sand with sharp edges. Farther along the route, as you reach the Delta, the desert turns into marsh. So Joseph and Mary, led by the priest, turned to the southwest, skirting the marshes, until they reached the Nile; then the priest departed south towards his own land in Upper Egypt (south is Upper in Egypt, and north is Lower, for that is the direction the Nile flows, north to the Great Sea), and the family and Brethren turned thence, following the course of the river on the rich farmland beside it, which is much easier than traversing desert.

It took many days for them to cross this great land and to reach the Nile, so I will leave the family in this narrative as they made this journey; and the reader of these words, I hope, will indulge me meanwhile in a digression about the history of the Essenes and the Great Brotherhood of mystics—for already they have played a large part in this drama that I am setting down, and to properly understand the rest of Yeshua's story and his later teachings, one must know at least some of this history.

I beg the reader's patience and will try not to make it tedious.

I will tell you the truth: the Essene Jews originated long, long ago: in Egypt, of an ancient mystical stream, although of course they did not then call themselves Essenes. (We did not even name ourselves Essenes; this was a label given us by others; we merely referred to ourselves as brothers and sisters of the *Yahad*.) We trace our origins to Pharaoh Thutmose III, who was inspired to join all the ancient mystery schools in the known world into a single body. Thus was formed the Great Brotherhood of mystics, philosophers, and initiates to which I have referred (and Sisterhood—whenever I say "Brotherhood," I am normally including women, for women were considered largely the equals of men in Egypt, and they are certainly our spiritual equals, as I have said.) Many women have been great teachers and High Priestesses. Yeshua learned much from the Essene High Priestess Judith and, even earlier in his life, from his teacher Salome. Yeshua would say towards the end of his life that one day there may even be a female avatar, if the world is ready and if we have not yet recognized the True Reality and turned from our selfish, materialistic ways. Simon Peter and Yeshua disagreed vehemently on this point regarding women. My father Jude would laugh when telling us the story. Whenever Peter said something that denigrated women, Yeshua's habit was to go share a special teaching with Mary of Magdala to put her in the position of having to teach Peter, which would greatly upset that man. He struggled to tolerate her as one of the inner circle, and having to learn from her was a test of Peter's stubbornness that he often failed.

Back to King Thutmose III. A few generations after him came the great Egyptian avatar, Amenhotep IV, who later took the name Akhenaten to honor the Aten, or sun disk. The Master Akhenaten, a Pharaoh of peace, was inspired to conceive of the Divine Being as one spirit. Yes! As I have written, *One God*. The one divinity was symbolized by the sun disk, but unlike worshiping the disk as an idol, the disk was merely a metaphor for God. God was not a person but a creative force, an energy, a consciousness, the bestower of Life itself. All are contained in God, and God exists in all of creation.

Naturally, in a country full of many gods, the Egyptian priests of Amun-Re, who wielded much power, would have none of it, and the Heretic Pharaoh, as they called Akhenaten, was eventually poisoned by an assassin; he died even as he was praying in his holy sanctum. However, Akhenaten had foreseen his betrayal and demise with great clarity—just as Yeshua was to see his. Akhenaten's star pupil, Ahmose or Moses, who had been brought up as his half-brother, rallied what followers he could—mostly others of his own people, the Hebrews, as most Egyptians were only too happy to return to the old religion and customs—and, at Akhenaten's request, Moses escaped Egypt so that their religion could perhaps grab a foothold elsewhere. The famous Jewish story of the Exodus is therefore only half true (although the Essenes love the tale of the Exodus: it is a good story!) The Israelites were never literal slaves as a people in Egypt, although some were certainly slaves; our ancestor Joseph of the coat of many colors held a high position in Pharaoh's court, and even the Torah will tell you that. But the Torah states that the Hebrews remained in Egypt some 430 years after Joseph's arrival until the Exodus. I think this was a copying mistake, for it was more accurately about forty-one generations. People try to say that Ramses II was the Pharaoh of the Exodus, but that is impossible: he reigned almost a thousand years after Joseph arrived. (But the story is improved if we claim the Hebrew God defeated a man as powerful as Ramses the Great!) Besides, there was more than one exodus: one took place not many generations after Joseph, but the largest one took place with Moses at Akhenaten's request. They chose Palestine, then called Canaan, for the simple reason that there were already Hebrews there, though they were not at the time all worshipers of a single god; and Akhenaten's grandfather, Yuya, was in fact a Hebrew descended from Joseph's line. Akhetnaten himself had Jewish blood. Canaan was the logical choice.

The hearer of these words must understand: Joseph's bloodline had remained one of status, since he had been vizier to the Pharaoh, and indeed I have also heard it speculated that the commoner (of high birth nonetheless) Queen Tye, who was Akhenaten's mother, was also of Joseph's line. Moses himself was beloved of Akhenaten. It was not Akhenaten's army that chased the people across the desert and perished in the Sea of Reeds (people on foot could traverse that area with relative ease; soldiers in chariots, on the other hand, were trapped in the marshes, where the wheels of the chariots became bogged down in the muck). No, it was the army of Akhenaten's usurpers who chased them, to destroy all the heretics, and who wished to set his son Tutankhaten on the throne—which they did, and the boy changed his name to Tutankhamun. This boy Pharaoh was forced to return the land to the old religion of many gods. And yet the Torah does not lie. It is still true to say the people of Egypt, both Egyptian and Jew, were enslaved. They were enslaved by false gods and capricious, corrupt priests. They were enslaved by materialism and rituals that had lost their meaning. They were enslaved by beliefs in magic and charms and meaningless gods carved out of stone.

I have always supposed that those who finally set down the Torah during the Babylonian Exile fashioned the story of the Exodus in the present way to encourage our people to take heart, and because the real story had long since been lost, but it is only a supposition. It doesn't explain the long-standing custom of the Passover. Yet every new nation needs its holy days and stories and customs to unite the tribes, and originally there had been twelve tribes, along with a few other followers of Akhenaten, who converted to the religion of Moses. Aten, Yahweh: the single god was the same One God, the Divine Presence, the creator, the light of the world. This has always been one of the great secrets of Essene knowledge and tradition.

Moses spread the idea of this single god in Canaan. Later on, others carried the teachings of the mystery schools across the Great Sea to the world of the Greeks, where Pythagoras one day founded his famous school in that land called Italia. The Essenes consider both Pythagoras and Moses as Masters. There have been other great Masters as well, in the Near and Far East, Persia, and

India. Together, all these streams converge, still even to this day, to form the Great Brotherhood. This is not to say the Great Brotherhood is perfectly cohesive by any means. Different cultures call for variations, but they are all variations on the same idea: God is one, and God is within us all. God surrounds us and animates us. I think about it as each of us being one of God's thoughts. He conceives us, so to speak, and we take material form as a realization of that thought. We live many lifetimes, first incarnating, then reincarnating, experiencing, evolving, and those who but seek within will find God and begin to remember they are of God—if that person is an earnest seeker. When one remembers he is of God, all things are possible. That person evolves beyond the material-human state and no longer needs to incarnate here. He continues in some other form, perhaps an etheric form, on a higher plane, or at least on a different plane, vibrating at a higher rate (I am thinking of Pythagoras here and his musical octaves), so that he would be unseen should he visit the physical-material plane, unless he chose to be visible, like the angels, or as Yeshua was miraculously able to do after his death.

I confess I tire. These abstractions are difficult to articulate to the uninitiated, especially in writing. And I again apologize for my poor Greek. I fear it plods.

The important thing to know is this: these are the underpinnings of the beliefs of Yeshua, called the Christ, for these are the things he was taught as an Essene. And to properly understand his teachings, one must understand that these are the views he held, the tradition from whence he arose. You must understand these things in order to have, as Yeshua so often put it, "ears to hear."

Beyond our Egyptian roots, the history of the origins of all the mystical streams is like a great mountain shrouded in clouds. There is a time told of when all the world was at peace and answered to a High Council of thirteen Elders. I do not know whether this is the same as the Atlantis of which Plato wrote or the people some of the Qumran Essenes refer to as the ancient Qualou. Mythologies collide. It is said that mankind's pride and selfishness began to corrupt the world and the Lord, dismayed, sent forth the deluge that forever altered the maps so that we would have to begin anew and relearn—or remember—how to reach union with the Divine, only this time to not abuse those powers attained. Of course that is the view of God as Punisher. I do not believe that. I believe he merely allows us to punish ourselves because of our own foolishness. We have the freedom to choose, and how else can we learn, if not from our poor mistakes? If we misuse power, misuse nature, there will be consequences, for the Great Nature that God has created has its Laws, and human beings are tasked with being nature's stewards, not its master. In any case, the story goes that the people who survived that great flood came down from the high mountains of Turkey into Egypt, where flowed the Nile, and where the lands were black and fertile and the harvests abundant near this river, and they passed along the knowledge they had in founding the mystery schools there. That is as much of the history as I know.

I will stop writing now that you know all of the necessary background, and move along with Yeshua's story in Egypt tomorrow. For now, I need to rest.

* * *

Mary, the babe, Joseph, and the Brethren were making their way towards Alexandria, the city founded by the Macedonian conqueror Alexander the Great, and a city of great learning, with its famous library that contained even copies of the Hebrew Torah, prophets, and writings translated into Greek a hundred or so years before by a group of seventy-two rabbis. So many Hebrews lived in Alexandria that there was a sizable Jewish Quarter in the city, but it was not to the city itself that the family traveled. At Alexandria, they would turn west and go the short distance to Lake Mareotis, where they would abide with the community of the *Therapeutae* in that place. (To make matters simple, think of the *Therapeutae* as Egyptian Essenes, although some became like monks, departed from the communities altogether, and were ascetics.) Today, some storytellers say the family went only as far as Zoan, or Tanis, in Egypt, which is not so. By this time, Zoan had long ceased being the capital city of Lower Egypt, which had been moved to Memphis, still during the time of the Pharaohs. Most of the Essene community from Zoan had relocated to Lake Mareotis to join the Eygptians.

Along the way the family passed near to Gizeh and saw, from afar, the three pyramids of that plateau. My grandfather Joseph, rough as he was, was still an Essene and therefore knew his Scripture well: he had himself attended the *yeshiva* at Mt. Carmel. Upon seeing the pyramids, my grandmother told me later, Joseph brought them to a halt and quoted Enoch:

"Observe you everything that takes place in the heaven, how they do not change their orbits, and the luminaries which are in the heaven, how they all rise and set in order each in its season, and transgress not against their appointed order. Now behold you the earth, and give heed to the things which take place upon it from first to last, how likewise constant they are, how none change. Take heed you, then, of how all the works of God appear."

This passage has been interpreted by many to mean "the laws of the heavens are as of those on the earth." The Divine Will is observable in His creations. Consequently, it is said the pyramids at Gizeh honor the Creator by mirroring on the ground the position of Orion's belt in the sky—Orion, that constellation that disappears for seventy days but reappears right at the time of the Nile's life-giving annual inundation. To the left of that constellation is Sirius, said to be home to departed Pharaohs. One never knows how true these old mythologies are, but who is to say where we go after death until we reincarnate? In any case, the Brethren, Mary, and Joseph, were interested to see, if only from a distance, the greatest of the pyramids, for that is where—if all went well—Yeshua would one day be initiated into the highest degree of the Great Brotherhood before commencing his ministry in Judea.

For now, he was just a babe, strapped to his mother as she rode along on a camel, a great, hairy beast with a hump and toes instead of hooves. They are creatures particularly suited to the desert, for they can go many days without water and possess long, long eyelashes that keep the sand from their eyes. They had procured for Mary the camel with the help of the Egyptian priest before he had departed. She had grown fond of it and given it the name Moses, because, she said, "he is leading me across the desert."

"And it is an interminably long journey," quipped one of the Brethren, and everyone laughed.

"At least it won't take us forty years," Mary said.

"Alas, there has been no manna of the Lord," Joseph said, reaching up to touch Mary's foot. "But we will be there soon now."

Finally, they reached Lake Mareotis and were warmly greeted, a room having been prepared for them in a house of one of the Elders. In that place, as they hid from Herod, Joseph could contribute his skills as a carpenter and stonemason both in the community and in Alexandria, and Mary could assist with the community's children and with teaching them when she was not tending to Yeshua.

I will write down how the Essene communities operate. All money is pooled into a fund and everything is shared. In this way, no one wants for anything; there are no rich and there are no poor. All who are able to work, do work. The old and the sick are tended to. The wise teach in the community school, each according to his or her special area of knowledge. Children gifted in certain areas of learning are given additional studies and are freed from helping as much as the others in the fields or from caring for the animals. Still they must contribute, and they are not seen as higher, or above, or better, than anyone else. The Divine grants his gifts to each individual. Some children are found to be better suited to an artisan's skills than, say, to animal husbandry. So they are given apprenticeship training in that area, in addition to their other duties. For the most part there is cheer and goodwill. Any disputes are handled by an elected Council of Elders. This is the basic working of every Essene community, including the ones at Mt. Carmel and the Community of the *Yahad* at Qumran. Students from other lands, members of the Great Brotherhood, often travel to any one of the Essene communities, where they are welcomed to study, as I have already written, and contribute the knowledge of their own lands in exchange for our knowledge.

An added benefit to the family in tarrying at Lake Mareotis was the proximity to Alexandria, for this made the library available, and my grandfather Joseph liked to go and hear the Jewish rabbis read from the Torah in Greek and would do so whenever he found work in that city. Bustling Alexandria was packed with pagan Greeks and Romans who worshiped various gods and goddesses—the Romans particularly seemed to love the Egyptian goddess Isis, adopting her as one of their own and repairing a great crumbling temple to her, both in Alexandria and in another place, much farther south in Upper Egypt on the island of Philae, near Elephantine Island where there was a small fortress and temple of Levites. These Jews were said to have once concealed the Ark of the Covenant before the destruction of Solomon's Temple. I write all this down to show that, although the Hebrews left Egypt, they never really did, not completely.

I am sorry for my wandering, and for yet another history lesson. Back to the narrative.

Yeshua's earliest years with the *Therapeutae* were not particularly remarkable: like any child, he crawled, he toddled, then he stood and walked. He learned quickly how to speak, picking up both Aramaic and Eygptian words with ease. As he grew older, Mary noted he had a keen eye and mind and a particular fondness for animals. Even wild ones would come to him if he sat down, was still, and then softly called them over. But he seemed much like any other child until he reached four years of age. My grandmother Mary used to tell this story with pride in her voice.

Yeshua had walked out from the community part of the way on the road towards Alexandria, to meet his father who had been in the city for the day working. Along the way, Yeshua happened upon some snares that had been set for birds. Some Egyptian boys were nearby and Yeshua demanded of them, "Who of you wishes to murder these innocent creatures?"

The boys were silent.

"The one who set these will also be caught in such a snare," Yeshua said, and he stepped closer to the snares and there found twelve dead sparrows.

Yeshua passed his hand over each of the birds, saying, "Go! Fly away!" and the birds loosened themselves and flew off, making a loud noise. "Remember me!" Yeshua called after them; a footnote that to this day never fails to make me laugh, because the Egyptian boys took what he said to mean them, and they ran off, afraid, when Yeshua had been addressing only the sparrows. And it was such a childlike thing to say to the birds, as if sparrows have memories. But I should not assume. For who knows the minds of sparrows?

This was Yeshua's first known miracle (the Egyptian boys told the story, and it spread, and when word reached the community, Yeshua confirmed it). The event was especially remarkable because Yeshua had as yet received no training in healing from the *Therapeutae*—although the curious youngster had perhaps watched more healings than anyone had been aware of. Also, the miracle was highly unusual because it appeared that Yeshua's will, and will alone, was strong enough to give him powers of healing—and not just healing, but that of Resurrection. Because of this miracle, Joseph and Mary—now pregnant with my uncle James—decided to tarry yet a while longer in Egypt, although word had long reached them that Herod had died. Now, at the suggestion of the Elders among the *Therapeutae,* they decided to take Yeshua to the community of *Therapeutae* at Lake Moeris, where animal healings were performed. Though there was no formal school there any longer, there were certainly wise and holy teachers —many of them having migrated there from Zoan, which is perhaps why the story of the whereabouts of the family gets a little confused. There Yeshua could continue to practice the art of healing, and James could be born, and then they could commence the long journey home.

* * *

Now, let me leave Yeshua at Lake Moeris for a moment, as he began learning the healing arts at the foot of his teacher Salome, and pause to contrast Yeshua's early years with those of his cousin, John the Baptizer.

John, being raised in Qumran, was—and there is no other way to put this—a hot-headed child. Perhaps it was because he was angry at the loss of his father. To explain this, I must go back a few years in time. Herod the Great, as one might imagine, had been enraged that the three wise men had not returned, as promised, to tell him where they had found the Messiah. Not knowing that Yeshua's family had fled to Egypt, Herod had sent soldiers to seek out this "new king of the Jews." However, there was no king to be found since the soldiers had no idea where to look, not even which town. Yet Herod did, somehow, find out—and to this day, no one knows how, but it was likely from a colluding priest—that Essene prophecy had foretold of two Messiahs: a priestly Messiah of the line of Levi, and a royal Messiah of the Davidic line. There were only so many actual

Levite priests at the Temple in Jerusalem any longer, since many of them served as rabbis in the land, in the synagogues, and had become Pharisees. So it was not difficult to locate Zacharias and ask to see his newborn son. Elizabeth, of course, had already departed to Qumran, in the hills, with John. Zacharias would merely say that his wife had the babe and that he, his presence being required in the Temple during that period, had no idea where they were. Herod was displeased with this answer, and so, right there in the Temple, his soldiers made threats and bullied the old man, to no avail. Finally they slew him, right between the altar and the Holy of Holies. It is said the blood of Zacharias made a pool that spread, staining the bottom of the curtain separating the two. Even the Sadducees were appalled that Herod would so desecrate the Temple he had put forth so many resources to renovate and expand.

But that was just it. To Herod, the Temple was not a holy place; it was nothing but a showplace, a monument to himself, a new wonder of the world. And the additional taxes he imposed on Jews paid for much of it.

Elizabeth grieved long over the loss of her husband, and John, being raised with a father killed so brutally by the king, grew up knowing he was different and therefore became zealous for the Law, praying to God for an end to the rule of the *Kittim* and their false Herodian king. Of course the absence of John's father was not as horrible as it might have been since the Brethren at Qumran considered all children as their own children, so there was no lack of a male figure to offer John guidance—if anything, there was a lack of women—but John remained quick to anger. It is said he once kicked a dog for nipping at his heel, and for this, John was punished. Boys are boys and sometimes get their entertainment from childish brawls or pulling the wings off of beetles or stomping on creeping insects, but this is because they do not yet understand pain and sometimes they are just curious about the natural world and its creatures. With John, it became clear early on that his frustration would need to be harnessed and redirected into anger for righteousness, anger for justice. This seemed right for the harbinger of the kingly Messiah, for someone to prepare the way by decrying the unrighteousness of the Jewish people and for all to repent so that the Kingdom of God could be restored to the Jews. Fortunately, John was also of good heart and wished to do well to honor his father, and he understood the gravity of his mission. Still, John never did learn to soften his tongue—his words, righteous or not, could cut like sharp blades of grass or stick into one like thorns.

Ironically, he would die for his sharp, honest tongue, not by the hand of Herod, but by Herod's son and by the manipulations of his wicked wife. But here I am, leaping far ahead of myself again.

I will take a break as the sun now sinks low in the sky and we are trying to conserve oil for our lamps. Tomorrow I will pick up the story of Yeshua at Lake Moeris and then the family's return to Nazareth in the Galilee.

* * *

Lake Moeris was several days' journey southeast of Alexandria, and therefore not much off of the road the family needed to travel on their way back to Palestine in any case. It was a good place to tarry until Mary gave birth to James.

One of the interesting things about the small community at Lake Moeris was the nearby Egyptian temple built to worship Sobek, the crocodile god. It was falling into disrepair, but the nearby city of Crocodilophilus was still a thriving center. There is a similar ancient temple, I am told, at a place much farther south along the Nile, called Kom Ombo, where the crocodile god was also worshiped. There, people went to be treated for various ailments, and the priests were actually physicians, each one specializing in various parts of the body.

Now, the Egyptians keep animals as pets because animals, especially cats, are revered, and their gods are given the attributes of various animals. But most priests will not take the healing of animals too seriously because it is also a common practice to kill certain animals—rarely cats, however; at one time it was an offense punishable by death to kill a cat—but the priests would sometimes slaughter and then mummify other animals, and finally even cats, to honor their deities. So the priests would not waste their skills healing any animal. Therefore, the Fayuum Oasis at Lake Moeris had become, over time, a special place for those who loved their pets to take them to be healed. In the center of Lake Moeris, there is an island that can be reached by the Egyptian boats made with papyrus reeds, which people would board with their beloved pets and be rowed out to where the animal healings were performed. And here is where the young Yeshua practiced healing. Here, he also became particularly fond of cats.

I should pause to discuss the Essene view of animals. Naturally they are God's creatures. According to the Torah, when humankind disobeyed the Lord and fell into sin, enmity developed between the human and animal kingdoms, and humans were to use certain animals for food—but only the clean ones. Among the Essenes, the meat most favored is salted fish. Other Essenes, who see no reason to stay in a fallen state if unnecessary, are vegetarians, relying on fruits, nuts, grains, milk, and honey for sustenance. Yeshua was one of these, as was John the Baptist. Followers of the Way such as I are mostly vegetarian, although I will occasionally eat salted fish. As a younger man, I would sometimes consume sacrificial lamb at the Passover meal if I were sharing the meal with non-Essene Jews. But I ate meat so little that even the Paschal lamb caused great pains in my stomach. Since I use my few sheep for the production of wool, I have befriended the animals, given them names, and cannot bear the thought of ever eating them, nor any of the lambs. Other

Essenes regularly ate meat if it was available. These were usually the soldiers at Qumran, who wished to be strong in case they were needed for battle. I am not sure how many of these, if any, are actually left, now that Qumran, Jerusalem, and Masada are laid waste. In any case, even the Essene soldiers, when consuming meat, had special pits outside the community structure where the animal bones were disposed of—akin to tombs for the animals, if it helps to think about it that way. It was a gesture of respect for the animals sacrificing their lives for the sustenance of men.

I do know that Yeshua, as a healer, found it particularly distasteful to eat animals since he would make them well. But he did not judge those who did, any more than he judged those who drank wine or strong drink. In fact he healed those who suffered from too often drunkenness, seeing it as an illness of karma. He healed these by forgiving them. But more on this later. From wine, Yeshua himself mostly abstained. Certainly he would sip a little when sharing the community cup. But I believe he tried to keep his body light and his mind clear. It is easier to attune with God this way.

Joseph, Mary, Yeshua, and the infant James tarried at Lake Moeris for about a year, Yeshua learning about the uses of various medicinal herbs and the mysteries of the laying on of hands. There were also two teachers of religions there, a married couple called Salome (whom I have mentioned and who was also a healer) and Elihu. They were originally of Zoan and were well traveled along the various caravan routes. Because Yeshua was so young, they kept their teachings simple, or foundational, but they introduced him to the Egyptian mysteries; the Brahmans; and the sayings of Siddhartha, called the Buddha; and Lao Tse Zsu, the Master of the Orient, although it is such a far distance to travel we still know very little of this man even today. Yeshua already knew the foundations of Judaism. More complex teachings would be for later. But later on in his life, Yeshua would sometimes repeat the words of the Buddha, saying things such as, "Even death is not to be feared if one has lived."

"He is a fast learner and a gifted healer," Salome told Mary. She laid her hands upon Yeshua's shoulders. "I would encourage this in him, for he could be a great healer of men."

Salome did not know that Yeshua was to be the Messiah. This information was still kept secret from most, for the child's safety. But Mary promised her his training would continue.

Thus, finally, the time came to depart. The family commenced the long return to Galilee.

Chapter Four

Rachel has made for me a good breakfast, and I slept well last night—a rare thing anymore, as I often awake in the darkness and toss and turn until I give up and go to my sanctum to pray. My spirit troubles me. This devastated land—what will become of us? At any time, the Romans could seize us and if not slaughter us, haul us away to Rome or Pompeii or to any of their cities to serve as slaves. Rachel is fetching enough that she would, I am without a doubt, be made to serve in a brothel. May God prevent this!

My prayers are fervent, sweat glistening on my brow. If I am lucky, sleepiness finally descends and I once again may sleep a bit more before sunrise. This night of sound sleep is truly a blessing; I return to my narrative refreshed. So—where did I leave off?

Ah, yes, the family was leaving Lake Moeris and the *Therapeutae*.

The family slowly crossed Egypt, now with a six-year-old and a toddler, and finally reached Judea. There they heard that Herod's three sons had been given Palestine, split into three sections: Archaleus had Idumea, Judea, and Samaria; Antipas the Galilee and Perea; and Philip the lands to the east of the Jordan. Unsure if Archaleus was even aware of a Messiah born into the House of David in Judea, and whether this Herod sought the boy as had his father, my grandfather decided to cross into Galilee through Archaleus's territories once again under cover of night. They passed through safely, into the Galilee, and resumed residence in Joseph's old house in Nazareth. Herod Antipas, who ruled the Galilee, would not be seeking a Messiah in that land.

Now, Nazareth is a tiny village of about two dozen families, an hour and a half's walk at most from Sepphoris, a city a person could smell well before he even arrived at its gates. This was where my grandfather Joseph found most of his work as a contractor, for everyone in Nazareth was poor and had no money; work in Nazareth was done in exchange for food or other goods. From his father, Yeshua began learning simple aspects of the trade of building, at Sepphoris largely with stone because Herod Antipas was then rebuilding that city since the Romans had leveled it after a rebellion—and then at the customary age of seven, Yeshua was sent to Mt. Carmel to begin studying the Torah at the School of Prophets. The Essenes are assiduous about learning, our *yeshivas* more rigorous than most. When I was a schoolboy, I did not appreciate that fact, but as an adult, I can easily see the value of being made to not just repeat a text by rote but to explain it. The Essenes do so love our *pesharim!* We are forever reinterpreting texts in light of new events.

One thing happened in Nazareth, however, that is worthy of note. Yeshua was still six years old. As I have written, he had a great fondness for animals, and one day the child noticed that a neighbor's dog was limping. He approached the dog to investigate.

"Stay back, Yeshua," said the neighboring man, who was called Amos. He was warily watching his dog as it limped in the street, leaving a trail of bloody prints. "He has cut his foot badly and may bite."

"He will not bite me," Yeshua said, and he knelt where he was, making chucking noises with his tongue.

The dog limped over to him.

Yeshua patted its head, then laid his own forehead on the dog's head for just a moment, his right hand meanwhile slowly moving down the dog's hind leg until it reached the injured foot. He lifted the paw and held it in his hand.

The dog licked Yeshua's face and began wagging its tail.

Yeshua laughed and got to his feet as the dog sprang away and ran, no longer lame, to its master.

Amos marveled over this thing and called out his thanks, but clearly the man was also afraid, for over the course of a few days, rumors began reaching Joseph and Mary of what Yeshua had done. Finally the patriarch of one of the oldest families of the town approached Joseph about the matter.

"What manner of child is your Yeshua?" the man asked, an edge in his voice that made my grandfather uncomfortable.

"What do you mean? He is but a boy."

"Amos says he healed his dog. By what means did he do this?" the man asked.

Joseph thought quickly and feigned a snort. "The dog had a thorn in its paw. All Yeshua did was take it out."

It was not a lie. It was a half-truth, for Yeshua, of course, had not only removed the thorn but had also healed the wound.

The man nodded thoughtfully, then seemed satisfied. "It is well then," he said finally. "We know of your sojourn in Egypt and feared the child had perhaps learned some kind of witch-craft."

Joseph laughed and clapped the man on the shoulder. "If my son knew of such magic, I would not have to work so hard. He could levitate stones and build houses for me as I sat and watched."

The man laughed also and took his leave.

Joseph heaved a sigh of relief.

But back at home, Joseph and Mary discussed this situation and decided to take Yeshua aside and speak with him.

"My son," Joseph told him. "You must be cautious. People do not know who you are."

"And people fear what they do not understand," Mary said.

Yeshua considered their words. "Should I have let the dog suffer?"

Joseph and Mary exchanged glances.

"No," Mary said. "But—perhaps do this work in secret, when others do not see."

Yeshua was troubled and addressed his father. "You spoke an

untruth and said I only removed a thorn."

"It was to deflect their fear, Yeshua. I would not see you harmed."

Yeshua nodded. "Yes, Father. But neither would I see you lie on my behalf. Bearing false witness is a sin."

At this, my grandparents were speechless. What did he want of them?

Still, there were no further incidents, and then Yeshua turned seven years of age.

* * *

The Mt. Carmel School of Prophets has a long and established history and, as I have suggested, is no typical Jewish *yeshiva*. It is said Elias himself founded the school where he had built the altar and defeated the priests of Baal, and that Pythagoras, after spending some twenty years or more studying the mysteries in Egypt and Chaldea, visited the Mt. Carmel school before returning home to Samos, then on to Italia, to found his own school. The mountain range itself is shaped like the holy triangle, with the apex facing the Mediterranean Sea and the western and eastern slopes branching off in either direction. There are many caves and precipices; the eastern slope drops off to the river below. The land is fertile and beautiful, with many pines, oaks, myrtle, carob, olive trees, and grape vines planted along terraces.

While Yeshua was there, the school was run by a gifted High Priestess and prophetess called Judith. Knowing precisely whom Yeshua was, she personally tutored him in many aspects of metaphysical studies. An elder named Jeremiah tutored Yeshua in Torah—or, more precisely, the Essene version of Torah, the true Torah, not the profane Torah that the Sadducees and scribes and Pharisees, with their extra writings, used to justify worship at only one place, the Temple in Jerusalem, and where animal sacrifices, not prayers, were the only method of true worship. (What an absurd idea, as if the Divine is not everywhere and in all places all at once and is confined to a single room in the Temple and cannot hear the prayers of all.) Yet Yeshua studied their Torah and prophets as well, fully aware that these writings were not set down until the Jewish exile in Babylon. Therefore that Torah was somewhat tainted by the cult practices of Mesopotamia. One must remember that, when the Persian liberator Cyrus conquered Babylon and allowed us to return to Judea, many of these same Jews chose to stay in Babylon, where they had acquired wealth.

While a student at Mt. Carmel, Yeshua was given a month off during certain seasons to return to Nazareth and help his father. He would travel with him to Sepphoris to work and earn money for the family, and this is where he learned Greek—beyond the few words and expressions he'd learned in Egypt, outside Alexandria—for Sepphoris was becoming almost just as Roman as Hebrew. Actually Sepphoris is where all my uncles learned Greek, for they all learned at least rudimentary stonemasonry, and you had to speak Greek well enough to bargain for a fair wage—although wages were never fair; over a third, sometimes almost half, was taken back in taxes to give the Romans and to Herod Antipas and then the annual tithe to the Sadducees ruling the Temple. As if any of these needed any more than they had! But that is the way of the rich; they can never have enough, Jew nor Gentile.

Anyway, it was in Sepphoris, upon a visit there on a roundabout way back from Capernaum to Jerusalem in my young adulthood, that I learned the secret of making the blue dye, that hue of which so many have tried, and failed, to copy.

I have digressed, of course.

The years passed, and Yeshua grew in wisdom and learning and was pleasing in the eyes of the Lord. This time flew by without incident.

Finally, Yeshua reached the age of twelve, the age for him to be examined by the priests. Most Jews save the examination for thirteen, but the Essenes view it this way: you are a year older after you have lived that year. So, when a person turns twelve, he has lived already twelve years and is commencing his thirteenth year. That is the proper year to be examined, but any time during that year is appropriate. The family waited for Passover since this was the only festival in Jerusalem they typically could afford to attend. Also, April is a pleasant month for travel. So the family—by then Joseph, Mary, Yeshua, James, Joses, and their sister Mary (my father, Jude, was not yet born, nor Simon, or Salome)—traveled down to Jerusalem to the Temple, along with many others making the trip from Galilee.

A most remarkable thing happened there.

Yeshua answered quite easily the questions put to him by the rabbis, and they were satisfied the boy was now responsible on his own for following the Law. The family departed the Temple and tarried overnight with a friend whose family celebrated the Feast of the Unleavened Bread, but also to welcome Yeshua to adulthood. In the morning, the many gathered together again to make the trip back to Galilee, and Yeshua was seen speaking with one of the men who would be traveling back with the group. At that time, my aunt Mary was but a toddler, so naturally my grandparents were more attentive to her needs—especially since Yeshua was now to be considered a man. They assumed Yeshua was among them and commenced the journey.

Well, he was not. When they finally realized he was missing, they turned back in panic to Jerusalem. How does one lose the Messiah? (That has been a family joke ever since.)

They found Yeshua where one would expect to find a Messiah: in the Temple. Actually not in the Temple, but on the Temple steps, outside the Huldah Gates, surrounded by several rabbis, arguing points of Torah and, of all things, cleanliness laws. Yeshua was disagreeing and saying that those not allowed into the Temple—not Gentiles, for even they had their own court inside—but Jews, the sick, the blind, the lame, the deformed—should be allowed into the Temple, for they were not.

"Are not these in even greater need of God's blessing?" he asked.

The rabbis marveled, of course, for they and the priests believed any malady is brought forth by the will of God for some sin that has been committed.

When my grandmother Mary used to tell this story, I could see her usual pride in her son. And it must have been something to see: this twelve-year-old boy being much like that great Greek philosopher Socrates, answering the rabbis and their questions with even greater questions, trying to get them to see for themselves the problems in their logic. Obviously, Yeshua's teacher, Jeremiah, had done well with him. A crowd had gathered, wondering over Yeshua's words.

There was a lull and Joseph took this opportunity to call for Yeshua. "Come, son," he said. "We were sick with worry, thinking you were lost. It's time to go home."

Yeshua looked at my grandfather and said, "How can I be lost in my Father's House? Is it not here that I belong?"

Yet, he got to his feet and thanked the rabbis and bid them farewell.

This, however, is how my grandparents knew that the time had finally come to let Yeshua go. It was now time for him to begin preparing more earnestly for his ministry, to cease living the carefree life of a child. And yet I curse those same steps, too, for it was there, some twenty years later or so, that members of the Sanhedrin would tell the people Pontius Pilate had condemned Yeshua to the cross.

Beth: The Travels and Initiation

Chapter Five

Yeshua's wisdom was so great it is often said nowadays, some forty-five years after his crucifixion, that he must have traveled around the world, learning all the wisdom of the sages, prior to beginning his ministry. As usual, this is only partly true. Much of his learning was "learning of the book" from the school at Mt. Carmel and when, after the incident in Jerusalem, he spent his thirteenth year at Qumran, where he first met his cousin, John the Baptizer, and learned many additional scrolls and readings from the teachers in that great Essene school. Some say Yeshua went to Rome, or to Greece to study the philosophers, or to some faraway province named Brittania, which the Romans have recently conquered, or to the very Far East to the highest mountain ranges. None of that is true.

Yet, Yeshua did travel, for that is common among members of the Great Brotherhood destined to become Masters. However, he deliberately kept his travels unknown, except for his later sojourn in Egypt, for, as I have written, many Jews live and study in Egypt and there is an entire Jewish Quarter in the city of Alexandria. No, he did not even tell the disciples who weren't his literal brothers, telling only certain Essene members of the one hundred and twenty, which included our family—for good reason. If the Jews thought his teachings defied Torah and had been influenced by the religious teachings of other cultures, they would not have listened to him. (Never mind that this was already true of the Torah and other writings.) No, most people, nor the disciples, knew not of the Great Brotherhood and that the Divine reveals himself in sundry ways. No one would have followed him or seen him as the Messiah. He would have been seen merely as yet one more false prophet claiming to be the Messiah. The irony, of course, is that this is what the Sanhedrin wound up thinking, and more, anyway.

So here is the truth as I know it. Now, I know it will be hard to believe of a Jewish peasant boy. I would take an oath, and swear to these things, but we do not swear, since one of Yeshua's teachings was to not take oaths; so I will just state that many of my family told me these things, and the Elders at Qumran confirmed these things, and when I was a child, I heard Yeshua himself refer to his travels. My uncle Yeshua more or less walked in the footsteps of the Master Pythagoras, only in reverse order. Specifically, commencing at the age of fourteen, Yeshua traveled first to India; then back to the near East, in Persia, the land of the Parthians, where he tarried awhile; but he then left that place when word reached him in his mid-twenties that his father Joseph had died. He returned to Nazareth, and this is when Yeshua met, for the first time, his brothers and sister who had not yet been born when he had departed on his journeys. Among these was my father, Jude. There Yeshua stayed a short while until he took his last journey back to Egypt, to receive his final preparations and initiation into Master there. Lest one think such travels are impossible, it is assuredly not so. My own father traveled as an apostle to India, back and forth, numerous times, by both land and sea. The caravan routes and sea routes are well established.

I will digress for a moment to write what my father's first impression of his older brother was. He said Yeshua was so sunburned from his travels that his skin was dark, a deep brown, and he was very thin. But his face was pleasing, and he had the gentlest of gray eyes—but that they flashed dark when he angered. When he smiled, it was as if the rays of the sun burst forth, lighting even the clouds of a storm. When he hugged my father and kissed his cheek, even though Jude was only twelve years of age, he felt Yeshua's holiness in his very bones. There is no other way to put it. It was like being enveloped into the bosom of love and compassion and complete understanding. Yeshua exuded this feeling at all times towards whomever he turned his attention to, except when he grew angry—but he was quick to forgive. I felt this warm feeling when I first met him but was too young to comprehend that this was unusual and that no one else I would meet again—not even my wife—would ever produce in me this same feeling. Now I feel humbled. I simply cannot explain. There are no words.

Anyway, it is difficult to say with precision what happened to Yeshua on his travels because no one accompanied him, so I have only the stories handed down that Yeshua shared with the family. He went to India first for the simple reason that there were six Hindus studying at Qumran while he was there, and their time came to return home, so he traveled with them. As I have written, the route itself is well known, comprised of a network of caravan routes for trade, and the route to India can be traveled in a single year, going at an easy pace. Later, when my father, Jude (then called Thomas *Didymus*), returned to India in Yeshua's stead to bring the good news and teach the Way, he traveled by sea all but one time, landing on the opposite side of India in that port city called Muciri, from whence he traveled to other places, establishing churches.

And now I hesitate, for it may be too soon, for the same reasons as Yeshua had, to share these things with all the world. There are great secrets and mysteries to be revealed. Is it given to me to record these things? Perhaps I should burn this day's writing—burn all that I have put down so far and begin the story in safer waters, with Yeshua's ministry, as did the scribe who wrote the book called Mark. Are not Yeshua's teachings the most important thing? Not the story of his whole life, and more? I am having such doubts! Doubts and fears that my words may be used for evil in some way; doubts and fears now that my words may bring harm to my family.

Well, I will stop now, as dusk approaches and the light is failing. Tomorrow is Sabbath. I will spend the day resting, praying, and meditating on this matter.

* * *

I have decided to continue, obviously, since you are reading this: for it feels right in my heart and my stomach, and I have reminded myself that Yeshua himself told me that one day I would set down his story as it was. I must trust the Divine to guide my words. I have prayed and asked that if I am to write down anything that is wrong, or is a misrepresentation, or that would do harm to Yeshua's memory, for God to stop my hand. Of course the Divine does not intervene, but I must trust in my inner master.

So, to India. There Yeshua tarried for five years in the east of that land at a place called Jagannath, listening to the ancient chants called the Vedas, and he learned about the tale of Krishna, the incarnation of the god Vishnu born to a virgin, and he later said, when teaching my uncles, "These stories where God is fractured into several gods, and then further into lesser gods, are much like those gods of the Greeks and Romans or Egyptian pantheons. They are all aspects of the one God. The mythologies please the people. In them the gods suffer and are jealous and war and do human things, except they have magic. They give the people hope." My father said Yeshua merely smiled when saying this, for to him all paths eventually lead to the One. Yeshua did not believe in all these gods, of course. His Jewishness never left him; he worshiped Yahweh. Not as a literal being, but as a Cosmic Essence. This is not blasphemy: it is why there was never any idol of Yahweh in the Holy of Holies. God is a presence, is timeless, and is the infinite spirit of Divinity, a divinity that is present in all of creation. Also, Yeshua always pointed out that one of the Hindu's main gods, Vishnu, was the god of compassion. There is no evil in compassion.

Their creator god was Brahma. And then there was Shiva, the Destroyer. Together the three comprise part of the usual trinity we see over and over (I am thinking of the Egyptian Osiris-Isis-

Horus). The three main Hindu gods together are aspects of the One Divinity, or a trinity, or the Brahman, the True Reality, which was well understood by the Hindu priests. Yeshua said the Hindus do not believe any religion is "true" or "false." He said that, like the Essenes, they believe God is God (except with the Hindus, they believe God may appear in different forms). They also believe, like us, that God is present within everyone and every living thing. And, like the less conservative and less literal-minded of us, wickedness is perceived as a lack of good: simply an absence of good. Nothing in and of itself is innately evil. God created nothing evil. Evil is always a choice—a choice made in the absence of good. As I have said, the Great Brotherhood shares many teachings; and once a person bores into the mystical teachings of a religion, or so I have found in my own studies, the religions all start to sound the same.

As proof of religions borrowing traditions, there is, near Jagannath, in India, on the coast of the sea, a place called Konarka, where the Hindus worship their sun god Surya (although the temple is a small one and will no doubt be rebuilt, Yeshua surmised.) Like the Egyptian deity Re, Surya is conceived of as crossing the sky during the day in a chariot. Furthermore, they give their chariot twelve wheels, for the twelve months or the twelve signs of the zodiac. This last idea is distinctly Persian.

Yeshua was accepted by the Brahmins, or priests, at least initially, because the Qumran Hindus had introduced him as a member of the Great Brotherhood and as a king destined to be a great Master among the Hebrews, and they could see for themselves that he was a holy man. From them he learned their methods of meditation and of opening the body's centers, which they call the spinning lotus flowers, each with a different name, color, and purpose. But here is the important part. Yeshua grasped in a fuller way the concept of karma, which had originated with them, or at least in their culture, for the Hindus themselves were undergoing a time of religious change. Of course, all the Essenes understand karma and reincarnation, but in India Yeshua came to develop a fuller understanding of karma, one beyond even that of the Hindus at that time. I will try to explain, because Yeshua's beliefs on this matter are the key to understanding many of his later teachings in his ministry among our people.

Most conceive of karma as simple cause, and then consequence. This is to say, what one gives out, one receives back. Therefore a man who hates much will be much hated. This makes only good sense: no one likes a person with a hateful spirit. If one does murder, a time will come when he will be murdered; if not in this life, in another. And so forth. This is how we all evolve and grow over many lifetimes until we reach perfection. And perfection is to merge once again with God, like a droplet of water returning to the immense ocean in which it belongs.

Yeshua loved all the Hindu teachings but came to disagree with the Brahmins on a single point. They believed a person born into a lower class or into poverty or illness must live out that karma and can do nothing to overcome it in the present lifetime. Indeed, to help them or teach them out of their situation is to interfere with the natural Law of karma. They must bear their burden. Now, consider what Yeshua said to the priests at the Temple when he was twelve. Did not the Sadducees believe much the same thing? (Though they did not call it karma.) They avoided the poor or the infirm or those they considered unclean because they felt Yahweh was punishing those persons, and who were they to defy Yahweh's justice? Is this not the same teaching: religious justification to reward those who need no reward, while denying happiness, the pursuit of the spiritual, and better circumstances to those most in need of them?

Yeshua rebelled against these beliefs, for he found them self-serving and hypocritical. He had also met, in the town outside the monastery, some traveling Buddhist monks with whom he had discussions. What, then, does a true Master, an avatar, do, when confronted by teachings that do not feel right to the heart? He prays, he fasts, he meditates, he converses with God, and God answers him. Yeshua came to believe that people do not learn from their karma if they merely suffer a miserable existence. Karma is not like paying a lifetime tax for the sins of a previous life. That is a punishment that teaches nothing, especially if the person cannot even remember the sin committed. Karma is intended to be overcome in life. And how is it overcome? Mark you this: for it is important: karma is overcome by forgiveness, both for the sinner and for the one sinned against. And when you do not forgive, you do yourself harm because you also pick up the karma of the other person. Anything you do not forgive will be visited, and revisited, and revisited upon your head, even over multiple lifetimes, until you learn to forgive it. This is why Yeshua forgave the Romans even as they nailed him to the tree, and he taught us to love even our enemies.

This is all I will write for now, because I will allow Yeshua's later sayings and parables to clarify this greatest of teachings.

Thus, ultimately, the Brahmins, as members of the upper class, disturbed Yeshua deeply. And of course it would. The Essenes have never held slaves, nor servants; slavery is most offensive to us. No man is better than another. And though the Brahmins did not have slaves by any means, there was a servant class, and by insisting those of the outcasts they called Untouchable stay as such and not be elevated and not be given religion except in teachings that forced them to resign themselves to a life of misery at the foot of the dung heap, Yeshua could not agree. He began to slip out of the monastery and go among these people and teach. I do not know if he healed, but it seems to me he would likely have done so.

So here was Yeshua, this young man just barely turned nineteen years of age and from a different country, disrespecting Law and tradition and teaching even those called Untouchable, and when I imagine this, I can began to see why some of the Brahmins came to regard him as arrogant. They called him to their chief Brahmin, who asked him to cease, but Yeshua refused. He offered to leave the monastery, but that was not acceptable since he had become popular and loved by the people of that town, and the Brahmins did not wish them to think they had sent him away.

Finally, Yeshua told my uncles, a young Brahmin not much older than he approached Yeshua in secret one afternoon and warned him of a plot. The two loved each other like brothers, having spent many hours together poring over the Upanishads and Bhagavad Gita and various codes of conduct and discussing their meaning. The young man, Ganid, spoke passable Aramaic and would translate for Yeshua the more difficult parts. Ganid told Yeshua he had overheard three of the older Brahmins in discussion over how to handle Yeshua, and one solution had been to hire an assassin to kill him in such a way that it would look like an accident. Ganid urged Yeshua to leave.

That very night, Yeshua slipped out of the monastery and began the long walk towards home. I believe he must have been more forlorn than afraid, unlike the fear of my grandparents when they fled to escape Herod. By morning Yeshua was many miles away, and the Brahmins' problem was solved. To this day no one knows if the plot would have actually been carried out, but as I have already suggested, great Masters or avatars are almost always met with resistance because they challenge the present social order and state of affairs.

Of course, Yeshua did not come directly home; he stopped at places along the way. Near the northwest border of India, he took refuge in a place called Srinagar, also called Kashmir, after a valley there, to tarry awhile with a group of followers of Siddhartha, otherwise called the Buddha. There was also a small community of Hebrews in this place—after the Assyrian scattering, the lost tribes are everywhere. Buddhism is a much newer religion, about only five hundred years old. And it is very different from other religions because the Buddha, or the Enlightened One, did not really teach belief in a God Being at all. He had not set out to found a new religion: his purpose had ultimately been to correct the missteps of the Brahmin priests and set that religion back on the right path—one of compassion and righteousness. The Hindu beliefs are so ancient that even the Hebrews of Srinagar also claimed lineage from them—meditate upon this: Brahma or Brahm and the similarity to Abram, who became Abraham, although Abraham was of Ur, a Chaldean. Are we not all related?

The Buddha's teachings centered on suffering and its relief—and Yeshua, yet so young, had already seen so much of it himself, feeling compassion for those in need and feeling frustration over the ways of the wealthy and how they turned away, in self-righteous indignation, from those who suffered. Yet there were also many similarities to the Hindus regarding meditation and opening the body's centers; a belief that the material world is illusion; and a belief that the light of the Cosmic Essence is present within each living thing.

I, personally, love the story of the Buddha, because it resonates with me so strongly. Do we not all suffer, and, like Job, perceiving no reason or fault for our sufferings, vainly ask the Lord why? The Buddha is said to have been born a wealthy prince who lived a sheltered life and was given every pleasure, but when he left the confines of his palace and saw the suffering of the people, he renounced his life of privilege. Just as Yeshua was to be tempted or tested prior to his ministry, the Buddha was tempted first to not set out on his path, because a life of power and being a king laid ahead of him; he had been born into the warrior class. He renounced even his wife and child, sacrificing a happy life with them to embark on his spiritual quest. For many years, he despaired, seeing reincarnation, even, as an endless wheel that turns and turns and each life is brought into suffering.

How to overcome the suffering? He studied with a guru who taught him meditation and told him to look within himself for the answers, that the self-reflective mind can be put to use to tame the mind and passions. Still the Buddha was not satisfied. Next he tried extreme asceticism, depriving his body of sleep, of food, of water; exposed to the elements, for many years, thinking that if he suffered badly enough he would find the key to learning how not to suffer. Still this did not work.

Finally, Buddha began to find his answer when meditating upon the natural world and the transitory nature of everything. Joy, he realized, is only to be found in the present moment, in appreciating the present moment. Having this insight, he realized he wanted to live. And to live, he had to eat. At that moment, a young girl approached him with a bowl of rice porridge. In compassion she offered it to him. From her action, he realized that is what we have to offer each other to ease the pain of suffering: the grace of compassion for our fellow creatures.

He ate, he bathed, he clothed himself, he left the ascetics. Then he went and sat under a fig tree to meditate, vowing to not move until he had found the answer to his question once and for all, by looking within. He reviewed his many past lives. He realized the problem of suffering lay in desire—that unquenchable flame of dissatisfaction. We suffer because we desire. Hence the answer to the problem of suffering is acceptance and to rid the self of unworthy desires, unrealistic expectations, and vain attachments. Nirvana, or to be awakened, means to accept all things, and in so doing, to recognize that everything is together connected. In that moment he became the Buddha.

More importantly, he realized that Nirvana is already here. One merely needs to open his eyes and see this.

He spent the rest of his life sharing this great teaching. The idea of a Creator or gods were not of importance to him. He had no dogma and no holy texts, although Yeshua said that stories of his life and sayings were beginning to be written down. The reader of my words will see, later, how at times Yeshua repeated his own version of Buddhist Sutras. But the Buddha himself merely spoke of the Four Noble Truths and the Eightfold Path that anyone can follow to obtain Enlightenment. We are all Buddhas—or can be. There are only three poisons in the way: greed, anger, and ignorance. In his lifetime, the Buddha gained many disciples and many were drawn to his teachings because he did not think the class system held any validity, nay, nor did even one's sex. All were welcomed to become monks or nuns in his monastery and were held in equal esteem. In this way his teachings were radical and freeing, for no Brahmins were required to intercede between the individual and that which was holy. That which was holy was already within everyone.

At Kashmir, then, Yeshua learned yet again of the Divine Spark within and of the healing nature of compassion. To compassion he linked his ideas of forgiveness and karma. The Buddhists came to love Yeshua and called him Issa; he tarried with them about two years. Refreshed and revitalized, Yeshua then returned to the old caravan route and began working his way back towards Palestine, through the land of the Persians, the land of the Chaldeans and the magi.

Chapter Six

Traveling back west over the mountainous terrain, Yeshua turned southward at the Indus Valley, having joined a caravan of travelers making their way from the very Far East into Persia with the Roman provinces as their ultimate destination. They traded silks, spices, jade, gems from India (among them rubies) and other goods with the Romans, who paid handsomely for such items, and indeed, even the Temple priests had need of gems such as rubies. Therefore men with swords traveled with the caravans, to protect the traders. In no hurry and enjoying their company, Yeshua wound his way through the mountain passes for many months, finally parting ways with one caravan in a place called the Bokhara Caves, known for secreting Jews during the time of the Assyrian invasion. More Jews had entered the area after the Babylonian invasion and the destruction of Solomon's First Temple, for it was well away from the Tigris and Euphrates Rivers. These caves were said to be a holy place, for here also had once been held the initiation rites of worshipers of the Persian sun god Mitra, often depicted as taming a bull.

As should be clear by now, religions share traditions. In Egypt was the celebrated Apis bull. In India, the Hindu god Shiva rode upon a white bull. Then there is the bull of the heavens, the constellation Taurus. Bulls have always been sacrificed upon altars to various gods. They are seen as symbols of strength, of fertility. One ancient cult was even said to practice a sport of bull leaping. And even now, the Romans, especially the soldiers, appear to be developing an entire new cult of Mithraic Mysteries, linking the bull to the sun worship of Sol Invictus, although Mithras is now turned into a Roman god in his own right; but they celebrate the sun god's birth date or incarnation on December 25th. It is a great pagan celebration called Saturnalia, a festival held here even in Pella, and as best as I can surmise,

Mithras is simply added to the mix, but they do not worship Mithras here. I hear that he is highly esteemed in Gaul. In any case, the noise of Saturnalia is at times deafening because there is a great feast and much drinking of wine and drumming and shaking of sistrums. As of late, at night during this week, I sometimes stop up my ears with leftover scraps of fabric just so I am able to sleep, so loud are their revelries!

But here I am, digressing once again. Later, when the prophet Zarathustra founded Zoroastrianism (as it is known in Greek), the earlier Persian god Mitra was swept into that religion and became an angel of the god, the all-seeing protector of Truth, not truth as in the opposite of lies, but Truth as in the reality of creation behind the illusion. But he was also seen as the guardian of cattle; thus, the bull. Ahura Mazda (basically meaning the God of Wisdom) became the One God, who manifests in the brightness of the sun. Yeshua saw these ancient caves, paid homage since members of the Great Brotherhood—respecting all religions—must do so, spent a few days and nights there reflecting, fasting, and meditating, then spent a short time resting and refreshing himself in the nearby city of Samarkand. He then resumed his journey, traveling to Persepolis—or to what remained of it. I must point out that travel through the Parthian Empire was relatively easy to do, if one was not Roman, since so many traveled along the caravan routes. And even to this day, the Romans and Persians still battle over that land, only now without actually fighting. Instead there is intrigue and assassinations and betrayals; there seems to be no end to the strife. I believe the Romans wish to out-conquer Alexander the Great. In the view of the Persians, the Greeks and the Romans are evil destroyers. At this time, therefore, the Persians are some of the greatest friends to the Jews.

In any case, at Persepolis, Yeshua's arrival had been anticipated by the Zoroastrian magi. Indeed, the one who had been sent to visit Yeshua in Bethlehem after his birth was still living and was now one of the Elders. His name was Balthazar. He greeted Yeshua with great joy. After embracing him, Balthazar said: "You were the tiniest of babes, but look at you now! I knew even then you would be a great man. Your eyes were open, and grave, and you watched me with great interest as I handed your gift to your mother." Then he looked long into Yeshua's eyes, his hands gripping Yeshua's shoulders. He himself became grave. Finally Balthazar said, "It is good that these shoulders are broad. They will one day carry the heaviest of burdens."

Yeshua was just short of twenty-two years of age.

As I have written, the Persians have always been great sages and astrologers. But they do not believe in a monastic life, living separate from the world. The world is meant to be lived in, in order to assist in conquering darkness. Their cosmology is very simple, black and white, no intermittent grays that create confusion. There is good, and there is evil. The One God, Ahura Mazda, is the unknowable Divine who can only be perceived in this world in good works because the God occupies the ideal and divine world of his original conception. Evil, or *druj,* attempts to undo the good in the material world and create chaos. (This idea is actually very similar to the Egyptian idea of *ma'at.*) Therefore, order is good. Knowledge is good, for acting in ignorance is lazy and selfish. The Persians are also somewhat like the Zealots and our apocalyptic Community of the *Yahad,* in their vision of an End Time, when good will finally battle evil, and good will triumph. Evil will be banished; the present world will end; Ahura Mazda will return to the earth and gather to him all the souls. And why should similar teachings not linger among us Hebrews? Mesopotamia, after all, is where our culture originated. Abraham was from Ur. If God is One, therefore God is God (I AM): he just has been given different names. So perhaps our ancestor Abraham spoke with Ahura Mazda. To be sure, Yeshua would entertain such ideas, pondering them very seriously and studying the ancient texts, although he always interpreted them through the lens of the Hebrew god Yahweh or 'El.

The Avesta and Gathas are the main sacred texts of the Zarathustrians, but unfortunately when Alexander the Great conquered Persepolis, he is said to have burned the library there in a bout of drunken stupidity, giving his men permission to burn even the palace, destroying others of the Persian texts. They completely looted the city, taking anything of value, killing the men, and keeping the women as slaves. So, the Egyptians might see Alexander as a God and a Pharaoh, which unites them with the Greeks, but the Persians, as I have written, do not.

Hence evil played a joke on the Persians, for to them fire is holy, yet it destroyed their great city. Nonetheless, the Persian magi still worship in temples with a fire always burning, tended by them, to represent the light that must never be extinguished: for one, it represents God, and second, it represents the Divinity within each person. They also practice sun gazing. Out of curiosity—and I know this sounds foolish—I tried sun gazing once. I stared into the sun until my eyes began watering and finally I had to look away. All I could see were bright white flashes and then yellow and red spots for quite some time. It was most unpleasant. Prayers, I think, are better. They do not make one blind. But the magi can stare at the sun for a long, long time and have an exalted experience. It occurs to me now that, perhaps when outer sight is removed, an inner sight awakens to take its place. Some have said Zarathustra first conceived of the One God when staring into a fire. And, as the story goes, did not God first appear to Moses in a burning bush? That would make perfect sense since he was, after all, the pupil of Akhenaten, who saw in the sun disk the One God: sun, light, fire, flames. And do not we Essenes also call ourselves the Sons of Light? A final thing worth writing down, which I believe I have already mentioned, is that the Zoroastrians had long anticipated a savior prophesied by Zoroaster himself. For centuries, the magi had been watching the skies for signs of his arrival. So, they had been as excited as us about the coming Messiah, which was why they had sent Balthazar with his gift of frankincense.

When Yeshua was there with Balthazar, I imagine Persepolis must have been much like the Jerusalem Temple is now, laid waste, sad, and in ruins. Yet it had been a great, great city, where people once came from all over the Persian Empire to give tribute to the king. The columns of the palace and great halls had been covered in gold and the ceilings made of the finest cedar from Lebanon. The main Gate of the Nations was guarded by two human-headed bulls with wings. Since so many of the Persians were nomadic, many lived in tents pitched outside the city, and these tents had woven carpets covering the ground and wall hangings that Yeshua spent much time describing, for they were very beautiful and of many colors. I have seen similar carpets in some of the forums here, but the Romans and Hellenized Jews seem to prefer tiles with mosaics for the floors of their houses. Most Jews certainly cannot afford such luxuries. We are content with our stone and dirt floors, and it is a luxury to us to sleep on a mat on the roof at night during the hot months. But carpets would be needed in tents since desert sand gets everywhere. I would try these old hands at carpet making if I thought I could sell what I made. Well, maybe in another life. Or perhaps my daughter will learn. In any case, all of this meandering is just to say that a part of my heart holds a great affection for the Persians. And I am not rare in this; even the prophet Ezra praised King Cyrus, who freed us from exile and returned to us the Temple vessels stolen by Nebuchadnezzar, that stubborn king who would not listen to the prophet Daniel. Or, rather, he would listen, be humbled, but then forget, returning to his old ways time and time again.

Yeshua and the magi walked solemnly through the ruins of Persepolis, viewing reliefs in the toppled stones that remained, pondering the rise and fall of civilizations; then Yeshua moved on with Balthazar and the other Zoroastrians to a nearby city about an hour's walk away, a place called Estakhr. It was here that he tarried two years, learning about the Persian religion and their methods of healing and divination, and in exchange he shared with them what he had learned.

Like the Hindus and like the Buddha, the prophet Zarathustra ate no meat, though vegetarianism was not a requirement of the religion. He also taught that animal sacrifices were wrong. He spoke of living righteously. In the material world, no one prospers without social justice. When creatures of God suffer, the world loses its balance, its harmony. Fortunately, each individual has been gifted by Ahura Mazda at birth with a good, uncorrupted mind. When a person sees injustice, he should speak out. The Zoroastrians also believe in three main pillars: the practice of good thoughts, good words, and good deeds. There is no predestination. God gave us the freedom to choose, and gave us solid minds to use with which to choose rightly. Satisfaction and reward come from doing the right thing for no more than the simple reason that it is the right thing. All our thoughts, if kept pure, will tell us the right thing to do. The two forces that may interfere with the purity of thought are greed and fear, both of which may motivate one towards unrighteous choices. Throughout his life, said Zarathustra, a person's choices are kept in a Book of Records. After death, one's soul lingers near his material body for three days, and then the dead person crosses the Bridge of Separation where there is a tallying up of good choices versus choices made in the absence of good. If the good outnumbers the bad, that person enters into the state of Right Consciousness. If not, that person enters into the state of Wrong Consciousness. Zarathustra believed in the immortality of the soul, but not in reincarnation. These ideas today have been adapted into, more or less, the Kingdom of Heaven or the fiery flames of Hell and perpetual torment, but they also are very much like the Egyptian view of the passage to the afterlife. One's heart is weighed on the scale against the feather of Ma'at. If the heart is light, that is, free of evil, the dead pass on into the realm of Osiris. If the heart is heavier than the feather, then that person is devoured by a beast. But what is interesting to me about Zoroastrianism is that, at the end of times, even those dead who are in the state of Wrong Consciousness will be returned to the God after all, for evil in the world will have been destroyed.

You will see that Yeshua told to the disciples a similar thing right before his ascension into heaven. The state of Right Consciousness is the better path to the Kingdom of Heaven.

During his two-year sojourn with the magi, Yeshua said there were two main concepts that struck a note within him. They both had to do with the power of thought. Since it is important to keep one's thoughts pure, for thought manifests in the world as deeds, he came to equate the two. One must therefore train oneself to banish evil thoughts from one's head, because once one has even had the thought, he or she has at least mentally committed the deed and thus it has already poisoned the heart. Since thought contains this kind of power, Yeshua also discovered that healing is considerably easier with people who believe in the powers of the healer. Faith that God is working through a person is part of the equation of thought and deed. Though it can be done, it is much more difficult to heal someone who does not have faith. So healing is best accomplished when the thoughts and faith of both healer and healed are as one.

I should add that no amount of faith and good thoughts can stave off the natural order of things, such as aging or getting sick when one drinks from a poisoned well, but you will later see how Yeshua got around some elements of natural law—or so it would seem—when he perceived karma was involved in the illness. Believe you me, if there were a way I could will away, through faith, the cold achiness of my joints, I would have done so years ago!

Hence Yeshua continued to grow in thought and in deed, and

in favor with the Lord, for he exhibited yet more miracles. One day, while out on a walk, he saw a lion and many men pursuing this lion, throwing javelins and pelting him with stones in order to slay him. Yeshua stilled them with his hand. "This lion," he said, "is more noble than you. These creatures of God were once our friends. Our cruelties over the generations have turned them into our enemies."

The desert dwellers must at first have thought him mad.

"Do him no harm," Yeshua commanded. "Do you not see how he flees from you, and is terrified by you?"

The lion then came to Yeshua and laid down at his feet, and Yeshua patted him. The people marveled over how his compassion extended to even ferocious beasts, and that even a lion could love him, purring at his feet like a domesticated cat.

Now, while Yeshua was away on his travels, as was required, he would write once a year to the Essene Council of Elders, and occasionally he would send letters home to my grandparents to let them know how he fared and where he was. The Sadducees say only the upper classes are literate, and that is mostly true, but even most poor Jews are able to read and write, at least enough to send a simple message. One day the news reached Yeshua that his father Joseph had died. As the eldest son, it was his responsibility to come home and see to the household. Thus, at age twenty-four, Yeshua ended his travels, with the exception of his final trip to Egypt for the initiation at Gizeh. Yeshua wrote home immediately to let his mother know he was on the way; he gave the letter to a trader on a caravan headed to Jerusalem and the Decapolis cities, and he set out on foot the next day. Balthazar was kind enough to give him a camel loaded down with provisions for his journey.

Yeshua sent other letters; I know not where they are, but the family still has in our possession the one that Yeshua wrote to his mother. I believe Simon probably holds it at present. In any case, I myself have read this letter, and I will set down what I remember of it. He wrote that he was sorry for his mother's grief, but to take heart since Joseph had been a good man, never accused even once of dishonesty or deceit or of breaking the laws of the Torah. He had been a good father, working hard for his living and teaching his sons his trade. And that he was even now in Heaven, with the Father of us all, where all righteous souls return after death to abide awhile before returning to this world. He encouraged Mary to not let her grief make her stray from the path of Love on which she had been set. Then he wrote something that I remember word-for-word, because it is almost a psalm it is so beautiful. He wrote, "Rise above the cares of earthly things and remember your life is given to those who still live with us here on earth. When your life is done, you will find it again in the morning sun, or even in the evening dew, as in the song of birds, the perfume of the flowers, and the lights of the stars at night."

And now I am thinking of my grandmother with tears.

Well. The rest of the letter said he would hurry home, not stopping at other places he had hoped to stop, with the exception of Babylon, the ruins of which naturally he had to see, to remember the sufferings of our people. But he would not tarry long, and it was not too much out of the way, for he planned to take the Royal Road, which was paved and fast to travel, then turn west across into Syria, then south on into Palestine. No doubt, he said, he would connect with another caravan, for the travelers had all treated him well. They would offer him sustenance when he shared his stories and would marvel at the wisdom of one so young. The common people, Yeshua said, no matter what land they come from, are in general pleasant and kind. No, it is those with power and riches who forget our common humanity.

There is a joke among the Hebrews that the Romans may build as many *latrinae* with comfortable seats and baths as they wish, with flowing water underneath to carry the waste away, but that which comes out of their bodies does not smell any less foul. Despite their power and their riches, they are also like any other human being. When I catch myself feeling self-righteous and judgmental, I try to remember this joke and apply it to myself. A man cannot be too humble; and, as Yeshua was to teach us later, "Blessed are the meek."

But as you can see, Yeshua's travels taught him much, and he increased in wisdom and goodness the entire time. Just as the Buddha can be seen as correcting or evolving the ideas of the Hindus, when the Brahmins left the right path, by addressing suffering and reminding them of compassion since compassion was, after all, a part of their teachings, so it seems to me that Zarathrusta evolved the early gods of the Mesopotamian religions, gods who merely wished to be appeased and had nothing to do with righteous living. Zarathrusta taught the people of good and right and the need for justice in all things. And so it seems to me that Yeshua was likewise inspired to evolve our god, the god of the Hebrews, to set us back on the right path, to turn us away from sin and slaughter and to remind us that God is Love, and to do the work of God is to do works of love. The Kingdom of Heaven is open to all the world over—for, the One God is God over all the world, over all the peoples, no matter what name God is given. Yeshua was setting out to follow in the footsteps of the Masters.

Chapter Seven

Many people of tiny Nazareth called out to Mary when Yeshua was spied, dusty and ragged, walking on sandals that should have been discarded (he had long since traded the camel for food), entering the town from the northern trail. Of course, these were the people who knew him, either family or other Essenes. They went up to him in great joy, embracing him, kissing his cheek, remarking over how much he had grown. They almost hadn't recognized him. He was twenty-five, after all, and the last they had seen him, he had been thirteen. At the noise, Mary left her spinning and came running. My father, who was almost thirteen years of age himself, still remembers his mother leaping into Yeshua's outstretched arms so that Yeshua almost fell over backwards. There was much laughter over this. Later that night, there was a modest welcoming feast, and some members of the family recall that Yeshua even allowed himself a small cup of new wine since it was the time of the crushing of the grapes, and a family in town had offered them some of the remaining first fruits of their labor for the celebration.

And then there were the gossipers, those who did not know. They grumbled behind their walls, in their courtyards. "What manner of son is this," they said, "who takes almost half a year to return to his father's home after his death?" These were those who fed the later rumors that Yeshua was not even the son of Joseph, for they said that if Yeshua were truly the son of Joseph, he would have come home within days. When speaking of Yeshua, later on they even omitted mention of Joseph altogether, as a sign of their disrespect. In this way "son of a fornicator" (because of his early birth) changed, over time, into "son of a harlot." The worst of these even accused Mary of fornication with a Roman of Sepphoris, but I think I have written that lie down already. All I can say to this is that, if there were ever any proof of such, the rabbis most certainly would have stoned my grandmother. But no, these cowards kept their viperous slander to themselves, never bringing forth a charge but instead allowing rumor to spread like a poison. Later, when Yeshua was telling the disciples what to expect when they went out into the world to spread the Word and the Way, he even said, "You will know your father and mother, but they will call you the son of a whore."

But that night, there was celebration. Yeshua met James's wife, Joanna, and Joses' new bride, Anna. My aunt Mary was at that time unmarried. Yeshua also met, for the first time, his siblings Jude, Simon, and Salome. James had filled Yeshua's place quite well in his absence. My grandmother Mary was provided for, and James and Joses had built two new rooms off the courtyard of the house. They were simple and small but at least offered them some measure of privacy. Their wives were helping Mary and my aunt with the smaller children, while Mary was teaching them spinning and tending to the few animals and the small plot of garden behind the house. Not much was grown, but oftentimes vegetables could be traded for a sheaf of wheat, or better yet, a small bag of wheat already ground, and bread could be made.

The family asked Yeshua about his travels, and since I have summarized them already, I need not repeat that information here. But they were most interested in his stories and also wanted to know what Babylon had been like, for of course we had had ancestors who had been exiled there. Babylon, like Persepolis, is also now in ruins. There the Mesopotamians had once worshiped their chief god, Bel, also called Marduk, although homage was given to other deities as well, such as Ishtar, for whom one of the city gates had been named. Yeshua said that while walking through the ruins, he could not help but think of the Psalm:

"By the rivers of Babylon, there we sat down and there we wept, when we remembered Zion. On the willow trees there we hung up our harps. For there our captors asked us for songs, and our tormentors asked for mirth, saying, 'Sing us one of the songs of Zion!'

"How could we sing the Lord's song in a foreign land? If I forget you, O Jerusalem, let my right hand wither! Let my tongue cling to the roof of my mouth, if I do not remember you, if I do not set Jerusalem above my highest joy."

It is a mournful psalm yet beautiful when sung. But mention of Jerusalem prompted Mary to ask if Yeshua intended to stay a while in Nazareth and take a wife, for she had several local women in mind as potential helpmates.

Yeshua was silent. Finally he said, "Mother, think of the story of the Brahmins I have just told you. I do not believe my ministry here will be any less dangerous. Only here, I am among my own people, and I will not seek to escape."

(Yes, even then Yeshua knew he would anger the Sadducees and those Pharisees who supported the priests and the Herodians, and that he would tax the patience of the Romans; he did not wish to draw a wife and children under their scrutiny, nor commit them to the grief he knew they would feel when he was persecuted. Today some preach that Yeshua was against marriage or remained chaste so as to not stain his soul by touching a woman, and all other sundry nonsense. On the contrary, he loved weddings and blessed those who married. He attended my uncle Simon's wedding in Cana with great joy, performing a miracle there when the wine jars ran dry so as to not bring embarrassment to his mother. No, when it came to marriage, Yeshua taught exactly what the Essenes taught: one of the three traps of Belial, or the Evil One, involves marriage, and that is the sin of polygamy and the sin of marriage between uncles and nieces, and, of course, the sin of adultery. The other two are hoarding, or the worship of, wealth; and defiling the Temple sanctuary. And therefore, Yeshua and John came down harshly on the Herodians and others for these practices, as you will see.)

But I digress once again.

"What do you mean, not marry?" James asked. "King David had a wife." He laughed. "Solomon perhaps had far too many."

"Don't fear the Romans. Surely the Lord will protect His Messiah," said Joses.

Yeshua did not answer.

"What will you do?" Mary asked, her voice almost a whisper.

"I will go to Qumran to fetch John, and we will travel to Egypt for our last instructions before our ministry." Yeshua raised his cup. "But let us not think about this now. I will stay here for a time to rest and visit and put some flesh back on these bones."

They stayed up talking until well after dark, and Yeshua went up to the roof to sleep.

* * *

Yeshua tarried about the span of a month. The only other things my father has told me of this time is that he seemed, except for his unusually kind and loving nature, just like anyone else. He helped his mother and sisters and sisters-in-law; he touched Anna's belly and told her she would soon conceive (which turned out to be true—for he would be my cousin Mattias), and on some days Yeshua walked with his brothers to Sepphoris to help lay stone. He also spent much time going on long walks and at night would go up to the roof at sundown to pray and then sleep. He was always up with the sun, saying prayers and then meditating, just like the Brethren at the Community of the *Yahad*, at Qumran. Finally, my father remarked that Yeshua sometimes would take his mother Mary aside for long conversations. During one such time, Mary was seen weeping as Yeshua comforted her. Everyone assumed then they were reminiscing about Joseph. Now I am not so sure. Now I think he may have been telling my grandmother more of what he foresaw for his upcoming ministry.

The day of his departure came. It would be about a three-day walk to Qumran, where Yeshua was expected. His cousin John would be ready to depart with him to Egypt. They would retrace the steps of Joseph and Mary, only this time they were not headed all the way north to Alexandria. This time they would stop at the City of the Sun that is called Heliopolis, or in the Hebrew writings called On, which is not strictly Essene or *Therapeutae;* it is, if you will, the "headquarters" of the Great Brotherhood. Here they would be tested and, if found worthy, initiated into the greatest of the mysteries. Yeshua was almost twenty-six years old; John had already reached that age. The family was not to see Yeshua for another five years. All the Essenes of Israel and Judea awaited their return from Egypt with great anticipation—Finally! The coming of the two prophesied Messiahs: the mighty warrior king of David and the legitimate priest of the line of Aaron. The Romans and their prefect would be ousted from the palace in Caesarea and from Herod's palace in Jerusalem; Herod Antipas the client king would be thrown down; the false priests would be expelled from the Temple; the promised land would be returned to her people; the covenant with God would be restored.

Obviously, none of this was to happen, for the Divine had an entirely different plan.

* * *

In Egypt, Heliopolis had once been a great city, with temples to the sun god Re, along with Pharaoh Akhenaten's temple to the Aten, called *Wetjes-Aton*. One cult of the bull was there, a bull said, if memory serves me, to represent an incarnation of Re. There had also been the Sanctuary of the Phoenix, a symbol of the Resurrection. The Egyptians have long believed in the immortality of the soul, except they believe that the physical body must be preserved so the soul may take up residence in it. Also the famed Benben Stone was in Heliopolis, said to have fallen from the heavens and resembling a pyramid, although more conical in shape. Others call it the Stone of Destiny and say it was the stone upon which Jacob laid his head when he slept and dreamed of the angels ascending and descending the ladder to the heavens. This stone is said to have many mysterious powers. Heliopolis had once been known far and wide for being such a place of wisdom that many great priests and philosophers took their learning there, among them, it is said, Pythagoras, Plato, and Solon, where Solon had there heard the priests' account of Atlantis. Even that weaver of glorious tales, Homer, was said to have spent time in Heliopolis. And in his day, our ancestor Joseph, of the coat of many colors, the vizier to Pharaoh, was married to the daughter of the High Priest of Heliopolis.

When John and Yeshua arrived, the city still stood, but it was largely in ruins because it had been abandoned after being burned by the Persians. A few obelisks still remained, but most of the monuments and grand sculptures had been pilfered by the Romans and moved to Alexandria. Now inhabited by only priests and other initiates, Heliopolis had long ceased being the main seat of learning, the great library having also been moved to Alexandria. The city surrounding the temple complex had been mostly deserted. The priests of the ancient Great Brotherhood had remained, however, because their initiation temple was at nearby Gizeh. The Leo Sphinx, facing east, and the underground passage to the Great Pyramid used to be widely known as parts of the initiation-temple complex, but knowledge of this was already beginning to be lost to the sands of time and history when Yeshua and John visited that place.

The original lion's head of the Sphinx had also been desecrated centuries before by a Pharaoh named Khafre, who had found the Sphinx buried up to its neck by blowing sand. (Some thousand or more years later, it is said, another Pharaoh, Thutmose IV, again had to remove the sand, and he erected a stele to himself by the chest of the Sphinx.) But Khafre had been worse. His men removed the sand, and Khafre turned the ancient carved limestone into a monument to himself by having his sculptors chisel down the original lion's head, replacing it with his own head and likeness. He had also built a pyramid as a tomb for himself next to the Great Pyramid, setting it upon a stone platform so that it appeared to be larger than the great one. It seems that man's vanity at times knows no bounds.

Yeshua and John, of course, could not say much of their trials and tests and the initiations there, for these things are kept secret. I confess I know not *any* details of John's stay in Heliopolis. In fact some have asked why Yeshua did not begin his ministry sooner than he did. It is for the reason that he had to wait for John. One may not become a priest until he has reached the age of thirty. Since the priestly Messiah was to herald the coming of the kingly Messiah, there is your answer. John had studied Torah at Qumran, and the reading of dreams, prophecies, and signs. Unlike Yeshua, he was not a fast learner. But once he grasped something, John understood it fully, and it stayed with him. When John's studies and initiations were completed, he traveled back to Qumran and, shortly thereafter, on his thirtieth birthday, he departed thence to the River Jordan, as had been planned.

On the other hand, Yeshua was able to share a little of his experiences at Heliopolis with the family, and I assume since he did so, it is permissible to write down what I remember. I confess, it is a fantastical story that my father told me. But perhaps that is the purpose of the ancient rituals, to imbue them with mystery and wonder. The tests themselves I surmise were adapted to challenge the dedication of each particular initiate. The first thing required was to meet with the hierophant for admission to the mystery school. Yeshua answered the questions put to him (he did not say what they were) with clarity and assurance. The hierophant listened to his answers, then said to him, "Rabbi of Israel, why do you come to us? You already have the knowledge of the gods. We are but men."

Yeshua answered that he wished to learn the wisdom of every hall of learning. He said, "It would please my Father for me to pass the hardest of any test you give to me—yes, even if takes me to where your dead are buried."

We all know of the Great Pyramid and that this was the place of the final initiation, so it was to this ancient tomb—or so all thought then that it had once been a tomb—that Yeshua alluded. But you must understand the importance of what Yeshua was saying. Under Torah, to venture into tombs is to make oneself unclean for seven days. Corpses render one ritually unclean. Even more so for a priest: they were not to touch the dead at all under any circumstances. To do so would be to force that priest to renounce the priesthood, so I am not sure how John handled this requirement, or if it was changed for him, or if he completed the last initiation. But Yeshua was dogged, and he seemed certain of what God wished of him even if it seemed to challenge God's own Laws. Ritual uncleanliness: well, he could always wash to purify himself. But as he was to later see, the Great Pyramid is not a tomb and never was.

The hierophant inclined his head. "Take then the vow of the Great Brotherhood."

Of course Yeshua could not share this promise with us, but I assume it was one of a "yes" or "no" nature. I write this because the Essenes do not make oaths or swear, for this is the Law of the Torah, although many non-Essene Jews repeatedly break this law. It is because we wish to always remain truthful, for one never knows what the future may hold. Contracts are different because they may always be renegotiated if the need arises, but vows and oaths are not permitted. That Yeshua was comfortable in making a vow speaks highly to the great intention of his soul. Or, as I have said, perhaps this vow was more a "yes" or "no" promise, a suggestion I made earlier. And I will write in all confidence that no one ever knew Yeshua to break a promise. For, what good is a person's word if he or she feels free to break it if ever an unanticipated contingency arises?

After Yeshua gave his word, the hierophant regarded him and said, "Rabbi of Israel, the greatest heights are reached by those who reach the farthest depths. You will one day reach the farthest of depths."

I confess I have no idea what that means. But it is said by some that, after Yeshua was crucified and died, and then resurrected, he descended into *Sheol,* the land of the dead, to tell the souls there of the good news: that the covenant with Yahweh was restored and that, by following the teachings of Yeshua, those there that were lost could be saved.

Well. It is an interpretation.

A priest then settled Yeshua into a comfortable but modest dwelling where he was to study their ancient teachings, pray, and meditate for three months. At that point, he would be given further instructions. Each day he was brought food and water that was clean for Jews, and no meat, but he was not to speak to this priest. He was allowed conversation with no one, nor was he to leave his dwelling. Thus all Yeshua knew of the outer goings-on in Heliopolis was what he could gather through his intuition and inner senses.

Three months passed. Then, one afternoon, after the priest delivered Yeshua's daily sustenance as was usual, he paused at the door as if considering. Yeshua looked at him. "Rabbi," the priest said finally, "I fear for you. Some of your Hebrew beliefs are antagonistic to the worship of Re. There are some here who wish to kill you. If not kill you, at least imprison you."

He came over to Yeshua and sat down on the mat beside him, speaking with great earnestness. "There are ways you may safely escape under cover of night," and he went on to give a method for stealing away from Heliopolis, leaving Egypt and returning safely to Palestine. "Soon you will be freed from the confines of this dwelling," he said. "When the priests approach you, you must tell them that you will stay here and serve the Temple forever, taking their instruction. Then by night I will come to you and help you to leave."

Yeshua looked into the man's eyes and smiled. "Begone, deceiver," he said.

The next day, Yeshua was summoned to appear before the hierophant. He placed his hand on Yeshua's head and handed him a small scroll upon which the Egyptian word "sincerity" was written. "You have passed the first test," the hierophant said. Then he smiled. "We know of your stay with the Brahmins and the danger you faced there. In fact, your old friend Ganid wishes you well."

Yeshua was happy to hear this news of Ganid.

The hierophant went on. "Your silence is now broken. You will continue your studies, but you may now leave your house to join us daily for our communal meal and the discussions of our teachings and practices afterwards." Because of differing food customs across cultures, at the communal meal people sat with those of their own lands or religion. As I have written, Jews have always remained in Egypt. There were three others aside from Yeshua and John when they were there. Together the five made one table. Among the initiates, there were Greeks, Persians, Hebrews, Indians, Egyptians, Libyans, and Africans from further south. To be accepted at Heliopolis, my father said, was a great honor.

The time thus passed, and Yeshua befriended all of the priests and Elders and other initiates, met some of the Masters, and was glad to be reunited with his cousin, John. It was forbidden, however, for anyone to speak of the tests, or of the various steps in the initiatory process, or to ask questions if an initiate disappeared, even if he or she was never to be seen again.

One night, a priestess knocked on Yeshua's door and entered his dwelling. "You must come with me," she commanded. Yeshua did as he was asked, even though the priestess tied a cloth around his head to cover his eyes. She took Yeshua by the arm and led him, this way and that way, many paces, down steps, down corridors, down more steps, turning to the left, turning to the right, going in great circles for all Yeshua knew, until they came to a chamber. Here the priestess removed the cloth from his eyes, and without a word, departed, slamming shut the door behind her and bolting it, leaving Yeshua in total darkness, completely alone.

He sat there many days, not knowing whether it was night or day. He was without food. Feeling his way around the chamber walls, he found a large stone jar of water. Thus he stayed, fasting and meditating, sometimes sleeping, sometimes hearing voices echoing from far away outside the chamber where he stayed.

He was finally startled from his sleep after many days had passed when a block in one wall of the chamber began scraping open. He saw the lights of two small oil lamps, and in through the opening stepped two men dressed in the garb of the Masters.

"We take pity on you, Rabbi of Israel," one said, and he handed Yeshua bread. They then sat down on the stone floor next to him and watched silently as he blessed the bread, broke, and ate.

"You are a holy man," the other said. "In the truest sense of that word. Therefore our hearts are grieved because of the suffering the hierophant has subjected you to."

"We were once like you," said the first. "We aspired to Truth and to Goodness and were willing to suffer these confinements and strange practices to attain the degree of blessedness which you seek."

The second Master shook his head as if weary. "It was our own vanity."

The first said, "Our eyes became opened after attaining the highest degree." He then laughed without mirth, more like a cry of pain. "Do you wish to know the *real* reason Heliopolis was burned? It is because the priests here are corrupted, nothing but common criminals. Do you really think the Persians, who saved your people, would so seek to destroy the holy places of Egypt?"

The second man said, "The priests here make sacrifices. Not just of animals, but of innocent children, men, and women—burning them as offerings—all to glorify their false gods."

"In horror and disgust we have left the confines of this wicked place," said the first. "We urge you to do the same, good Rabbi."

Yeshua asked, "How came you into this chamber?"

"Beneath these walls are many hidden ways, and since we were priests and Masters, we have spent months and years within this labyrinth, knowing all the corridors and secret passageways."

"Then you are traitors," Yeshua said. "The small lights you carry are the greatest light you bring. I will not listen."

"Do not be surprised when they throw even you on the pyre," the first warned as they rose to their feet and exited the way they had come, pulling the stone back into place and leaving Yeshua once again in darkness.

A few days later, the priestess returned and led Yeshua from the chamber without covering his eyes with a cloth. It was indeed an underground labyrinth. The priestess took him to the hierophant. Once more the hierophant placed his hand upon Yeshua's head and handed him a scroll. On this scroll was written the Egyptian word for "justice."

The hierophant said, "You are wise, and just, that you are able to discern evil when it is disguised as good. Now, return to the communal table and eat your fill. You must be very hungry."

At table Yeshua was greeted by many welcomes and smiles. He noticed that John was absent, but this did not trouble him. He was likely undergoing one of his own initiatory tests. He trusted his cousin with all his heart.

More time passed. Upon the date of one year of joining the Heliopolis School of Mysteries, Yeshua was rewarded by being taken from his modest dwelling and given a new one. It was a chamber rich in furnishings and decorations. The ceilings and walls were painted blue and gold, and the room blazoned with light from many gold and silver oil lamps. One wall contained a shelf filled with scrolls written by many Masters of the past. He was even given a bed: a wooden piece of furniture, painted gold, with several thick woven mats stretched between the two ends. For his head he was provided with what the Greeks used, a cushion made of cloth stuffed with feathers and embroidered with threads of blue and gold. The entire chamber smelled of lotus flowers, for lotus oil bubbled in an incense burner in one corner.

The priest who took Yeshua there bowed to him. "Rabbi of Israel, we congratulate you."

Yeshua also bowed.

The priest straightened, shaking his head to indicate no. "You must now learn to accept reverence," he said, not unkindly. "We never offer it lightly. You have remained here a year, passing two degrees, and most do not make it past the first." The priest then gestured to the scrolls. "You are to study these works of our Masters and continue to attend the communal meal and discussions."

Yeshua told the family he had never lived in such luxury, nor slept as soundly as he ever had in that chamber of comforts. Indeed, during the days as he studied the scrolls, a priest would come in and offer him an unusual drink of heated water infused with herbs and sweetened with honey. Every day people drank much beer in Egypt, for barley was a staple crop. The priests often drank wine infused with the flower of the blue lily. However, abstaining from strong drink, Yeshua drank nothing but water and this new drink the priest would bring him. He said it was very bitter, but the honey made it good.

After some time had passed, one day a different priest came in, bowed to Yeshua, and stacked a few new scrolls onto the shelf of scrolls. He paused to survey the surroundings.

"Rabbi of Israel," he said, his voice filled with awe. "Look at the grandeur of this room. You have found great favor with the hierophant for him to have given such a room to you."

"I know this not," Yeshua said.

"But it is true!" the priest said. "They speak much of you, of your travels and miracles and healings in foreign lands. They say you are a great philosopher and the greatest of mystics and teachers. They say even the gods do your bidding."

"That is surely blasphemy," Yeshua said. "It is the other way around. I do the bidding of the One God."

"Then this is a great new teaching! You are the Messiah of Israel. You should leave this school and go found your own, even greater school. Think of the fame and power and wealth that would come to you. Think of the love the people would have for you. Your destiny is to be a great King, is it not?"

Yeshua said nothing.

The priest gave a small shrug and left the room.

Yeshua was troubled by this conversation. Was this to be the destiny of the Messiah? He had merely sought the wisdom of Solomon, but even Solomon had built the great First Temple and amassed vast wealth. What good Yeshua could do with such wealth! He could restore to the peasants the land seized from them by the rich who had lent them money so the poor could pay their taxes. He would pay off their debts and give the peasants back their lands. He could see to it that no one, from Galilee to Judea, was homeless or hungered any longer or possessed no cloak or sandals. He could raise a great army and drive out the Romans. He could restore the Levites and true sons of Zadok and Aaron to the Temple and install John as High Priest. Was this not what the people Israel expected of their Messiah?

For many days Yeshua wrestled with this question. He meditated; he prayed. Much later on, to my father and my uncles, Yeshua admitted that Ambition was a great king indeed.

One day the priest returned with a new scroll to add to the shelf. Then he turned and bowed to Yeshua with reverence.

"Master Rabbi," he said, making a show of humility, "May I be the first you will accept into your Great School?"

"Please stand up. I am not your Master," Yeshua said.

The priest straightened and regarded him.

Yeshua said, "The wealth, the honor, and the fame of earth are nothing but the trinkets of an hour. When this short span of earthly life has all been measured out, those things will be buried in the tombs, nay, even in the ground, with the bones of the dead." He gestured in the direction of Gizeh. "Even the greatest of tombs have been robbed of their riches. Doing the will of God is what will enter men and women into His Kingdom."

The priest nodded and turned to go.

"Wait," Yeshua called.

He stopped.

"I wish to thank you," Yeshua said, "for this great contest that raged within myself. And I thank God that my greater self prevailed."

The priest inclined his head again and took his leave.

The next day, the priest returned and brought Yeshua to the hierophant. Once again the hierophant placed one hand upon Yeshua's head and handed him a small scroll. This time the word written upon it was "faith."

The hierophant said, "You have now completed the first three degrees towards Master of our Great Brotherhood. Three remain, each of which takes one year to complete. In your fifth year, you will study your final degree under my tutelage. Then will come the final great test. Remain steadfast, O Rabbi of Israel."

Thus ended the three great temptations. The rest of the degrees had to do with the mysteries and with the development of the soul and its capabilities, and Yeshua had been forbidden to share any information at all about those degrees. However, his later teachings and works that I will set down may point towards some of what he learned, as well as I am able to articulate these things. Yet, some of his sayings remain mysterious, and I still ponder them to this day.

For now, I will stop and resume tomorrow, for the story of the Great Pyramid initiation deserves a parchment of its own.

Chapter Eight

Yeshua was returned to his more modest dwelling, and the three years passed swiftly. My father said he pressed Yeshua several times to divulge something of those years, but he would say no more, except for a story—from which of necessity he omitted much—about his final initiation. At the communal meals, sometimes Yeshua would see John; sometimes he would not. At some point during the fifth year, John disappeared for good, and Yeshua assumed he had completed his studies and returned to Qumran. This bothered Yeshua not, for had he not himself told the hierophant at the beginning that he wished to be given the hardest of their tests?

"Either that," Yeshua said much later, after the death of John, "or he was the better man than I, and it took him a shorter time to learn and to vocalize the teachings and to complete the degrees. It is true John was never reluctant to speak. He articulated his beliefs and feelings clearly."

How kind my uncle was. Everyone knew John had possessed a loud, indiscreet voice. Yet this trait, and his temper, had also made John the perfect Prophet, just like those of old, his words thundering in the wilderness, calling the people to repent.

Yeshua began his studies with the hierophant. He was able to say that some of the work was reviewing or sharpening information already learned in his travels, such as slowing down the breathing during meditation, opening the body's centers, developing the gift of foreknowledge, reading dreams and signs, and communicating with the Divine. But there was a mysterious, non-physical and non-material element to this last degree that Yeshua was forbidden to explain to the uninitiated. All Yeshua would say is that the world we see and touch is not the entire world, for we are limited by our human senses. Since I am familiar with Plato's allegory of the cave, I understand what my uncle Yeshua was saying, but no matter how much I meditate and burn sandalwood and try to open my body's centers, my mind perceives nothing but blank things or white dots or sometimes, blobs of pulsing colors. My thoughts also continually interrupt when I try to quiet my mind. I believe I have done good in my life, helping others, never turning away one in need, following Torah and teaching the Way of Yeshua our Messiah, but perhaps I am a failure.

Then I am tempted to be like some, who curse our bodies and see them as a trap that separates us from God.

Still, Yeshua very clearly taught us: "The body is not evil. It is but one part of the True Reality. But you do not need to die to visit the other parts and to see God."

It is so frustrating to not experience for myself what he knew. Then envy interrupts my thoughts, and I think, spitefully, that perhaps in Egypt they gave him some medicine that made him see visions.

Yet how could such a good and holy man be like one who is drugged and possessed? He would not even take strong drink. But he ate so little, and fasted so often. Perhaps fasting provided him the visions.

I pray for insight, but it does not come. I am left with nothing but trust in my uncle, faith in his words and in God.

I am sorry for this tangent. I suppose I am thinking out loud, in my words here on parchment. This will have to be one of those things I strike out.

Back to Yeshua's story.

When the hierophant was satisfied Yeshua had grasped all there was to grasp, Yeshua was given the final great initiation into Master of the Brotherhood. Once again, he could not tell us much, since the rite is secret, but I will tell you what he told the family.

The initiation took place the night of a full moon. At dusk, Yeshua was led back down into that great labyrinth, though this time with his eyes uncovered. There were several priests and priestesses and the hierophant himself. Only small oil lamps and candles were used to light the way, so all was dim. They walked, Yeshua said, for at least an hour or more, or so it seemed. Then they ascended a flight of stairs and pushed up a stone and emerged into the night, next to the Nile. The cool breeze stirred the hairs on Yeshua's arms and the expanse of night sky sparkled with stars and the one large cloudy, milky swath that cleaved the sky much as the Nile parts that land into east and west.

They stepped into a waiting felucca and crossed the great river, which was inky black in the night. All was silent except for the sound of the oars being dipped into the water, for even though it was a still night, the current flowed, as always, towards the Delta. Nevertheless the full moon laid a trace of light across the deep channel, and Yeshua watched the wake of the boat, the concentric circles of the dips made by the oars and how they then dispersed into the larger current. How this great river directed everything in this land! The year centered on the inundation and the water's retreat, irrigation, planting, and harvest. All the major temples and temple complexes were near to the Nile, or had been at one time, for over the centuries the riverbed itself shifted and moved, and then shifted again, as if beckoning the people to follow it to newer, fresher, unblemished soil that the great river would fertilize.

They made land and climbed out of the boat. Again they walked a ways, came to a small structure by a sycamore tree where there flowed a stream, and once they were inside the structure, two priests heaved aside a stone, and they descended again below ground. The candles and lamps were relit and once more they moved in darkness, walking for several hours in the stifling dimness. Still, there were air shafts, since occasionally Yeshua could feel fresh air hit his skin for a few paces at regular intervals. Finally they reached another stone staircase, ascended this, and exited onto the Gizeh Plateau. From the position of the moon in the sky, Yeshua guessed that it was well after midnight. They had traveled many miles, and he was weary.

They had emerged by the temple that had been constructed for the Sphinx. The night was still clear and the stars shone more brightly, and with the full moon, it was light enough that the lamps and candles could be extinguished. The group walked over to the Sphinx to the altar that stands between its paws. The brass of its mighty claws glistened in the moonlight.

Here Yeshua took the first vow.

Next a doorway was opened in the Sphinx's chest, and they descended to a hypostyle hall, with many columns with hieroglyphs and passageways going off in sundry directions. The lamps and candles were once again lit.

They proceeded down one long passageway for many thousands of paces until they reached a second subterranean room where there was a statue and sarcophagus, the dwelling of Osiris. Here Yeshua took a second vow.

Finally, they left the chamber and began moving up a slanted passageway. There were no more stairs. At times they had to bend over, for the ceiling was quite low. At some point, perhaps because of the angle, it became clear to Yeshua that they were inside the Great Pyramid. The going was steep and proceeded slowly. The blackness was pitch. There was no speaking, but it was the responsibility of each priest or priestess to ensure the person behind stayed with them. If one tripped and fell, the other helped him up. Yeshua's place was in the middle of the line. The passageways were so narrow in some spots that he could easily place both hands on the granite walls on either side of him; at the steepest points, his fingers found handholds in the walls he used to help propel himself forward and upwards. Many times they had to bend over and worm their way through. Although it was well past midnight and the night air outside the pyramid was cool, inside their footsteps kicked up dust in the oppressive heat, so at times breathing was difficult.

They reached a straight passageway and turned to the right, entering yet another small chamber with an altar. The hierophant lit frankincense, and here Yeshua took a third vow.

Then they left this chamber by the way they had come, turning right yet again, and began climbing a grand gallery, where finally they could stand at full height. The priests and priestesses began vocalizing sounds that vibrated the very walls and echoed throughout the passageways of the entire pyramid, and Yeshua said his skin even vibrated. It was then that Yeshua realized the pyramid had never been an actual tomb. It was a temple, and this gallery was a sound chamber for raising energy. With each step forward, his body felt lighter and lighter. Never had he been in a place with such acoustics, no, not even in the Roman amphitheatre in Sepphoris. The sounds were almost deafening, and at one point Yeshua said he heard the roar of a lion, as if the Sphinx itself were permitting entry.

They reached the final chamber and turned to the left, ducking low, to enter it. Within was another sarcophagus. The hierophant commanded Yeshua to climb into it and repose. He gave Yeshua further instructions; then he and the priests and priestesses departed, leaving Yeshua in darkness, alone in the pyramid, alone in the sarcophagus.

Yeshua could never say what these final instructions entailed. All he would say was that the initiation in the Great Pyramid is an experience of death from which one emerges born again. From that point on, Yeshua said, he never had reason to fear death. Indeed, he said, no one need *ever* fear death. Death does not exist.

Gimel: The Ministry

Chapter Nine

It was the thirteenth year of the reign of Tiberius Caesar. Pontius Pilate was the prefect of Judea, Herod the Great's son Archelaus having been deposed by Rome for incompetence, while Herod Antipas remained tetrarch of Galilee. In Jerusalem, Joseph Caiaphas was the High Priest, appointed by Pilate, and Caiaphas' father-in-law Annas was the chief of the Sanhedrin. Together they worked with Pilate to keep the peace in Jerusalem, much to the dismay of the people, who abhorred this collaboration but nevertheless feared to speak out against the priests of the Temple.

Into this milieu strode John, whom the people came to call the Baptist, who preached at the Jordan River. This was not far from Qumran actually, at that place where the Jordan flows into the Dead Sea. He had stationed himself within sight of Mt. Nebo because that mountain was where Moses was said to have been allowed by God a look at the Promised Land before he died.

Which reminds me! How can it be that some say the Torah was written—I mean written just as I am writing here, dipping pen into ink I have made from soot and scratching on a piece of parchment—I have lost my thought. Old brain. Ah. How can the Torah have been written by Moses himself? In it Moses refers to his own death and burial. It is possible he initially chiseled parts of the Law himself into stone, after they were first broken, parts such as the *Aseret ha-D'varim* (Ten Declarations), long since lost with the Ark of the Covenant. He was certainly up on Mt. Sinai long enough to do so, putting those down as the Lord revealed them to him. But all the Laws the Pharisees love to squabble over most certainly were not written by Moses himself, for there are also repetitions. They were an oral tradition, finally parts written down, lost, one book found by a priest under Josiah's reign, and then the whole rewritten later. The present version of the Laws, the Prophets, and Other Writings was composed, as I have said before, in Babylon during the Exile so that we would not forget our teachings and traditions. And the various factions still argue over the books: which are legitimate, which should be ignored? Some treat the words as if they were all dictated by God Himself, as if God were bursting with new ideas to give to his chosen people. But no, not even circumcision was exclusive to the people of Israel as the story of Abraham would have us believe; the Egyptians have practiced circumcision for millennia. But Moses, in honoring Akhenaten the Master, his teacher, wanted the people of the One God to be known in Canaan by the continuation of this tradition, for it was a symbol of cleanness and purity. Therefore I write here that even the five books of the Torah are not to be taken literally, or not entirely so, since much of it was woven together by various priests refashioning myths that explained the state of humanity and the world and the place of the Jews within it.

One thing Yeshua mentioned, my father said, upon my uncle's return from Persia is that the magi had told him of a Sumerian legend called the Epic of Gilgamesh. It was written in the ancient Akkadian tongue and one part was about a king named Utnapishtim. One of the gods told him to build a great circular ark so that this king, his family, and the animals he took, two-by-two, aboard the ark would survive the Flood. It predates our own story of Noah. As for the creation, no one else was there living to set that story down. Moreover, did the children of Adam and Eve bear children together? Whom did Cain marry? His own sister? If not, from whence sprang the other tribes in the land? At Qumran we argued these things incessantly.

In truth, in a way, I like this startling, albeit disturbing, thought of incest among the first peoples, for it makes all human beings true brothers and sisters, but of course it is rather absurd. No one knows how God created this world, its creatures, its grasses and plants and vines and trees bearing fruit, and the creeping things, and the birds of the air, and man and woman.

No one knows how God made the stars and all the heavenly bodies. It is the greatest of all mysteries, which is why all cultures have their myths. Our Jewish myths are beautiful. They contain lessons for living in righteousness, warnings against repeating mistakes—although this seems the nature of humankind, to forget its history and repeat our errors. Human history is the ever-unfolding tale of ambition, greed, and the lust for power contrasting with the human need to understand—nay, see, God. We are created but one level below the angels; but even the evil one is a fallen angel. Humanity is the history of us fighting with our own inner and conflicting natures. We are a vast sea, roiling, seething, thundering against shores, yearning for calm.

But back to my point. All of the revisions of the earliest Word is why the Essenes believe the Torah has been spoiled, with too many additions and interpretations of priests added, and stories refashioned to fit the beliefs of whatever scribe was writing, and now the Pharisees—I should say *some* of the Pharisees. Many of them are upright men. But some of them take an almost vicious glee in insisting their interpretation of the Law is the only true one. As an example, they take the simple command to "honor the Sabbath" and turn it into "do no work on the Sabbath." That is fine; a day of rest and reflection is good; but then they want to argue over what constitutes work. So we get such rules given as "walk no more than one thousand paces on the Sabbath"—as if walking is work! Is walking for an hour to reach a quiet place by a stream, to repose under the shade of a tree, to offer thanks to God for the beauty He has created, work and a sin?

Indeed, there was once a Pharisee from Damascus who became an Essene, first joining the sect at Damascus, then moving down to Qumran, where he wrote a document in which he imagined a New Jerusalem, with Laws even more complex and stricter than anything the Pharisees have concocted. Truthfully we Essenes are assiduous about purity, but he suggested that one must not even defecate on the Sabbath. Let me explain this. Though much of the *halakhic* laws in the Qumran scrolls are very similar to the usual Torah, there are some differences. Ritual purity was indeed very important to the Qumran Essenes, but not so much to other sects of Essenes. A part of one *halakhic* scroll that became ignored, and actually a subject of some ridicule at Qumran, was this former Pharisaic scribe's description of the "Ideal Jerusalem," in which he made the entire city itself into a Temple. Some of the laws were most puzzling, such as no sexual union, even between man and wife, within the city, and no defecating or urinating within the city walls. Since one could walk only so many paces on the Sabbath, or else it would be considered work, this rule basically meant that no one could relieve himself or herself on the Sabbath! A rule conceived in madness indeed—the brother was dismissed from the community, a rare thing. I saw this Scroll at Qumran, for it was used as instructive. Though parts were still valued, the rest the teachers used to demonstrate what happens to the minds of men when the letter of the Law becomes more important than the spirit of the Law. The mind becomes like that of a burrowing creature lost in tunnels below ground with no recollection of how to find its way out.

"We strive to be holy, but we are still human beings," was a common saying of the teachers at Qumran. So here is the truth. In Qumran, outside the main community dining area, there was a room very like unto a Roman *latrinae.* This was used for urination. Defecation was done by walking some paces from the community buildings out into a private area, digging a pit, then covering the waste over. Upon joining the community, in fact, every man was given a small shovel for precisely this purpose. But walking away from the community to defecate was just to control the smell! Afterwards, if you were going back into the community building, you were required to step down into one of the pools to wash, for the entire building was considered a Temple and all of us as priests. We did our best to replenish the water in these mikvot, but sometimes even they became something one hesitated to walk into. I would walk down, stay the required time, and get out as quickly as I could. And I will tell you: many of the brothers did this same thing. But such are the sacrifices one makes when living in the desert, where there is little water. We conserved fresh rain water in barrels made for this purpose, and also constructed a large water tower for this purpose, but more often than not, we had to bring living water in from the spring at Ein Feshka, which was where most of our crops were grown, since the dry riverbed to which we had built an aqueduct at most flooded once or twice a year. And so you see, even in our own community, there were those whose literalism and rigidity interfered with their common sense.

So you begin to see why Yeshua and John were sorely needed. The Israelites needed freeing in so many ways. Blind obedience to the sayings of men that are then written down and taken as the words of God Himself turns many away from the real intentions of the Divine Presence.

Hence, John began teaching and baptizing on the River Jordan. He called for repentance, to prepare the way of the Lord. Most famously he cried out, "Even now the ax is at the roots of the tree!" The Kingdom of God hastened near. They say John lived like a wild man, but that is an exaggeration. He did wear a piece of camel's hair, though. He was inspired to do so by the Egyptian priests of Re in Heliopolis who wore a drape of leopard's skin over their shoulders. But John would kill no animal, so he must have settled for what he could find. He did live in a nearby cave. He ate wild honey, carob, and cooked cakes of oil he slapped down on heated stones. Thus he lived, preached, baptized, and waited, collecting to him some few who would later be disciples to both him and to Yeshua.

John's call for repentance and the coming Son of Man who would restore to Israel a right relationship to God, ushering in the Kingdom of Heaven, struck a chord with many of the dispossessed and downtrodden. They flocked to see him and be baptized to wash away their sins. This was different from the washing in the baths we call *mikvot* to make someone ritually clean. No, like the purifications of the Master Moria El at Lake Moeris in Egypt, this was a cleaning and clearing of the very soul. Later Yeshua explained it to the family as a cleaning of forgiveness made on all planes of reality, material and immaterial: the here, the now, the past, wherever the soul has been and will ever be. It is a fresh start, a freeing from negative karma. Of course one must not then go forth and commit acts leading to more negative karma. It is difficult to explain. But if one loves God and acts with good will towards all, hating none and forgiving all, his soul remains free, and a free and ascended soul gains entry to the Kingdom of Heaven.

Eventually John grew in such popularity that word of the crowds he attracted reached the ears of Pontius Pilate in Caesarea, so Pilate sent soldiers from the garrison in Jerusalem to observe. But all they heard was "Repent! The Kingdom of Heaven is near!" and naught about overthrowing the Romans, so Pilate left John alone. Politics are sticky and gummy as tar. On the one hand, any gathering of large numbers of Jews could be dangerous, especially if their teacher urged insurrection. On the other hand, to imprison or execute John could start a rebellion since he was popular. Thus Pilate did the prudent thing. Already the peace was shaky and many false Messiahs and Zealots had been caught and crucified. He chose to leave John alone since he had not spoken of overthrowing the Romans.

Then the Sadducees, hearing also of John, sent some few priests and a rabbi to the Jordan River to discover from John his purpose.

"Who are you?" they demanded of him, and John, perceiving the real reason for their curiosity, answered, "I am not the Messiah you seek."

"Then who are you? Elias?"

"I am not."

"If you are not Elias or the prophet of whom Moses spoke, then who are you? What are we to say to those who sent us to ask?"

John quoted the prophet Isaiah. "I am the voice of one crying in the wilderness: make straight the way of the Holy One."

The Pharisee that was among them was annoyed. "Stop speaking in circles. If you are not Elias, and if you are not the Messiah, upon what authority do you baptize?"

John's temper flashed. He said, "I baptize with water to wash away the sins of those who confess them, in order to prepare the Way. But there is One coming who will baptize with water *and* with fire! He who is coming is preferred before me, and his shoe's latchet I am unfit to unloose."

The men looked at each other and decided John was just another false prophet, a poor peasant man who had lost his mind, and was no one to take heed of.

Meanwhile, having completed his final initiation, Yeshua made his way back to Palestine to reconnect with John at the appointed place. He arrived at the Jordan one day in the tenth month as John was preaching and baptizing. He stopped at the water's edge to watch until John noticed him. Then he waded out into the water and stood next to his cousin.

"Baptize me, John," Yeshua said.

John shook his head. "Who am I," he asked, "to baptize you?"

"I am a man," Yeshua said. "And therefore I am not without sin." He leaned in closer so no one could hear. "And you are the priest; I am the king. Did not Aaron often speak for Moses? Are we not both Messiahs, cousin?" Stepping back, Yeshua said, "Suffer it to be so, for it is to us both given to fulfill all righteousness."

John bowed his head, then put one arm around Yeshua to brace against his back and the other onto his chest to hold him steady. He then immersed Yeshua backwards into the water.

"It was cold!" Yeshua told the family later, laughing. But then he waxed somber. As he came up out of the water, he said, he saw a great, blinding light and heard the beating wings of a bird. He felt a shudder pass throughout his body and then came a voice: "You are my son, my beloved, in whom I have been well pleased, and today I have begotten you," which echoes, of course, the second of the Psalms. The moment passed, and Yeshua stood in the river, shaking his head, sending beads of water flying from his hair.

From John's point of view, he had seen the clouds part and a crown of light with twelve rays surrounding Yeshua's head, and everyone, including those on shore, saw the bird. It had been, in fact, a descending dove. It did not quite alight on Yeshua's head before flying off.

Of certainty this was a sign.

Of certainty this was when the Holy Breath descended upon Yeshua, after so much arduous preparation, for God had found him a worthy vessel through which to do His works. That day, the Lord adopted Yeshua as his own begotten son.

Later that evening, Yeshua and John sat together with John's four disciples and shared a meal. This was when Yeshua first met Simon Peter, the Rock; Simon's brother Andrew; Philip; and Nathanael, whose mother and father had traveled to Judea from the land of the Nubians and whose skin was so black it shone. After the meal, Yeshua and John went off to the side together to plan for the beginning of their ministry. Their initial thinking was to send out a great call for repentance across Israel and Judea, as if the territories were once again a single united kingdom, as under David, and to baptize as many as they could in preparation for the Kingdom of Heaven and the arrival of the Son of Man, who would separate the good from the evil and usher in the cycle of the great Piscean age. Yeshua had traveled and learned among the peaceful Masters of the Great Brotherhood for so long that he could not imagine ushering in the Kingdom of Heaven by war. But first Yeshua wished to travel to Galilee to attend the wedding of his brother Simon in Cana. Then he would visit his family in Nazareth. Upon his return to the Jordan River, Yeshua and John would then switch places. John, as priest, would move north to baptize in the Galilee, and Yeshua, as king, would take John's place closer to Jerusalem. This John well understood. He said he would get a message to the Essene Council of Elders to apprise them of their plans.

The next morning, Yeshua set off to Cana.

Hence the long-awaited time had arrived. When they received John's message, the Essene Council of Elders met to discuss plans for the future and how the Brethren might assist. It seemed good that Yeshua's family, since he was to be king, have a family tomb. Normally the poor did not have tombs since they could not afford them, and they were simply buried in the dirt with the head facing towards Jerusalem. But this did not seem proper or fitting for a king. As I have written, money was collected from the various Essene communities and a builder hired to hew a simple tomb in the rock outside Jerusalem about a half hour's walk south of the city, towards Bethlehem. It was a simple affair, absent the Greek columns and other decorations typically added by the wealthy. It had only one small central court and six loculi. To honor Yeshua's position as Master in the Great Brotherhood, as I have written, a pyramid shape with a sun was carved over the doorway. The bones of Yeshua's father Joseph were dug up from the ground in Nazareth, brought down to this tomb, and placed into an ossuary. A few more plain ossuaries to one day contain the rest of the family were made by an artisan and set inside the tomb; then it was sealed. More ossuaries would be added later.

A former Essene turned merchant, a man named Joseph of Arimathea, agreed to set aside part of his lands for this tomb. Although he was no longer an Essene, he remained a faithful Jew and friend to the Essenes, which was good because he commanded great respect in Jerusalem, even having friends in the Sanhedrin. I doubt they knew of his association with the Essenes. But naturally Joseph knew of the prophesied Messiah, and when the Council of Elders informed him the Messiah had come, Joseph was willing to do what he could to assist.

One day Yeshua would be laid in this very tomb.

Chapter Ten

Since John's disciple Nathanael's Nubian parents now lived in Cana, and Cana was not that far southeast of Capernaum, where Peter and Andrew resided, these three decided to travel with Yeshua, both to visit their homes and to become better acquainted with Yeshua. John had told them that now that Yeshua was here, "I must decrease and he must increase," although it was made plain their missions were the same. Philip remained with John.

On the way, Yeshua invited the three disciples to the wedding feast, since the marriage was, after all, that of his youngest brother Simon, and to not invite them would be discourteous.

Some background. While Yeshua was in Egypt, my father Jude had married and his wife, Sarah, had quickly borne two sons. These were my brothers James and Zoker. Then she bore me. At the wedding of my uncle Simon, Yeshua first laid his eyes upon me, although I was but a babe in arms and of course remember nothing of this. I am told that, even as an infant, I favored my mother, with a broad face and aquiline nose. I look more Greek than Jew!

In Yeshua's absence, James as the second eldest had taken charge of matters of the patriarch and had arranged, with my grandmother Mary's advice, a marriage contract for Simon. The young maiden of Cana, called Rachel, was the only remaining child and daughter of a widowed man whose two sons, both Zealots, had been caught up in a skirmish a few years prior and been slain by the Romans. Having no sons to inherit his house, he was agreeable to marrying his daughter to a man who would not take his daughter out of his house, as was the usual custom, and also waive the bride price. The house in Nazareth, already holding a dozen people, would require another addition built if Simon brought his wife and expected children to live there. Thus,

Mary and James asked Simon if he would consent to living in Cana in a house that would one day be his own. Simon laid eyes on the young Rachel and readily assented. Since the house and the widower's goods served as Rachel's dowry, Mary and James assumed the costs of the wedding feast. After the feast, Simon would remain with his wife and the widower and be as his son. This was an agreement that suited all.

When Yeshua arrived in Cana, the consummation of the marriage had taken place, and the feast had already commenced. If you are unfamiliar with Jewish customs, the marriage celebration prior to the final feast goes on for as long as a week. So there is much food and drink prepared, and Mary and her daughters-in-law had spent numerous hours making breads and vegetable dishes, washing and cutting fruits, roasting meats, purchasing the finest flour for making cakes. They had continued cooking in shifts throughout the ceremony so that all would be ready for the feast, when the largest number of guests would arrive. For the feast itself, they had hired servants and stewards, as was also customary.

Yeshua said he had no trouble finding the house because the noise from the celebration was so loud he and the disciples could hear it from two thousand strides away. No doubt he was just making a joke, but when he appeared in the courtyard another cry went up at the sight of him. His mother and brothers rushed up to kiss and embrace him. Someone pushed a cup of wine into his hand. Such a fuss was made that he finally had to remind them, "This is Simon and his bride's day—and," looking around, "where is Simon?" And then there was joking that he and the bride had returned to the bridal chamber.

"The bed cloth was stained with her blood," James told Yeshua, clapping his brother's shoulder as they walked to a table and sat to eat. He said this not because James was proud of any pain his brother had caused his new young wife. This was because a lack of blood sometimes led to trouble, accusations of non-virginity, stoning in some cases among the crueler members of the wealthy classes. Knowing my uncle Simon, I doubt he would have made much of a lack of blood, but its presence on the bed cloth is generally a relief to all, and cause even for celebration and ululation in some cultures, where they display the cloth for all to see. I am told it is a female rite of passage.

Nathanael asked if he might go and fetch his family to join the celebration, and James, flushed with wine, said, "Yes! You must! Any friend of my brother is our family," and so you see how it went.

Instruments were brought out and music commenced; people danced, drank, and ate, and Simon reappeared and danced with his bride, who, against custom, he drew forth from the bridal chamber, her body still adorned with henna; but no one minded; the celebrating continued for some hours. Even Yeshua danced. Indeed, he taught the guests a celebratory dance of the Egyptians, although I believe more people stumbled than danced as it required much leaping.

Then Mary approached Yeshua and drew him aside. "We have run out of wine." She looked at him anxiously. To run out of wine before the feast was over would not reflect well on the family and keeping to our end of the contract.

Yeshua understood what she was asking him. "Dear woman," he said, "what have I to do with this? It is not my time." He meant he had not yet intended to begin his ministry. He also meant he did not wish to perform a miracle and astound the guests, drawing attention away from Simon and his bride on a day set aside for them.

Yeshua then looked around the courtyard at the guests. "But I have myself added at least a dozen guests you did not expect." He sighed, then nodded.

Mary found the four servants, brought them to Yeshua and said to them, "Do whatever he tells you, but do so quietly." She departed, for the widower was calling her over.

Yeshua said to them, "Take the six stone jars for washing and fill them with water. Take them to the chief steward, draw some out, and say nothing."

They did as he asked, then returned to their serving.

The chief steward sipped that which had been drawn out from the first jar and exclaimed, loudly enough for many to hear: "Wondrous wine!" He found Mary with the widower and heaped praise upon her. "Most serve the best wine first and then switch to the inferior. But you have saved the best for the last."

The widower was pleased, and went himself and drew a cup of the wine for Mary.

All of this had been done without notice by the guests.

Yes, my uncle loved my grandmother, and she loved him. Over the years, she told us this story many times, long after Yeshua was dead and up unto the day she transitioned and was laid in the tomb herself.

* * *

After the feast, the next day Peter and Andrew returned to Capernaum to tarry awhile until Yeshua came for them; Nathanael remained with his family; and Yeshua departed to Nazareth with his mother, brothers, sisters, and the rest of us. His thinking was that he would commence his ministry in Nazareth, for this was where he was known by the several families of Essenes who resided there and who knew of his mission. The week passed peacefully, much as it had when Yeshua visited from his return from Persia and India, only this time he told stories of Egypt. Again he slept on a mat on the roof, arising with the sun to pray and going up to the roof to pray each night as the sun set. There was a feeling of anticipation in the house, with James, Joses, and my father Jude pressing Yeshua for details about what he planned to say in the synagogue, but Yeshua bade them to wait.

Sabbath arrived, and that morning Yeshua donned the white garment of the Essenes and a prayer shawl with the tassels of a rabbi we call a *tzitzit*. From that point on, he was to always wear these, and his cloak for cold weather was also white. His garments also indicated he was an Essene—sometimes they called us "the men in white"—which could be one additional reason the Pharisees and Sadducees always challenged him on his teachings throughout his ministry. With his white garments, his skin, which was dark because he was always in the sun, looked even darker. One of my earliest memories, in fact, is of Yeshua, and how I was fascinated by the contrast between his clothing and his skin.

In any case, the family went with Yeshua the next morning up to the synagogue, which in poor Nazareth was really nothing but a large tent pitched by the town's Levite brother, who kept several scrolls of the Torah and the Prophets. This tent stood on a knoll above the town. If at least ten men were present, there would be a meeting. Usually what happened, after a prayer, a blessing, and the singing of some psalms that the Levite had chosen, was that someone of the town who could read would select a passage to read aloud, and a discussion of its meaning would follow. If no one stepped forth to read, the Levite himself would choose a passage and read. Sometimes attendance was sparse if there was no issue the town faced, and sometimes, if there were not ten men, there was no meeting at all. One is not compelled by the Law to attend a synagogue on the Sabbath. The only Law was to not work and to use the Sabbath as a day of rest. Some say this was because the Lord rested on the seventh day of creation. Others say it is to honor the Lord for freeing the Jewish people from slavery in Egypt. The Essenes wished not to quibble over this, and we just say it is a day honoring both, for both reasons are given in the Torah. In any case, word seemed to have spread around the town that Yeshua would be reading, for the little synagogue bulged with attendees. The inside was filled with the men, so the women sat on the ground outside the tent.

Once it appeared that there would be no more arrivals, the Levite stood and gave thanks to the Lord for the Sabbath and proceeded as was usual. Finally he was concluded and asked if someone wished to read.

Everyone turned to look at him, so Yeshua stood and came forward.

"Isaiah," Yeshua said.

The Levite nodded, went over to the scrolls, found the one he wanted, and laid it on the stone table that had been fashioned for this purpose. He stepped to the side as Yeshua searched quickly through the scroll for the passage he wished.

Finding it, Yeshua read aloud: "The Spirit of the Lord is upon me, because he has anointed me to bring glad tidings to the poor. He has sent me to proclaim liberty to captives and recovery of sight to the blind, to let the oppressed go free, and to proclaim a year acceptable to the Lord."

Yeshua rolled up the scroll and returned it to the Levite. Then, facing the crowd, he said: "Truly, I say unto you, this day this prophecy is fulfilled in me."

Now, this story has been exaggerated, and distorted far away from the truth, and what happened afterwards was not quite as ugly as some have claimed. Many of the town were interested and wished to hear more. But among those in the town who did not know, these sounded like the words of a man who had taken leave of his senses, or at least was puffed up with self-importance.

There came some murmuring from the back of the tent. Finally a man stood up. "What do you mean?"

"I mean," Yeshua said simply, "that the Lord wishes me to do His bidding and return his lost sheep to the fold."

Some laughter broke out. Another man stood. "Well, then, shall I go fetch my old grandfather, who can hardly see, and you can restore to him his sight?"

There was much laughter at this. My father said he began to feel a horrible clenching in his stomach. This was not as they had expected.

"You do not listen," Yeshua said. "Your unbelief will not serve you, nor the father of your father."

"What is that? Some kind of curse?" That man's brother got to his feet.

"Who do you think you are?" someone then cried loudly from the back. "Aren't you the son of that Mary? And aren't your brothers and sisters even now here with us?"

"Likely more half-brothers and -sisters, since no one knows his father," another shouted.

Yeshua raised his hand for peace, but there was to be no peace, since half the crowd was now mocking him. The Levite stood and called for silence, but there was to be no silence. Now there was just yelling and pushing, and some started to come forward to throw Yeshua out of the tent as if he were a misbehaving child.

My uncles and a few others of the Essene men got in the way.

"Are you calling my mother a whore?" Joses asked. He was ready to serve justice with his fists.

"Stop!" James pushed one man away. "Stop!" he said, pushing another. He grabbed Yeshua by the arm and began pulling him away. "We came not here to fight."

My uncles led Yeshua out of the tent, Joses helped my grandmother to her feet, and the rest of the family followed them, feeling humiliation as taunts and jeers chased them down the road.

"Even his family thinks he's crazy," people said; and others called after them, "Make way for the great Prophet!"

But this was nothing. As Yeshua said later, prophets are never accepted in their own hometowns. No, it was what came once they got home that is the part of the story that seems never to be told.

* * *

Joses was filled with fury. In the courtyard, everyone was seated, but Joses came behind Yeshua, grabbed him by the shoulders and shook him. "What kind of Messiah will allow his own mother to be thus insulted?"

Yeshua removed Joses' hands and said quietly, "Brother, you do not understand."

Joses cursed him and turned his back. He went over to the corner of the courtyard to fetch the wine jar.

"Yeshua," James said, "David was a great king, defeating all enemies. If you are to take this land back from the Romans, you cannot be soft. You must roar like the lion."

Joses turned, his cup filled. "Why did they not teach him at Qumran how to do battle?" He gulped from his cup, grimaced, then spat at his own feet. "I do not understand the purpose of these…" he waved his other hand. "These travels and gathering of spiritual knowledge. A priest has never been a king. I thought John was the priest."

"You misunderstand the nature of the battle," Yeshua said.

"Then you would do well to explain to us," my father said. "We cannot live here and be ridiculed."

"You will *all* suffer much," Yeshua said. "And be persecuted for my sake."

Joses snorted, and James and Jude shook their heads.

"My son," Mary said. "You must tell them."

Yeshua sighed, looked up to heaven, then back down. He stroked his beard. "Brothers," he said. "This is a bloodless fight. This is a fight against evil, and for the saving of souls."

"The bandits of this land make better sense than you," Joses said.

"That is enough, Joses," Mary said. Her voice took on an edge that was rarely heard.

Yeshua stood. "John is but a herald for me. I am but a herald for the coming Son of Man. The Son of Man will pass judgment on the people, removing those unworthy of the Kingdom of Heaven, and restore to Israel the land of the covenant. With that restoration, I become King, and John becomes High Priest."

"So you expect the Lord to give the Kingdom to you?" Joses asked. He finally sat.

"If I am worthy. I must remain without sin and strive to be pure of thought. It is written, 'Thou shalt not kill.' Israel has always been imperfect, her kings doing battle, and the Lord has shown great patience. But His plan has always been for that of a people who live in peace and follow the Law. I show the way by my example."

James said, doubt inscribed across his face, "It will be difficult for that message to take hold amongst the people. It is not what they expect of the Messiah."

"Which is why," Yeshua said, sitting back down, "I will show the Lord's favor by doing good deeds in His name: healing the sick, feeding the poor, restoring sight to the blind, casting out demons that oppress the soul. Even," he said, "if need be, raising the dead."

Joses pointed at his cup. "Have you been drinking this? Perhaps at night as we are all sleeping?"

Yeshua laughed. "But my brother, I can do these things."

"Well," Joses said. "Then so can I."

That was enough for my grandmother. She reached over and pulled Joses' ear as if he were only five or six. "All of you," she said. "Listen to me.

"Your brother is a gifted healer and prophet, and he has been raised and trained to be such. He is the Lord's chosen. Last week—do you remember the wine you drank at Simon's wedding feast? The last good wine? I tell you, there was no wine. None remained. Yeshua changed water into wine for my sake."

My three uncles looked at Yeshua with astonishment.

"When your father and I were with Yeshua in Egypt, even as

a child he wrought miracles. He healed wounded and sick animals, and this I saw for myself. When he tells me he did healings on his travels, I believe him."

"Wait, then," my father said. "If this is so, then why—" and he turned to Yeshua, "did you not ask the man in the synagogue to bring to you his blind father? And put their mocking to shame?"

"It is not for me to shame others," Yeshua said. "I do not heal or work miracles as a magician, for coins or to impress or astound. I do those things only when it is right and good to do so."

James shook his head again. "This is truly not at all what the people are expecting of the Messiah."

"I must do my best to win over as many as I can until the Son of Man arrives," Yeshua said.

"And this Son of Man," my father Jude asked, "is that angel of the Lord foreseen by the Prophet Daniel, and he is not to be confused with the Messiah the people look towards?"

This was a fair question, because sometimes the Scripture uses "Sons of Men" to refer to angelic beings, and other times "Son of Man" means "Messiah," "King," or "Anointed One."

"Yes," Yeshua said. "They are different. Now you understand."

To this day, I do not think Joses was fully convinced until Yeshua reappeared after his crucifixion. It was for this reason he chose to stay with his wife, Anna, in Capernaum, residing at Simon Peter's, while James and Jude joined Yeshua as disciples. Simon, of course, could not join without breaking his marriage contract, so he stayed in Cana, but he remained one of the one hundred and twenty—followers who knew of Yeshua's true mission.

It would not suffice after this for the family to stay in Nazareth or for Yeshua to set up his center of ministry there when half the town denigrated him as a *mamzer*. Later on, the nature of Yeshua's ministry, and some of his interpretations of Torah, lost him some of the Essene Brethren as well, those of the apocalyptic view that the Messiah himself as the Son of Man would slay evil with weapons. As well, they believed his interpretation of Torah too lax. These were the Brethren that later joined the Zealots and fled to Jerusalem or Masada, instead of coming with us to the Decapolis. They were among those I think of today as "the literalists," those Jews who criticized Yeshua for breaking the third of the commandments by healing on the Sabbath.

Hence, the family spent two days to themselves, preparing food for the journey and packing up their scant belongings that could be moved. Only James's wife left the house to draw water from the well. On the third evening, my family quietly abandoned the house at Nazareth to make the journey to Capernaum.

The wicked ones said they fled in embarrassment and for Mary's sin being exposed.

Chapter Eleven

Reaching Capernaum, the family went to Simon Peter's house, where Peter lived with his wife, their son Mark, his wife's mother, and his brother Andrew. They were fishermen and made a good living, although they worked very hard, long hours when they weren't with John the Baptizer, and taxes were a hardship. Peter knew two other fishermen in the city, who were also brothers, and who had wished to join with John but had been unable to do so because they had needed at that time to care for their aging father. These were James and John, the sons of Zebedee.

All collected with Yeshua at Peter's home that evening to discuss the matter before them.

"I will go forth to the River Jordan in the south where John baptizes now," Yeshua said. "Peter, Andrew, James, and his brother John will come with me." He smiled. "I will make you four into fishers of men."

Living arrangements and care for those who would remain needed to be determined. Simon Peter offered up his home in exchange for Yeshua's family taking care of his wife, son, and mother-in-law. Yeshua also agreed that his family would bring food to Zebedee every day and take care of his household. John the Baptist would be coming up with Philip to Aenon, near to Salim, a major crossroads between the Galilee, Decapolis, and Perea territories. It would be a good place to capture the attention of many, and the living waters there were abundant. When all was settled and a routine established in Capernaum, Yeshua's brothers James and Jude would then join John the Baptist. Joses would be left as the male of the household. If needed, James and Jude could leave John for short spells to come back to Capernaum. My uncle Simon, in Cana, could also come to visit on occasion and help if the need arose. The women would tend the gardens at both houses to grow food and spin to make money. They could also see to the animals. Joses was amenable to learning how to cast nets from Simon Peter's boat, and Simon knew of two other fishermen who would help Joses for wages since they owned no fishing vessel.

"Be generous with these men," Yeshua told Joses. "For they are poor. Keep what you need but pay out the rest, lest you fall prey to the love of money, which is the root of all evil."

Now let me pause to write down how Yeshua's ministry with his disciples actually operated. There is an impression that all Yeshua ever did was wander with his disciples from town to town, preaching on the outskirts as his disciples stood by. This is assuredly untrue. The disciples had families and some of them wives and children. They did not just leave their homes for three years, never to return the entire time. On the contrary, the disciples frequently went back home if they were needed, as did Yeshua. Capernaum wound up being a kind of "headquarters" for Yeshua during his ministry, except for two times, when he chose to be alone, away from the wicked gaze of Herod Antipas, reviewing Scriptures, praying, and meditating upon what the Lord required of him, while he sent out disciples to preach and heal in his stead. But more on this when I reach that part of the story.

Everything thus settled, Yeshua with his four traveled the three days south to John the Baptist, told him of the plans, and John was satisfied. "I love that you give me your own brothers," he told Yeshua. He paused, his eyes warm as he regarded his cousin, then he added an afterthought. "They are also my cousins, but we are all brothers in the eyes of the Lord. I will instruct them in our teachings." The two embraced, and the next morning, John and Philip proceeded north.

Therefore Yeshua was in the south, baptizing and calling for repentance in John's place. "Repent!" he cried out. "The day of the Lord draws near." And he baptized the people to wash away their sins.

"Now there are *two* of these crazy ones," the priests, scribes, and rabbis of Jerusalem grumbled into their beards, although some of the Pharisees kept a watchful eye on Yeshua as he attracted more and more attention. But no one acted.

One day, after preaching and baptizing, and the crowds were dispersed, a man approached Yeshua and pleaded for help. He had held back, standing afar off, for he was a leper. "Lord," said the man, "if you will, you can make me clean."

Yeshua reached out and gently grasped his arm. "I will." He closed his eyes and concentrated. "Be you clean."

The man was healed, his sores and skin clearing before the very eyes of the four disciples.

Yeshua said, "See that you tell no one of this. Go your way in peace."

"Master, what of the priests at the Temple? The gifts as Moses commanded—"

Yeshua shook his head and took the man by his shoulders. "You *are* cleansed. Our Father has blessed you. He requires of you no sacrifice."

Relief crossed the man's face, for he was poor. "Lord, will you baptize me before I go?"

Yeshua regarded him. "Do you repent of all your sins?"

"I do, Lord."

Yeshua took him down to the river and baptized him, reminded him to observe the Law and will of God, and sent the man on his way.

The four disciples marveled at this miracle, and marveled all the more that Yeshua wished it kept hidden. As for Yeshua's not paying the Temple priests and sacrificing animals and undergoing eight days of ritual cleansing and all else, they did not marvel. The Temple was so corrupted it was throwing good money after bad. This, indeed, was one of the main reasons those from Galilee were so often judged harshly by the priests. Few could afford to be continually traveling down to the Temple to sacrifice this and that animal, changing money, and tithing. Even once a year at Passover was a hardship. And as I have written, the Essenes had long since done away with animal sacrifices.

And thus came to an end that year, according to the calendar, and the next year began. Thus far it had been only several months into Yeshua's ministry.

Now, my story must here shift to John the Baptizer in the north, where, as I said, he baptized at Aenon. Herod Antipas was king over the territories there. This Herod was not unlike his father, a man who was a client king installed by the Roman emperor, and perceived by many of the people to not sit rightfully on his throne, for he most certainly was not of the line of David. Therefore when word came to his ear that there was a man preaching that the true king was to soon come and that the people must repent, Herod perceived John as a threat. The more people crowded to John, the more anxiety-ridden Herod became. He was just as paranoid as his father! Finally, he sent his men to arrest John.

But John was no fool. At night his disciples, now among them my uncle James and my father, kept vigil in shifts. The local people, on the side of John, also kept watch and would warn the disciples if Herod's men were coming. John and the three would then slip over the border into the Decapolis territory west of the Jordan, where Herod did not reign. Not far—perhaps three hours' walk—there was a cave near to the brook called Cherith, which is south of Pella, where I now reside. When I was younger, I often visited that place, to pray and to remember. This cave is where John, my uncle, my father, and Philip would tarry awhile, waiting for the soldiers to abandon their searches and leave. They then would come back across the border and resume calling for repentance and baptizing.

This worked for some months until Herod, whom later Yeshua was to call "that fox," sent his men dressed in the clothes of peasants, and they caught John unawares. They seized John, and Herod had John removed to his fortress at Machaeras, which is far away to the east on the Dead Sea, for Herod feared if he kept John imprisoned in the area close by, the people would rise up in an attempt to free him.

It is true that John had insinuated to the people that Herod was not their true king, which to the Romans is of certainty sedition. But John meant that Herod Antipas, aside from the other reasons, was not fit to be king because, John declared, "This son of a half-Jew does not keep to the Law." Now, that is nothing but the truth. Some years before, Antipas' brother had divorced his wife, and Antipas took her to himself to marry. This may be done only lawfully, according to Torah, if the brother has died and left no heir. The brother, Philip, was alive and well, ruling over his own Roman tetrarchy. Hence, Herod Antipas lived in what to us is sin, adultery with his sister-in-law. This woman, Herodias, was said to be most beautiful, but she was just as crafty a fox as her brother-husband.

My uncle James, my father Jude, and Philip hastened to the south to tell Yeshua of these happenings. They found him and the disciples in John's old cave near the Jordan.

Upon receiving the news, Yeshua put his face into his hands and was much aggrieved.

"I believe Herod is afraid to actually kill John," my father said, to lessen Yeshua's grief. "He fears the people would revolt if he did this thing. So John's life, at least, is probably safe in the dungeon."

Yeshua was quiet a long while, then looked at the men surrounding him. Finally he said, "Evil will test us in many ways. We must remain ever vigilant and save as many souls as we can before the angel of the Lord arrives." He got to his feet. "I will go to pray. In the morning, we will depart for Capernaum. But I will leave the route and go to Cana to fetch Nathanael."

"All of us, Master? Should some stay to continue baptizing?"

This was asked by a new disciple Yeshua had called to him, a man called Judas Iscariot. He had been born in the small village of Cariot in southern Judea, and his father was named Simon, but Simon of Cariot had moved to Jerusalem and was now a well-to-do merchant. Since Judas was good with numbers, Yeshua had made him the group's treasurer, holding the meager money they pooled, for sometimes a wealthier new follower of the Way would donate to them coins. Later on, my father said, if they ever passed a person begging, Yeshua would stop and ask Judas what money they could part with. At least half the time, there was so little money that Judas would not be able to answer honestly—that is to say, nothing. Many times they had no idea from whence their next meal would come. Yeshua would then smile, ask for Judas' purse, reach into it, and even if it was the last coin, he would take that coin and give it to the beggar.

"We ate this morning. This man has not yet eaten today."

By the end of Yeshua's ministry, Judas would simply hand over the purse whenever Yeshua stopped, unless it was empty. In that case, Yeshua would squat before the beggar and bless him. "The Lord will send sustenance to you soon."

He would rise, and they would be on their way.

"But one time," my father said, "we had no sooner gone twenty paces when the wife of a wealthy merchant turned the corner, saw the beggar, and tossed him a few coins. To this day," he said, "I believe every one of those poor we saw ate before the sun set."

But back to the story at hand.

"Yes, Judas, all of us," Yeshua said, and went off a ways into the wilderness to pray.

* * *

Yeshua wasn't long in Cana. He told Nathanael when they would be departing and stayed with his brother Simon and his new wife. Simon later said Yeshua spent the time either praying or meditating, or going to the synagogue to study the Scriptures. The Levite there was pleased to allow him to pore over the scrolls. With John now in prison, it seemed obvious that something needed to be done. Perhaps, Yeshua feared, he and John were not going about their ministry as the Lord wished. The Council of Elders at Qumran had no answers for Yeshua, Simon told us; so they sent a message to advise him to act as our Teacher of Righteousness had done and to search the prophets. Yeshua must have found his answer, for he gathered Nathanael and returned straightaway to Capernaum and called the disciples to him. Assembled, the disciples now numbered nine.

"We need three more disciples, one for each of the twelve tribes of Israel," Yeshua said. "When the Son of Man arrives and restores the Kingdom, I shall rule over all. The disciples will each govern the old territories of Israel and Judea."

"Wouldn't you need just eleven, then?" Judas Iscariot asked. "The Levites held no lands."

Yeshua smiled at him. "Yes, Judas. I need one disciple to sit at my right hand and be the king's advisor."

"What of John? Shall we attempt to free him?" asked Nathanael.

"This is something we cannot accomplish," Yeshua said, "for it would mean the spilling of blood." He sighed and spread his hands, palms up. "Yes, this distresses me." He looked around the table. "But Herod allows visitors, so I will send you, Nathanael, to see John and to comfort him in his imprisonment."

The disciples all nodded their agreement.

"What next, Master?" Simon Peter asked.

"Judas and Jude, my brother. Your names are too similar. Also the two James'," said Yeshua. "To avoid confusion, I give nicknames. Jude, you will be called Thomas, for it means 'twin.' And everyone says we look much like each other."

"Thomas," my father said. *"Didymus."* As I've said, we do

speak Greek.

"I fear," my uncle James said, laughing. "What name do you have in mind for me?"

"Nothing," said Yeshua. "You will remain James. The son of Zebedee will be called 'My heart,' for his brother John is also my beloved."

Everyone laughed, and Yeshua looked at James of Zebedee with fondness in his eyes. "Thaddeus is therefore your name, James."

"If this is your wish," Thaddeus said.

Simon Peter said, "'Heart' and 'Twin' are good names. He calls me 'Rock' for no reason." This was Peter's nickname, *Cephas*. I know these many names can become confusing; and therefore as much as possible I use "my father" when I mean Jude/Thomas *Didymus*, "my uncle" when I mean James, and Simon Peter for *Cephas*.

"One day you shall see why I call you Rock," Yeshua said, with some amusement, for Simon Peter, my father said, was actually pouting like a child who has broken a toy.

Philip clapped Simon on his shoulder.

"Now hear me," Yeshua said, turning serious. "The times have been interpreted. The Son of Man hastens near. I say unto you, none of you will die until you see the Kingdom of God come with power. We must act with greater urgency."

"What shall we do?" my father, now Thomas, asked.

"The final age of wickedness in this land shall end, and the will of God shall be done on earth. Without John the Baptizer, my message must be stronger and louder, for we must save as many souls as we can. Therefore I will take the teachings to the people. It is no longer enough to teach repentance and to baptize. I must teach them how to live the Law of our Father. We will travel together for a time so you can learn how to teach the Way, but then you shall fan out across the land in twos."

The disciples agreed.

Yeshua stood. "Go out, now, into Capernaum and the closer locales, and announce to as many as will hear that I will be teaching outside Capernaum in the morning, on the hill. Come back and we will eat together. For now I will go prepare my thoughts."

The disciples exited Peter's house and went among the people to pique their interest in this new interpreter of the Law.

* * *

In the mid-morning, on the outskirts of Capernaum, Yeshua climbed the small hill, wearing the white linen garment of the Essenes and his *tzitzit* with its four tassels, and waited as the people gathered to hear him. When all were assembled, he opened his mouth to speak, and the people quieted.

"Behold," Yeshua said, "the Kingdom of Heaven arrives forthwith. I say unto you, repent, and be saved, do good works, and with the Lord you will receive many blessings. Yea, I tell you that:

"Blessed are you poor, for yours is the Kingdom of Heaven.

"Blessed are those of you who mourn, for you shall be comforted.

"Blessed are the meek among you, for you shall inherit the earth.

"Blessed are those that hunger and thirst for righteousness, for they shall be satisfied.

"Blessed are the pure in heart, for they shall see God.

"Blessed are the merciful, for in return they shall obtain mercy.

"Blessed are the peacemakers, for they shall be called the children of God.

"Blessed are those who are persecuted for righteousness' sake, for theirs is the Kingdom of Heaven.

"Blessed are you when men revile you and persecute you and

utter all manner of evil against you falsely on my account. Rather, be glad, for your reward in heaven will be great. And remember: men also persecuted the prophets who came before me."

Here Yeshua paused. My father said he and James had been watching the crowd, fearful of another confrontation as in Nazareth, but that did not happen. He did hear some murmuring, but it was more in the manner of awe. For, not only did Yeshua's face seem to radiate joy as he spoke, but the people said also, "He speaks as one with authority."

Let me pause also to write that these blessings of Yeshua were not original to him. A very similar list appears in one of the scrolls at Qumran. Of course, throughout his ministry, Yeshua adapted Scripture at times so that it would make better sense to the people, but many Essenes can tell you that they would recognize these words, from texts that are not known outside our community. For now, I have fervently prayed, the scrolls were not destroyed when Qumran was laid waste and remain safely hidden from the *Kittim,* along with other treasures that were buried to be sold and used later to minister to those in need. If they are gone . . . I grieve at even the thought. It would be such a loss. Generations of composing, copying, and scholarship: an entire history of a people. I cannot bear to think of it.

Yeshua continued. "You are the salt of the earth; but if salt has lost its taste, how shall its saltiness be restored? It is no longer good for anything, except to be thrown out and trodden under foot by men. Therefore never lose your hope.

"You are the light of the world. A city set on a hill cannot be hid. Nor do men light a lamp and put it under a bushel, but they set it upon a stand, and it gives light to all in the house. Let your light so shine before all, that they may see your good works and give glory to your Father who is in heaven.

"Now let me tell you this. Some will speak evil against me and say that I have come to abolish the Law and the prophets. Take heed of me: this I deny most surely. For I have come not to abolish the Law and prophets but to fulfill them. For, truly, I say unto you, that until heaven and earth pass away and the Kingdom is restored, not one iota, nor one dot, nor one stroke of the pen will pass from the Law until all is accomplished."

The crowd was pressing closer to hear, so Yeshua took a few steps towards them and raised his voice even louder.

"Therefore mark you this: any prophet who teaches to relax the Law and the commandments shall be called least in the Kingdom of Heaven. But he who follows the Law and teaches men so, he shall be called great in the Kingdom of Heaven.

"For I tell you, your righteousness must *exceed* that of the scribes and Pharisees and other interpreters of the Law, lest you never enter the Kingdom of Heaven." Here Yeshua paused for breath.

Someone in the crowd called out a question. "But how does a person exceed even the rabbis in righteousness?"

Yeshua faced this man. "I thank you for your question. This," he said, addressing the crowd once again, "is how to be righteous.

"You have heard that it was said to the men of old, 'You shall not kill; and whoever kills shall be liable to judgment.' But I say to you that everyone who is even angry with his brother or sister shall be liable to judgment. Whoever insults another shall be liable to God's council of angels, and whoever says, 'You fool!' shall be liable to the hell of fire.

"When you go to offer your gift to the Lord at the altar, and there you remember that your brother has something against you, leave your gift there. Go, be first reconciled to your brother. Then come back and offer your gift."

Yeshua began pacing slowly as he spoke, as if he were ticking off the rules and examples he had prepared. You will see in his examples, if you pay close attention to them, that he speaks of the benefits of keeping good karma and practicing right thinking, the things he had learned so many years before in India and Persia.

"If you are accused of not paying a debt," Yeshua continued, "make friends quickly with your accuser, while you are going with him to court, lest your accuser hand you over to the judge, and the judge to the guard, and you be put in prison. One who fails to do this, I say to you truly, will never leave prison until he has paid the last penny. It is preferable to work out terms with a friend.

"You have also heard the Law, in which it says, 'You shall not commit adultery.' But I say to you that everyone who looks at a woman lustfully has already committed adultery with her in his heart."

There was a little laughter in the crowd. "But Master," another man called out, "we are but men, with natural urgings of the flesh. How does one control his own thoughts?"

"Yes," said Yeshua, stopping and addressing him directly. "But this is exactly what you must try, and try, and continue to try, until it takes no effort, and then you have reached perfection in the eyes of the Lord."

He looked up, to all assembled, and went on. "Listen to me: if your right eye causes you to sin, pluck it out and throw it away; it is better that you lose one of your members than that your whole body be thrown into hell. And if your right hand causes you to sin, cut it off and throw it away; it is better that you lose one of your members than that your whole body be thrown into hell. In this manner you control your own salvation. For you are free.

"It was also written, 'Whosoever divorces his wife, let him give her a certificate of divorce. But I say to you that every man who divorces his wife, except on the ground of unchastity, makes her an adulteress and dooms her, for no other man will have her, and how shall she live? Or, if perchance a man will have her, that man then commits adultery. Beware of your actions and how they may bring harm unto others. Let not us rip asunder that which our Father has brought together.

"Again you have heard that it was said to the men of old, 'You shall not swear falsely, but shall perform to the Lord what you have sworn.' But I say to you, Do not swear at all, either by heaven, for it is the throne of God, or by the earth, for it is His footstool, or by the holy city of Jerusalem, for it is the city of the great King to come. Neither swear by your own head, for you do not control your physical body, only your thoughts. You cannot make one hair white or black. Nay, let what you say be simply 'Yes' or 'No'; anything more than this comes from evil, for you cannot know what things of the future may change your circumstances and make you break your swear, bringing harm to you and to others.

"You have also heard that it was said, 'An eye for an eye and a tooth for a tooth.' But I say to you, Do not resist one who is evil. But if anyone strikes you on the right cheek, turn to him the other also; and, if anyone would sue you and take your coat, let him have your cloak also."

Yeshua paused again for breath, and another man called out a question. "Rabbi, what of the Roman soldier, who daily vexes me by making me carry his bag for a mile every day? I am not his slave. This bag must weigh five stone. After a mile, it feels as if I am carrying twice that."

"My brother," Yeshua said to him, "if he forces you to go one mile, go with him two miles. Then you are free, for you have chosen the second mile." He smiled at the man. "You may also gain the friendship of the Roman. Or at the very least, his respect."

Facing the crowd again, Yeshua said, "Give to those who beg from you, and do not refuse one who would borrow from you. Show kindness during these troubling times, for you know not when you may need someone to return this same kindness to you.

"You have also heard that it was said, 'You shall love your

neighbor and hate your enemy.' But I say unto you, Love your enemies and pray for those who persecute you, so that you may be sons and daughters of your Father who is in heaven. For, the Lord makes the sun rise on both the evil and the good, and sends rain on both the just and unjust. The gifts of the Father are offered to all.

"Of certainty if you love only those who love you, what reward have you? Do not even tax collectors do the same? And if you salute only your own brethren, what more are you doing than others? Do not even the Gentiles do the same?

"You, therefore, must be perfect, even as your Father in heaven is perfect."

Here Yeshua ended.

Later, my uncles James said that, if he had harbored any doubts about Yeshua's greatness before then, they vanished with this teaching on the hill at Capernaum. My father concurred. And the teaching was pleasing to the people, for many crowded around Yeshua afterwards, asking him questions about particular quandaries in which they found themselves, and seeking his advice. Some sought his blessing, which he gave.

Finally the crowd left, and Yeshua appeared drained. He sat on the ground, his brow furrowed as if concentrating. He closed his eyes, his face relaxing. Philip took this opportunity to bring a woman to Yeshua, a young woman who had listened to the teaching.

"Yeshua, Master," Philip said. "This is my sister, Mary. She has been a follower of John the Baptizer."

Yeshua opened his eyes, looked up at the woman, and smiled. "Mary. It is a good name, my mother's name."

The woman smiled back. Did I mention that she was breathtakingly beautiful? Olive skin, black hair, black eyes that sparkled with intelligence, and dressed in the colorful silks of a city family, not the poor threadbare linen of the country peasant farmers. Her head covering was plain white, however, and her body free of other ornamentation.

"Rabbi," she said, "I enjoyed what you had to say. These are different, but good, teachings. I am inspired by you to do better in my life."

Yeshua got to his feet. He embraced Mary and kissed her cheek. "Then you must join us to break bread, my sister."

This is the nature of Jews. If you invite someone to eat with you, then you are inviting them into your family. Therefore one of the greatest insults is to be able to say of someone, "We broke bread together, yet look what he did to me!" To be invited to a meal is an honor, a mark of trust.

The disciples began walking back towards Capernaum. They were all hungry, having eaten sparsely in the morning because all of them had been nervous.

"And what city are you from?" Yeshua asked Mary.

"Magdala," she said. "It is not far, which is why my brother asked me to come."

Mary of Magdala was never to leave them after that. She remained by Yeshua, as devoted a disciple as any. Though she was never counted as one of the twelve, for women could not rule over provinces, she did teach, and she was a member of the seventy, which, of course, makes her (like me) also of the one hundred and twenty. Her parents on occasion would send letters telling Mary and Philip that they were practicing madness, following this itinerant rabbi, yet enclose money for their well-being. The two would immediately donate this money to the group, handing it over to Judas Iscariot.

That afternoon, the bread, lentils, honey, fruit, and olives were particularly good, my father said. Finally they felt their Messiah had arrived—though no one as yet dared to speak that word.

Chapter Twelve

The next morning, Nathanael set out towards Herod's fort at Machaeras, to visit with John the Baptizer in prison. Yeshua decided to walk down with Joses to the Sea of Galilee to see Simon Peter's boat and help Joses mend nets. I think he may have been trying to win his brother's love again since Joses was one to hold onto a grudge for a time. Still, Joses seemed to like his new life as a fisherman, and Yeshua later said he felt Joses' heart begin softening as some of the people of Capernaum, going about their morning business, recognized Yeshua from the day before and hailed him as "rabbi."

Down at the waterfront, some boats were still coming in with their morning catches. The sun shone slanting onto the water, lighting the tops of the waves so the sea seemed flecked by the sparkle of jewels. The fishermen hoisted their nets from the boats and dumped their fish onto the shore, where helpers gathered them into bushels. These they carried over to a man in a small stone building, who weighed the fish on a scale, writing down numbers next to names, then collecting coins.

"Tax collector," Joses said, with scorn in his voice. "You always must stay a day or more ahead, for the Romans must first have their tax before you even sell your catch. If you have a day of bad luck selling, you must then go into debt and pray you can net and sell enough fish the next day to catch up."

Yeshua nodded. "I heard of a practice such as this in Egypt. The farmers would be taxed based on measurements taken of how high the Nile River ran. The amount of crops they could grow would be calculated. This tax they owed—even if their crops failed."

"It's theft," Joses said.

He and Yeshua leaned together against Simon Peter's boat and were quiet as they mended the nets. The holes had to be close enough together that only small fish could slip through while the larger ones remained trapped. To save valuable net, mending often required stitching with a needle made out of bone and knotting, then re-knotting, then knotting yet again. As he worked, Yeshua's eyes watched all—but he seemed particularly interested in the doings of the tax collector.

When he and Joses were done, they began the walk back up the hill. Then Yeshua put his hand on Joses' arm and said, "Wait for me."

He walked back a ways and over to the tax collector's hut.

"Peace be to you, brother," Yeshua said to him.

The man looked up, startled.

"And to you," he finally said, caution in his voice.

"People are unkind to you," Yeshua said. "Tell me—you are a Hebrew. Why do you collude with the Romans by taking taxes for them?"

The man sighed.

"I came not here to bother you," Yeshua said. "I am just curious, and my heart goes out to you."

The man said, "I have not much choice. I do not fish. I am no artisan or builder. My family is poor. The Romans pay me fairly."

"Is this what you wish to do?" Yeshua asked.

The man laughed. "No!" After a pause, he added, "I'd hoped to perhaps save enough money to one day buy some sheep."

Yeshua smiled at him. "What is your name?"

"Matthew, son of Levi."

"Son of Levi, follow me. And I will help you herd many lost sheep."

It appears Matthew required no coaxing. Or perhaps he saw whatever it was in Yeshua that so many saw. Still yet, perhaps it was merely kindness for once from a fellow Jew that compelled him. But, Matthew put his things away and closed and barred the door to the hut.

When Joses saw them coming, he scowled but said nothing.

And thus the disciples numbered ten.

* * *

When the three arrived at Simon Peter's house, Simon met them at the entryway with his wife. "My Lord," said he, his face stricken. His wife tugged at Yeshua's sleeve. Simon gently pulled her away, holding her close to himself. "Master," he said. "My mother-in-law is very sick, burning with fever."

"Let me see her," Yeshua said.

The disciples had clearly been waiting for Yeshua's return, as they all followed them to the mother-in-law's room, crowding around the doorway to watch.

The sick woman was on the floor, on her mat, covered with a blanket, taking shallow breaths. She would take no water to slake her thirst, for it would not stay down. The room stank of vomit and other foulness. My grandmother Mary was dabbing at her face with a cool cloth to ease her fever, but when Mary saw Yeshua, she rose and stepped to the side. "She was well last night," Mary said. "We found her thus this morning."

Yeshua knelt and placed his hand on the woman's forehead. "Woman," he said. "Will you believe the will of the Lord works through me?"

She was too weak to manage more than a slight nod.

Yeshua said: "Then be healed." He touched the top of her head, then her forehead, then her heart.

He stood, and as he did so, the woman's fever broke. She began to sweat with such profusion her blanket and clothes were drenched. Her breathing became deep and regular. After another moment, she sat up and looked around herself as if confused. Mary handed her the cloth and the woman began wiping her face.

Simon Peter's wife broke into tears. She freed herself from her husband's grasp and hugged Yeshua. Yeshua smiled and kissed the top of her head. "All is well, daughter," he said.

The sick woman stood. "I am hungry."

"No," Mary said. "Please sit back down."

"Bring her food, and water to drink," Yeshua said. "Then light a lamp in this room and give thanks to our Father. Clear away the sickness and wash those things she has touched."

"Thank you, Master Yeshua," Simon Peter said. Yeshua touched his arm as he left the room, the disciples parting to make way for him.

My father said that Joses looked astonished, as did the new disciple Matthew.

* * *

Now, in the Galilee were bandits and also the Sicarii, so named after the *sicae,* the thin, easily hidden daggers they carried. The Zealots were not yet organized as a group, but the Sicarii were later to join them as one of their many factions. The Sicarii were, in a word, assassins. They were notorious for blending in with the crowds in public gatherings, approaching their target, plunging the dagger in quickly, then concealing the dagger in their cloaks and disappearing into the crowd. It is a lie that they targeted mostly Romans. Romans are not easy targets. No, for the most part they targeted Jews considered Roman sympathizers, mostly Herodians and the wealthy Jews who benefitted from collusion with the Romans. Someone like Matthew, although he worked for the Romans as a tax collector, was poor and had not enough influence to be worth risking capture and crucifixion for. But in Capernaum there did reside a Roman centurion of some influence, for he had friends in Caesarea and among Pilate's praetorian guard.

It was the next day.

"This Roman," Simon Peter was telling Yeshua and the disciples, "is actually a good man. Yes!" he added, seeing doubt on the faces of some. "Our synagogue used to be crumbling. This man paid to have it rebuilt for us."

"What does he expect in return?" asked Judas Iscariot.

"Not a thing. He is well traveled and wise, and has seen the many things his Empire has done," Simon Peter said. "He is loyal to Rome—do not misunderstand me. He has been raised up in the ranks and been made a citizen. He serves here now for Herod."

"I think," Andrew said, "he tries to right some of the wrongs done to us."

"I would like to meet this man," Yeshua said.

"It would not be difficult. He often comes to the synagogue to sit outside and listen to the discussions. I think it pleases him to know he has provided the place."

As I have said before, only ten men are required for a meeting. In Nazareth, which is just a tiny village, there was perhaps just one meeting a week. But in Capernaum, which is much larger, the synagogue (especially being a pleasant, solid structure, not just a tent) was more a center of community. People would drop by during the day to see if anything of interest was going on. There was always one scheduled meeting on the Sabbath, but the rabbi, if asked, could say prayers and give blessings and name hymns to be sung on any day.

Yeshua got to his feet. "I have not yet visited your synagogue," he said. "Which is grievously wrong. Let us go see it."

The disciples filed out, along with Mary of Magdala, with Simon Peter and his brother, Andrew, leading the way. It was not far.

A cry of welcome went up when Yeshua entered the synagogue, for many recognized him from the few days prior, and word of him was beginning to spread. "Teacher!" they greeted him. "What have you to say to us today?"

Yeshua greeted them, and sat down in the place they gestured for him to sit, and he looked around the room at all the faces. His eyes lingered briefly on one man who was red of beard and wore a hooded cloak. Then Yeshua stroked his own beard a moment, thinking. Finally he said, "I will tell you a story of the coming Kingdom of Heaven." He said:

"The Kingdom of Heaven may be compared to a man who sowed good seed in his field. But, at night, as everyone slept, his enemy came and sowed weeds among the wheat, and then he stole away. So when the plants came up and bore grain, then the weeds appeared as well. The servants of the man came and said to him, 'Master, did you not sow good seed in your field? Where, then, did all these weeds come from?'

"The man answered, 'An enemy has done this.'

"The servants asked, 'Shall we go then and gather up the weeds?'

"The man said, 'No, for in gathering the weeds, you would uproot the wheat along with them. Let both of them grow together until the harvest; and at harvest time, I will tell the reapers to collect the weeds first and bind them in bundles to be burned. And then the wheat may be gathered and put into my barn.'"

Yeshua paused, and the listeners looked at him askance.

"Until the Kingdom of Heaven arrives," Yeshua said, "the good and the bad must together coexist. Do not despair over the bad. Plenty of good has been sown. Indeed, the Kingdom of Heaven even now begins to sprout forth. Take heart, my brothers and sisters. However, see to it you are one of the good. This is something to do even now."

"How do we become like the good seed, so that we enter into God's Kingdom?" This question came from Mary of Magdala, and some of the men frowned at her for speaking first.

Yeshua raised a finger and shook his head. "Do not chastise her," he said. "Mary is blessed and her question is a good one. Now listen:

"If your leaders say to you, 'Look, the Kingdom is in heaven,' then the birds of the heaven will precede you. If they say to you, 'It is in the sea,' then the fish will precede you. Rather, the Kingdom of Heaven is inside you and it is outside you. Look into your own heart and your eyes will be opened.

"When you know yourselves, then you will be known to the Father; and you will understand that you are children of the living Father. But if you do not know yourselves, then you dwell in poverty, and you are poverty."

The man with the hooded cloak and red beard spoke. "How does one know himself?"

Yeshua regarded him. "Look at what is in your heart. Look at your actions. Look at your speech. How do they align? *Do* they align? Are they of God?"

The man looked down at his feet.

"This thing you are considering," Yeshua said to him. "Do it not, for it is not of the Father, and your heart knows this."

My father said that everyone at this point was utterly confused and did not understand the exchange between the two.

Yeshua got to his feet. He thanked the listeners and took his leave.

Outside, he turned to Simon Peter. "You are right: it is a good synagogue. I will have to thank the Roman when we do meet."

The man with the red beard came out, seeking Yeshua. "Master," he said. "May we speak?"

The group watched as Yeshua and the man stepped to the side and conversed in earnest. After a while, the man wept. Finally Yeshua placed one hand on the man's head and the other over his heart. He looked skyward and cried out, "Asmodeus! Leave him!" The man's knees buckled and Yeshua reached out to hold him up. He steadied. Then there they stood a while, conversing a little more.

The two came back over. "My friends, this is Simon, a new disciple." He smiled at Simon Peter. "It is a good name, is it not?"

Simon Peter laughed.

Yeshua turned to the man, gesturing at Simon Peter. "His name is also Simon, but I call him Peter, so we shall call you Simon the Zealot: for you are, at heart, zealous for the Law—which is good, when your zeal is well directed."

Simon the Zealot seemed pleased.

Thus the number of disciples was brought to eleven.

Much, much later, my father said, Simon confided in him what had transpired that day. Simon had been a Sicarii. He had come to the synagogue that very day with the mission to kill the Roman centurion and to not depart Capernaum until he had, although most certainly it would have been a mission of suicide. He no longer cared. Yeshua had cast out the demon that was torturing his soul, for the Romans had killed Simon's family a few years previously. He had over the years assassinated seven men, and the centurion of Capernaum was supposed to be his eighth. The demon expelled was the demon of revenge, wrath, and fury.

How Yeshua had known what was in his heart he could not say.

"What I can say," Simon said, "was that the Master put love back into my heart."

* * *

Word of Yeshua was beginning to spread into the local cities and villages, so the next day Yeshua summoned the disciples, and Mary of Magdala, and now even Simon Peter's mother-in-law, who wished to come, and some few others of Capernaum who saw them begin walking out, and followed.

They walked a few hours to a plain outside of Magdala and there paused to take rest and eat. After a time, Yeshua bid the disciples to go into the city and tell the people he would be speaking. He would meditate and pray as he waited.

Even Mary went into the city, to find her family and friends, for among Mary's acquaintances were wealthy merchants, some even close to the court of Herod. Surely they would give money to support the ministry of this great new Teacher, if they would only but hear him.

After a few hours, a large crowd had amassed, and it was not nearly as hot, since the sun was over halfway through its descent to the horizon. Yeshua opened his mouth to speak. He spoke the same words as his earlier sermon on the knoll outside Capernaum, so I will not repeat that part here. But now he embellished his words and added more to the end, after bidding the people to strive for perfection in their thoughts and deeds. He said:

"Beware of practicing your piety before others so that you are seen by them, for then you have no reward from your Father in heaven. A person's true piety is seen in those things he does in secret.

"Likewise, whenever you give alms, do not sound a trumpet before you, as the hypocrites do in the synagogues and in the streets, so that they may be praised by others. Truly I tell you, they have already received their reward, in this present world. But when you give alms, do not let your left hand know what your right hand is doing, so that your alms may be done in secret. Your Father who sees in secret will reward you."

I must interject to write down that Judas Iscariot told the disciples afterwards that with these words, he finally understood why Yeshua would sometimes take his purse and pull out coins without even looking at them to hand to the poor. Once he gave an entire silver drachma to a man begging when there were smaller coins that would have easily paid for several meals. "That man must have thought he'd won a large wager at one of Herod's Hippodromes," Judas joked. The disciples all laughed at the very idea, for only wealthy Jews influenced by the Greeks attended theatrical performances or chariot races or the games. Indeed, the rich inhabited a different country than did the poor, although they shared the same land.

Back to the teachings. Yeshua went on:

"And whenever you pray, do not be like the hypocrites; for they love to stand up and pray in the synagogues and at the street corners, so that they may be seen by others. Truly I tell you, they have received their reward. But whenever you pray, go into your room and pray to your Father who is in secret; and your Father who sees in secret will reward you."

"Master," a man called out from the audience. "I have heard your friend John the Baptizer taught his followers a prayer. Would you tell it to us?"

"Yes," Yeshua said. "For it is a good prayer, not heaped up with empty phrases such as the Gentiles add to their prayers. They seem to think that the more they speak, the more likely they will be heard. Do not be like them, for your Father already knows what you need before you ask him. Pray then in this way:

Our Father in heaven,

Hallowed be your name.

Your Kingdom come.

Your will be done, on earth as it is in heaven.

Give us this day our daily bread.

And forgive us our debts, as we also have forgiven our debtors.

And do not bring us to the time of trial,

But deliver us from evil.

"For, my brothers and sisters, if you forgive others their sins against you, your heavenly Father will also forgive you; but if you do not forgive others, neither will your Father forgive your sins."

Now do you see? My uncle was speaking of karmic debt, not only debts involving money. He had already spoken to that point, in his advice to become a friend of the person to whom you owed money. The material things of this world—especially wealth—were one of Yeshua's least concerns. His purpose was to save as many souls as he could, to open the hearts of the hardened, before the Kingdom of God arrived. And thus he continued, imploring the people, for he could see that Mary had indeed drawn from the city some people of great wealth:

"Do not store up for yourselves treasures on earth, where moth and rust consume and where thieves break in and steal; but store up for yourself treasures in heaven, where neither moth nor rust consumes and where thieves do not break in and steal. For where your treasure is, there your heart will be also.

"I tell you that no one can serve two masters; for a slave will either hate the one and love the other, or be devoted to the one and despise the other. You cannot serve God and wealth.

"Therefore I tell you, do not worry about your life, what you will eat or what you will drink, or about your body, what you will wear. Is not life more than food, and the body more than clothing? Look at the birds of the air; they neither sow nor reap nor gather into barns, and yet your heavenly Father feeds them. Are you not of more value than they? And can any of you by worrying add a single hour to your span of life? And why do you worry about clothing? Consider the lilies of the field—" and here he gestured at the flowers on the plain, "how they grow; they neither toil nor spin, nor weave; yet I tell you, even Solomon in all his glory was not clothed like one of these.

"Strive first for the Kingdom of God and for his righteousness. Do not worry about tomorrow, for tomorrow will bring worries of its own. Today's trouble is enough for today."

As you might expect, one of the wealthy hearers was puzzled by this teaching and bade if he might speak. Yeshua set his eyes upon him and said, "Yes, brother."

The man said, "I have a wife, and children, and my children have children. Is it not wise that I set to the side some inheritance for them? By the sweat of my brow I have earned my fortune honestly. Are you not advising idleness, in saying that the Lord will provide?"

"Oh you of little faith," Yeshua said to him. "I did not say to not work and to never toil. I said only to not obsess over these things and to, rather, have faith in our Father. I see so many worry, 'What shall we eat?' or 'What will we drink?' or 'What shall we wear?' Yet these are the worries of the Gentiles, who strive for all these worldly things. I am saying God knows our needs and will provide for those who are righteous."

"So the idle beggar who does no work is not righteous," the man said.

Yeshua locked eyes with him a moment. "Can you read that man's heart and are you able to read the story of his life?"

Yeshua took a step backwards and raised his voice for all to hear. "Do not judge, so that you may not be judged. For with the judgment you make, you will be judged, and the measure you give will be the measure you get. Why do you see the speck in your neighbor's eye, but do not notice the log in your own eye? Or how can you say to your neighbor, 'Let me take the speck out of your eye,' while the log is in your own eye? You hypocrite, first take the log out of your own eye, and then you will see clearly to take the speck out of your neighbor's eye."

The man looked troubled, for he had been rebuked. Yeshua's tone softened.

"My brother. Ask, and it will be given you; search, and you will find; knock, and the door will be opened for you. For everyone who asks receives, and everyone who searches finds, and for everyone who knocks, the door will be opened. Is there anyone among you who, if your child asks for bread, will give a stone? Or if the child asks for a fish, will give a snake? If you, then, know how to give good gifts to your children, how much more will your Father in heaven give good things to those who ask him!

"Therefore in everything, I say, Do unto others as you would have them do to you; for this is the Law and the prophets."

Now Yeshua was finished, so he ended with a parable. Again he raised his voice so all could hear.

"Everyone then who hears these words of mine and acts on them will be like a wise man who built his house on rock. The rain fell, the floods came, and the winds blew and beat on that house, but it did not fall, because it had been founded on rock. And everyone who hears these words of mine and does not act on them will be like a foolish man who built his house on sand. The rain fell, and the floods came, and the winds blew and beat against that house, and it fell—and great was its fall!"

Afterwards, as before, many came to Yeshua to ask for his blessing or for words of advice, but the sun hastened towards the horizon and the disciples urged him to depart. Yeshua got to his feet and said, "I will. But first let me speak with this man." And he walked over towards the rich man who had been questioning him, and had lingered off to the side, his countenance obscured by the clouds of consternation.

"Master," said the man. "I have been moved by your words."

Yeshua put his hand on the man's shoulder. "Your Father in heaven knocks even now upon your heart."

"I would follow you. What must I do?"

Yeshua said, "Take all that you have, and sell it, and give the money to the poor. Find me in Capernaum and join us."

"Sell all? And give it away?"

Yeshua nodded.

"Not even give it to my sons?"

"Cannot your sons provide for themselves?"

The man scratched his head. He shifted his weight, back and forth, back and forth, considering. Finally he sighed. "This thing I cannot do." He turned and walked away.

Yeshua watched him with sadness inscribed on his face. Then he said to the disciples, "Indeed I tell you, it is much easier for a camel to pass through the loop in a rope than it is for a rich man to enter the Kingdom of Heaven."

Mary of Magdala looked stricken. "He is my cousin, a good man. I had hoped—"

"Never lose hope," Yeshua said, and he kissed her cheek. "The seed has been planted; it is good seed; it may sprout yet."

He turned, and to all, he said, "Mark you this: the Father resides in all of us. If you bring forth that which is within you, it will save you. If you do not bring it forth, it will destroy you. Now let us go."

They began the walk back to Simon Peter's house.

* * *

When they reached Capernaum, the Roman centurion, the same man who had paid for the synagogue to be built, awaited them. He rushed towards them in the manner of great urgency.

"Lord," he said to Yeshua, "I have heard much of you. I have a slave whom I dearly love. He is lying at home paralyzed, in great distress."

"I will come and cure him," Yeshua said.

The centurion stayed him. "Master, I am not worthy to have you come under my roof. Speak only the word, and my slave will be healed. For I am a man of authority, with soldiers under me; and I say to one, 'Go,' and he goes. To another I say, 'Come,' and he comes. To my slave I say 'Do this,' and he does it. Say the word, and I know it will be done."

Yeshua looked at the man, amazed. "In no one in all Israel have I seen such faith. Go, let it be done for you according to your religion."

The centurion bowed. Yes! This Gentile Roman centurion, a pagan, bowed to our Lord.

He said, "I will send this slave to you, to be your servant."

"What is his name?"

"Bartholomew."

Yeshua said, "Let it be done."

They proceeded to Simon Peter's house, and within the hour, the slave Bartholomew knocked at the door and was admitted. He fell at Yeshua's feet, thanking him for curing him. "How may I serve you, Lord? For I am told you are now my Master."

"Rise," Yeshua said.

Bartholomew stood.

Yeshua said to him, "I have no slaves. In the Kingdom of Heaven all persons are of equal rank. Follow me, as one of my disciples."

And henceforth, Bartholomew was deeply devoted to Yeshua, for it was because of Yeshua he had been made free. And thus the number of disciples became twelve.

Chapter Thirteen

The time had come to depart Capernaum and the north side of the Sea of Galilee, Yeshua had decided. He suggested using Simon Peter's and the sons of Zebedee's boats for the crossing, to minister to those on the southeastern side of the sea.

"What of our fishing?" Joses asked.

"Bring your helpers. You and they can take the boats back. If the need arises, we can walk our way across the countryside and visit the villages on our return. Or, you fish at night anyway; we could meet you if you return at sunrise."

If you are unfamiliar with the Sea of Galilee, which some today refer to as the Tiberias Sea, it is more a large lake than a sea like that Great Sea to the west, called the Mediterranean. Depending on the wind, you can sail from one end to the other in about two hours. So Yeshua was asking nothing of Joses that would pose a difficulty.

Thus, the next morning, Yeshua and the disciples and Mary of Magdala boarded the two boats, and Joses took them southeast from Capernaum. (Yeshua had asked the women to stay, since the land to the east was full of Gentiles, but Mary gave Yeshua what the disciples came to call her "look of the devil," so Yeshua laughed and told her she was welcome to join them.) They made shore in that country which is called the land of the Gadarenes. There were some Hebrews there who had been long lost, serving the Gentiles in the cities of the Decapolis. Yeshua and the group intended to walk up to the village called Gesemar, and, if successful, to continue on to the city of Gadara itself.

As they clambered ashore, however, having to wade through shallow water since there was no harbor or port where they sought to make land—they avoided the harbor town, for it was packed with Gentiles—they saw that a nearby ridge inland was dotted with caves and tombs. The hewn tombs were jammed close together for the saving of space, and, my father said, the disciples' pace slowed with trepidation the closer they approached them on the climb. A heaviness hung in the air. Yet Yeshua moved forward, climbing steadily.

Gesemar was a small settlement at the top of the ridge; Gadara itself is much farther inland. The group had almost crested the hill just before the final climb when screams from the tombs nearby stopped them. These were ghastly loud and otherworldly.

"Lord," Philip said. "Is that some phantom? Crying in torment?"

Yeshua shook his head. "No. This is a man." He listened again. "Actually, it is two men. But you are right that they suffer torment."

Yeshua left the path and strode towards the tombs, following the screams.

The disciples and Mary hesitated, then followed at a safe distance.

Two men, exceedingly fierce like wild beasts, shrieking, eyes rolling back in their heads, ran towards Yeshua as if two of the Roman Furies. One reached down and picked up a boulder that no man should have been able to lift and hurled it at Yeshua, who merely stepped to one side as it struck the ground and rolled on past.

The other man, his mouth foaming, cried out, "What have you come here for, Child of God? Have you come here to torment us before the time?"

"It is the time," said Yeshua. He raised his hand to call forth that which possessed the two demoniacs.

"Stop! It is not the end of times."

"It is the end for this legion of you who have taken possession of these men."

Now, a herd of swine was feeding at some distance from them. The demons begged of Yeshua, "If you cast us out, send us into the herd of swine."

Yeshua inclined his head and commanded, "Go then!"

So they came out of the men and entered the swine; and of a sudden, the whole herd rushed down the bank and hurled themselves into the sea, perishing in the water. Some nearby swineherds, observing all of this, hastened to the settlement and told the people the story.

Yeshua and the disciples returned to the path and completed the climb to Gesamar, but the people met them and stopped them from entering their village. "Leave us," they pleaded.

There were both Gentiles and Hebrews in this crowd, and the swineherds led them, shaking with rage. These were Hebrews, upset that they had lost their herd. Yeshua questioned them.

"Why do you live in such a way as to invite evil into your lives? You house yourselves near death, to the uncleanness of tombs. You herd swine, the most unclean of beasts, whose flesh may not be eaten nor whose skin should be handled, according to the Law of Moses, and yet you do these things for the making of money."

"We do not eat it. We only sell it. Now depart from us!"

"Do you not see that your deeds tell the evil one he is welcome here? Temptation comes to us each day, unbidden. Is not that enough? Why do you bid evil to come?"

Some of the Gentiles began collecting stones to throw at them.

Simon Peter plucked at Yeshua's sleeve. "Master," he said, "let us leave this place."

With some reluctance, Yeshua agreed. "Peace be to you all. Tend to the men from the tombs. They can now do you no harm."

With that, they all turned and began walking back down the hill, but after they had departed some thirty paces, one man saw fit to throw a stone after them anyway. It bounced, harmless, off Andrew's shoulder.

"It seems we are not welcome in this land," Judas Iscariot said, to which Yeshua answered, "Any good seed that was planted here has long since been stamped out by the Greek

Syrians."

Reaching the bottom of the hill, however, their sadness was replaced with joy when they saw that Joses and his helpers had not ventured too far out into the sea, for they had decided to try the fishing in this area, a place to which they seldom came. The disciples waved and shouted, so the two boats were rowed back to the shore to pick them up. Being almost mid-afternoon, the fishing had not been good in any case, for the nets were too easily seen by the fish.

Joses looked at the horizon. "There is ample time to make it back." He pointed at a few clouds gathering in the distance. "We may have rain fall upon us, however."

They set the sails, caught the wind, and began the journey back across the sea.

Now I confess, I have sometimes wondered about the floating carcasses of the dead swine. Surely Joses and his helpers must have seen them, but my uncles and father never mentioned this. I cannot imagine the swineherds left the swine to decompose in the sea and poison the water. No, they must have returned, with helpers, to drag out as many as they could and butcher the meat to be sold. The Gentiles here in Pella tell me that swine meat is very good when smoked, and that the fat is sweet. The thought of eating a pig that rolls around in its own dung, though—it makes me nauseous. I have also been to this site on the Sea of Galilee, and I must say that there are not a great many tombs to be seen, only hills and no village. Perhaps some earthquake—these lands often shake—has altered the landscape. Or perhaps my father and uncle mixed up the place. But, this is how they told me the story.

Well. Yeshua was exhausted from the day's work, and it was his custom to meditate when he needed to revitalize himself, but since that was not possible on the boats, he laid down in the stern and rested his head upon the ballast pillow.

My father said Yeshua was sleeping soundly, as unconscious a rock as Simon Peter—I am sorry. This is a family joke. I am not insulting Peter. He was a good man. He could just be a little thick-headed. (For that matter, in all fairness, so can I.)

Back to the story. As Yeshua was sleeping, the winds picked up until they became a storm, rocking the boats. Water began sloshing over the sides as the boats pitched back and forth, and the disciples became sore afraid of being swamped. Windstorms are not uncommon on the Sea of Galilee, but one this strong was not. Still Yeshua slept on, even with water in the bottom, soaking his garment. The windstorm did not let up, growing only stronger. Finally Philip and Bartholomew shook Yeshua to rouse him.

"Lord! Save us! We will perish!"

Yeshua sat up, groggy from sleep. "Why do you fear a little wind? Do you have no faith at all?" He raised one hand to rebuke the wind and sea. "Hush. Be quiet."

There was dead calm.

Yeshua laid his head back down and was soon sleeping again.

They all looked at each other, amazed, wondering what sort of man Yeshua was, that he could bid even the sea and the wind to follow his command.

Finally, Joses shrugged. "Well," he said. "Lower the sail. Now we will have to row."

Fortunately, Capernaum was within sight. They made land with no further trouble.

* * *

Now, the Pharisees of Capernaum did not like Yeshua. My father said this was understandable, for Yeshua was gaining popularity in the town as a rabbi, and he was not one of the Pharisees. And they were sticklers about the Law, not just to the Torah, but to their own second Torah, an oral tradition that they had themselves created. And Yeshua, the interloper, did not fear to point out to them that their "laws" and interpretations were of men, and not of the Father.

I bring this up because, when the boats landed and were tied up to the mooring stones, and Yeshua stepped ashore, there was a group of men waiting for him with a man upon a bed they had made of an old sail tied between two pieces of wood. There must have been some discussion in the synagogue beforehand, or a wager placed—casting lots is not forbidden in the Torah, though of course the Pharisees frown on that as well—or there was some plan of which no one was aware, for several of the Pharisees were also with them.

The bearers of the bed set the paralyzed man down on the ground before Yeshua. One man stepped forward and said, "Rabbi, this is my brother. He was born crippled; his limbs are useless to him. Will you make him whole?"

Yeshua knelt and examined the man, who dared not speak but whose eyes implored the Master for help. "Take heart, my son," said Yeshua, touching his brow. "Your sins are forgiven you." Clearly, Yeshua saw the man's affliction from birth as one of karma. This was not always so—sometimes bad things simply happen of their own accord—but I am afraid I am not sure how Yeshua was able to tell the difference.

At Yeshua's words, the Pharisees were outraged. "What blasphemy is this? Only God can forgive sins."

Yeshua stood. "Which is easier?" he asked them. "To forgive sins or to say, 'Rise and walk'?"

One of the Pharisees came close and actually shook a finger in Yeshua's face. "*You* cannot forgive sins."

"The Son of Man does indeed have the authority to forgive sins," Yeshua said. He raised his voice so the other Pharisees could hear. "Hear me now, you hypocrites. The Father wishes this of us. Forgive sinners—for it is the greatest of gifts we can bestow." He looked down at the man on the stretcher. "Rise, then, and walk."

The man sat up, feeling at his own limbs as if he were astonished to find them attached. He swung his legs around, tested the ground by tapping it gingerly with first one foot, and then the other; and then he got slowly to his feet. Like a toddler just learning to walk, he was unsteady, but he tottered a few steps forward. A smile split his face and he raised his arms. "I can walk! I can walk!" He turned to Yeshua. "Bless you, Rabbi, for this miracle of miracles."

All were amazed, and some began to glorify God.

The Pharisees snorted their disbelief. "We are not fooled by the tricks of magicians. You have paid to have this circus performed." They walked away, waving their hands dismissively and muttering into their beards.

The man who was the brother said to the small crowd that had now gathered, "This was no trick. I have known my own brother since birth." He turned to Yeshua. "Thank you, Rabbi. The Lord works through you."

"The Father can likewise work through you," Yeshua said. "Yea, I say to you that faith can move even mountains."

And all marveled that Yeshua claimed that any human could do works such as he.

* * *

But the Pharisees of Capernaum would not let the incident go. They spoke evil of Yeshua in that town, claiming if his works were not magic, they were then of Beelzebub or of some other devil or demon. These words angered the disciples, for twice now they had seen Yeshua cast out demons. One does not cast out demons in the name of a demon. That makes no sense.

"Well," Yeshua said with his usual calm. "We will go to the synagogue and see if these rabbis can be reasoned with."

But the synagogue was largely deserted at this particular hour. However, since there were a few men there, and now with

Yeshua and the disciples exceeding the ten men required for a meeting, Yeshua sat and began to teach.

"The Pharisees and the scholars," he said, "have taken the keys of knowledge and have hidden them. They have not entered, nor have they allowed those who want to enter to do so."

John asked, "Entered where? Here? The synagogue?"

"No, beloved. The Kingdom of Heaven."

John's brother Thaddeus asked, "What, exactly, is the Kingdom of Heaven, Master?"

"The Father's Kingdom is like a merchant who had a supply of merchandise and then found a pearl. That merchant was prudent; he sold the merchandise and bought the single pearl for himself. So also with you, seek his treasure that is unfailing, that is enduring, where no moth comes to devour and no worm destroys."

They were all confused, so Yeshua tried again.

"The person who enters the Kingdom is like a wise fisherman who cast his net into the sea and drew it up from the sea full of little fish. Among them the wise fisherman discovered a fine large fish. He threw all the little fish back into the sea and with no difficulty chose the large fish. Whoever has ears to hear should hear."

My father later said, laughing, that apparently none of them had the ears to hear, for many times Yeshua's parables and sayings made no sense to them. In fact, he said, they once asked him directly why he spoke in parables instead of just speaking plainly, but Yeshua's answer was equally obscure. "Something," my father said, "about not overwhelming children with the calculations the Egyptians used to build the Great Pyramid."

Musing on it now, I think I may understand what my uncle Yeshua was getting at. Truth, when it shatters all previously held beliefs, must be imparted in small pieces. And some will resist the truth no matter what, for the cause that they are distracted by unimportant things or are committed to believing untruths for self-serving reasons. So truth is like the merchant's pearl or the large fish. You must rejoice when you find it and reject all else that detracts from it. Finding and accepting the truth takes great effort, which is why so few will enter into the Kingdom. Still, Yeshua was here to give us the truth, which he did in bits and pieces, challenging us to look within, to keep seeking. I think he did not wish to deliver the truth as a dogma. The truth is a personal path and makes sense only to one who has realized it.

I myself still seek the truth. I still knock. I pray I will understand before I die.

But I am of good cheer of late. If I do not understand, I will come back and try again. Unless, of course, the Kingdom comes, and then I pray that I will be found to have been worthy enough.

Naturally I digress. Perhaps this is another thing to strike out when I recopy. Back to my story.

As Yeshua was teaching these things, one of the elder rabbis of the synagogue entered in a hurry. At first the disciples braced themselves for a battle of heated words and more accusations of blasphemy. But no, the rabbi knelt in front of Yeshua and begged of him: "My daughter is dying of some fast-working sickness. Will you come and lay your hands on her, so she will live?"

Yeshua got to his feet and he and the disciples followed the man out into the street, and down the way towards his house.

Along the route, there was a woman who had suffered from hemorrhages nigh onto twelve years. She could see that Yeshua was in a rush and did not wish to slow his pace. She thought to herself, *If I but touch his cloak, I will be made well.* So she came up behind him in the crowd and touched one of his tassels. This was, of course, bold of her because bleeding women are considered unclean.

Yeshua stopped and turned, as if in surprise. When he saw the woman, he smiled. "Take heart, daughter," he said. "Your faith has made you well."

And, indeed, she was well.

Then he turned back and continued on.

Reaching the rabbi's house, the disciples saw that the courtyard was already full of the man's family, weeping, and some played songs of mourning on their flutes. "Cease you this," Yeshua told them all. "The little girl is not dead. She only sleeps."

Some faces held hope; others of them laughed at Yeshua and called him delusional, for they had seen the girl dead with their own eyes. They were waiting for some of the women to return with oils to anoint the body.

"Take me to her," Yeshua said, and the rabbi took him to a room in his house. "Leave us," Yeshua said, and he went in and was alone with the girl.

This next part is how my father told the story, for no one was there to witness it, but it is probably based on the later observation of the raising of Lazarus, which was done in front of many witnesses. So saying, the story goes, Yeshua took the little girl's hand and said to her, "*Talitha koum*," which means, "Little girl, arise!"

The girl, who was but twelve, woke as if from sleeping, and got up, and Yeshua led her back out to the courtyard. The rabbi embraced Yeshua, weeping. He released Yeshua and said to him, "I will tell my brethren that you are indeed a holy man, blessed by the Lord." But Yeshua said, "No. Tell no one of this."

I ask you, was this humility on Yeshua's part? Or did he know a miracle such as this would certainly reach the ears of Herod Antipas and endanger him? Or, rather, did he know human nature so well that once you tell people not to say a thing, they go right out and blast it on trumpets to the world?

For news of this miracle spread rapidly.

* * *

The next day, as dusk approached, Nathanael appeared at Simon Peter's, back from his visit with John the Baptist. He was hungry, not having eaten that day, so Peter's wife brought out some salt fish, bread, lentils, and oil for dipping, even though all the rest had already eaten.

"What news of my cousin?" asked Yeshua, after Nathanael's pace of eating had slowed.

Nathanael put down his piece of bread and shook his head. "It is dismal. Herod keeps him below grounds, in a dungeon that is cold and damp, and John is chained by one foot so that he can move about only so many paces. He must relieve himself in the corner, and there are rats. The stench is unbearable. He does get food once a day but it is often stale or on the verge of rotten. They give him so little he finds himself forced to gnaw the meat from the bones he is given." This was indeed a terrible thing, since John ate no meat.

Nathanael scooped lentils onto his bread and bit into it.

Yeshua sighed. Philip, Simon Peter, and Andrew, who, like Nathanael, had been disciples of John if you'll remember, were greatly distressed.

"We should kill Herod," Simon Peter said. "And rescue John."

"No. No, Peter," Yeshua said. "That is the way of evil. Even John would not wish it."

"Can we take food to him?" Bartholomew asked.

"Perhaps," Nathanael shrugged. "If it is plain and nothing Herod's guards would want for themselves."

"How fares John's spirit?" Yeshua asked.

Nathanael heaved out a breath. "I'm afraid, Master," he said, looking into Yeshua's eyes. "He asks me to ask you if you are the one, or if we should wait for another."

"This pains my heart," said Yeshua, and he seemed much aggrieved. Then he cheered. "We will send John a message that will salve his heart. One that Herod and his guards will not understand."

Yeshua stood and surveyed the group. "Stay with us a while, Nathanael. You have done well. I will send Philip. And with him the Sons of Thunder, who will confirm what Philip says."

Yeshua's nickname, by the way, for the sons of Zebedee, John and James, was "Sons of Thunder," because at times they, like Simon Peter, could be hot-headed. Well, John the beloved was of gentler temperament, but compared to James, or Thaddeus, he was indeed as soft and fuzzy as a lamb.

"Here is what you will say to John: that which you have seen and heard. Say that the blind see, the lame walk, the lepers are cured, the deaf hear, the dead are raised, and to the poor is brought the good news." This, of course, was straight out of Isaiah and was a clear "yes, I am he; do not lose hope" to John, but this would mean nothing to Herod.

"And take him plain food, as Nathanael suggests."

Yeshua paused a moment as if thinking. At last he said, "The trials sent by evil could break any man. Do not think ill of John for his doubt. John is the man of whom the Scriptures said, 'I will send my messenger before you, and he shall prepare the way.' John is a Prophet—no, more than a Prophet. Of all who have gone before him, none is greater than he.

"But I tell you this: even the most insignificant person in the Kingdom of God will be greater than John."

And since the sun was setting, Yeshua went to the ladder and climbed up to the roof to pray. He stayed there the remainder of the night.

* * *

Philip, John, and Thaddeus set out in the morning with a basket of food prepared by my grandmother, Mary of Magdala, and Simon Peter's wife, to give to John, along with food for two days for the three. "When you return, if we are not here, wait for us," Yeshua told them. "For in a few days, we will travel to the villages near Jerusalem. It will soon be *Shavu'ot*, the time of the wheat harvest. And I will also go myself to Qumran, for there are scrolls kept there which are nowhere else."

Matthew said, astonished, "Aren't the Essenes worse than the Pharisees? What have you to do with them? I thought you wore white to show your holiness."

My uncle James, my father, and Yeshua looked at each other. Yeshua said to Matthew, "What is said of the Essenes is mostly untrue. And a Master belongs to all sects, not only to one." And he left it at that.

When Yeshua and the rest of the disciples and followers (including some now from Capernaum) departed, they took the usual three-day route from the Galilee towards Jerusalem that most follow, the way that skirts Samaria. This route basically follows a flat road running parallel to the Jordan, with stops along the way. This trip was uneventful except for a stop overnight at Jericho, from whence Yeshua planned to walk the eight miles to nearby Qumran the next day. The group was to travel on without him, to Jerusalem for the feast, then go on to Bethany, where Yeshua would rejoin them, and he would preach, for it was now time to bring the Way to Judea.

Word had reached Jericho that Yeshua and his followers were on their way into the city. A crowd gathered, some bringing their sick, to greet him. And there were many people likewise en route to Jerusalem for *Shavu'ot*, to celebrate the first fruits, that their number added to the crowd. There was one man, named Zacchaeus, who wished to see Yeshua with his own eyes, for he had heard of him as a teacher and worker of miracles. However, Zacchaeus was short of stature and could not see because of the press of people. So he ran ahead, and he climbed into a sycamore tree just inside the city gate.

Now Zacchaeus was hated in Jericho because he was, like Matthew, a tax collector. Only, Zacchaeus was rich and held a much higher position than had Matthew. He was one of the despised customs house officials, who were notorious for their thievery; for under Herod the Great, Jericho had become a center of trade. As an example, these publicans would accuse someone bringing in goods of smuggling merchandise, when it was not so, but they would promise to say nothing if they were paid a bribe. The entire system of taxation was a ziggurat of extortion. The Romans extracted a set amount of taxes from their managers; so these turned and extracted money from the publicans unfairly in order to make up any shortfall; and the publicans swindled the common people to make up the difference, in addition to more.

Indeed, greed begets greed, but it is always the poor who suffer most.

Now, just outside the city, a blind man was sitting by the roadside begging. When he heard the crowd going by, he asked what was happening. "It's Yeshua of Nazareth! The rabbi and healer—he passes by."

So the blind man shouted, "Yeshua, son of David, have mercy on me!" Those lining the road in front of him admonished him to be silent, for they were in Judea now, and to be called a son of David was akin to calling Yeshua a king, or it could be taken as such; but the blind man shouted even more loudly, "Son of David, have mercy on me!"

Yeshua, hearing him, stopped. He asked that the man be brought to him.

The people then stepped out of the way, and helped the blind man to his feet, and said to him, "Take comfort; he calls for you." They brought him to Yeshua.

Yeshua asked him, "Brother, what do you wish that I do for you?"

He said, "Lord, let me see again."

Yeshua said, "Receive your sight; your faith has saved you."

Immediately the man regained his sight, rubbing his eyes and squinting, blinking in astonishment, then rubbing his eyes again and peering around him, finally breaking into a joyous smile. He joined the crowd following Yeshua into the city, glorifying God; and all the people who had seen this miracle praised the Lord.

This included Zacchaeus, who had seen all from his perch in the tree.

When Yeshua entered the city and came to the sycamore, he stopped and looked up. "Zacchaeus," he called, "hurry and come down; for I must stay at your house today."

Zacchaeus, in such eagerness he scratched himself in his haste, came down and was happy to welcome Yeshua and the disciples.

This pleased the people not. They grumbled and complained, for Yeshua was going to stay in the house of this thieving sinner.

Zacchaeus was humiliated by their accusations, and also, I think, somewhat in awe of being in the presence of my uncle. Along the way to his house, Zacchaeus told Yeshua, "Half my possessions, Lord, I will give to the poor; and if I have defrauded anyone of anything, I will pay back four times as much."

This pleased Yeshua and he said to him, as he entered the man's home, "Today salvation has come to your house, for you as well are a son of Abraham. The Son of Man came to seek out and to save the lost sheep."

But then came the rabbis, the Pharisees who led the synagogues of Jericho, having been told what was happening. They stood outside the house and said to the disciples, "Why do you follow this man? He eats with tax collectors and sinners." For in Zacchaeus' house were some of his friends, who reveled without moderation, and a half-dozen women of questionable virtue.

This offended Matthew, who entered the house to tell Yeshua what the Pharisees were saying. Yeshua excused himself to his host and went outside to face the Pharisees.

"Listen to me, you who do not understand the will of the Father. Those who are well have no need of a physician, but only those who are sick. Study on this saying: 'I desire mercy, not sacrifice.' For I have come to call not the righteous but the sinners."

With that, he turned away and went back inside.

Zacchaeus bade him to please invite in his disciples, and his mother and sisters and Mary of Magdala. There was food and wine aplenty at this time of *Shavu'ot*, along with couches and cushions and floor mats to accommodate all.

That night they all ate well for a change and slept in comfort.

* * *

The next morning, all departed as planned, and Yeshua went down to the Dead Sea, also called the Salt Sea, to the Essene settlement at Qumran. Of course no one knows exactly what happened there, but my father said that he and James had asked him in private what had transpired. Again Yeshua was seeking the advice of the Council of Elders, for he was troubled by John's continued imprisonment. Was John to stay there until the angel of the Lord arrived? The Council had no answers beyond their earlier one: "Be ye like the Teacher of Righteousness, Anointed One, and seek out your answer in the prophecies." So Yeshua went to the library near the scriptorium and pored again over the scrolls.

For those who may not know, if I have not mentioned this already, there are more scrolls and writings at Qumran than is possible for any single person to read, unless that person devotes his or her life to such a task. There is the Torah, and the Prophets, and the Psalms and other writings; then there are the interpretive writings of the Hebrews, and then there are the scrolls composed at Qumran. Everything is collected, but not everything is believed. There is no single collection of writings that any group of Jews agrees fully upon, except for the five books of the Torah, and as I have explained, even the Pharisees add their own tradition of oral law to the Torah. The groups don't agree even about basic things, such as Resurrection after death. The Pharisees believe in Resurrection at the last judgment, and they believe in predestination or fate. The Sadducees believe in no Resurrection, that death is death. There is no fate, but there is free will. The Essenes, as I have said, accept Reincarnation. We do believe in free will, therefore (why else reincarnate, unless to learn from past mistakes and continue evolving towards perfection?), yet we also believe in prophecy, which is a kind of fate. How things get muddled when there are too many interpreters!

It strikes me that it would be so much easier, and much less dispute, if there were a single accepted collection of Hebrew writings: the wheat. And the chaff separated out and discarded. But who can decide what is wheat and what is chaff? Are not all writings inspired? Alas, there is no such precedent as agreement among the Jews, and now I see the followers of Yeshua, Jew and Gentile, falling into the same deep pit. Unless something changes, and human beings can learn to agree, I can already plainly see that the followers of the Way will continue this fracturing into different sects as well, and some will no doubt persecute each other just as the sects of Jews have persecuted and condemned each other, unless the Kingdom of God arrives soon.

It is disheartening.

The Essenes hold dear the prophets Isaiah, Daniel, Habakkuk, Zacharias, the prophecies of David and Solomon in the songs, the prophecy of the battle of good versus evil as laid out in The War Scroll (inspired by the Zathustrians of the Brotherhood), Enoch-Elijah-Elisha, Jubilees, and others. Of certainty Yeshua knew all the Messianic prophecies in the book of the rule of the congregation; the book of Melchizedek, anticipated to be the angel that would judge the world; and sayings of the Hymns of Thanksgiving. But of all the prophets, Isaiah is held to be the greatest. We all know Isaiah, even I, who, I freely admit, was not the most assiduous of students.

Yeshua told James and Jude that he asked for, and received, a copy of Isaiah. This he wished to read, and re-read, and study and meditate upon. For ease of carrying, the Elders gave to him a short but long scroll written not on parchment but on papyrus. This he was able to fit into a small bag that he entrusted to Judas Iscariot to carry whenever Yeshua was in the presence of the disciples. Otherwise Yeshua slung the bag over his shoulder, or tied it about his waist, and carried it himself.

It is, of course, not unusual for Jews to wear Scriptures, but an entire scroll was something new.

In five days, Yeshua joined the group on the outskirts of Bethany, where they awaited him.

Chapter Fourteen

In Bethany was an Essene household headed by a woman named Martha. She lived there with her younger brother, Lazarus, and her dear friend Miriam; but, they called Miriam "sister" since she was also an Essene, and none of the three were married—which, of course, is not uncommon among Essenes, but which is yet one more of the many reasons the Essenes were thought unorthodox. Had not God commanded us to be fruitful and multiply? However, as I have written, even I once thought I would remain unmarried, until I was smitten by my wife as if she had clubbed me over the head with a mace. Well, it was to the house of Martha that the Elders of the Qumran Sons of Light suggested Yeshua would find hospitality.

But first he wished to teach the people of Bethany, so as was now his custom, Yeshua sent the disciples into the town to tell the people he was here and to come listen. When the people were gathered, he delivered his usual teachings about the Kingdom of God and concluded with:

"Therefore, come to me, all you that are weary and are carrying heavy burdens, and I will give you rest. Take my yoke upon you, and learn from me; for I am gentle and humble in heart, and you will find rest for your souls. For my yoke is easy, and my burden is light."

Such a message of hope! So unlike the fires of Hades and damnations that so many priests and rabbis and the false messiahs of that day, and to this day, continually proclaim. Even John the Baptist had been wont with his biting tongue to rail against the Temple priests and call them "pits of vipers" and "hosts of Belial" and the like. But it was very rare, rare indeed, for Yeshua to condemn anyone with any kind of judgment, beyond that of hypocrisy; although there was a double insult for Jews that was embedded in that word since it was one used to describe the Gentile actors in Hellenistic theater, people of two faces.

The usual questions about the Kingdom of Heaven came from the crowd, and at Bethany Yeshua repeated the parable of the weeds in the field. But he also told two new parables which have become well known by word of mouth, so I will write them here. He said:

"The Kingdom of Heaven is like a mustard seed that someone took and sowed in his field. It is the smallest of all the seeds, but when it has grown it is the greatest of shrubs and becomes a tree, so that the birds of the air come and make nests in its branches.

"Or, the Kingdom of Heaven is like a small amount of yeast that a woman took and mixed in with three measures of flour—until all of it was leavened."

A woman in the crowed remarked, "That which is sown in the heart grows into the greatest of harvests," and Yeshua turned to look at her.

"Yes, daughter," he said. "You are indeed close to the Kingdom of the Lord." She was a tall woman with raven hair she covered with a plain white *mitpachat.* Yeshua stepped towards her and laid a hand on her shoulder. "What is your name?"

"Martha," said she.

Isn't that wonderful? Yeshua did not even need to seek out the household of Martha, for she came right to him, herself, Miriam, and Lazarus, all of whom had stood in the crowd and drunk in his words like parched travelers crossing the desert.

Sabbath approached, and the sun was beginning to sink in the sky. The people departed to go home, the women rushing to prepare food for that night and the following day.

Naturally, Martha invited Yeshua and the disciples and others close to him to her house, where they sat in the courtyard relaxing after everyone's feet had been washed and they had taken some refreshment. Since it was not yet summer, there was not fresh fruit, but there was plentiful barley and Lazarus had made beer. It had not fermented long and was not strong, but Yeshua declined and asked for water, which was brought to him. Miriam then sat at Yeshua's feet, still thirsting for his words. Martha busied herself preparing the meal.

The disciples asked Yeshua to explain the parables, so Yeshua—perhaps he was beginning to tire of the same questions—finally gave them the meaning of the parable of the weeds. "I am the one," he said, "who sows the good seed; the field in which the seed is sown is the world; the weeds are those that do evil; and the enemy who sowed the weeds in the field is the evil one. The harvest time is the end of times, when the angels—who are the reapers—come to gather up those who do good works. Just as the weeds are then collected and burned, so will it be at the end of the age. Then the righteous will shine like the sun in the Kingdom of their Father."

Miriam said, "The wolf and the lamb shall feed together; the lion shall eat straw like the ox; but the serpent—its food shall be dust! They shall not hurt or destroy on all my holy mountain, says the Lord."

Yeshua reached down and touched her cheek, for she had quoted the prophet Isaiah. Miriam was unlike the tall, confident Martha. She was small of stature, even for a woman; and whereas Martha could easily look a man in the face, Miriam kept her eyes downcast and blushed at Yeshua's touch.

Now Martha, in the meantime, was scurrying to and fro, preparing food for the group. She was trying to both listen and work, but distracted she could not do both, and she became frustrated because Sabbath would soon commence. Finally she entered the room and said, trying to keep exasperation from her voice, "Lord, we are your hosts. Do you not care that Miriam has left me to do all the work by myself? Tell her to help me."

Miriam started to rise, but Yeshua stayed her with his hand. "Martha," he said. He met her eyes and they looked at each other a moment. "Martha, you are distracted by many tasks, and yes, you worry about a great many things. But truly there is *need* of only one thing. Miriam has chosen this thing, and I will not deprive her of it."

Martha understood, but she looked weary. Mary of Magdala broke custom and got to her feet. She offered to help Martha in Miriam's place. At first Martha protested, but Mary said, "I am with the Master always. Let your dear sister listen."

And so it was, the women joining forces to accomplish a task the way they always do, and in a way, my Rachel tells me, much unappreciated by men because so much of what they do is unseen and appears conjured as if by magic and not by effort; and before long, laid out upon a mat were many dishes, and all ate and enjoyed, and afterwards rested since it was now Sabbath.

After the meal, Martha came and sat next to Miriam and put her arms around her and embraced her, sorrowful for her short temper. Miriam kissed her cheek. My uncle James and my father said their affection for each other was apparent, and beautiful to behold.

Yeshua merely smiled at the two women and said, "Anyone who does not know love does not know God, for God is love. I say to all here, this household is blessed."

The evening ended on this happy note as if one had plucked a string on a harp, and all retired to sleep. There was ample room, for Martha was a woman of means, her house having even two stories, and indeed even its own *mikvah*. No one ever said, but my supposition is that Martha had received an inheritance of some kind, or Lazarus had and had turned it over to her. Or, perhaps, she had once been married to a wealthy man but he had divorced her, and according to the marriage contract he bestowed on her enough wealth to live comfortably the rest of her days. In any case, as is typical of Essenes, the money was shared, and Martha, as head of the household, was known in Bethany for helping the poor. Indeed, when the group departed the day after Sabbath, Martha gave to Yeshua one hundred shekels, which, shortly after, as you will see, he put to good use.

* * *

It was the morning of Sabbath, but since Yeshua had taught the people the day before, he did not wish to go to the synagogue to cause a disturbance. There are some who say to this day that he went out of his way to provoke the rabbis, but he did not. Or so my uncle James and my father insist. No, they say, the rabbis seemed to go out of their way to provoke Yeshua.

For after the people had departed the synagogue, some came to Yeshua, for they all knew he was staying in Martha's house. With them they brought a *tekton* like Yeshua's own father Joseph, a stonemason with a withered hand, and there were some Pharisees in this crowd. To accuse Yeshua, these Pharisees presented the man to him and asked, "Is it lawful to cure on the Sabbath, teacher?"

Yeshua said to them, "Suppose one of you has only one sheep and it falls into a pit on the Sabbath; will you not lay hold of it and lift it out? How much more valuable is a human being than a sheep? So I say to you, it is lawful to do good on the Sabbath."

Then he said to the man, "Stretch forth your hand."

The man stretched it out, and it was restored, the withered hand now as sound as the other.

All marveled, especially the healed man, who blessed God for Yeshua, for now he could again earn his bread; but the Pharisees were angry, for in their minds, Yeshua had done work and had broken the commandment. It is said they left and began conspiring how to destroy Yeshua, but this was of no matter, for Yeshua and the disciples and followers all left Martha's house at the break of dawn the next morning, after Yeshua had said his sunrise prayers.

* * *

They had departed Bethany not far when Philip and the two sons of Zebedee caught up to them, having run and walked, run and walked, without much sleep, from the north.

"What is the meaning of this?" Mary of Magdala called out at the sight of her brother on the road ahead, and the disciples broke into a run to greet them.

Yeshua came up slowly, his face inscrutable. There had been not enough time for them to get to John and then travel down to Bethany.

"Don't stand there like pillars of stone," said Simon Peter. "Tell us!"

"Master," Philip said, and tried to speak, but he burst into tears. Yeshua came to him, drew him close, and held him until he calmed.

John, the beloved one, broke the news. "Lord, we never made it to Machaerus. Word came to us that Herod has taken off John's head."

"So we hastened to you," Thaddeus said.

Mary gasped, as did some of the men, and my grandmother Mary wailed and sank to the dirt, weeping with storms of tears. You must remember, she was there after John's birth, and helped her cousin with him the first six months of his life, so her attachment to John was nigh unto the same she had for her own children.

Eventually the story emerged. Herod Antipas, it was said, had left his palace at Tiberias and gone to his fort at Machaerus to hold a banquet and grand celebration to mark the day of his forty-eighth birth. As Andrew had said some time before, Herod feared to do more than hold John in his dungeons because he did not wish to risk an uprising. But his wife, Herodias, held great malice in her heart towards John for his insults of her and their incestuous marriage. She bid her daughter, Salome, to perform a—the words used I cannot repeat. I will just write "suggestive." This maiden did a suggestive dance to the flutes, timbrels, and pounding of the drums during the celebration, keeping time even with the clapping and whoops of the men of the court, pleasing Herod greatly.

Rashly, and much drunk with wine, Herod promised her, in front of the whole court, that he would grant to her whatever she wished, up to half his kingdom, for this shameful performance.

The young woman asked her mother what she should ask of Herod, and Herodias whispered the answer in her ear. The girl told Herod:

"Bring me the head of the man John, the one they call the Baptizer."

Herod, it is said, was at first concerned about doing this thing, but he could not break his word in front of the entire court, so he bade his soldiers to do as she asked. Then he seemed no longer to care. They say when he saw John's head held by the hair before Salome, he laughed and made a joke: "I see a prophet bleeds like any man, and now his mouth pleases me more, for it makes no more noise."

"This Herod," said Yeshua, "is as worse a fox as his father."

I still grieve for John. He, too, is my kinsman, after all. What had his last moments of life felt like, whilst he had been doubting, wondering if all the prophecies were wrong, and the Kingdom of God had not arrived? Of certainty the Messianic High Priest was not supposed to die. He must have thought God had abandoned him, and perhaps John blamed himself, for not doing enough, for not saving enough souls. Perhaps he thought he had displeased God. If only Philip and the brothers had gotten there in time to tell John of Yeshua's miracles! But they had not. Therefore I think, as the soldiers forced him to his knees and one raised his sword to take his head, John's last thought must have been, *Why, Lord?*

* * *

Last night my daughter Rachel could see that I was distressed, scratching here on this goat skin and seeing the many pieces of parchment I have now filled.

"Father," she said, "you will make yourself sick."

I read to her the part about the death of John and she grieved with me a time, then brought to me a meager cup of pomegranate juice.

"John lives, in heaven, with Yeshua, and with God," she said.

"And with all the angels," I said, and patted her hand.

But, nothing in this world changes. How long must we wait? How long until the children of Israel are restored to the Kingdom? I then think, in my impatience with God I sin. There must be something I do not yet see.

I will return to my story the day after tomorrow, for Sabbath arrives at dusk.

* * *

They all sat a time on the side of the road in small groups, some discussing John, and some quiet. Yeshua was off by an acacia tree, alone. Finally he rose and called the disciples to him.

"I am going back to Capernaum, for I have angered the Pharisees here," he said. "And there I will leave the women with Joses."

Mary of Magdala opened her mouth to protest, but Yeshua silenced her with a look of great seriousness.

"I need to be in solitude for a time," he said. "To think and to pray. I will go to the cave in the Decapolis where John hid from Herod, for there I will be safe."

"And what of us?" Simon Peter asked.

"You I will send by twos, across Judea, then back up to the Galilee, to teach the people. You have listened to enough of my teachings to deliver them to others. But go nowhere near the Gentiles, and enter no town of the Samaritans. Go rather to the lost sheep of Israel."

He paused, considering, then spoke again. "Now, listen. To you I give authority over unclean spirits, to cast them out, and to cure every disease and sickness. Do so in my name." He then passed by the disciples, touching the forehead of each one. "You must have faith that I have given this authority to you."

He then asked Judas Iscariot for the purse, and he divided among the disciples all the money in it, most of it given by Martha. "This should be more than enough to feed yourselves in the absence of hospitality, but it is mainly to give to the poor. Do not hoard this money; give of it freely, as you see that I have done. Trust in the Lord to provide for you."

And then he must have thought of John, for Yeshua spoke unto them as if he were going away for good:

"See, I am sending you out like sheep into the midst of wolves; so be wise as serpents and innocent as doves. Beware of them, for they may hand you over to councils and flog you in their synagogues; and you may be dragged before governors and kings because of me, as a testimony to them and the Gentiles. When they hand you over, do not worry about what you are to say; for what you are to say will be given to you at that time; for it is not you who speak, but the spirit of your Father speaking through you.

"Indeed, brother may betray brother to death, and a father his child, and children will rise against parents and have them put to death; and you will be hated by many because of my name. But the one who endures to the end will be saved. When they persecute you in one town, flee to the next, and shake off the dust from your feet as you leave. For truly I tell you, you will not have gone through all the towns of Israel until the Son of Man comes."

"Master," said Bartholomew, "who are we to do these things in your name?"

Yeshua answered him: "A disciple is not above the teacher,

nor a slave above the master, as you say. But it is enough for the disciple to be like the teacher, and the slave to be like the master. Remember they have said I do the work of Beelzebub. Therefore, be not surprised when they malign you all the more."

"But if they kill us, Lord, as was done to John. . ." And these were the words of Andrew.

"Yes," said Judas Iscariot. "You go to hide, but send us out in the light of day."

"Andrew, have no fear of them; for nothing is covered up that will not be uncovered, and nothing secret that will not become known. Do not fear those who kill the body but cannot kill the soul; rather fear for him who can destroy both his own soul and body in hell. Are not two sparrows sold for a penny? Yet not one of them will fall to the ground apart from your Father. And even the hairs of your head are all counted. So do not be afraid; you are of more value than many sparrows."

To Judas, he said simply, "I will not be long. It is not so much to hide as to be away from the chatter, for I would speak with my Father. And I would like to remember my cousin in a place where he was safe, when his spirit was among us in human form."

"Therefore," Yeshua said, "know that whoever welcomes you welcomes me, and whoever welcomes me welcomes the one who lives in me. Whoever welcomes a prophet in the name of a prophet will receive a prophet's reward. Whoever welcomes a righteous person in the name of a righteous person will receive the reward of the righteous."

A family passed by on the road, with no fewer than six children. They were on their way to Jerusalem, and the children were shouting and playing at games as they went. Yeshua gestured towards them.

"And whoever," he said, "gives even a cup of cold water to one of these little ones in the name of a disciple—truly I tell you, none of these will lose their reward."

The disciples were satisfied; and they broke off into twos, the three sets of brothers together; Philip and Nathanael together; Matthew and Bartholomew together; and Judas Iscariot together with Simon the Zealot. Thus the word of Yeshua was spread to towns such as Hebron, Beth-Shemesh, Gath, Amasa, and so on, even up to the border of Samaria at Bethel.

With this, Yeshua turned and departed towards Capernaum, the women following him, along with the others from Capernaum and some few more he had gathered to him along the way. But some of these left and went back to their own towns.

Yeshua tarried in the cave of John for seven weeks; studying Isaiah, praying, meditating, and fasting. When he emerged and returned to the disciples, all of whom had safely ministered to Judea before returning to Galilee, he was gaunt and some of the hairs on his head and in his beard had begun turning gray. My father said some of the light was gone from his eyes, but perhaps this was only because he was malnourished, having eaten only that which he could find. But he seemed renewed in purpose, more determined than ever to take his message as far and wide as he could.

"As if he knew his time was short," my father had mused aloud, when telling me this story. "Yes," he said to me, seeing me frown. "As if he knew his time was short."

Chapter Fifteen

It was well into the second year of Yeshua's ministry, and he and the disciples now set off at a rapid pace. Many in Galilee were overjoyed that Yeshua was back, and crowds now flocked to him whenever word spread he was speaking. And always, always, they brought their sick, or possessed, or paralyzed, and Yeshua would heal them. There were so many miracles of this kind that I think to write them all down would become dull in the repetition. So I will record only the ones that, for some reason or other, were unusual or striking. And to every place that Yeshua traveled, the number of his followers increased, for some would leave their homes and go with him from village to town. Crowds that at one time were only some forty or fifty became four hundred or five hundred, and those crowds grew at times even into the thousands, if he were near to a city.

Therefore what was inevitable came to occur, and this was that word of Yeshua traveled to the ears of Herod Antipas, and Herod heard of his miracles and was afraid that John the Baptist, whom he had killed, had been reincarnated in Yeshua. So the Herodians looked upon Yeshua with both fear and wrath. Yet Yeshua spoke not against Herod; therefore there was an unspoken truce between them. As I look back at the reign of this Herod, he was not really as terrible, nor as great, as his father. His father had numerous grand building projects; but he also did not care for the religious sensitivities of his subjects, putting the idols of pagans into holy places. His son? Well, his son by comparison had only minor building projects, but he did not taunt his subjects with things like pagan idols. Then again, he did not have the entire kingdom, as had his father. Herod Antipas had only the Galilee and Perea. Had he had Judea, things may have been different. For, great men do great but can also do horrible things; yet mediocre men are but mediocre, and do mediocre things.

Likewise the Pharisees did not like Yeshua's interpretations of the Law, so thirstily they drank up the rumors that Yeshua was the son of a harlot, and was a magician, or that he did his miracles in the name of some demon or the evil one. One time, in Bethsaida, which is near to Capernaum, Yeshua was involved in a quarrel with the Pharisees of that town. It was Sabbath, and Yeshua and the disciples were hungry, so they had walked through the grain fields to glean as is lawful to do, and they had plucked heads of grain to eat. The Pharisees said to them, "Look, you have done what is not lawful to do on the Sabbath," that is, to harvest.

And Yeshua said unto them, "Have you not read what King David did when he and his companions were hungry? He entered the House of God and ate the shewbread of the Divine Presence, which was not lawful for him or his companions to eat, but only for the priests. Why have you also not read into the Law that on the Sabbath the priests in the Temple break the Sabbath? But in your minds they are guiltless."

Yeshua then smiled at them. "Truly, I teach the people as you do, and I say to you that reading Scripture and discussing and interpreting Scripture is more labor than plucking and eating a few heads of grain. But something greater than even the Temple is here. But if you had known what this means, 'I desire mercy and not sacrifice,' you would not have condemned the guiltless. The Son of Man is lord of the Sabbath."

"What arrogance!" they said of him, and Yeshua continued on to Capernaum, for there they all intended to stay the night at Simon Peter's house, so some of the disciples could visit with their families. My father says I was growing well. My uncle Yeshua often held me on his lap or tickled me or held my fists in his hands over my head, moving behind me to help me totter across the floor. Of course, I can remember none of this.

My older brothers, James and Zoker, were three and four already, and Joses' own son, Mattias, was of seven years; the three, and Simon Peter's son Mark, ran around being nuisances to all the women, and to Joses, but Joses sometimes let them come down to the boats to help with cleaning and salting fish to sell if there had not been a large catch. (Otherwise, they often sold their fish to one of the *garum* makers, for this sauce was often exported and the *Kittim,* or the Romans, loved it.) I write the word "help" with irony because Joses and his men probably spent more time making sure the boys did not cut themselves, or go into the sea too far and drown. I know Joses has probably not come off well in this narrative that I set down. I do not mean to make him sound thus. He was a good man. He just had trouble seeing his brother as the Messiah, viewing Yeshua as only a rabbi and miracle worker. But later, my father told me Yeshua had told James and him, "Joses helps me. This is enough." And, of course, later he was to completely accept his brother as the Messiah.

Back to my story. There was another incident with the Pharisees. This was when Yeshua had healed a demoniac who was blind and deaf, and some in the crowd marveled and were asking, "Could it be true? Could this be the Son of David of the prophecy?" and the Pharisees denied this with vehemence. Then one, finally, said in Yeshua's own hearing that he cast out demons and healed only by the hand of Beelzebub.

Yeshua pounced like a cat, which has been hiding in the weeds and getting its haunches ready, pounces on a mouse. "Every kingdom divided against itself," he said, "is laid waste, and no city or house divided against itself will stand. If Satan casts out Satan, as you say, he is divided against himself; how then will his kingdom stand? If I cast out demons by Beelzebub, by whom do your exorcists cast them out? Therefore they will be your judges."

The Pharisees were displeased, but knew not how to answer. Since others were still gathered about and could hear, Yeshua continued with his voice raised:

"But if it is by the Spirit of God that I cast out demons, then the Kingdom of God has come to you. Or how can one enter a strong man's house and plunder his property, without first tying up the strong man? Then indeed the house can be plundered. Whoever is not with me is against me, and whoever does not gather with me scatters. Therefore I tell you, people will be forgiven for every sin and blasphemy, but blasphemy against the Spirit, ah," and here he raised a hand and shook a finger in warning, "now that will not be forgiven. Whoever speaks a word against me will be forgiven, but whoever speaks against the Holy Breath will not be forgiven, either in this age or the age to come."

"You are saying that God's Spirit works within you," said one Pharisee, but my father said he meant it not rudely but only doubtfully.

Yeshua addressed him. "Consider: either make the tree good, and its fruit good; or make the tree bad, and its fruit bad; for the tree is known by its fruit. What fruit is harvested from me?"

Then he addressed them all: "You brood of vipers! How can you speak good things, when evil is in your hearts? For out of the abundance of the heart the mouth speaks. The good person brings good things out of a good treasure, and the evil person brings evil things out of an evil treasure. I tell you, on the Day of Judgment you will have to give an account for every careless word you utter; for by your words you will be either justified, or by your words you will be condemned."

The doubting Pharisee seemed thoughtful. Then he said, "Teacher, can you give us a sign? So that we shall know if the Lord, indeed, is with you."

Yeshua tilted his head and seemed amused. And I suppose it makes sense that he would be, for after all the good he had done, what more sign could anyone need? But the unbelief of some was—and still is—so very great. So he answered him:

"An evil and adulterous generation asks for a sign, but no sign will be given to it except for the sign of Jonah. For just as Jonah was three days and three nights in the belly of the great fish, so for three days and nights the Son of Man will be in the heart of the earth. I tell you, something greater than Jonah is here!"

Well, this sounded like nonsense to everyone, the sign of Jonah. What had that old tale to do with anything, other than that Jonah had gotten the people of Nineveh to repent? So the Pharisees and scribes went away, and the crowd dispersed, and Yeshua and the disciples and followers moved along to the next village.

Now I must point out that this was a slightly different teaching that Yeshua was now giving. At first he had said the Kingdom of God would be coming, and soon. Now he was implying the Kingdom of God was here. This puzzles me still. I think that something came to him when he was fasting and talking with God in John's cave, but that something was not yet clear. And "brood of vipers" sounded like words John the Baptizer would have said, not the Yeshua of the previous year.

* * *

And then Yeshua went down to the Sea of Galilee to teach the people, but they numbered so many that Yeshua climbed into Joses' boat, which was tied to the shore, and taught the people from there. His teachings were the same, but on this day he added a new parable that is similar to the parable of the weeds. It went thus:

"Listen! A sower went out to sow. And as he sowed, some seeds fell on the path, and the birds came and ate them up. Other seeds fell on rocky ground, where they did not have much soil, and they sprang up quickly, since they had no depth of soil. But when the sun rose, they were scorched; and since they had no root, they withered away. Other seeds fell among thorns, and the thorns grew up and choked them. Other seeds fell on good soil and brought forth grain, some a hundredfold, some sixty, some thirty. Let anyone with ears listen!"

After he had taught for a time, Yeshua was weary and bade Joses and his men take him and his disciples and Mary of Magdala—who was always with them . . . I confess I tire of writing the "disciples and Mary." In every way she was a thirteenth disciple, but only twelve were needed for the twelve tribes. Therefore: henceforth when I say "the disciples," assume you that Mary of Magdala was there, unless I write otherwise. Often my grandmother Mary was there as well, and even Simon Peter's mother-in-law, if they were both not required at the house. While I am wandering aimlessly with this pen, I should also mention that my aunt Salome was now of marriageable age, and arrangements were being made for her to marry, in a year, a man named Yeshua (it is a common name, which is why so often men are identified as being of a place or as the "son of," to help prevent confusion. This Yeshua, of Capernaum, was the son of Shimon). My aunt Mary had married a man named Benjamin the previous year. But she was now living in her husband Benjamin's house, as was, and mostly remains, the custom.

I am glad my Rachel's husband does not mind living with us, for which he and Rachel will inherit my church-house.

Apologies, and back to focusing on my story. Joses and his men therefore sailed Yeshua and the disciples over to the other side of the lake, so that they might rest, free from the pressing crowds. It was a calm day, with a mild wind, so the boats sailed close together, and as they sailed, the disciples again asked Yeshua why he spoke to the people in parables, because even they, the disciples, at times had trouble fully understanding them.

Yeshua said, "To you it is given to know the secrets of the Kingdom of Heaven, but to them it has not been given. For to those who have, more will be given, and they will have an abundance; but from those who have nothing, even what they have will be taken away. The reason I speak to them in parables is that 'seeing they do not perceive, and hearing they do not listen, nor do they understand.'" He quoted the prophet.

"I thought," said Simon Peter, "you taught the opposite: those who have much will lose everything, for they have received their reward; those who are poor are blessed and will gain their reward."

"I am speaking now of those in whom my words do find purchase. For we are all born with the inner light. Once it is perceived, my words fan it into a flame; but those who do not perceive will be consumed by the flame," Yeshua said.

He put his hand over the bow and scooped out water to splash upon his face, for the day was hot.

"I do this," he said, "to fulfill the prophecy of Isaiah that says:

'You will indeed listen, but never understand,
and you will indeed look, but never perceive.
For this people's heart has grown dull,
And their ears are hard of hearing,
And they have shut their eyes; so that they might not
Look with their eyes, and listen with their ears,
And understand with their heart and turn—
And I would heal them.'"

He said to the disciples, "But blessed are your eyes, for they see; and your ears, for they hear. Truly I tell you, many prophets and righteous people longed to see what you see, but did not see it, and to hear what you hear, but did not hear it."

My father said these words troubled him, for Yeshua spoke of things as if they were already past, and his ministry was over. Indeed, he said, since returning from John's cave, Yeshua had continued to drop hints such as this that some sort of end was near. But they did not understand, and they assumed Yeshua meant the coming Kingdom of Heaven when all would be judged.

Then Yeshua explained to them the parable of the sower: "When anyone hears the word of the Kingdom and does not understand it, the evil one comes and snatches away what is sown in his heart; this is what was sown on the path. As for what was sown on rocky ground, this is the one who hears the word and immediately receives it with joy; yet such a person has no root, but endures only for a while, and when trouble or persecution arises on account of the word, that person immediately falls away. As for what was sown among thorns, this is the one who hears the word, but the cares of the world and the lure of wealth choke the word, and it yields nothing. But as for what was sown on good soil, this is the one who hears the word and understands it, who indeed bears fruit and yields, in one case a hundredfold, in another sixty, and in another thirty."

He looked at the disciples. "Have you understood all this?"

And they answered, "Yes."

Finally they made shore and climbed out of the boats and went and found the shades of several trees and sat to rest. Some lay down to nap. Since Yeshua did not intend to stay long, Joses and his men also got out and laid down to rest in the heat of the day. However, resting was not to be, at least not for long. For as I have said, the Sea of Galilee is in reality a large lake. Thus it did not take but a few hours for the people from the other side, who had departed once Yeshua and the disciples departed on the boats, with even more joining the crowd along the way, to cross the distance along the northern shoreline and find Yeshua and the disciples on the other side. Many had brought their sick, so Yeshua, in his compassion, rose up to go among them and cure them.

Finally, dusk approached. The disciples came up to Yeshua and said, "This is a deserted place, and the hour is now late; send the crowds away so that they may go into the villages and buy food for themselves."

Yeshua said, "They need not go away. You give them something to eat."

Matthew said, "But all we have in the boat is a basket with five loaves and two fish."

"Bring them to me," Yeshua said. "And tell the crowds to sit down on the grass."

Once this was done, Yeshua reached into the basket and put his hands on the fish and the stacked loaves. He looked up to heaven, and blessed the fish and broke the loaves, and gave them to the disciples, and the disciples distributed all among the crowds, the basket never emptying. And all ate and were filled; and afterwards, the disciples gathered up what was left of the pieces of bread, twelve baskets full. And my father said that those who ate were about five thousand people.

I think he was exaggerating the number, but this was indeed a great miracle. He never did say what happened to the leftover bread, whether it vanished back from whence it appeared, or whether they carried it back in the boats to Capernaum and gave it to the people. The latter seems more likely, if they did not leave it as food for the birds.

Well. After all of this, Yeshua was indeed exhausted, since he had not gotten much time for rest and the quiet that he had needed. So he bade the disciples to go back with Joses and the men on the boats and told them he would rejoin them, for the sun was setting and he wished to pray. They did as he asked.

But once the sails had been set, another windstorm blew up, although it was nowhere near to the one they had faced before, when Yeshua was sleeping in the boat. The problem was that the sails were useless to them, for the wind was so strong against them that they could not advance, so finally, they took down the sails and commenced rowing. They were about halfway across the sea when the disciples spotted a white figure coming towards them on the water. They were terrified, saying, "It is a phantom!" And they pointed, and they cried out in fear.

Then they heard Yeshua's voice calling to them: "Take heart, it is me; do not be afraid."

They ceased rowing and watched him approach, walking across the water as if it were land. As he neared, Simon Peter, emboldened, called out, "Lord, command me to come to you on the water." Yeshua said, "Come." So Peter got out of the boat, started walking on the water, and going towards Yeshua. But then he felt a gust of strong wind, and became afraid, and beginning to sink, cried out, "Lord, save me!" Yeshua reached out his hand and caught him; he helped Peter into the boat, then climbed in himself.

Sitting, Yeshua looked at Simon Peter and chuckled. "You of little faith, why did you doubt?"

And the disciples had now seen too much to doubt any longer, and they worshiped Yeshua, saying, "Truly you are the begotten Son of God."

Do you know what strikes me most about the story of this miracle? It is that Simon Peter, a plain human being like you or me, was able to walk on the water just as Yeshua had, for the few moments in which he had believed he could. Was this faith only in Yeshua's command? Or was Yeshua trying to show them that, with faith in the Divine, any person could do as Yeshua did? Or if we but realize our own Divinity within, we, too, can do as Yeshua did?

I have much faith! I believe fully in the Divine Consciousness of God, that He lives in each of us. And yet I cannot walk upon water, nor perform miraculous healings, nor create an abundant vineyard from one bunch of grapes. I know not how to have more faith. But I endure; writing of this, I am inspired to keep trying to grow my faith more, until the day I cease to breathe.

* * *

And now, having spread the word among all of Galilee, and the disciples having spread it in Judea, Yeshua decided to minister to other lost sheep of the Hebrews, so they all departed Capernaum and ventured northwest towards Phoenicia and Syria. He wished to visit Tyre and Sidon and then to come back south, turning sharply to the left to travel west towards Caesarea Philippi, that new Hebrew city of Gentiles (such as my current home, Pella, is, only it is in the Decapolis territory and very old).

Though they had carried with them some loaves of bread, they never carried much, for Yeshua always said to trust in the bounty of the Father. Therefore, one day they were walking through the fields, plucking grain to eat, and then eating of it, when they encountered some Pharisees, not of the local village, but from Jerusalem, apparently returning from some errand on which they had been sent by the priests. They accosted Yeshua, asking him: "Why do you and your disciples break the tradition of the Elders? For they do not wash their hands before they eat."

Yeshua answered them by saying, "And why do you break the commandment of God for the sake of your tradition? For God said, 'Honor your father and your mother,' and, 'Whoever speaks evil of father or mother must surely die.' But, you say that whoever tells his father or mother, 'Whatever support you might have had from me is given to God,' then that person need not honor the father. So, for the sake of your tradition, you make void the word of God."

The Pharisees liked not this answer, for he had accused them of greed. There were also some people of the local village nearby who had come out to see Yeshua, and hearing his words, they laughed at the Pharisees.

Yeshua offered them some of the grain they had gathered, for he knew their journey ahead was long, and he wished them to eat with him. But they stepped back as if he had offered them a basket of snakes.

"You hypocrites!" Yeshua said. "Isaiah prophesied rightly about you when he said:

'This people honors me with their lips,
But their hearts are far from me;
In vain do they worship me,
Teaching human precepts as doctrines.'"

Turning to the small crowd that sat observing all of this, he said, loudly, "Listen and understand: it is not what goes into the mouth that defiles a person, but it is what comes out of the mouth that defiles."

The Pharisees, in their usual way, waved their hands dismissively and turned away, continuing on their journey. Yeshua looked after them and seemed both angry and sad at once. Then he turned on the road himself and they resumed their own journey towards Tyre.

"Master," said Judas Iscariot, "you greatly offended those Pharisees." And he and some of the other disciples laughed, just as the people had laughed.

Yeshua said, "Every plant that my heavenly Father has not planted will be uprooted. Let them alone; they are blind guides of the blind. And if one blind person guides another, both will fall into a pit."

But Simon Peter said, "Explain the parable to us."

Yeshua stopped and slapped Peter on the arm, but only in play, as two boys slap one another with no intention of harm. "Are you also still without understanding?"

So he explained to the disciples: "Do you not see that whatever goes into the mouth enters the stomach, and goes out into the sewer? But what comes out of the mouth proceeds from the heart, and this is what defiles. For out of the heart comes evil intentions, murder, adultery, fornication, theft, false witness, slander. These are what defile a person, but to eat with unwashed hands—" and he stopped to laugh, as if he found the entire idea absurd. "Eating with unwashed hands does not defile a person."

He was right, you know. For Yeshua had traveled in many lands, as I have written, and seen many customs, some of which were most strange; and he had no doubt eaten many times without washing his hands, out of sheer necessity due to the scarcity of water. Yet there he stood, the holiest prophet in all the world. Had the Father stricken him down? No. Had he lost favor in our Father's eyes? No. Therefore I write this: the rules of men are sometimes as substantial as the wisps that fly from a dandelion. To condemn and persecute people for infractions of such laws is every bit as absurd as Yeshua was saying. I say to you, his message was one of freedom—and was not freedom for our people the purpose of the Messiah?

Word of Yeshua had reached Tyre before he and the disciples had even neared that city, and the same was true of Sidon, because of the many healings he did along the way; but his mission was to minister to the Hebrews, so within those cities he visited only the synagogues and some local houses. There is nothing new to report of this time except for an exchange that occurred with a Phoenician-Syrian woman outside of Tyre when they departed that city. She came running up behind them on the road, shouting, "Have mercy on me, Lord, Son of David! My daughter is tormented by a demon!"

But Yeshua, deep in thought, ignored this woman and kept walking.

She continued shouting as she approached them, "Mercy, Master!"

She made such a loud noise that my father said, "Send her away." For he had a head that ached that morning, but Yeshua would not heal him because it was his own fault for drinking too much wine. I hasten to add that my father was never a drunkard, but he had not much of a head for wine, being an Essene and not drinking it often.

And the other disciples chimed in, "Yes, send her away, for she keeps shouting after us."

But she caught up to them, and came around and fell at Yeshua's feet and repeated her plea for mercy, and to heal her daughter.

Yeshua said, "I was sent only to the lost sheep of the house of Israel."

She remained where she was, at his feet, but she looked up at him and said, "Please, I beseech you, Master, have mercy."

He said, and I think his reluctance may have been because he remembered the inhospitality with which the Gadarenes had treated him: "It is not fair to take the children's food and throw it to the dogs."

She met his eyes and said, "Yes, Lord, yet even the dogs eat the crumbs that fall from their master's table."

Yeshua broke into a smile, and he was much delighted with her answer, and he drew her to her feet. "Woman," he said, "great is your faith! Let it be done for you as you wish." And her daughter was healed.

* * *

On the way to Caesarea Philippi, again they met some Pharisees on the road, and with these were also some Sadducees. Clearly they had heard of Yeshua (as most of the land had by now, and beginning even into other lands), and in conversation with him these were polite and made no accusations. However, they did ask Yeshua if he could show them a sign from heaven, to prove that the Lord was with him.

Yeshua said to them, "When it is evening, you say, 'It will be fair weather, for the sky is red.' And in the morning, 'It will be stormy today, for the sky is red and threatening.' You know how to interpret the appearance of the sky, but you cannot interpret the signs of the times. An evil and adulterous generation asks for a sign, but no sign will be given to it except the sign of Jonah."

Then he left them and went away. And all the disciples wondered yet again what he meant by the sign of Jonah, but no one dared to ask, for it seemed to them he tired of having to always explain to them the meaning of his parables and sayings, and of the Pharisees always asking of him a sign.

They reached the district of Caesarea Philippi that day, and on the road, Yeshua was deep in thought. He was often like that, said my father. He would be silent for hours, retreating into himself. During these times, the disciples would hang back and walk together, giving him solitude as they talked among themselves. Sometimes, however, Mary of Magdala would walk with him in silence. Yeshua seemed not to mind. Sometimes he would place his arm around her, or kiss her on the cheek. Do not misunderstand these words I write. The two loved each other, but not in the way a man loves a woman and a woman loves a man. Or, perhaps they did love each other in this way, but chose to not act on these feelings. As for the other disciples, the rest were too talkative to bear these long periods of quiet.

But then Yeshua opened his mouth to speak, so the disciples caught up to him, and he asked them, as they walked along, "Tell me, who do people say that I am?"

Philip said, "Herod Antipas thinks you are the reincarnation of John the Baptist."

"Others say Elias or Jeremiah, or one of the other prophets," Andrew said.

Yeshua stopped walking and regarded them. "But who do you say that I am?"

Nathanael said, "You are like a just messenger."

Matthew said, "You are like a wise philosopher."

Yeshua looked at his brothers. They knew not what to say, for they knew perfectly well who and what he was. Finally my father said, "Rabbi, my mouth is utterly unable to say what you are like."

At this, Yeshua smiled, for his answer was clever. "Jude," he said, "I am not your rabbi. Because you have drunk my words, you have become intoxicated from the bubbling spring that I have tended. I would speak with you in private, however, in a few moments."

He asked the others, "Any other comparisons?"

Simon Peter spoke up. "You are the Messiah, the Son of the

living God."

And Yeshua said, "Blessed are you, Simon Peter! For flesh and blood has not revealed this to you, but my Father in heaven. And Peter is a good name for you indeed, for on this rock I will build my Church, and the gates of Hades will not prevail against it. I will give you the keys of the Kingdom of Heaven, and whatever you bind on earth will be bound in heaven, and whatever you loose on earth will be loosed in heaven."

He looked at all the disciples and said, "Do not yet tell anyone that I am the Messiah."

He turned and began walking again, and my father stayed with him. When my father returned to the disciples, they asked him to reveal what Yeshua had told him. My father said, "If I tell you one of the sayings he spoke to me, you will pick up rocks and stone me, and fire will come from the rocks and consume you."

They never asked again.

But later, when my father was alone with his brother James, he spoke freely of what Yeshua had said to him. My father told him, "Yeshua said that I, too, was correct: that it is impossible to articulate the nature of the Divine."

"He called himself God?" James asked. His face fell with worry and confusion.

"No, that is not what he meant. But you see why I would not tell the others," my father said. "And why I said they would stone me if I did."

James nodded.

"But there is something he wanted me to tell you," my father said, "for he said I understood well enough to articulate it in a manner that you would understand."

"I'm not without intelligence," my uncle James said, offended.

"He did not mean that, either," my father said. "I think when he said I was intoxicated by the bubbling stream which he tended, he meant—" and my father searched for words. "He meant a kind of ecstasy of the Holy Spirit. He once caught me praying—and he apologized, and left me alone with God. Another time I found him watching me when I was doing nothing but sitting and looking."

"I know you are not drunk, or I would think you were," James said.

My father smiled at his older brother. "Now you sound like Joses."

At this, they both laughed.

"But do you know what I mean?" my father asked him. "When you are sitting sometimes in a beautiful place, with the flowers blooming and the air perfumed by their scent, and the sky is a deep blue, and the trees' leaves shake gently in the wind as if the air were greeting each one in turn, and you feel as if you, and the wind, and the earth, the trees, the flowers, and everything, are as one."

James nodded. "You say it well."

"I think that is all he meant" my father said. "A personal experience of oneness with God."

"Ah. I understand."

"So, here is, more or less, what Yeshua said to me. He said, 'I am the embodied will of the Holy Spirit, who begot me at my baptism, and who speaks through me. You must impress upon your brother the nature of my work, for he will take my place. If he listens to the still, small voice that proceeds from his heart, and that gives him feelings in his stomach, then he will be doing my will, and the will of our Father. But he must listen carefully, and separate the head from the heart. This is the thing that demands the most effort and prayer, and the setting aside of personal desires.'"

This, James understood, but both were troubled; for once again it sounded as if Yeshua knew his presence among us was coming to an end. But this end did not sound like the end of times. Therefore, what did he mean?

Chapter Sixteen

From this time onwards, Yeshua began to tell the disciples that he must go to Jerusalem and undergo great suffering at the hands of the Elders and chief priests and scribes, and that he would be put to death. So finally my uncle and father understood the hints and sayings he had made, but they were even more troubled.

Simon Peter took Yeshua to one side and dared to rebuke him, saying, "God forbid it, Lord! This must never happen to you."

Yeshua said to Peter, "Get behind me, Satan!"

Peter looked stricken, so Yeshua's tone softened. He said, "You are a stumbling block to me; for you are setting your mind not on divine things but on human things."

So dying was not a thing that Yeshua wished to do; else, Simon Peter's words would not have been an obstacle or temptation to him. And who cannot understand that? What man or woman wishes to suffer and die?

I have thought on this much. All I can write is a speculation: that what Yeshua had found, when he had fasted and meditated and prayed in John's cave, poring over his copy of Isaiah given to him by the council at Qumran, must have been the prophecy that is set down in Isaiah in the fifty-third section. It is hard to say exactly what Yeshua was thinking. Perhaps he thought if he died, as was prophesied, and as had happened to John the Baptizer, though no one had ever before seen this prophecy to be about the Messiah, this act, with him serving as the sacrificial lamb, would usher in the Kingdom of Heaven, for the Lord would surely be wrathful at such a gift, much as he had been displeased with the gift of Cain. But that is the view of God as Punisher, which, as I have written, the Essenes did not particularly embrace. Or perhaps God had told him the Kingdom would not come quite yet, for too many of the people were unworthy or unready, not heeding his message, and God wished not to take so many souls. It is difficult to say. I still ponder the question of the need for Yeshua to die in the manner he did. If God desired mercy, not sacrifice, then why would God desire the sacrifice of both his kingly and priestly Messiahs? Perhaps some answer will come to me by the time I have finished writing this narrative.

In any case, after having told the disciples this thing, Yeshua told them: "If any want to become my followers, let them deny themselves and take up their cross and follow me. For those who want to save their life will lose it, and those who lose their life for my sake will find it. For what will it profit them if they gain the whole world but forfeit their life? Or what will they give in return for their life?"

And then Yeshua reminded them their suffering for his sake would not be for long: "For the Son of Man is to come with his angels in the glory of his father, and then he will repay everyone for what has been done. Truly I tell you, there are some standing here who will not taste death before they see the Son of Man coming in his Kingdom."

Oh, Yeshua, my uncle, you were wrong! That generation has died, and the next generation is dying now. This is why I think perhaps the Cosmic Divinity altered the course of history, for the people of Israel hardened their hearts and did not heed the words of his begotten Son. In his mercy, perhaps, the Lord has granted us a reprieve, and he still waits to see if the seeds planted by Yeshua will take root, and spring forth from the soil, and bear a more bountiful harvest than the one present. God is not a Punisher but is full of Mercy.

* * *

After ministering in Caesarea Philippi, they left that place and began the journey back to Capernaum. They stopped for the night in a desolate area at the foot of a mountain, about a day's walk from Thella. Just as the disciples were beginning to lie down and roll themselves into their cloaks, Yeshua summoned my uncle James, Simon Peter, and John to him. "Come with me," he said, and the three followed him up the mountain.

At the crest, Yeshua departed from them and went to the edge, where he stood. As the disciples watched, marveling, Yeshua raised his arms above his head, then lowered them, crossing them over his heart in supplication. His head bowed, he became slowly transfigured before them, and his face shone like the sun, and his garment, which was already white, became dazzlingly bright.

At this sight, the three men dropped to their knees in awe. But then two figures appeared alongside Yeshua, figures of light that grew more sharply into focus until they appeared as men. Both wore garments of white, and one, like Moses, carried a staff. The other appeared like Elias, from descriptions of that great prophet. The two beings of light spoke with Yeshua, but the disciples could not hear what was said. Next a bright cloud descended and overshadowed the three, Yeshua, Moses, and Elias, and a voice came from the cloud which said, "This is my Son, the beloved; with him I am well pleased; listen to him!"

When the disciples heard this, they pressed their faces to the ground and were overcome with fear. But Yeshua came and touched them, saying, "Get up, and do not be afraid." And when they looked up, they saw no one except Yeshua himself alone.

"Lord," said Simon Peter. "It was good for us to be here, to see this thing. If you wish, I will build here three altars, one for you, one for Moses, and one for Elias."

Yeshua smiled at him and said no, this was not required, and as they descended from the mountain, he told them to tell no one of what they had seen, until after he had died.

So I will write more of this later.

John asked, "Master, why do the scribes say that Elias must come first?"

Yeshua said, "Elias is indeed coming and will restore all things; but I tell you that Elias has already come, and they did not recognize him, but they did to him whatever they pleased. So also the Son of Man is about to suffer at their hands." Then the disciples understood that he was speaking of John the Baptizer.

When my uncle and father told me this story, I did not understand why my father was not one of the three, instead of John, for my father knew Yeshua was the Messiah, and Simon Peter had recognized this on his own, but John had not known. My uncle James answered my question.

"Yeshua was forming the three pillars of his Church. The eldest of his brothers would lead. And on my right hand would be Peter. On my left would be John. More than one brother would be . . ." and here he sought for words. He shrugged. "It would be too much like the Gentiles or the Herodians, where all the kings are of one family, and the princes are made to govern provinces or made generals to conquer more territories. As for Simon Peter, as you know, he is a great leader and a man of charisma, but he is also quick to anger and impulsive. To temper him, the best choice was John, the beloved one, who is gentler of nature than Peter and not so quick to anger and more thoughtful. But he is not so gentle that he wilts like a flower in want of water."

This made sense to me, so I was satisfied. I am but a man. I do not like to think that my father was slighred.

* * *

Finally, they arrived near to Capernaum; word had reached the town that Yeshua was coming, for many came out to greet him. One was a man who had come all the way north from Beersheba, and he knelt before Yeshua, and he said, "Lord, have mercy on my son, for he is an epileptic and he suffers terribly; he often falls into the fire and often into the water. And I brought him to your disciples when they were in Judea, but they could not cure him."

Yeshua said, for all to hear, "You faithless and perverse generation, how much longer must I be with you? How much longer must I put up with you?"

Even then he was turning weary, for he preached and taught and healed and still the people did not repent. All they did was ask for miracles from him.

To the man, he said, "Bring your son to me."

So the man brought his son, who ceaselessly twitched and made guttural sounds with his mouth, and Yeshua rebuked the demon within him; and it came out of him, and the boy was healed instantly.

Later, in private at Simon Peter's house, the disciples asked Yeshua, "Why could we not cast the demon out?"

"Because of your little faith," Yeshua said. "For truly I tell you, if you have faith the size of a mustard seed, you will say to this mountain, 'Move from here to there,' and it will move; and nothing will be impossible to you."

And now I feel I should discuss demons, for it occurs to me that they have appeared much in this narrative. Some human beings truly are possessed by strange, evil entities, like the two Gadarean men in the tombs, and Yeshua would cast these out. But most of the time when people came to him to say they had a demon afflicting them, it was not really an entity that did this. It is, and I think I wrote of this very early on in this narrative, a superstition. It was some illness they believed was caused by an evil presence that was being visited on them, for this is how afflictions of the body are often explained. But I think perhaps such superstitions are nothing more than the punishment inflicted by a guilty conscience. Or perhaps these are the illnesses of karma. But if their faith in Yeshua was as strong, or stronger, than their belief in the demon, just his touch could cure them. I think of it as Yeshua erasing the evil in their own minds that was causing the illness. This was why he so often would say, "Your belief has made you well." It was essentially the truth.

They made themselves well.

Of course, broken legs or arms or bleeding or leprosy and things such as this Yeshua healed of his own power—or, more accurately, of his own faith in the Father or his attunement with the Divine Consciousness—but as he had learned from the Zoroastrians, healing was still much easier the more faith the person he was curing held. But if the healer and the one who would be healed both lack faith—woe to that person!

I have healed some few by appealing to the Father and the laying on of my hands, but I confess it does not always work. Then I resort to the various herbal medicines such as the Essenes kept in the grottoes. These often relieve pain, or itching, or rashes, and the like. Sometimes I tell people to go visit the healing waters of the Salt Sea. I always encourage them to pray and to ask their family and friends to pray for them. Sometimes it works, and I refuse to take coins for such a service. But I have never been able to heal a person, other than that of a forlorn spirit, through the forgiveness of sins. Yeshua was very special in that way.

These are things my uncle and father explained to me, and they also appear in the Essene teachings.

* * *

Now they were only in Capernaum a day before the collectors of the Temple tax came to Simon Peter when they saw him returned, for Peter was down at the boat landing with Joses inspecting some repair work Joses and his helpers had done. They reminded Peter he owed his annual tax. And then they added, "And what of your teacher? Does he not pay the tax? "

"Yes, he does," said Peter, to get them to go away. "I will get the money and bring it to you tomorrow."

Of course, Peter did not have the money but perhaps he was hoping Judas Iscariot carried enough in the purse.

Back at his house, Peter brought up the tax to Yeshua, and

Yeshua asked him, "What do you think, Simon? From whom do kings of the earth take toll or tribute? From their own children or from others'?"

Peter chuckled. "From others' children."

"Then the children of kings are free," Yeshua said, and this made them both laugh because, of course, Yeshua was descended from King David.

"But let us not offend them," Yeshua said. "Go back to the lake, and cast out a hook. Take the first fish that comes up; and when you open its mouth, you will find a shekel. Take it and give them this coin to pay for you and me."

And so it was done.

When Peter returned the next morning after paying the tax, Yeshua and the disciples were gathered in the courtyard, where Yeshua was speaking to them the sayings of the prophet Daniel regarding the Kingdom of Heaven. I should say that the Pharisees did not like much the words of Daniel and the coming End Time, for many were friends to the Herodians and liked things just as they were, so they took Daniel out of the Prophets and put him with the minor Writings; so, too, the Sadducees, for the Herodians among them were even worse since they did not believe in the Resurrection of the body. As the wealthy Temple priests, they in particular were happy with things just as they were.

In the meantime, the countryside groaned under the weight of their taxes: taxes to Rome, taxes to Herod, taxes for the Temple. Never had all Israel been subjected to such tax. Sometimes, and I think I wrote this down before, the amount could approach almost half of one's annual earnings. Thus the farmers, who had owned land, were forced to sell it to the rich so they could pay their taxes; and then these farmers were forced to farm their own land and turn over their crops to the wealthy landowner, who allowed them only a portion to keep. And still they owed the tax! Meanwhile the landowners took their crops and loaded them onto merchant ships and made much money sending the food into other lands.

I think of a donkey, which can carry a light burden. But say its owner keeps adding to the burden, and adding, and adding more, until one day he lays a cloth over the whole to keep it secure; and the weight of this light cloth is the very thing that makes the donkey collapse and fall, one leg having snapped. The donkey is then put to death, for it is no longer useful. These are the people of Israel.

Then the owner procures a new donkey, and begins anew, placing on a burden, and then adding, and then adding, and so on until the new donkey meets the same fate. The owner represents the leaders of Israel: the Romans, the Herodians, and all who collude with them and profit from Roman rule.

Ha! I have just made up my own parable.

But you can see why, even then, the Zealots and the Sicarii were beginning to increase in number. Yet, every rebellion had up to this time in the story been quashed, and many people had been crucified.

Back to the story. The disciples asked Yeshua who would be greatest in the coming Kingdom of God. Yeshua answered, my father told me, by reaching out to stop me, for I had been just about to run by, as my brothers James and Zoker were chasing me, whilst Simon Peter's son, Mark, chased after them. Yeshua lifted me onto his lap.

"Truly I tell you," he said, "unless you change and become like children, you will never enter the Kingdom of Heaven. Whoever becomes humble like this child is the greatest in the Kingdom of Heaven. Whoever welcomes one such child in my name welcomes me.

"If any of you put a stumbling block before one of these little ones who believe in me, it would be better for you if a great millstone were fastened around your neck and you were drowned in the depth of the sea. Woe to the world because of stumbling blocks! Occasions for stumbling are bound to come, but woe to the one by whom the stumbling block comes!"

It is for this reason that I tried never to stand in the way of my own daughter. I taught her the Way of her great-uncle, but it was her decision alone whether or not to believe, and to follow those of the Way. Our philosophy is to open up the door to all, and offer admittance to all without judgment. But neither do we cast stones and curses after one who does not enter through the door. We would help up a man who has fallen in the street even if he does speak ill of us. And of certainty we would never trip a person who is on the road, or place an obstruction in the road to harm him. In matters of social equality, the door is also opened to all. No man or woman, no Jew or Gentile, no rich or poor, is better than another and due more than any other. I think that Paul, with whom, later on, we so disagreed on many things, even understood Yeshua's sayings well enough to write down much the same, in one of his letters, as this last thing that I have written.

Therefore Yeshua continued, "Take care that you do not despise one of these little ones; for I tell you, in heaven their angels continually see the face of my Father." This is yet another Essene teaching, as I have written before. Every person is born with an angel as a spiritual guide and protector. Over the years I have come to think my own angel may hint at the course I should take by giving me feelings in my stomach when I consider various solutions to problems. Or perhaps this is the Master Within.

I chat much today, and for this I apologize. Again this is the kind of thing I write that I suppose I will strike out later.

Yeshua then asked the disciples a question in the form of a parable: "What you do think? If a shepherd has a hundred sheep, and one of them has gone astray, does he not leave the ninety-nine on the mountains and go in search of the one that went astray? And if he finds it, truly I tell you, he rejoices over it more than over the ninety-nine that never went astray. So it is not the will of your Father in heaven that one of these little ones should be lost."

The disciples understood this well. In the Kingdom of Heaven, no one was greater, and everyone was received with joy. I was now playing with Yeshua's tassel, so he stopped my hand with his, then kissed my cheek and continued.

"If another member of the church sins against you, go and point out the fault when the two of you are alone. If the member listens to you, you have regained that one. But if you are not listened to, take one or two others along with you, so that every word may be confirmed by the evidence of two or three witnesses. If the member refuses to listen to them, tell it to the church; and if the offender refuses to listen to the church, let such a one be to you as a Gentile and—" here he pointed at Matthew and said: "A tax collector!"

They all laughed, including Matthew.

"Do not persecute that person. All is restored in the Kingdom of Heaven. Truly I tell you, whatever you bind on earth will be bound in heaven, and whatever you loose on earth will be loosed in heaven. Again, I tell you, if two of you agree on earth about anything you ask, it will be done for you by my Father in heaven. For where two or three are gathered in my name, I am there among them."

Yeshua set me down, for I was starting to wriggle and squirm, and off I went to find my brothers and Mark.

Simon Peter asked, "So, Lord, if another member of the church sins against me, how often should I forgive? As many as seven times?"

Yeshua said, "Not seven times, but, I tell you, seventy-seven times!"

Which, of course, is forever, or to always forgive. This is simply karma. But Yeshua told to the disciples a parable to illustrate this point. "Now, listen," he said:

"The Kingdom of Heaven may be compared to a king who wished to settle accounts with his slaves. When he began the reckoning, one who owed him ten thousand talents was brought to him; and as he could not pay, his lord ordered him to be sold, together with his wife and children and all his possessions, and payment to be made. So the slave fell on his knees before him, saying, 'Have patience with me, and I will pay you everything.' And out of pity for him, the lord of that slave released him and forgave him the debt.

"But that same slave, as he went out, came upon one of his fellow slaves who owed him a hundred denarii; and seizing him by the throat, he said, 'Pay what you owe.' Then his fellow slave fell down and pleaded with him, 'Have patience with me, and I will pay you.' But he refused; then he went and threw him into prison until he would pay that debt.

"When his fellow slaves saw what had happened, they were greatly distressed, and they went and reported to their lord all that had taken place. Then his lord summoned him and said to him, 'You wicked slave! I forgave you all that debt because you pleaded with me. Should you not have had mercy on your fellow slave, as I had mercy on you?' And in anger his lord handed him over to be tortured until he would pay his entire debt. So, my heavenly Father will also do to every one of you, if you do not forgive your brother or sister from your heart."

Now, unless you understand not the numbers in this parable, depending on the land in which you reside, a talent is just a little more than fifteen years' worth of wages for a laborer. Ten thousand talents is a greatly exaggerated sum. A denarius is the common daily wage for a laborer. So, one hundred denarii is by comparison a very small sum. Heed you well this parable, for it is most instructive.

Now, it was almost March, and Yeshua next reminded the disciples that he would be going to Jerusalem for Passover in April, where he would be persecuted, and mocked, and put to death. He wished to spend this last month alone, traveling with his face covered so he would not be recognized except to those he chose, and doing the Father's work without the crowds continually following him. Therefore, over the next few days, he sent out the disciples, with fifty-eight more men and women who had sometimes followed him from town to town, to total seventy teachers. He split them into groups of five, so all but two groups were led by one disciple. Mary of Magdala led one of these groups, and his own mother, Mary, led the last. Yeshua gave them the same instructions as he had given the disciples before he went to John's cave after he had heard of John's beheading. But this time he specifically included Samaria, for, as he said, "There are lost sheep among them as well." All were to meet back in Capernaum at the end of March.

So, they did as they were instructed. To this day, no one really knows what Yeshua did during this time, except for going to Caesarea, a thing he mentioned to the disciples later. In retrospect, I believe he may have tested several Roman cities, to see how the Gentiles might receive him. And I would not be surprised if he had also spent part of this time praying, fasting, meditating, and preparing his spirit for the trial that was soon to beset him.

* * *

Finally came the appointed time. Much was to happen in these last two weeks of Yeshua's earthly existence, and much of the family traveled along. James and his wife, and my father and mother, came. Joses and his wife stayed in Capernaum, however, for Zebedee was unable to travel; and my uncle Simon could not, for he was still bound to Cana until his wife's father passed on. My aunt Salome and her new husband came, for he wished to observe the Passover; but my aunt Mary stayed with her husband, for she had recently conceived and was often sick. All together, traveling to Jerusalem was therefore much of the family, including my two brothers and me, Simon Peter's son, Mark, and Joses' son, Mattias. Mattias had been attending the *yeshiva* in Capernaum to learn Torah, but it was already past time for him to be attending an Essene school, so Joses wished the family to send him to the Ein Kerem school after Passover. Ultimately this is what my brothers and I did as well, when we were old enough. We went to the school at Ein Kerem; my brothers Zoker and James married, however, when one was sixteen and the other fifteen. In contrast, I, at that time, did not wish to marry and instead continued my studies and then went on to Qumran. But now I am well ahead of myself, so I will return to the story at hand.

Also in the group were all the disciples, including Mary of Magdala, and Simon Peter's wife (but his mother-in-law stayed behind to help Joses and his wife with Zebedee), and some others among the seventy that had been sent out, and some brought their wives and children. Therefore this group from Galilee numbered close to a hundred people in total.

We all set off early, about ten days ahead of the Passover, for it is a three-day journey, and Yeshua wished to avoid the crowds of pilgrims that would be on the road. He also sent my uncle James ahead to Qumran with a note for the Council of Elders, and he was to rejoin us outside Jericho with their response.

Now, it will be difficult for me to set down this next part. Lately my health has not been as robust. Perhaps it is grief. In remembering my uncle with such detail, I believe I have come to love him even more, a thing I had thought impossible. If only it had been God's will to have him with us a little longer! Perhaps more hearts would have been unhardened, and more would have repented.

But the ways of God remain shrouded in mystery, and still we struggle to see through the shroud to the Truth.

Chapter Seventeen

The usual route from the Galilee (from Capernaum) takes one around the sea on the western side, to the bottom or southern end of the sea, where one then connects with the road that runs by the Jordan River. I have perhaps already described this route; sometimes this old mind fails me in recollection. But anyway, as I wrote yesterday, my uncle James was sent ahead to Qumran; and, traveling with so many, we wound up taking four days instead of the usual three. The trip was eventful, for some sort of incident happened each day along the route.

The first was in a small village I recall not the name of, but it was between Magdala and Tiberias. The Pharisees of that place heard that Yeshua was outside the town, having brought the group to a halt to eat bread and rest a bit before continuing on, so they brought to him a woman who had been found taken in adultery. They had her hands bound together with a cloth and had clearly been holding her in a cell overnight. Now by the Law, it was proper to stone her to death for this crime. But I will say that stoning was done much less often than some think, if they derive their impressions of Jews solely from reading our Torah. Many rabbis say the Law lists the punishments in increasing severity just as an indication of the seriousness of the crime. Therefore stoning was not a requirement; more often than not, floggings were meted out instead for punishment. This was particularly so in Judea, where the Romans had put themselves and no one else in charge of decisions involving capital punishment. In Galilee, where Herod Antipas ruled, he did not much care what the rabbis did, so long as they did not challenge his authority.

But I believe they brought the woman to Yeshua just to see what he would say. And, of course, the man with whom she had been adulterous was nowhere in sight. Apparently they had decided to overlook his part in the crime.

These Pharisees threw the woman to the ground near to Yeshua, and some began gathering stones. The woman was terrified, and crying out, and begging for mercy.

Several of these Pharisees stepped towards Yeshua. "Teacher," they said, "this woman is adulterous, and the Law calls for stoning. Are you in agreement that we should follow the Law?"

Yeshua squatted down, and using his forefinger, wrote something in the dust, as if he were making random marks while thinking this problem through. Finally he stood and addressed them so all could hear:

"Follow the Law as it is written. But I say to you, he who is without sin, let him cast the first stone."

The Pharisees, and the men who had come out with them, all stood as if struck dumb. One man then stepped towards the woman and raised his arm as if to throw his stone, then seemed to think better of it and let the stone drop to the ground.

As if one, they all turned together and went back into the village, leaving the woman cowering on the ground, covering her head with her arms and afraid to look up.

Yeshua approached her and touched her shoulder. "Woman," he said, "where are your accusers?"

She removed her arms from covering her face and turned to look behind her. Seeing no one but Yeshua, she sat up, then grabbed Yeshua's legs and began begging him for his mercy.

"Woman," he said. "My child. Stop. Rise."

He helped her to her feet.

"Those who would condemn you have departed. Neither will I condemn you. Go, then, and sin no more."

The group went on its way.

I have always loved this story. When I was told it, I asked my father what my uncle had written in the dust. He smiled at me, pleased I had latched onto this detail.

"He'd written in Aramaic," my father, Jude, said. "It said 'I desire mercy, not sacrifice.'"

So, once again, Yeshua had quoted the prophet Hosea.

* * *

The next day, they drew abreast to the land of the Samaritans. Seldom do Jews venture into their country, for they do not follow the Law. They have their own Torah, and indeed their own Temple, on Mt. Gerizim, for they believe that mountain to be the location of the House of the Lord, not Jerusalem.

Now, you may have heard this story told, and I can reasonably be assured you have heard the exaggerated version that is shared around. That version sets the story at Shechem, and the well as Jacob's well. That makes for a nice story, but it is not true. Yeshua did not venture but a few miles off the Jordan road, taking six of the disciples with him carrying empty water skins, for he had been told of a well there by some of the seventy he had sent out the month before. It is true they could have more easily drawn the water from the Jordan, so I believe Yeshua ventured into Samaria because he saw doing so to be his duty. After all, as Messiah, he was to bring the Word to all the lost sheep. And what better place to find Samaritans than at a well outside one of their towns?

For it is true that wells or springs are a most popular meeting place. If you have read your Torah, you know this thing. Moses met his wife at a well. Jacob met his wife at a spring. Isaac's servant found Isaac's wife at a well. Indeed, it is a common joke among Jews that wells are a good place to meet eligible maidens. If she favors you, she will dip you out a drink.

So, most waited by the road, resting as Yeshua and the disciples went off to get water.

As they approached the well, after about an hour of walking, Yeshua saw that a woman was there drawing water, so he stayed the disciples and approached her alone. This part of the story is actually humorous, for I do believe the Samaritan woman at first thought Yeshua was interested in her as a wife.

He hailed her and asked her if she would dip him out a drink.

She looked at him as if he had sprouted a third eye in the middle of his forehead, like one of Homer's Cyclops, only with two normal eyes as well.

"Now why," she asked him, noting his garment, "would I give a drink to a Jewish rabbi? You people hate us."

"Woman," said Yeshua, "I carry no hate in my heart."

She pointed at Mt. Gerizim. "Then I will tell you that the true Temple of the Lord resides there, not in that den of charlatans in Jerusalem." She hoisted up one skin of water and set it to the side; hooked onto the rope another, and began letting it down into the well. "Which, I will add," she said, "we Samaritans offered to help your people rebuild when they returned from Babylon, but you were too holy to accept our help."

She had more mouth than Mary of Magdala! But Yeshua was not disturbed.

"That was indeed a grievous error," said Yeshua. "But I am thirsty. Will you not draw me a cup? For if you knew who it is who speaks with you, you would have asked him for a drink instead, and he would have given you living water."

Then that woman had the audacity to flirt with the Master. "You, Lord, have nothing to draw with, and the well is deep."

Well. If that was not her being flirtatious, then she was being insulting. But she was also curious. "What is this 'living water?'"

Yeshua pointed to the well. "Everyone who drinks of that water will be thirsty again. But those who drink of the water I offer will never thirst, for it is a spring that wells up to eternal life."

The Samaritan woman gave a small laugh, but she played along with Yeshua in this game. "By all means, Lord, give me some of this living water so that I don't have to keep coming back to this place every day to draw more."

Yeshua said, "Go fetch your husband."

She said, "I have no husband."

"Indeed you do not," Yeshua said. "You have had five husbands, and the current one with whom you live is not your husband."

Her cheeks reddened. "Who has been telling you these rumors?"

"Am I not correct?"

She would not answer at first. Finally she asked, "What are you—a prophet?"

Yeshua answered, "I am he of whose coming was foretold."

"The Messiah?"

Yeshua did not answer this question, but he said, "A time is coming, and is now even here, in which the Jews bring salvation to the world. It will not matter if a temple is on your mountain or on Mt. Zion. The Spirit of the Lord is everywhere, within you, outside you—" and he pointed again, "in that rock, and in this tree."

"What is your name, Prophet?"

"Yeshua, son of Joseph of Nazareth."

Her eyes registered surprise. "I have heard of you! You are the miracle worker." Her eyes narrowed. "They say nothing good ever comes out of Nazareth. Some say you are a magician." Nevertheless, she picked up a small cup that was attached to the skin she had already drawn out, released and dipped, and handed it to Yeshua, who drank.

She pulled up her last skin of water, retrieved her cup from Yeshua, and then picked up both skins to carry back into her village.

"Thank you for the water, daughter," Yeshua said. "And when you hear my name again, remember me, and listen to the teachings."

She called back over her shoulder, "I will."

Yeshua smiled after her, then turned and gestured for the disciples to come over and fill their water bags. This was indeed a bit difficult since the woman had not lied—the water was deep—but the work was accomplished by lowering Bartholomew, the lightest of them, into the well as the two Simons held his feet. That must have been a sight to see!

The bags filled, they returned to the group, rested a time, and they all resumed the journey.

* * *

The next day they had just passed near to that city called Gigal when the group encountered several boys tormenting a cat for sport. They had buried it up to its head and were tossing stones at the poor creature.

"Stop this cruelty!" Yeshua said, and the boys looked at him befuddled.

"It's only a cat," said one.

"It is a creature of God," Yeshua said, kneeling down and digging around the animal to free it. He then passed his hand over the cat's head, healing its wounds, which included a gash over one of its eyes. Then he lifted the cat into his arms, and bringing it over to the boys, held and stroked its fur as he spoke to them.

"If you desire to find mercy from our Father in heaven," he said, "then you must show mercy to even the least of his creatures."

"How did you do that?" asked another of the boys, marveling over the healed animal. For, whereas before it had also been scrawny, and wild, now its fur was full, and the cat was tamed and purred.

Yeshua handed the cat to this boy. "I say unto you, if you give love, you will receive love, and love is the creator of all miracles. But if you withhold love, you will see death. What is your name?"

"David, son of Barnabas," said the young man.

Yeshua smiled. "It is a good name. See that you live up to it, and that you match the goodness of your father."

Yeshua resumed walking and we all followed. To the day he told me this story, my father said, he had no idea how Yeshua knew who the boy's father was. But later, this boy's father, Barnabas, was to be important in the Church; indeed, he traveled to Rome before even Simon Peter. This was Barnabas of Cypress, who had only recently moved his family to Jericho.

* * *

They did not enter into Jericho this time, for Herod Antipas was said to be just beyond there in one of his palaces, for he, as was customary, would be coming into Jerusalem for the Passover, as already had Pontius Pilate, along with Pilate's three legions of soldiers from Caesarea, in order to enforce the peace. I should write "their peace." For there was no peace among the Jews of the land, and Passover often was cause for strife or rioting as the people remembered their enslavement in Egypt and Moses' triumph over Pharaoh, and so they rose up in protest. (Of course the Essenes know better, as I set down very early in this narrative. But this does not mean some of the Essenes would not rise up with the Zealots, as they shared the same cause: freedom for Israel.)

Outside Jericho, however, the crowds did flock to Yeshua, and he stopped to cure many of their afflictions. Then, as the disciples had come to expect, came some Pharisees with their verbal snares to try and catch Yeshua.

"Rabbi," they asked him, "is it lawful for a man to divorce his wife for any cause?"

Notice you that these hypocrites did not ask if it was lawful for a woman to divorce her husband for any cause.

But since these Pharisees were forever divorcing their wives in order that they might marry into a richer family, sometimes leaving their wives with very little means to make their way—and unmarriageable in the eyes of many, for they were no longer virgins—Yeshua gave them the standard teaching of the Essenes.

"Have you not read," he asked them, "that the one who made them at the beginning 'made them male and female,' and said, 'For this reason a man shall leave his father and mother and be joined to his wife, and the two shall become one flesh'? So they are no longer two, and are one. Therefore what God has joined together, let no one separate."

This is important to mark so that you understand: Yeshua quoted the first story of the creation as written in Torah, not the second. The second says that the woman was created from the rib of the man. That story the Essenes reject, for it is often used as a means to justify what amounts to the enslavement of women, and the Essenes do not believe in slavery or forced servitude of any kind, as I have written before.

But the Pharisees were not satisfied with this answer, because, as I have said, many of them enjoyed being able to divorce their wives if they found a replacement who could improve their status. "Why then," they asked Yeshua, "did Moses command us to give a certificate of dismissal and to divorce her?"

"Because," Yeshua said, "you were so hard-hearted that Moses allowed you to divorce your wives, but from the beginning it was not so. And I say to you, whoever divorces his wife, except for unchastity, and marries another commits adultery."

Yeshua held his ground, and bravely so, I must say, for he had just publicly stood with John the Baptizer when Antipas, his murderer, was but a few miles away, and these Pharisaic Herodians without question would take these words back to him.

The group resumed travel, and now we were traveling uphill,

but I will tell you the truth: my father and mother had been quarreling over some trivial thing that very morning. So my father said to Yeshua—and he was only kidding, for the two had resolved the issue to their satisfaction, but her sharp words still stung in his ears—"If such is the case with a man and his wife, it is better not to marry!"

All within earshot laughed, including my mother.

But Yeshua took the words seriously and said, "Not everyone can accept this teaching, but only those to whom it is given. For there are eunuchs who have been so from birth, and there are eunuchs who have been made eunuchs by others, and there are eunuchs who have made themselves eunuchs for the sake of the Kingdom of Heaven. Let anyone accept this who can."

Now let me write down the meaning of this teaching as my father explained it to me. Yeshua, who had remained chaste so as to not bring grief to a wife and children, had not castrated himself. Neither do the chaste brethren at Qumran. But Yeshua was saying that Nature itself, which God has made, at times appears to bend its own rules. Some men are born eunuchs, or infertile, just as some women are born with their wombs closed. This does not mean they are mistakes of God or are suffering the wrath of God for some past sin, as the Pharisees and temple priests would have us think. It is simply natural. Other men are deliberately castrated, usually by some rich man with an assortment of concubines who wishes the eunuch to guard them and not intimately know them; others are castrated by some Romans or Greeks who wish certain boys to retain their angelic voices for singing, or to be in their theater, and who sometimes even force those boys to take on the role of women for sexual favors. These boys are always slaves, acting at the whim of their masters. That is unnatural, an abuse, and an abomination.

Yeshua, in choosing chastity, was not saying that his state was preferable or holier than the state of marriage. For, chastity is also unnatural. However, when chosen for the sake of doing good, that is a blessed thing to be admired. But chastity is not required, for if it were, human beings would, obviously, cease to exist.

"In the Kingdom of Heaven," my father explained to me, "there are no males or females. One's body parts are a reality of this worldly, material plane. This is one reason Yeshua sometimes lost patience with Simon Peter when he would insult Mary of Magdala and say she was a woman and could not do this thing or that thing."

"But women are weaker," I'd said.

My father laughed and pinched my cheek. "Do not say that to your mother! And," he said as an afterthought, "one day you may see a woman give birth. Men fear this thing, as if they were viewing death, and they think it makes them unclean. I say, I challenge those men to give birth themselves, and then say whether women are weak."

I must add here that, much later on, I saw my own Rachel lose my grandson in childbirth, and almost her own life, and I no longer say childish things such as "women are weaker."

"The Master," said my father, "tried explaining the Kingdom of Heaven to Simon Peter and to all the disciples, many times. But as you know, putting the inexpressible into words is a difficult task. He said to us that in the Kingdom women would be made into men, and that indeed he had already made Mary of Magdala male, but Peter was unable to make any sense of it. He is very literal-minded."

I am not sure that even I fully grasp this teaching. Therefore, here is how I think of it. On this plane, we have gendered even the angels when we speak of them. But they do not appear as male or female. They appear as beings of light. Light, of certainty, is neither male nor female. So perhaps what has been split apart on the material plane is put back together in the Kingdom. As I think on it, I believe Yeshua tried to live his life here as if he were already in the Kingdom. But, he was realistic and acknowledged many were not able to do this; yet, he never said that not being chaste was sinful or "less" in some way.

It is so hard to explain to the uninitiated! But remember his parable of the sower. Some seed yielded thirtyfold, some sixty, some a hundred. But all that yielded did yield some measure, and all of these were gathered into the Kingdom. So woe goes only to those who yield nothing.

* * *

And now they reached that place where James was to meet them, past Jericho and on the road up to Jerusalem. James was already there, bearing a message from the council of Elders at Qumran. As it would be Sabbath at dusk, they had to hasten to Bethany, where they would abide at the home of an Essene named Jonathan until the morning of the first day of the new week. From thence they would enter into Jerusalem for the Week of the Passover.

Simon still has in his possession this message from the Elders, although the piece of papyrus has gotten somewhat dirty and cracked. Thereupon was written: "We no longer say to you, 'Be like the Teacher of Righteousness.' You are the Teacher of Righteousness, like your ancestor David, the adopted Son of God and the Messiah of all Israel. Your word is our instruction. You will find those things, as you have asked of us, to be done. Within Jerusalem, the house of Eleazar will be found ready for you." It is indeed a cryptic message; but once you learn the story, you will understand it. The Essenes were of necessity good at hiding in plain sight, even up unto their last days. As I have written, the wealthy merchant Joseph of Arimathea, though of his own choice no longer an Essene, still was a pious and generous ally. A friend to many, he served also as ears in the Holy City, knowing certain members of the Sanhedrin, particularly a kindly rabbi named Nicodemus. This Nicodemus was a Pharisee, but he was not a friend to the Herodians. And, of course, several Essene families lived near the Essene Gate.

Back to the story. Now, obviously, Jonathan was not able to house the entire group; we all pitched tents outside the town and Jonathan gave room to Yeshua and his mother. But Jonathan did see to it that all had food to eat and that water was replenished. Thus Sabbath was spent calmly and in peace. Shortly after Sabbath ended on the seventh day, however, a man appeared at the camp, seeking Yeshua with a message from Martha. This man was sent to the house of Jonathan.

"Lord," relayed this man to Yeshua, "Martha and Miriam bid you hasten to them. Lazarus is very ill, even on his deathbed."

Yeshua thought upon this, for he loved Lazarus as one of his own brothers, and Martha and Miriam as his sisters. But God called him to Jerusalem. So he said to the man, "Tell Martha I will be there as soon as I can."

Disappointed, the man turned to go, but Yeshua stopped him with a hand on his arm. "Tell Martha that where there is despair, the glory of God hides but just around the corner. Take heart; I have work to do, but soon I will be there."

And Yeshua retreated into prayer and meditation.

To this day, I wonder about this. Yeshua was in Bethany; Lazarus and Martha's house was not far; why did Yeshua not go to heal him? It seems callous, to let them grieve for a few days to prove a point. And yet his message to Martha was to take heart and that he would come. For, of course, those who called Yeshua a magician produced their own magicians to work miracles; and they scoffed at any raising of the dead, saying that the resurrected person was surely not dead to begin with. Particularly this last came from the Sadducees, who did not believe in any Resurrection. They believed not even in *Sheol*, saying a dead man was dead and would always remain dead. This was most unlike the Sons of Zadok at Qumran, who believed not only in a Resurrection of the Righteous at the Time of the End, but in reincarnation until the Time of the End, when all souls are reunited with God, as it was in the beginning. For the Essenes see the world not so much as its being sinful because God banished Adam and Eve from paradise; it is more as if the world is sinful because Adam and Eve banished God from it by breaking God's commandment. Thus we try to return God's light to the world by following God's commandments.

If Followers of the Way of Yeshua do not always agree, this is nothing new. Neither do most Jews.

* * *

In the morning, the group departed Bethany and walked to Bethphage, which is on the Mount of Olives just outside Jerusalem. Yeshua sent Simon Peter and his brother Andrew ahead, telling them they would find a young donkey tied to a tree just off the road. They were to free this donkey and bring it to him; if anyone was to ask them about it, they were just to say, "The Lord has need of it," and all would be well. I see the hand of the Qumran Elders in this, for Yeshua would ride the donkey into Jerusalem, to fulfill the prophet, who wrote: "Behold, tell the daughter of Zion, look, your king is coming to you, humble, and mounted on a donkey." The other disciples, except for his brothers and Mary of Magdala, he sent ahead towards the city to announce that Yeshua was coming, and to cut palm fronds so believers in him could greet him much in the way the Maccabees, who restored the Temple from the Seleucids, were once greeted. Those occupying Seleucids had so Hellenized the city of Jerusalem an idol of Zeus had been placed on the altar!

On the way, my uncle James asked Yeshua if he was not overdoing it, for surely Pilate, the Herodians, the Temple priests, and their allies among the rabbis would interpret this action as those of a Zealot inciting the people to riot. "Pilate will nail you to a tree," James said. "Are you sure your pride is not guiding this action?"

Yeshua answered, "My aim is to do the will of our Father and not my own will." Still, the question bothered him, for he also said, "I concede that often it can be hard to tell the difference."

"How do you tell?"

"I fast, I pray, I meditate, I listen to my inner heart, I listen to my feelings. I examine my motivations. And I ask the Lord and my angels to guide me."

James nodded. "And inviting death is necessary? This is not what is expected of the Messiah."

"I do not wish to die to this life. But if the Lord wills it, then I must, if my death would unharden the hearts of those who do not yet understand."

"Understand what thing, Yeshua?"

"That there is more to us than this earthly world, which is like unto a single grain of sand in all the deserts combined, or to a single beam from a solitary star in all the heavens."

"Is there no way to demonstrate that beyond dying yourself?"

"There will be Lazarus and the sign of Jonah."

My uncle James sighed, for there Yeshua was, speaking again in riddles. So he just said, "The people expect not a Messiah who is a martyr. They expect the kingdom of Israel to be restored."

And then there were Andrew and Peter with the donkey. Yeshua climbed upon the donkey's back and patted its neck. He looked at James. "Have I ever been what is expected?"

James laughed and gently slapped the donkey's flanks to get him moving.

"No," said James. "You of certainty have not."

* * *

Now I must digress a moment to describe Jerusalem, as it was then, to anyone who suffers from the impression that it was some sort of Jewish peasant town where people threw their sewage into the streets. On the contrary, Jerusalem is a well-established city, a different world altogether from that of humble Galilee or even simpler towns in Judea. Most of the disciples had been there at some point, for a Passover or some other festival such as the Feast of the Tabernacles, but even I, whenever I went into Jerusalem before its destruction, after being at some other place for a time, had to stop to marvel at all I saw before I became re-accustomed to it. (Well, I was young. And imagine a young man in his twenties entering there, after spending a few years isolated in the desert at Qumran.) There were so many people, especially around the time of the Passover when pilgrims from many lands thronged and filled the city to bursting; and, there were sundry types of buildings, ranging from the elaborate palace of Herod the Great, where the Roman governor Pilate lived when he came down from Caesarea, the other half of which was Antipas' palace, to the wealthy homes of the Upper City, to the slightly less elaborate houses of the merchants, to the plain stone houses of most people. But the truly poor had no houses, not in that city. They lived outside the city walls or in the surrounding countryside. And then there was the grand Temple, still under construction almost up until the time the Romans leveled it. Six years completed and then gone—all that work, all that tax money squeezed out of us, for nothing!

The Temple was grand, indeed, and even Yeshua said this, as grand as anything he had ever seen in any of his travels. Its polished white marble stones gleamed and the gold gilt shone and sparkled if the sun was bright. There were many gates and steps and columns and stone arches, all a great display of wealth, where the uninvited poor and maimed and blind sat outside in the streets and begged for alms. But this was only part of the reason Yeshua was to become angry in the Temple, which I will write of soon. He'd seen this injustice before, when he was only twelve.

In Jerusalem there was much elaborate stonework on display, and not just on the Temple itself. The artisan stoneworkers also made elaborate tiles with many geometrical shapes that adorned the houses of the wealthy in the Upper City. And, of course, they carved the outer tombs and the ossuaries of the wealthy, some of them very elaborate, the outer tombs with Greek columns and the ossuaries decorated with designs of rosettes and flowers, leaves, vines, bunches of grapes, pomegranates, horns of plenty, and the like. Even tables made of stone were fashioned, which were rectangular or circular, and were supported by one pillar carved in the manner of a Greek column with the same sorts of adornments. These were tall tables that supported vessels or objects of art. There were also lower, round tables that held drinks, and the rich reclined around these on couches when eating. Most Jews in Jerusalem could not afford such things, of course, and ate like everyone else in the country did, reclining or sitting on the floor, gathered around a mat, everyone sharing the dishes laid out in front of them, although some may have had small tables made of scrap wood, for wood was too precious to waste. But even the wealthy Martha never bought for herself and her family something as frivolous as a table. She had only a most beautiful mat, which was long, and which she brought out for banquets. Even I, now, have only this simple wooden table I banged together with wooden nails and scrap wood I scrounged or purchased, so I would have a place to write this narrative.

Stone vessels, however, carved from limestone, were very common all over the land, and many were for sale in Jerusalem. These were, of course, very useful, for stone is not porous as clay pottery is, and you have to throw away any clay vessel that becomes unclean. Stone can be cleaned ritually if there is any question of contamination and reused forever. So, the forums in Jerusalem contained many stone vessels for sale: cups, plates, bowls, and jars of numerous shapes and sizes. The very fancy ones of marble or alabaster, of course, you would look away from, for those were for the rich, and some of these were also carved with elaborate designs.

There were also the pottery makers, and their shops and stalls. These made all sorts of jars and pots for cooking, and the better-quality ones could be found even painted with bright colors with symmetrical motifs. And there were glass workers, who worked first with molds and later on also with tubes. They made many fine, small jars for holding such things as perfumes. Larger ones could be used for oils, but they were not very practical. Other things they made were twisted sticks for wealthy women to use to apply cosmetics, or game pieces, and other such things.

Yes, you could spend an entire day just walking through the two forums of Jerusalem, looking at all the wares, the cloth and garments, woven mats, jewelry, spices, incense, foods of all sorts, and wines, although some of the food and wine made available were not clean for Jews, but were for non-Jews; and, sometimes even Roman soldiers from the Antonia Fortress by the Temple, which was called "the castle," could be seen when wandering through the forums. I would sometimes buy dates or figs as I walked through the forums. I particularly like dates, for they are like unto a mix of carob and dried grapes all in one bite.

And then proof of our conquest resided in Jerusalem, in the ruins of a Greek-style gymnasium for boys, who had wrestled naked, and in those of a hippodrome, where chariot races had once been held during the time of the Seleucids. Most Jews had never gone to these places, but the Hellenized ones had, and they also attended plays; indeed, there stood even then in Jerusalem a new grand theater for the rich to attend plays—so, once again, the vast divide between the rich and the poor could be seen in these things. And aside from their mocking of God's Laws, this display of those who had many things, contrasting with those who had very little to nothing, was the reason the Zealots hated the Romans and the Herodians and any who colluded with them, many of whom were Pharisees, and all of whom were the Sadducee families of Temple priests. The true Sons of Zadok were at Qumran.

Now back to the story at hand.

Yeshua made his way on the donkey down the slopes of the Mount of Olives, the disciples, and the family, and then other people along the way joining in, shouting:

"Hosanna to the Son of David!

Blessed is the one who comes in the name of the Lord!

Hosanna in the highest heaven!"

And they took off their cloaks, and spread them on the road, so that Yeshua might ride over them. More people cut palm fronds to distribute among the crowd.

Yeshua entered the city by the southern gate, which is called the Susa Gate, and the people's cheers grew louder, and many asked, "Who is this man?" and others answered, "This is the prophet Yeshua from Nazareth of Galilee!" for his reputation had preceded him. The crowd grew as even more people came out to see and to cheer and to wave the palm fronds that had been cut.

And Yeshua greeted them, and waved to the crowds, and the disciples' hearts were filled with joy at this great welcome. My father lifted me to his shoulders so that I could see. I remember laughing, and shouting "Hosanna!" with the people, even though I had no comprehension of the importance of what I was seeing.

I also could see, from their height on the Antonia Fortress, the Roman soldiers looking down upon this scene, and I could also see the Temple priests lining the walls of the Temple observing the happenings below, with great interest written upon their brows.

Dalet: The Crucifixion and Resurrection

Chapter Eighteen

The crowd was already thinning as Yeshua rode up to the Temple, where he jumped down from the donkey and patted its nose. I tugged at my father's sleeve, wanting to ride on the donkey myself.

"No, son," he said. "The donkey is not ours." And he had no sooner said this when a man stepped out from the crowd, and taking the donkey's lead from Andrew, began guiding it away, after whispering a word in Andrew's ear, for him to tell the Lord.

"I would pray," Yeshua said to the crowds, and therefore, seeing no more would happen this day, they departed back to their work and their businesses. At this point, the Roman soldiers and the priests lost interest as well and returned to their doings.

Now, no one could enter the Temple beyond the Court of Gentiles if he or she was ritually unclean, and none of our crowd had bathed. So if Yeshua prayed in the Temple that day, he did so only privately inside his heart, for none of our group went beyond the Court of the Gentiles. And that was sufficient, for Yeshua was merely observing and making plans for the next day. As for me, I had never been in such a place and my mouth was agape at all the noise, and the splendor, and all the comings and goings. But my young eyes drank in much, which I will set down for you tomorrow.

When we all left the Temple, Yeshua spoke with Andrew and then gave instructions. To the disciples, he said to go to the next road over, where they would find a man carrying a load of barley. They were to follow this man to the house of Eleazar. "I will join you shortly," he said, "for I have a few small things to accomplish."

To the women (except for Mary of Magdala, whom, as I have said, was treated as one of the disciples), he instructed them, along with the extended families of the disciples, to leave the city and return to Bethany. "We will return there to you tomorrow," he said. To his mother Mary he gave a special task. "Send word reminding Martha that I will come, and that all will be well." And therefore I was not witness to the events of that night and the next day. But my uncle James and my father told me all, later when I was older and able to understand.

So, they dispersed as they were told, and the disciples followed the man to Eleazar's house, and there they awaited the Master. I know not of certainty what Yeshua was doing during this brief absence, but given later events, I suspect he had sought out and spoken with Joseph of Arimathea. This would not have looked suspicious to anyone, for Joseph was a popular merchant, dealing in hard-to-find materials, such as tin, for he owned two merchant ships which he berthed in Caesarea, as well as being the owner of many olive groves. And he was well-liked by even the peasants, for he paid his laborers fairly. Indeed, if any of his laborers was unable to pay his taxes or tithes, he would give them extra coin to do so—I write give, not lend. He also did this thing without lecturing them about their laziness or lack of thrift, for he knew perfectly well how hard they worked and how humbly they lived. This Joseph was a good and righteous man.

At Eleazar's house, the disciples sat with Yeshua, when he arrived, to break bread and eat the dishes Eleazar's wife brought to them, and they asked Yeshua if he would be eating the Passover with them four nights hence, for they would buy a lamb and take it for consecration by the Temple priests if so.

"I will not eat the Paschal lamb with you," Yeshua said. And of course he would not; he ate no meat, and believed not in animal sacrifices; although as I have said, he did not condemn those who did. But he did say, "In three nights, however, I would share a meal here with you all. And I remind you that the Son of Man will be handed over to the *Kittim,* and I will suffer and die."

For, I believe Yeshua's thinking had evolved from what he had thought was his earlier mission, and he had come to see dying as his duty in fulfilling prophecy. There is, indeed, a prophecy among the *pesharim* of the Essenes, a gloss to Isaiah, if memory serves me. It speaks of the Messiah being pierced. For, it was the practice of the Essenes to read the Prophets and apply their sayings to the present day. Yeshua's dying does explain why the Kingdom of Heaven did not arrive with the Messiah—which makes even Paul correct, in theory, when he called Yeshua the "first fruits" of the coming Resurrection of all the righteous. But it still does not explain why the Kingdom has not yet come, except, as other *pesharim* claim, that evil would temporarily rule after the coming of the Messiah, but that ultimately the Messiah would prevail.

We have yet to see the Kingdom, and I, of course, digress once more. I suppose I am just sorrowful that my uncle had to die at all.

That night, Bartholomew asked Yeshua how anyone could enter the Kingdom of Heaven, if even the Messiah sent by God had to suffer and die. Yeshua answered him frankly: "For mortals it is impossible, but for God, all things are possible."

Then Simon Peter, always of literal mind, asked him, "Look, we have left everything and followed you. What then will we have?"

Yeshua said to them, "Truly I tell you, at the renewal of all things, when the Son of Man is seated on the throne of his glory, you who have followed me will also sit on twelve thrones, judging the twelve tribes of Israel. And everyone who has left houses or brothers or sisters or father or mother or children or fields, for my name's sake, will receive a hundred-fold, and will inherit eternal life. But many who are first will be last, and the last will be first."

And to explain this last, he told them a parable.

"For the Kingdom of Heaven," he said, "is like a landowner who went out early in the morning to hire laborers for his vineyard. After agreeing with the laborers for the usual daily wage, he sent them into his vineyard. When he went out about nine o'clock, he saw others standing idle in the marketplace; and he said to them, 'You also go into the vineyard, and I will pay you whatever is right.' So they went. When he went out again about noon and about three o'clock, he did the same.

"And about five o'clock he went out and found others standing around; and he said to them, 'Why are you standing here idle all day?' They said to him, 'Because no one has hired us.' He said to them, 'You also go into the vineyard.' Now when evening came, the owner of the vineyard said to his manager, 'Call the laborers and give them their pay, beginning with the last and then going to the first.' When those hired about five o'clock came, each of them received the usual daily wage. Now when the first came, they thought they would receive more; but each of them also received the usual daily wage.

"And when they received it, they grumbled against the landowner, saying, 'These last worked only one hour, and you have made them equal to us who have borne the burden of the day and the scorching heat.' But he replied to one of them, 'Friend, I am doing you no wrong; did you not agree with me for the usual daily wage? Take what belongs to you and go; I choose to give to this last the same as I give to you. Am I not allowed to do what I choose with what belongs to me? Or are you envious because I am generous?'

"So," Yeshua concluded, "the last will be first, and the first will be last."

The meal thus finished, Yeshua went to pray; and the disciples scattered themselves about the house on mats or rolling up into their cloaks, to sleep and be ready for the morrow.

Now, I think Yeshua may have told this story because already he could imagine the disciples, after his death, arguing over who should get the greatest reward, or the largest honor in heaven, or placing themselves as older followers of the Way over the newer followers of the Way, when in truth, in the Kingdom of Heaven, all are equal because all are saved. You who read my words, then, take heed yourself, for it is a good lesson and one I remind myself of often: do not count up your good works and compare yourselves to others; and do not count up how much you have tithed to the Church and compare yourselves to others. For such is folly: you will either count yourself as better than another or chastise yourself as being worse than another, and no one can make this judgment but God himself.

And now I am reminded of another thing that happened in Jerusalem, not this day, nor the next, but two days hence, but I might as well set it down here because it has also to do with this same subject. In the Temple, of course, especially at the time of the Passover, when there are many pilgrims and many to observe them, the scribes and the Pharisees love to say long prayers to demonstrate their devotion; and they and their wealthy Herodian friends make a grand show of adding large sums of money to the treasury. So Yeshua and the disciples had been watching this display of piety, for they by then had been ritually cleansed and had passed by the balustrade.

Then came a poor old widow, who added two small copper coins to the treasury, which are together worth a penny. Some of the wealthy who observed this sneered at her, for they had given considerably more.

But Yeshua said to the disciples, "Do you see this? They look at her with haughtiness for the poverty of her gift. But truly I say to you, this poor widow has put in more than all of those who are contributing to the treasury. For all of them have contributed out of their abundance; but she out of her poverty has put in everything she had, all she had to live on."

The disciples understood and blessed the woman in their hearts.

And while I have made a digression on this subject, there is one other story I might as well write down now, for it also fits. This had actually happened on the Jordan road to Jerusalem, not long after Yeshua had visited with the Samaritan woman at the well and the Pharisees outside Jericho were trying to trip Yeshua up with their verbal snares. It is another parable that Yeshua told to the disciples to pass the time as they walked along. In this story, a man had been traveling on the road and was attacked by bandits who stripped him of his property and left him for dead. He lay there, unconscious and bleeding, and a priest passed by. The priest, seeing him, moved to the far side of the road and paid him no mind. Shortly after, a Levite passed by, and, seeing him, also moved to the far side of the road and paid him no mind.

Then a Samaritan passed by, and seeing the man, stopped and dismounted, and finding the man barely clinging to life, treated and bound his wounds and took him to his house to care for him until he was healed.

"Who," Yeshua asked them, "is the best neighbor?"

Of course all said the Samaritan, for the Samaritan had shown the injured man mercy.

In general people interpret this story to mean that Samaritans should not be hated and that we should treat others well, but there is an entire other layer of meaning to this parable. Note that the two who ignored the wounded man are priests. They ignored the man because they felt they must. A priest may not touch the unclean—especially, according to the Law, not a corpse—and for all they knew, the man was dead. So they did not assist because they believed it to be God's will to not assist, lest they be ritually unclean and unable to serve the Lord.

Yeshua was saying that it was God's will to assist, that compassion for others always is the greatest of the Laws. Sometimes one is called upon to break a lesser law in order to fulfill the greater law. He pressed this point so many times: do no harm, show compassion, love your neighbor, even saying numerous times that the entire Law can be reduced to merely two: Love God, and treat others in the way you would like to be treated.

But so many ears just did not hear, and it seems to me that, the closer Yeshua moved to his last days, the more and more he tried to open the eyes of the disciples to this most great of his teachings.

* * *

And now the next day dawned, and after prayers and a meal, Yeshua gathered to him the disciples and announced to them his plan. My father said the eyes of Judas Iscariot were joyous at his words, as were those of Simon the Zealot. "Finally," my father said, "those two were getting what they wanted: none of this dying and suffering Messiah. They wanted a Messiah of the House of King David, one who would fight to restore the land."

To Eleazar, Yeshua said they would return to him the following day, for that night they must return to Bethany; but though they would eat with him, they would be spending the last two nights before the Passover outside the city walls, for his own protection and that of his wife.

"For they will come for me," Yeshua said, and Eleazar bowed his head to Yeshua in reverence.

"As you wish, Master," he said, "but I would willingly die for your sake."

"You are blessed among men!" Yeshua said, and embraced him, and then he and the disciples took their leave, for there was work to be done in the Temple.

Now I will describe for you the Temple, which had once been great under Solomon, until it was destroyed by the Babylonians; and when it was rebuilt after the exile was much humbler; but then Herod the Great came along and, to placate the Jews and bring glory to himself, began reconstructing it as the grandest of monuments.

One of Herod's tasks was to further level the Temple Mount, most cleverly because the mountain Moriah was not even by any means, so he laid foundation stones of varying size, along with fill, to make all flush. The Temple was then added to upon this, and new areas constructed or renovated. The structure was divided into multiple courts, and there were numerous staircases and arches and gates that led into the first court, which was the Court of the Gentiles. This was as far as non-Jews were allowed to go. The Court of the Gentiles was enormous, surrounded by colonnades and benches where rabbis could teach. The court was surrounded by two porches, one called the Royal Porch and the other, smaller one, Solomon's Porch (said to be part of the original Temple of Solomon).

The next upper level was the Sanctuary, which consisted of three courts atop one another. The first was the Court of Women, which was as far into the Temple that Jewish women were allowed to go. Therefore the treasury was here, for women also to make their tithes. Depending on what money you were offering—the Temple tax or a gift; a sin offering or some other contribution—you placed your money into the appropriate chest.

Next was the Court of the Israelites, a comparatively small court where men went to offer their sacrifices to the priests; and then there was the Court of Levites and the larger Court of Priests and the Great Court, all on one level. Within the Great Court was the altar for burnt offerings and marble tables for butchering; and within this Court was the Holy House containing the Holy of Holies, the final level, where only the High Priest could venture once a year. It is said there was much gold and marble in this part of the Temple, and I would say that is correct, for one could see it from the top of the Mount of Olives.

But that day, Yeshua was interested only in the Court of the Gentiles. For it was here, the previous day, he had seen things most upsetting to him, which I will try my best to explain. First of all, the Temple priests would not accept any coin that had an image or idol upon it, for this broke the commandment of the Lord. Or at least this had once been the claim. Since the only coin they would now accept was the shekel that was struck in Tyre and highly regarded for its purity of silver, and had images aplenty on either side of it, I leave you to draw your own conclusion about their motives. Therefore, with pilgrims coming from all over the land, and from outside the land, moneychangers were set up within the Court of the Gentiles to exchange these coins for Jewish shekels or other types of coin. Everyone knew the moneychangers were, as a lot, thieves and charlatans. They would charge a fee for changing money; they would have unbalanced scales for the measuring out of copper, silver, and gold. The priests tolerated this practice even though it fleeced the people.

And then, in the Court of Gentiles, were sundry unblemished animals for sacrifice—lambs, goats, doves or pigeons, mainly; and they were in pens and cages, bleating or crying out in fear and misery, and these animals were also for sale, for no one was able to bring a lamb, for instance, all the way from Galilee or another land altogether. It was most impractical.

Worse of all was—how do I describe this? The smells, the crowds, the movements to and fro, and the ruckus of the place. Men shouting their services, animals crying out, the stench of blood and incense from the upper courts, the smell of burning meat. The place felt unholy. And it was just this that Yeshua intended to protest.

He and the disciples entered the Court of Gentiles, and Yeshua stationed a few of the disciples at each of the gates, to prevent anyone from entering or leaving. Then he stood in the center of all and cried out in a great voice:

"It is written,
'My house shall be called a house of prayer';
But you are making it a den of robbers."

With this, Yeshua set to work overturning the tables of the

moneychangers, scattering coins in all directions. He opened pens and cages and freed the animals for sale and kicked over the seats of those who sold them, the whole time crying that the House of the Father had been defiled.

The noise of yelling men and freed animals attracted the priests, who came running down from the level above, many of them covered in blood from the sacrifices; and then they began shouting also; and the soldiers at the Antonia Castle began lining the walls and looking down upon the scene. The ones in the Tower set arrows to their bows in warning.

Simon Peter and James came to Yeshua and said, "It is time to depart," so the disciples gathered together and hastened from that place.

Outside the Temple, the streets remained calm. There were some lame, who, upon seeing Yeshua, cried out to him, so he healed them, and others in the street, among them children, cried out, "Hosanna to the Son of David!" A few outraged priests who had followed Yeshua out of the Temple to chastise him were further angered by these words. They accosted Yeshua, saying to him, "Do you hear what these are saying?" For everyone knew the Messiah that would overthrow Rome was to be a Son of David.

Yeshua said to these priests, "Yes, I hear them; have you never read, 'Out of the mouths of infants and nursing babies you have prepared praise for yourself?'"

He turned on his heel and shook off the dust from his feet, right in front of the priests; and then he and the disciples finally departed for Bethany.

* * *

When they reached Bethphage, there awaiting them were Martha and Miriam, dressed in mourning and wailing. They came up to Yeshua and Martha said, "Lord, had you come when I first sent,

Lazarus would be alive. But now he has laid in the tomb for nigh onto three days."

Yeshua said, "Did not my mother tell you all would be well? Your brother will rise again."

But Martha was not comforted, for she thought Yeshua spoke of the End Times and the Resurrection of the Dead.

As they approached Bethany, however, many streamed out of their houses to grieve with Martha and Miriam; for their family was loved, and the people felt the loss of Lazarus deeply. Yeshua was so moved by their tears that he also wept.

"Take me to the tomb," Yeshua said to Martha, and they took him there. Then he commanded some men with them, "Roll back the stone."

"Oh, Master," Miriam said. "We anointed him with oils and spices, but he will not smell good at this point, for surely his body begins to decay."

Yeshua smiled at her and patted her arm. "Wait here, daughter."

With the stone rolled back, Yeshua stepped towards the open tomb and looked up to heaven, praying. Then he lowered his eyes and looked directly into the tomb. He cried, "Lazarus! Come out!"

Within a minute, Lazarus, dressed in his shroud, came stumbling out of the tomb, confused, much as a man who has just woken up from a deep sleep stumbles in the night. His shroud was torn and filthy, and the stench of rotting flesh caused all but Yeshua to raise their hands to cover their faces, even as they gasped at the sight of him.

Yeshua stepped forward, taking Lazarus' arm to steady him and then led him to Martha and Miriam. "See that he bathes and is dressed in fresh garments."

Lazarus stood, blinking and dazed.

Many fell to their knees, marveling, and praising Yeshua for this great miracle. But Yeshua said, "Do not praise me, for I have done nothing. Praise our Father in Heaven, for this work is his."

And he departed to the house of Martha, with all the disciples.

* * *

Martha and Miriam were overjoyed, and prepared a great banquet to celebrate the return of Lazarus. While they were feasting, Miriam came to Yeshua with an alabaster jar of spikenard, which is a very costly ointment from India, and she poured it on his head as he sat at the meal.

This troubled Judas Iscariot, who said, "Why this waste? For this ointment could have been sold for a large sum, and the money given to the poor."

But Yeshua said, "Why do you trouble the woman? She has performed a good service for me. For you always have the poor with you, but you will not always have me. By pouring this ointment on my body, she has prepared me for burial. Truly I tell you, wherever this good news is proclaimed in the whole world, what she has done will be told in remembrance of her."

Judas and some of the disciples shook their heads, for they understood not why Yeshua kept saying he was to die, but they kept their peace.

Now, as instructed, after Lazarus was raised, he came with Yeshua and the disciples to Martha's house, bathed, and dressed himself in a new garment. He managed to eat a little of the feast. But the young man seemed greatly troubled, and unable to speak but a few words. After the meal, the disciples decided to sit quietly with him and bother him not, for obviously he had experienced much.

When Yeshua came down from the roof after his sundown prayers, he had wished peace upon everyone and was going to the room Martha had set aside for him, when Lazarus leaped to his feet, pulling at Yeshua's fringe.

"Master," he said. "Let me stay with you."

Everyone was surprised except for Yeshua. "Yes. Of certainty." He took Lazarus' arm and led him into the room, and they shut the door.

My father said everyone exchanged looks, but it was the Master, after all, who never sinned. My father supposed that Lazarus, just back from the dead, was perhaps afraid he'd die again, and wanted Yeshua near to him to bring him back, else he might never sleep.

The morning was a different story.

The two emerged uncustomarily late from the room, well after sunrise, and it appeared they had spent the entire night together.

No one said anything—how could they? It was the Lord.

But finally Judas Iscariot ventured the question they all had on their minds. "Master," he said. "I do not understand this night with Lazarus. It appears—" he stopped to search for words that would not offend. He could not think of any.

Yeshua looked at Judas. "You are asking me if we lay together, and knew one another."

"No," Judas said, reddening, so he hid his face. "I am not accusing you."

"But you are asking me to tell you there was no sin."

Judas was ashamed.

"There was no sin," Yeshua said. He put one arm around Lazarus and addressed them all. "This man has experienced death. He has seen things you have not seen, nor do you remember, but he remembers them, and understood them not. He sought my counsel."

All looked relieved.

"That which is good appears evil when evil is invited into the heart," said Yeshua. "That is my first rebuke. But I have another teaching this morning: Believe it is sin, and it is sin. I say unto you, not all sin is sin."

"What do you mean, Lord?" Andrew asked. "This sounds like

a riddle."

"Had I loved Lazarus as a man loves a woman, is that sinful?"

They concluded that Yeshua was testing them.

"Yes," Simon Peter said. "The Law clearly states so. A man who lies with another man is an abomination to the Lord."

Yeshua rebuked Simon. "Have I taught you nothing?"

Simon Peter sat down, his face embarrassed, but plainly not understanding why he was rebuked.

Yeshua addressed them all again. "Have I not taught you all well? Have I not shown you the Law was made for man, but not man for the Law? Do you think my Father in heaven will judge me for healing on the Sabbath?"

They shook their heads no.

"Have I not, according to the Law, been like a eunuch, as I have said, and remained chaste and broken the command to be 'fruitful and multiply?'"

"You have, Master," said Nathanael. "But you have done so for a greater good."

"I ask you, then, do you think my Father in heaven will judge me if I loved another man?"

Judas Iscariot said, "Yes, Lord, I do. Which is why you don't. The Law is very clear on this matter. It is an abomination."

Yeshua said, "No! More than any commandment, my Father loves that which is good."

"Are you mad, my brother?" James asked. "A man lying with a man is not good. Lying with a woman is to plant seed in the woman, to grow a child. The spilling of seed is the waste of life, the sin of Onan, so God struck him dead. A man lying with a man is base lust, with no purpose or purchase, like that of the Romans and the Greeks, who lie even with young boys, and who lie with harlots in their temples."

"In your ignorance you discern no difference, James," said Yeshua. He then spoke unto them a parable. "There are four rams but no ewes. Two of the rams become like unto friends, and their owner finds it of no use to separate them. They bleat and complain when they are apart. So the owner lets them stay together. But one day the owner buys a new sheep. He adds her to his herd. The other two rams mate with her, and she conceives. But the two rams who love each other stay with each other and it is as if the ewe does not exist. You see this in the fields with all creatures of God—some cover one another with no purchase. Does the owner then kill his two rams? He who has ears to hear, let him hear."

"But Lord," said John. "They are beasts, not men. And maybe a different ewe in her season would interest one of the other two rams."

"I kick my dog away from my leg all the time," said Matthew, and everyone laughed. "That is not love."

"A dog and a man are two different creatures!" Yeshua said.

"A man and a woman are two different creatures," said my father, and all laughed again.

Yeshua sighed, and he tried once more. "When the seventy were out ministering, one day I preached on a hillside, to a small group of people, near to Caesarea; and there were Roman soldiers and a centurion keeping watch. Afterwards, two of the Roman soldiers, appearing brutish with armor and shield and spear, came to me, for they would speak. They asked of God's Kingdom. They called me Master, and asked of me questions greater than those I have been asked of many rabbis. For soldiers, they were traveled, and learned, and spoke of philosophies; for they were freed Greek slaves and had joined Caesar's army to earn Roman citizenship, and it came to pass that they spoke of Egypt.

"I tired, so I sat down and they sat with me. I was hungry and thirsty, and one gave me water from his pouch. The other found bread and grapes in his bag and gave them to me. We spoke for some time of Egypt, and they were astonished to learn I had taken some of my teaching in that place. They actually knew of

Thales, and of Solon, and Socrates, Plato, Aristotle . . . philosophers I have been unable to discuss with anyone in this land, except for some at Qumran, for anything that is Greek the Pharisees and scribes and Sadducees will view as sinful, unless it suits their purpose to say otherwise.

"As we spoke, I observed the two men were great friends and companions. Yes, as they looked upon each other, I could see they perceived in each other a reflection of their own virtue. A beacon, like the great Pharos lighthouse of Alexandria, so pure was the love in their hearts. Is this not different from abusing slave boys who give not their consent? Is this not different from staining the beauty of my Father's gift of love by consorting with any harlot in a temple of evil? Shall I sit in judgment of these two men, who showed to me hospitality?"

No one knew what to say. It was true he had also refused to condemn the adulterous woman, who had, by Law, clearly sinned.

Then Yeshua said, "Would you sit in judgment of Martha and Miriam, after all the good they have done unto you, and unto me?"

Lazarus, who all along must have known the true nature of his sister's relationship, became pale and frightened as all the disciples looked stunned. Silence hung over the room, pressing down upon them.

Then Mary of Magdala leapt to her feet and spoke, defying each of the men with her look. "No, Lord," she said. "I would not! Martha and Miriam are my dear sisters. I would not allow one of these to harm a single hair on either's head."

"So then," Yeshua said. "Judge not, for you never know what is in the heart of another, or what karma is theirs, or what worries they have; or why my Father has made them the way they are, as he has made some eunuchs the way they are; lest you be judged unfairly by one who knows not what lies in your heart, or what you have suffered, or what troubles you at night."

Then Yeshua left the room, and Lazarus followed, for the two were famished and wished to break their fast, and Martha had just taken fresh barley bread from the fire.

I append to this story the thought—and it is just a thought of mine; I cannot say that it is the truth—that perhaps this teaching, and Yeshua's accepting Miriam's gift of spikenard the night before, were the very things that pushed Judas Iscariot out of the fold, and to betray his Master. There is also more to tell of the experience of Lazarus, that I heard from Lazarus' own lips years later. But of these things I will write later.

No, I must first append my own reaction to this story, for when my father told it to me, I thought about it for many days. It is a story that is dangerous and therefore it needs a *pesher* like unto the writings at Qumran. Indeed this is one of those things I may strike out of this narrative when I return to copy it over, because so many would not understand and would condemn the Master as blasphemous. Then again, many already do! But perhaps I will not strike it out, for Miriam and Martha are long dead, and no evil can come to them now. The Lord blessed them many times, and I cannot see them rejected from the Kingdom of Heaven. And indeed, I see not how their intimate friendship spilled seed or broke the Law of Moses, beyond "be fruitful and multiply," and as Yeshua said, even he did not marry and was chaste: a thing that was also unnatural.

But it is a most strange teaching, and I think this must be how the Pharisees sometimes felt when Yeshua challenged them on points of the Law. I try to imagine myself loving a man, and I just cannot. But neither can my stomach abide the thought of calling love something evil.

And yet that is the interpretation of Yeshua's words. The Law was given to human beings as the Rule to join Israel as one community. But times arise when the Law is more divisive than unifying, and brings harm when the Lord desires mercy. This makes the problem of acting in righteousness difficult, and a tremendous challenge. If there is no set of rules that carries with it no teeth or punishment, would not all act in utter selfishness? Would not the community of man be chaotic and riotous, with people robbing each other, killing each other, striking and insulting each other in drunkenness? So there must be laws. Yet as Yeshua showed us, sometimes the Law is not the greatest good in a particular situation. It would have been evil, and cruel, to stone the adulterous woman. Is not her shame punishment enough? Is atoning to her husband not punishment enough? And how do I know that her husband does not also commit adultery, or strikes her, or abuses her in some other way? Likewise, it would have been wrong to let the man with the withered hand go unhealed, even if it was the Sabbath. The man was in need—did God not prefer the greater good to be done?

Therefore my interpretation is that some line of righteousness must be drawn in a place. I think Yeshua established where that line lies. In all things, if you are righteous, do unto others as you would have them do unto you. If someone does something that harms another, the Council of Elders and the Law can have their say. A righteous person would take his just punishment: but the facts must be known and the punishment just. But if someone does something that does not harm anyone else, who are we to judge? And if someone does something out of love, and it harms no one else, even all the more who are we to judge?

I loved my wife dearly, and saw her beauty and her virtues, and it was partly for her sake I left Qumran. Had I been forbidden to love her, I would have been most aggrieved. I would not have liked to be told our love was a sin. Therefore, this is how I think about it.

Later, this teaching will be important, for when my uncle James led the early Church, the Elders at Qumran did not agree with his allowing a few Gentiles into the Church, for they had no other building; for the Elders saw God's Covenant to be solely with the Jews; and it is why James opposed them when they urged him to turn the self-professed apostle Paul over to the Sanhedrin. It would have been a death sentence for Paul, which James saw as unmerciful in the eyes of the Lord. Nevertheless, since Paul taught blasphemous things, he was never appointed as an apostle by James, nor given by him a letter of certification verifying Paul's teachings were the true teachings of the Way.

But now I have leaped far, far ahead of myself, so I must put this narrative away for the day, for it is long past dusk and our supply of oil once again runs low.

Chapter Nineteen

When Yeshua was ready, he sent James, Simon Peter, and John to go and gather together the family and the disciples' families; any other followers, including Martha, Miriam, and Lazarus; and some other Essenes from the Community of the *Yahad* who had arrived and were now staying with Jonathan; and all were gathered together outside Bethany, for he would speak.

"The time has arrived," he said. "I will go now into Jerusalem, where I will preach and heal and draw to me those who will hear me. But on the morrow, I will be handed over to the Sanhedrin, who will in turn hand me over to the Romans. I will be nailed to one of their crosses."

At this time, this was nothing new to the disciples, except for only a few additional details, but those to whom this was complete news were disturbed and protested this thing, saying, "Surely not, Master," and such like, until Yeshua raised his hand to silence them.

"It is written, 'It is the will of the Lord to crush him with pain.' And that he, the Messiah, who is believed in, will 'make his life an offering for sin.'"

Miriam, who seemed to have memorized all of Isaiah, then called out the passage:

"He was oppressed, and he was afflicted,
yet he did not open his mouth;
like a lamb that is led to the slaughter,
and like a sheep that before its shearers is silent,
So he did not open his mouth."

And therefore, to this day, I write now that I wonder if, all along, Martha and Miriam did not somehow know of Yeshua's plan, since Miriam had anointed him the previous night with oil for burial, as Yeshua had said to Judas Iscariot. But this I was never able to ascertain for fact.

Of more, Yeshua would not say, other than to invite any who wished to come to journey into Jerusalem with him. "But I would have you as witnesses to the crucifixion," he said. "So those who come not, come you at least the morning of the Passover, before the Sabbath begins."

Therefore it sounded to all like some miracle was planned: perhaps this, finally, was when the Kingdom of Heaven would arrive, and that the Son of Man would come on the clouds and save Yeshua from the cross. Speculation abounded, but as I have written, Yeshua would say no more. Others wondered if this was the reason some of the Qumran brethren were there—that the warrior brothers, secretly armed like the Sicarii, would come into the city and attack the *Kittim* and the collaborators when the angels came, to be among the righteous Sons of Light fighting the oppressors. How perfect, for this to be at the Passover, when all were celebrating the Exodus and their freedom from enslavement in Egypt! (Again you must remember: not all in this group were Essenes.)

And so, many came into the city that day, and scattered about to stay with friends or relatives, or returned to Bethany (it is but two miles from Jerusalem) on both nights and returned, as directed, on the morning of the Passover. This is what most had intended to do anyway, to make a sacrifice and eat of the Paschal lamb the evening when Passover started. And because Passover began on Thursday, the fifth day, from dusk to dusk was one day; and then dusk to dusk was the second day, Friday into Saturday, the usual Sabbath. Therefore in that year there were two Sabbaths, back-to-back. So, the women were all especially busy preparing food to last the course of two full days.

I, naturally, being just shy of four years, understood not a thing except that there was an air of excitement surrounding us, and much chatter and talk. At one point along the route into the city, Yeshua came over to say goodbye and to wish us peace, along with my father and uncle James. This was the moment in which Yeshua laid his hands on my head, and blessed me, and told me that I would one day write down his story. My mother smiled at these words and kissed my cheek. She, my grandmother, my aunt Salome, and James's wife, Joanna, all had their hands full taking care of me, my brothers, Mattias, Mark, and a few other children whom I forget now to whom they even belonged! This was how large our crowd had become. Yeshua and the disciples then departed to go ahead to the Temple—a place I wanted to see again, because it was like unto a white and golden maze, with stairs and corridors and columns, and when we arrived, there was a man in a tunic and unusual head covering standing on a stone that jutted out over the street, and he blew into a *shofar,* or ram's horn.

I tugged at my grandmother's hand. "Why does he do that?"

She smiled down at me with her eyes, which crinkled at the corners, then lifted me up and held me in one arm and kissed my forehead before setting me back down (for I was getting too big to be continually carried, even if I did slow down everyone's steps). "It is blown mostly to mark the new year," she said. "But they blow it now to announce the nearness of the Passover."

"Or to announce the arrival of Antipas from his winter castle," said another in the crowd, and this brought laughter.

Well, I should return to Yeshua's story and stop writing about myself. I tell this story only to show how everyone knew the Temple priests had been corrupted by the Romans. In challenging them, and in challenging the Pharisees, Yeshua was only daring to say what everyone else already thought, except for the collaborators themselves.

Oh, and I will also write down this, in order to be clear. Each night I returned with my brothers, my cousin Mattias, and the women of Yeshua's family to the house of Martha in Bethany, who had been kind enough to offer it. So I was not a personal witness to any of the things that happened in Jerusalem at that time—except for a short period during the crucifixion when I was at Eleazar's house with my father, uncle, and the disciples, until they, concerned for our safety, sent all the women and children away. Therefore this part of the story, as has most of the narrative up to this point, been told to me by either my father or by my uncle James, who, of course, were there and saw it all, unless I indicate otherwise.

* * *

Upon arriving in Jerusalem, Yeshua first went to Eleazar's house to let him know that he and the disciples would be eating with him again that night, and also the next. Eleazar was pleased and once more offered his house for them to stay in, but again Yeshua declined. "I would not put you and your wife in danger," he said in parting, and Eleazar accompanied him to the door, where outside in the street—or halfway in the street—was a man lying drunk, and it could not have been even nine o'clock in the morning.

Yeshua looked at this man.

"My neighbor," said Eleazar, with sadness in his voice. "Truly, he is a good man. But he is not in a good way, and he sins with too much drunkenness."

This is hardly an unknown sight, a man taken with too much strong drink; the two Simons hoisted the man up and pulled him completely out of the street and propped him in front of his doorway, for the door was bolted shut from the inside. He was so drunk he could not stand, and he had soiled himself. His eyelids fluttered open when he was being moved, and he muttered something that no one could understand.

Yeshua went to him and squatted in front of him. "Brother," he said. He put his hand on the man's shoulder. "It pains me to see you thus."

The man's eyes fluttered open, and he regarded Yeshua. His mouth tried to speak, but he could not. His eyes closed.

Yeshua shook him gently until he opened his eyes again.

"This is not my Father's plan for you," Yeshua said. "The loss of your child is a terrible thing to suffer. But your wife needs you, for she also suffers."

The man still could not speak, but his eyes welled up with tears.

Yeshua said, "I tell you, your sins are forgiven you."

The man spoke. "How did you know—" and then he saw Eleazar, and assumed Eleazar had told Yeshua of his troubles. But he was completely restored, and no longer drunk, and he got to his feet. "I am disgusting," he said, seeing that he was filthy, and stank. He knocked on his own door.

A woman's voice came from within. "Go away, you—" Well, I cannot write the words, for it was a most unseemly curse.

"I have my senses back," called the man, and his voice was meek.

After a minute, the door was unbolted, and the wife opened the door to him, took one look at him, and grabbed his arm and pulled him in, shutting the door again. More yelling and curses were heard, and they were all from this woman.

Many of the disciples had been amused by this entire scene, and now some burst into outright laughter. Yeshua merely smiled at them. "He has been uncompassionate, and he has judged many. So now he judges himself harshly, and he cannot bear his own flaws, and blames himself for every woe that comes his way. So, I say unto you: if your compassion does not include yourself, it is incomplete."

Now this last was a saying of Siddhartha, the Buddha, and to me it is clear Yeshua was speaking of the karma of a former life the man had led, but I know these things only from studying later at Qumran, where there was a group of Buddha followers from the Great Brotherhood.

You may also wonder if this man ever drank again. Years later, when we lived in the house of Eleazar, Eleazar confirmed that he did not. Indeed, I even met the man, and he and his wife, who were elderly then, were happy. His name was Judah, the wife Sarai. He was a maker of pottery. They were good Jews. But he did not believe in Yeshua as Messiah, for Yeshua had been crucified, and that was not what was expected of the Messiah. Judah had no memory of Yeshua healing him, nor did he believe us when we told him he had. But he did not mind the followers of Yeshua and shared bread with us often, or gave us clay vessels to use in our church. Indeed, Judah was the very man who warned us when Saul was coming, and finding us not there, Saul broke the altar and cups of the communion in his rage.

But again I have leaped far ahead of myself.

* * *

That day, Yeshua went to the Temple, and was teaching, and people came to listen because they had heard of this prophet from Galilee, and others remembered his entry into Jerusalem two days prior. But then the chief priests and Elders came to him and asked, "By what authority are you doing these things, and who gave you this authority?"

Yeshua said to them, "I will also ask you one question; if you tell me the answer, then I will tell you by what authority I do these things."

They agreed, so Yeshua asked of them: "Did the baptism of John come from heaven, or was it of human origin?"

And they stepped to the side to argue with one another, saying, "If we say 'From heaven,' he will say, 'Why then did you not believe him?' But if we say 'Of human origin,' it will anger the crowd; for all regard John as a prophet." So they came back to Yeshua and said, "We do not know."

Yeshua said, "Neither, then, will I tell you by what authority I am doing these things."

This pleased them not, and they were beginning to walk away

when Yeshua got to his feet and challenged them, but not quite with the anger of John. "Tell me," he called after them, so they paused. "What do you think of this question?

"A man had two sons; he went to the first and said, 'Son, go and work in the vineyard today.' He answered, 'I will not'; but later he changed his mind and went. The father went to the second and said the same; and he answered, 'I go, sir'; but he did not go. Which of the two did the will of his father?"

They said, "The first."

Yeshua said to them, "Truly I tell you, the tax collectors and the prostitutes are going into the Kingdom of God ahead of you. For John came to you in the way of righteousness and you did not believe him, but the tax collectors and the prostitutes believed him; and even after you saw it, you did not change your minds and believe him."

From their faces it was clear they knew they had been insulted, but they did not understand how they were like unto the second son. So Yeshua said, "Listen to another parable.

"There was a landowner who planted a vineyard, put a fence around it, dug a wine press in it, and built a watchtower. Then he leased it to tenants and went to another country. When the harvest time had come, he sent his slaves to the tenants to collect his produce. But the tenants seized his slaves and beat one, killed another, and stoned another. Again he sent other slaves, more than the first; and they treated them in the same way. Finally he sent his son to them, saying, 'They will respect my son.' But when the tenants saw the son, they said to themselves, 'This is the heir; come, let us kill him and get his inheritance.' So they seized him, threw him out of the vineyard, and killed him. Now, when the owner of the vineyard comes, what will he do to those tenants?"

They said to Yeshua, "He will put those tenants to a miserable death, and lease the vineyard to other tenants who will give him the produce at the harvest time."

Yeshua smiled at them. "Have you never read in the Scriptures: 'The stone that the builders rejected has become the cornerstone; this was the Lord's doing, and it is amazing in our eyes'?"

Now here is the interpretation: Yeshua is, like King David, the begotten son of God, the Messiah; and he is the cornerstone; and he is the son due the inheritance. But these priests and Elders were not following him. So he said: "Therefore I will tell you, the Kingdom of God will be taken away from you and given to a people that produce the fruits of the Kingdom. The one who falls on this stone will be broken to pieces; and it will crush anyone on whom it falls."

So Yeshua outright told them they were not favored in God's eyes on account of their evil works and their rejection of John and him. They waved their hands at him as usual and went away, wishing they could arrest him, but since he was surrounded by so many who saw him as a prophet, they dared not. Therefore the Herodian Pharisees among them began plotting how they might entrap him and have grounds for his arrest.

Yeshua taught the people far into the day, and finally he tired and was getting ready to leave when the Pharisees, having concocted a plan, sent some of their disciples to Yeshua, saying, "Good Teacher, we know that you are sincere, and teach the way of God in accordance with truth, and show deference to no one; for you do not regard people with partiality. Tell us, then, what you think. Is it lawful to pay taxes to the Emperor of Rome, or not?"

But Yeshua, aware of their malice, asked them, "Why call you me 'good'? For there is only one who is good, and that is the Father. But since you must put me to the test, show me the coin used for the tax."

They gave him a denarius.

Yeshua studied the coin and then asked, "Whose head is this, and whose title?"

They answered, "It is that of the Emperor Tiberias."

"Well, then," Yeshua said, and he tossed the coin back to the man who had handed it over. "Give therefore to the emperor the things that are the emperor's, and give to God the things that are God's."

Now this was a clever answer, for he did not say directly to pay no taxes. But anyone knows that the land of Israel is ours by covenant with the Lord; so if any taxes are owed, they are owed to God and never to the Emperor of Rome. So the Pharisees marveled at his quick-thinking mind, for he was unlike any Zealot they had ever met; and they left him and went away.

Therefore some Sadducees came, not so much to ensnare him as to mock him with a parable of their own. As I have written before, the Sadducees do not believe in Resurrection; so they asked Yeshua a question, saying, "Teacher, Moses said, 'If a man dies childless, his brother shall marry the widow, and raise up children for his brother.' Now there were seven brothers among us; the first married and died childless, leaving the widow to his brother. The second did the same, so also the third, down to the seventh. Last of all, the woman herself died. In the Resurrection, then, whose wife of the seven will she be? For all of them had married her."

Yeshua answered them, "You are wrong, because you know neither the Scriptures nor the power of God. For in the Resurrection they neither marry nor are given in marriage, but are like angels in heaven. And as for the Resurrection of the dead, have you not read what was said to you by God, 'I am the God of Abraham, the God of Isaac, and the God of Jacob?' He is God not of the dead but of the living."

Now this was a remarkable teaching indeed, for he had just said Abraham, Isaac, and Jacob were not dead, and in comparing the resurrected to the angels, he was also saying human beings were not, ultimately, of a sex. At least, that is my interpretation, for it fits with earlier things he had said.

And then, seeing the Sadducees silenced, here came the Pharisees again, this time with a teacher of the Law, hoping to catch Yeshua for blasphemy. "Teacher," this lawyer asked, "which commandment in the Law is the greatest?"

Yeshua said, "'Hear, O Israel, the Lord your God is One. You shall love the Lord your God with all your heart, and with all your soul, and with all your mind.' This is the greatest and first commandment. And a second is like it: 'You shall love your neighbor as yourself.' On these two commandments hang all the Law and the prophets."

With this the teacher of the Law agreed, and they could not argue; and therefore Yeshua left them for that day. When he and the disciples left the Temple, they took a roundabout way to Eleazar's house to ensure they were not followed. Then they entered into his house and ate. From there they retired to the Mount of Olives, to that garden called Gethsemane, or the place of the olive presses, where they rolled up in their cloaks and slept for the night.

Meanwhile, word of the day's happenings in the Temple came to the ears of the High Priest Caiaphas, and many members of the Sanhedrin gathered informally in Caiaphas' house in the Upper City to discuss what they might do with Yeshua. This information came to us later, from Joseph of Arimathea, who had gotten the story from Nicodemus. Many of the Sanhedrin saw Yeshua as a threat and wished to arrest him by stealth and kill him. Others, among them Nicodemus, said no, that the man had broken no laws. Still others agreed that something must be done, but not now, during the festival of the Passover, for then there might be a riot among the people, which would anger Pilate and bring his wrath down upon their own heads. They departed that night with the question unsettled.

This was the last night Yeshua was to ever sleep as a living human being on this earth.

* * *

The next morning, they rose, and as Eleazar had sent them off from his house with food to carry, Yeshua and the disciples ate of this for their morning meal. Then they went back into Jerusalem and to the Temple, where Yeshua resumed teaching the people. Judas Iscariot seemed restless and angry, but no one knew why, and when asked, he said, "I am well, only tired."

Of course, what the disciples did not know then was that, in secret, he had stolen away the night before, when all slept, and visited the High Priest and offered to hand Yeshua over to him, when the opportunity presented itself. It could not be done in the Temple in plain view, lest a riot be provoked. For this action, Caiaphas paid him thirty pieces of silver. But, more on the motives of Judas later.

In the Temple, Yeshua taught the people, saying, "The scribes and the Pharisees sit on Moses' seat; therefore, do whatever they teach you and follow it; but do not do as they do, for they do not practice what they teach. They tie up heavy burdens for the people, hard to bear, and lay them on the shoulders of others; but they themselves are unwilling to lift a finger to move them. They do all their deeds to be seen by others; for they make their phylacteries broad and their fringes long. They love to have the place of honor at banquets and the best seats in the synagogues, and to be greeted with respect in the marketplaces, and to have people call them rabbi."

And, of course, hearing these words, the Pharisees and some of the scribes stepped closer, so that they might hear, for they still sought a way to entrap Yeshua.

Yeshua continued, "But you are not to be called rabbi, for you have one teacher, and you are all students. And call no one your father on earth, for you have but one Father—the one in heaven. Nor are you to be called instructors, for you have but one instructor, the Messiah. The greatest among you will be your servant. All who exalt themselves will be humbled, and all who humble themselves will be exalted."

There came a mumble of discontent from the Pharisees, so Yeshua got to his feet and confronted them directly. This day he was like his cousin John, for he cried out many harsh words. He said:

"Woe to you, Pharisees, scribes, hypocrites! For you lock people out of the Kingdom of Heaven. For you do not go in yourselves, and when others are going in, you stop them. Woe to you, scribes and Pharisees, hypocrites! For you cross sea and land to make a single convert, and you make the new convert twice as much a child of hell as yourselves."

He stepped towards them, as if he were daring them to lay hands on him and arrest him.

"Woe to you, blind guides, who say, 'Whoever swears by the sanctuary is bound by nothing, but whoever swears by the gold of the sanctuary is bound by the oath.' You blind fools! For which is greater, the gold or the sanctuary that has made the gold sacred? And you say, 'Whoever swears by the altar is bound by nothing, but whoever swears by the gift that is on the altar is bound by the oath.' How blind you are! For which is greater, the gift or the altar that makes the gift sacred? So whoever swears by the altar, swears by it and everything on it; and whoever swears by the sanctuary, swears by it and by the one who dwells in it; and whoever swears by heaven, swears by the throne of God and by the one who is seated upon it.

"Woe to you, scribes and Pharisees, hypocrites! For you tithe mint, dill, and cumin, and have neglected the weightier matters of the Law: justice and mercy and faith. It is these you ought to have practiced without neglecting the others. You blind guides! You strain out a gnat but swallow a camel!"

Naturally the Pharisees were not going to stand and listen to this condemnation of them, so they turned and began walking across the Court, away from him. Yeshua cried after them:

"Woe to you, scribes and Pharisees, hypocrites! For you clean the outside of the cup and of the plate, but inside they are full of greed and self-indulgence. You blind Pharisee! First clean the inside of the cup, so that the outside also may become clean.

"Woe to you, scribes and Pharisees, hypocrites! For you are like whitewashed tombs, which on the outside look beautiful, but inside they are full of the bones of the dead and all kinds of filth. So you also on the outside look righteous to others, but inside you are full of hypocrisy and lawlessness."

And now he ceased, for they were gone from him and could no longer hear his words.

My father said to him, "You invite trouble."

Yeshua regarded him and laid a hand on his shoulder. "Someone must get them to see that they are forever adhering to the letter of the Law in order to retain their holiness in the eyes of men; meanwhile they forever ignore the spirit of the Law, which destroys their holiness in the eyes of the Lord."

"I do not think they have the ears to hear," said my uncle James, and since all the disciples seemed afraid of a confrontation, Yeshua led them out of the Temple.

"Look at this place," said Simon Peter, as they came down the right-hand side of the great staircase at the Huldah Gates. He had paused to look up at the vastness of the Temple. "All this gilt and polished stone."

"Mark you this," Yeshua said to them. "Truly I tell you, not one stone will be left upon another; all will be thrown down."

When they reached the street, there was a blind man begging. Judas Iscariot reached for the purse to hand to Yeshua to give the man coins, but Yeshua declined. He squatted instead in front of the man.

"Would you like your sight restored?" he asked him.

The man laughed. "Either I or my mother and father have sinned, for I have been thus since birth."

"Any sin has been forgiven you," Yeshua told him.

But the man shook his head, and his sight was not restored, for he did not believe. Therefore Yeshua made a great show for him, that he might believe. He spat loudly onto the ground so that the man would hear him working, and then he made a mud paste by mixing his saliva with the dirt. This mud he spread over the man's eyes.

"Now we will take you to wash in the Pool of Siloam," Yeshua said, and he helped the man to his feet. "Your sight will return."

The disciples followed Yeshua and the man down to the pool, where many bathed before going into the Temple. This pool was continually fed by water that came from the spring outside the city, through the canal that was dug by Hezekiah prior to his repelling the Assyrian siege. Yeshua led the man down the steps into the water of the pool and bade him to wash.

The man did as he was asked.

Now there were many there who knew this man, having seen him daily outside the Temple begging. So these also watched, with great curiosity.

The man scrubbed at his eyes, and splashed water onto his face, then opened his eyes, blinking in the sunlight. Immediately he covered his eyes with his hands, for the light was too great. Then he removed them slowly, letting in a little light at a time as his eyes adjusted. Finally he put his hands down altogether.

"I can see! I can see!" he cried out.

He went to look for Yeshua, to thank him, the story goes, but Yeshua and the disciples had already slipped back into the crowds and were on their way out of the city. I have always loved this story, for it shows how important faith truly is in the making of miracles.

* * *

They went onto the Mount of Olives and sat to eat the rest of the leftover loaves, and the disciples, remembering that Yeshua had told them that even the Temple would be destroyed, asked Yeshua of the End of Times.

"Tell us," Andrew asked, "when will this be, and what will be the sign of the coming Son of Man and the end of the age?"

Yeshua answered them, "Beware that no one leads you astray. For many will come in my name, saying, 'I am the Messiah!' and they will lead many astray. And you will hear of wars and rumors of wars; see that you are not alarmed; for this must take place, but the end is not yet. For nation will rise against nation, and kingdom against kingdom, and there will be famines and earthquakes in various places: all this is but the beginning of the birth pangs."

"So the End will not be now? Why must you let the Romans hang you?" Simon Peter asked.

"It is written, so it is the will of the Lord," said Yeshua.

"I do not see the purpose," said Judas Iscariot, and he picked up a pebble and threw it at a tree, where it hit, bounced off, and rolled.

"The will of God is not to be questioned. 'By his bruises we are healed,'" said Yeshua, quoting his beloved Isaiah. "'The Lord has laid on him the iniquity of us all.'"

All were silent.

"I am not the only one to suffer, as I have told you," Yeshua said. "No, even you will be handed over to be tortured and put to death, and you will be hated by all nations because of my name. Then many will fall away, and they will betray one another and hate one another. And many false prophets will arise and lead many astray. And because of the increase of lawlessness, the love of many will grow cold. But the one who endures to the end will be saved. And this good news of the Kingdom will be proclaimed throughout the world, as a testimony to all the nations; and then the End will come."

"But when?" asked Nathanael.

"Truly I tell you, as I have said before, this generation will not pass away until all these things have taken place. Heaven and earth will pass away, but my words will not pass away.

"But about that day and hour no one knows, neither the angels of heaven, but only the Father. For as the days of Noah were, so will be the coming of the Son of Man. For as in those days before the flood they were eating and drinking, marrying and giving in marriage, until the day Noah entered the ark, and they knew nothing until the flood came and swept them all away, so too will be the coming of the Son of Man. Then two will be in the field; one will be taken and one will be left. Two women will be grinding grain together; one will be taken and one will be left. Keep awake therefore, for you do not know on what day your Lord is coming. But understand this: if the owner of the house had known in what part of the night the thief was coming, he would have stayed awake and would not have let his house be broken into. Therefore you also must be ready, for the Son of Man is coming at an unexpected hour."

"And to be ready, what must we do?" asked Bartholomew.

Yeshua smiled at him. "Who then is the faithful and wise slave, whom his master has put in charge of his household, to give the other slaves their allowance of food at the proper time? Blessed is that slave whom his master will find at work when he arrives. Truly I tell you, he will put that one in charge of all his possessions. Therefore, take you always good and righteous actions. But if that wicked slave says to himself, 'My master is delayed,' and he begins to beat his fellow slaves, and eats and drinks with drunkards, the master of that slave will come on a day when he does not expect him and at an hour that he does not know. He will cut him in pieces and put him with the hypocrites, where there will be weeping and gnashing of teeth."

Mary of Magdala was sitting with her head leaning back against her brother Philip. Philip asked, "Master, how will the judging take place?"

"When the Son of Man comes in his glory, and all the angels

with him, then he will sit on the throne of his glory. All the nations will be gathered before him, and he will separate people one from another as a shepherd separates the sheep from the goats, and he will put the sheep at his right hand and the goats at the left.

"Then the king will say to those at his right hand, 'Come, you that are blessed by our Father, inherit the Kingdom prepared for you from the foundation of the world; for I was hungry and you gave me food, I was thirsty and you gave me something to drink, I was a stranger and you welcomed me, I was naked and you gave me clothing, I was sick and you took care of me, I was in prison and you visited me.' Then the righteous will answer him, 'Lord, when was it that we saw you hungry and gave you food, or thirsty and gave you something to drink? And when was it that we saw you a stranger and welcomed you, or naked and gave you clothing? And when was it that we saw you sick or in prison and visited you?' And the king will answer them, 'Truly I tell you, just as you did it to one of the least of these who are members of my family, you did it to me.'

"Then he will say to those at his left hand, 'You that are accursed, depart from me into the eternal fire prepared for the Devil and his angels; for I was hungry and you gave me no food, I was thirsty and you gave me nothing to drink, I was a stranger and you did not welcome me, naked and you did not give me clothing, sick and in prison and you did not visit me.' Then they also will answer, 'Lord, when was it that we saw you hungry or thirsty or a stranger or naked or sick or in prison, and did not take care of you?' Then he will answer them, 'Truly I tell you, just as you did not do it to one of the least of these, you did not do it to me.' And these will go away into eternal punishment, but the righteous into eternal life."

They all sat a while, in silence, thinking about these things that Yeshua had said. Then Yeshua suggested they rest a little, under the trees in the heat of the day, and sleep if possible, for, he said, "The night will be long."

Yeshua went off a ways and sat, leaning against a tree and closing his eyes, but my father said he could not tell if he actually slept or was only meditating.

And thus the afternoon was spent until the sun began to dip below the horizon, and all gathered back together to go to Eleazar's house for the meal that was there prepared for them.

* * *

They had gathered at Eleazor's, the twelve and Mary of Magdala, and also Eleazar and finally his wife, whom Yeshua bade to sit and join them and to stop running to and fro waiting on them. For she had prepared a grand feast indeed, of two kinds of bread, one barley and one wheat, many stacked loaves of each; olives, carob, lentils, and vegetables; dried fruits from the marketplace; spiced herbs in oil for dipping; and the meat of a goat, for those who ate meat; and several jars of wine.

Yeshua did not eat much but seemed to enjoy watching the others.

When they were near to satiety, Yeshua said, 'Truly I tell you, one of you will hand me over."

Everyone looked up from their eating, alarmed and distressed. And they began to say to him, bursting out with almost one voice, "Surely not I, Lord?"

And Yeshua just shook his head. "You will know. But all of you will desert me this night, for it is written, 'I will strike the shepherd, and the sheep of the flock will be scattered.'"

Peter said, "Even if all become deserters because of you, I will never desert you!"

Yeshua looked at him, and his smile was almost tender. "Truly I tell you, Peter, this very night, before the cock crows, you will deny me three times."

Peter shook his head no. "Even though I must die with you, I will not deny you."

And all the other disciples agreed they would do the same.

After all of this, James, who reclined next to Yeshua, whispered to him, "Which one?"

Yeshua whispered back to his brother, "The one who has dipped his hand into the bowl with me will betray me." So he waited, and when Judas Iscariot went to dip his bread, Yeshua did also. Therefore, my uncle James knew first.

"It explains his mood," James said. Yeshua nodded in agreement.

"Now," Yeshua said, addressing them all, "I would hear a hymn. Let us sing a hymn of thanksgiving to the Lord."

"Which one, Lord?" asked Mary of Magdala, for she always started the hymns when they sang them, having a sweeter voice than any and the ability to begin on the right note.

"The one hundred and sixteenth."

So Mary began: "I love the Lord, because he has heard my voice and my supplications . . ."

When the hymn was finished, Yeshua took up one of the jars of wine and poured out wine into his cup. Then he blessed the cup of wine, saying, "Thank you, Lord, for the holy vine of David, your servant. To you be the glory forever." He then took a small sip from the cup and handed it to James. "All drink this in remembrance of me."

When all had sipped, Yeshua took up one of the loaves of bread, and after blessing it, he broke it, and he ate of a piece and handed the loaf to James. "All eat this bread in remembrance of me."

Once all had eaten of the bread, Yeshua thanked them and said, "I have done this as a sign of the New Covenant, our restored covenant with God so that you may not fall away." He then said to Judas Iscariot: "Go, now, and do what you must do."

Judas got to his feet and departed without a word. My father said later that Judas did not protest, nor did he even try to sneak away. His face was inscrutable, beyond the same restless and angry look he had worn on it all that day.

The meal finished, Yeshua rose and thanked Eleazar and his wife, and embraced them both. They then left his house, and returned to the Mount of Olives, and to Gethsemane, where they would wait.

And now I add a short note to this story of Yeshua's last supper. Much later, when I was at Qumran, I found a scroll with a listing of things that the Messiah would do at the End of Times. Among the last things, it stated that the Messiah would preside over a communal meal. So again, Yeshua was following the Prophets, and the Essene writings, in order that he might fulfill them. It is, as I have written previously, the way of the Essenes, who believe in predestination. But again, although things are preordained, one's freedom to choose can "un-ordain" events, so to speak. I know this sounds like a contradiction, and therefore some among the Essenes deny the existence of free will. It is also worth noting that, aside from referring to themselves as the "Sons of Light," the Essenes, anticipating the End Times, also sometimes referred to themselves as the "Community of the New Covenant."

So, you must understand that Yeshua did that which he believed was the will of the Father in heaven. But, he *chose* to do these things.

Chapter Twenty

Therefore, just as they had the previous night, they returned to Gethsemane; except as time passed and as the moon rose higher in the sky, Yeshua seemed to become more and more troubled. The disciples rolled themselves up into their cloaks and were settling down to sleep, but Yeshua was restless, first lying down, then sitting up and leaning against an olive tree, and finally getting to his feet to waken the disciples. "Sit here and keep watch," he said. "I am going over there to pray." He took with him James, Peter, and John.

Yeshua was agitated in spirit and said to the three, "I am deeply grieved, even to death; remain here and stay awake with me."

And going a little further, he threw himself on the ground and prayed. My uncle James was able to hear some of his words, though he tried to not overhear, for Yeshua had taught that a person should pray in private.

Yeshua prayed, "My Father, if it is possible, let this cup pass from me; yet not what I want but what you want." He lowered his voice and began mumbling, though with some fervor. Time passed.

Then Yeshua got up and walked back to the three and found them sleeping. He said to Peter, "So, could you not stay awake with me one hour? Stay awake and pray that you may not also come into the time of trial; the spirit indeed is willing, but the flesh is weak."

The three propped themselves against trees and tried to force their eyes to remain open. Again my uncle could hear some of Yeshua's words.

"My Father, if this cannot pass unless I drink it, your will be done." Then his voice lowered and James could hear no more, and he found himself nodding off to sleep again. He startled, and wakening, could hear Yeshua still praying. He tried to keep himself awake, but his eyelids were heavy.

Finally Yeshua came and woke them. "Are you still sleeping and taking your rest? See, the hour is at hand, and the Son of Man is handed over into the hands of sinners. Get up, let us be going. See, I am about to be handed over."

He was still saying these words when Judas Iscariot arrived, and a group of Temple guards with swords and clubs, among them some of the chief priests and Elders. Now, Judas had apparently given them a sign to identify Yeshua to those who arrested him, else they may have mistaken my father for Yeshua: that is how closely the two resembled one another. The sign was a kiss.

Hence Judas came up to Yeshua, saying, "Greetings, Rabbi!" and he kissed Yeshua's cheek.

Yeshua said to him, "Friend, you have done what you were here to do."

Judas disappeared into the night, never to be seen again. (But I will write more of him later.)

Then the Temple guards came and laid hands on Yeshua and arrested him. By now all the disciples had gathered near, and when Simon the Zealot saw what was happening, he drew a short sword and struck the man who was the slave of the High Priest, taking off a part of the man's ear.

Yeshua stayed Simon. "No! Put your sword back into its place; for all who take the sword will perish by the sword."

"But Lord—"

"No," said Yeshua. He reached forward and touched the slave's ear, which ceased bleeding. He then turned and addressed the disciples.

"This must be as it is. How else will the Scriptures be fulfilled, which say it must happen in this way?"

Truly, as I have said, as the Messiah, Yeshua was convinced his path was cleared before him and he was doing only what God required of him. I confess I understand the disciples; for still I struggle with this idea. How could God allow such a thing? How could God even want such a thing? But later, the deacon Barnabas, whom I mentioned before when his young son was tormenting a cat, said something that made me think. He said that it had also made no sense for God to require of Abraham the sacrifice of his son Isaac. And indeed, God had, at the last minute, sent the angel to stop it from happening. Jews have always read that story as God's testing Abraham's love for him. So now, perhaps, Barnabas concluded, God was going through with the sacrifice of his own begotten son, the anointed one, to prove to humankind his love for us.

I write now that I wish human beings did not require such a proof!

But, Simon put away his sword—nobody ever told me why he was carrying a sword, but he had been a Sicarii, so perhaps he could not bring himself to feel safe without a weapon, especially with Yeshua lately speaking of the troubles to come.

Yeshua raised his voice and said to the crowd of priests and Temple guards—and to some Roman soldiers as well, who stood well off, but who had also been sent in case there was trouble—"Have you come out with swords and clubs to arrest me as though I were a bandit? Day after day I sat in the Temple teaching, and you did not arrest me. But all this has taken place, so that the scriptures of the prophets may be fulfilled."

The disciples had not even noticed the Roman soldiers until now. Upon seeing them, they feared greatly, including even Simon the Zealot. They deserted Yeshua and fled.

My uncle and my father were not proud of this. "We abandoned him in his hour of need," my father told me later. He heaved a sigh. "But I think he wished us to, and told us we would, for had we also been arrested with him that night, surely the High Priest Caiaphas would have wiped out Yeshua's movement altogether." He tugged at his beard. "Or perhaps I am just trying to make myself feel better. I will tell you this," he said, and paused, searching for words. "People say how blessed we are, having known Yeshua personally. I agree that we are blessed. But we also carry with us the burden of atonement. This shame and this sorrow I will carry to my grave."

This burden was carried by each of the twelve, minus Judas Iscariot, who was to carry a different burden.

As it turned out, the disciples wound up back at the house of Eleazar, for it was the logical place to go. Simon Peter, however, proved to be the bravest—or the most foolish—of them all. Yeshua was taken to the house of Caiaphas, in whose house Caiaphas and Annas had gathered to them those scribes and Elders who did their bidding. Peter followed at a distance, indeed daring to enter into the courtyard of the High Priest, where guards, servants, and some others were gathered around a fire warming themselves. He even sat with the guards and had idle conversation with them. He wanted to see how the situation would end.

Never mind that any matter of importance was supposed to be discussed by the Sanhedrin in the Hall of Hewn Stones in the Temple. Never mind that for any matter of grave importance—as surely this was—the entire Sanhedrin of seventy-one men was supposed to sit in judgment. Therefore the entire proceeding was a farce, like one of the Greek comedies the rich priests and their families were accustomed to seeing in the Jerusalem amphitheatre.

The hearing took place, therefore, late at night, and early in the morning hours, in an unlawful way at the house of Caiaphas. They were in a large banquet room just off the courtyard, so Peter was able to hear much of what was going on, but he bit back enraged words and put on a blank face so as to not be discovered.

"The whole council was trying to find a reason to put Yeshua to death," he told the disciples later. "They even brought forth many false witnesses to testify, saying he was a magician or did miracles in the name of Beelzebub, or flouted the Law, and raised their voices when nothing with proof could be found to condemn him.

"But then two came forward and said, 'This man said that he would destroy the Temple of God and build it up again in three days.'

"Caiaphas stood and addressed Yeshua himself, saying, 'Have you no answer? What is the meaning of these words they use to testify against you?'

"Yeshua said nothing.

"Then Caiaphas said, 'I put you under oath to the living God: tell us if you are the Messiah, the Chosen One of God.'

"Yeshua said to him, 'You have said so. But I tell you, the time comes when you will see the Son of Man seated at the right hand of Power and coming on the clouds of heaven.'"

Now, there is no blasphemy in this, for everyone knew this prophecy, and there had been many false Messiahs before, and many to come later. None was ever killed for blasphemy. But it was convenient for Caiaphas to see it as such from Yeshua, for he had spoken out against them, and also insulted his friends among the Pharisees, in the Temple.

Thus, said Peter, Caiaphas made a great show of tearing at his clothes and crying out, "He has blasphemed! Why do we still need witnesses? You have now heard his blasphemy from his own mouth. What is your verdict?"

And Caiaphas' Lower Sanhedrin of nodding puppets said, "He deserves death."

Then the members spat in Yeshua's face, and some struck him with their fists, saying, "Prophesy to us, you Messiah! Who is it that just struck you?"

They bound Yeshua, and some guards within the house took Yeshua down to stay the rest of the night in the cell in Caiaphas' cellar.

Peter had sat in the courtyard listening, while pretending to not listen, the whole time. But now a servant-girl came to him and said, "You were also with Yeshua the Galilean."

And because the Temple guards were still there, Peter denied it before them all, saying, "I do not know what you are talking about."

He got up and departed the courtyard, but once he reached the porch, yet another servant-girl saw him, and she said to the bystanders, "This man was with Yeshua of Nazareth, for I recognize him from the Temple."

Again Peter denied it with an oath, saying, "I do not know the man!"

Then one of the bystanders said, "Certainly you are one of his disciples, for your Galilean accent betrays you."

Peter began to curse, and he swore another oath, "I do not know the man!"

He reached the street and, as he was walking away, the cock crowed, for a sliver of sun had appeared in the eastern sky. Then Simon Peter remembered what Yeshua had said: "Before the cock crows, you will deny me three times."

Poor Peter. He wept bitterly during the telling of this story to those disciples who had already gathered at Eleazar's house, for this was where he went next. They comforted him and eased his conscience as best they could. "It was plain Yeshua had forgiven you before it even happened," they said. And, "All will be well. The angel of the Lord will save Yeshua." And, "Yeshua will perform some miracle; you will see."

Now morning had dawned, and the rest of the disciples straggled in, but all were too afraid to go out lest they be captured and tried as conspirators with Yeshua. And, from Peter's story, it was clear that they, no more than Yeshua had, would not receive a fair hearing. Eleazar's wife brought them food, but they were not hungry. Their faces were wracked with worry, and their stomachs clenched in knots.

* * *

Not long after sunrise, the Temple guards dragged Yeshua from the cell in the basement of Caiaphas' house and took him to the Praetorium, or the governor's house, to be tried in front of Pontius Pilate. Caiaphas explained to Pilate that Yeshua claimed to be the Messiah, or the King of the Jews.

Now let me digress to tell you of this prefect—governor, essentially, of Judea—whose name was Pontius Pilate. He was only of the equestrian class of Romans and was said to hate his post in tiny Judea. He was of such unimportance in his own Empire he answered not even to Caesar; he answered to the Roman legate of Syria, upon whom he was to call if there was an uprising that Pilate's legions could not put down. When Pilate first arrived in Judea, he was completely in ignorance of Jewish customs (this was when Yeshua was still in Egypt). That man had entered Jerusalem with Roman standards bearing the image of Caesar and he wanted to place them all over the city, which, as you can imagine, threw all Jerusalem into an uproar, for images and idols are not permitted under the Law. The Temple priests tried to reason with him using flattery and tact, but Pilate did not care. His standards would hang.

So the people revolted not by fighting, for that would be folly, but by marching to Caesarea and lying in the streets, and they would not be moved. At first Pilate seemed amused by this and said, "Let them die, then, in the streets," but after five days he became annoyed with the "absurdities of these people," and finally he had the standards removed. But I do not think he ever forgot this thing. He ignored the Jews as much as he could, staying in his palace in Caesarea, enjoying his pools and his views of the Great Sea. He came only to Jerusalem when his presence was absolutely required, such as during festivals and particularly during the Passover, which, as I have written already, was a time when revolts were wont to break out. For the man had but one job in Judea, and one job only: to enforce the *Pax Romana*, or the peace.

His own secondary purpose was to steal or make for himself as much money as he could, so he happily took bribes and expected gifts of money or other goods in exchange for appointments, such as tax collecting, or the office of High Priest. Pilate and the Annas family of Sadducean priests were great friends, if Jews and Gentiles then could be said to be friends. Therefore, Pilate himself had appointed the High Priest Caiaphas, at the request of Caiaphas' father-in-law, Annas. So anything Caiaphas or Annas asked of Pilate, so long as it would not bring trouble upon Pilate, these two priests received. And anything they received, a portion went to Pilate. Indeed, when Pilate sent an extra unblemished kid every year to be sacrificed to the Hebrew God in the Temple, this was done by the priests. A lamb was also sacrificed to Yahweh on the altar every day, by order of the Emperor of Rome. Now, I cannot say this was something new, for Herod the Great, a Jew only by marriage, as I have written, and therefore at best a half-Jew or a converted Jew, but not a Jew by birth because his mother was some Arabian princess, and certainly he was not of the line of David and thereby was a false king, did this thing as well. This practice, and compliance by the priests, was one of the many reasons the Brethren at Qumran had wholly rejected the Temple. To them, making sacrifices for foreigners on the altar was breaking the Law. The Temple was for Jews and for those who worshiped solely Yahweh, and these pagans worshiped other gods, thereby breaking the first of the commandments.

Therefore, who was this Yeshua that Caiaphas clearly wished to dispense with? If two Jews were merely arguing about God, why would Pilate care? It had nothing to do with him, or with Rome. And thus you will see the clever hand of Caiaphas in the accusation brought to Pilate: Yeshua was being called the Messiah, the Son of David, the King of the Jews. Now this was sedition, the words of a traitor, for only the Romans could appoint a king.

My uncle James said that Yeshua had no trial, not in the way one would think of a trial or a hearing in front of the Sanhedrin. The verdict was made before he even appeared before Pilate. His accusers gathered with Pilate outside the Praetorium on the stone pavement called Gabbatha, for it was unlawful for Jews to enter the house of a Gentile lest they be made unclean. Pilate watched from his judgment seat as Yeshua was pushed in front of him; he stood in front of the prefect for less than a minute. "They tell me you are the King of the Jews," he said to Yeshua. "Is this what you say?"

"So say you," answered Yeshua.

Pilate laughed. "Take him away," he said. "Crucify him." For he was anxious, no doubt, to get back inside to his wife and his wine.

And that was the end of it. The Annas family got what they wanted; the Herodians got what they wanted; and Pilate got what he wanted: no trouble during the Passover, a quick crushing of a possible rebellion. And lest anyone get any more ideas during the Passover, the presence of the crucified rebel leader on Golgotha, in full view of the city before the Passover commenced, would deter any more trouble.

The Jews of the city were outraged, for they knew that Yeshua had never spoken overtly against Rome or even against Herod Antipas, but they knew he had criticized the Jewish collaborators. At the same time, their hopes for a Messiah were also dashed in this thing: the Messiah was to overthrow Rome and restore the kingdom to Israel, but this man Yeshua was now being dragged off to be crucified like a common criminal. So now it seemed he was just one more false Messiah among many: although, perhaps like John the Baptizer, the powers-that-ruled were again killing a Jewish prophet, and most unjustly.

The Sanhedrin announced the verdict of Pilate on the steps of the Temple, thus washing their hands of the blood of Yeshua: his death was decreed by Rome, not by them. The people who heard this news wept and cried out in protest, but Caiaphas assured them there was nothing he could do.

But we knew the truth.

Now, my family would of course not allow my brothers or me to watch my uncle being put to death, and the disciples were afraid of being captured and crucified for sedition as well, so they stayed hidden at the house of Eleazar; indeed, there they hid for almost a week. However, Yeshua's mother, my grandmother Mary, went to be with him, for the presence of the family would be expected. For a few minutes of argument, my uncle James and my father tried insisting on going as well since they felt it was their place to do so also, but both relented when everyone disagreed. It was too risky: doubly so, perhaps, as brothers of the man being crucified for being a traitor to Rome, for they might claim to be next in line to be "King of the Jews." But the women were safe. Therefore, Mary of Magdala went as well, along with my aunt Salome, for one was a sister, and Mary was not viewed as one of the disciples and could also claim to be a sister if the need arose; and it would not be a horrible lie, they all reasoned, because we did call her sister.

All others of the family stayed at Eleazar's.

There is a story that the sons of Zebedee, especially John the Beloved, were at the cross, but they were not; there is another that James was at the cross, but he was not; for the reasons stated. None of the disciples were at the cross: no, they were hiding for their lives, and praying, and hoping that the angel of the Lord would descend and save Yeshua from death or that by some miracle, he would descend from the cross alive, fully healed, and that the Kingdom of Heaven would finally arrive.

Therefore this next that I set down is from the mouth of my grandmother, Mary. Mary of Magdala and my aunt Salome confirmed these things, and, of course, there were many other witnesses as well who will confirm that Yeshua did die on the cross. I write this because others try to say that Yeshua did not die, that he had merely lost consciousness, and that when he was taken to the tomb, he was bathed in healing ointments and revived. That is absurd. The Romans had done many crucifixions. They certainly knew when a man was or was not dead. If time was of the essence—as it would be this day, the day of the actual beginning of the Feast of the Passover—they would simply break the crucified man's legs so that he could no longer bear his own weight and would quickly suffocate to death, not being able to lift himself up so as to take in breaths.

Crucifixion—what a horrible way to die! I confess, I am getting upset even as I write this down. Not just on behalf of my uncle Yeshua, but on behalf of all Jews who have been put to death in this cruel manner. Later in my life I was to see my share of crucified men: bandits and other rebels, Zealots who were fighting for the freedom of Israel. Sometimes these men were scourged so severely beforehand that they did not last long on the cross, and this was actually a merciful thing. For those who were nailed up that were not already half dead were destined to suffer sometimes more than a day and night of agony, and, in extreme cases, for many days. And if no one came forth to claim the body, which happened more than I care to admit—for fear of the *Kittim*, or the Romans, was a powerful thing, and to claim a body might associate one with the condemned—then the crucified man was simply left hanging there, dead, for the scavengers to eat, the birds pecking out the eyes and eating of the upper portions, and the dogs jumping up and pulling off flesh and eating from the bottom. It was a ghastly sight to behold.

The Romans reused, whenever possible, the same trees for crucifixion, so when it came time to crucify another, if a body still happened to be hanging there, they merely knocked it down, scattering the bones at the foot of the tree, and then kicking the bones out of the way—as if that had not been an actual person, with a father, a mother, a wife, perhaps children. And this is why Golgotha was named the way it was: the place of the skull, for many bones lay scattered about on that hill. It was a most unclean and ghastly place.

I must pause. My heart pains me as I write these things. I will return to this narrative tomorrow.

* * *

Rachel is concerned, for she says my skin begins to take on a pallor, so yesterday she insisted I take a day of rest, and I admit I feel better for it. I told her that I am writing a difficult part and that of certainty it is taxing upon my spirit. She says today she will check upon me often and make me stop if I don't look well.

Therefore I return now to the story as told me by my grandmother Mary.

No one really knows how many lashes were given to Yeshua, she said, but when he finally appeared on the street, from the small courtyard north of the Praetorium where the scourgings were carried out, where the condemned were bound helpless with their arms around a pillar, Yeshua's back was like raw meat, and blood ran down his body. He was carrying the crossbeam that would be secured to the tree, and he was weak and already stumbling from the scourging. I must also point out that he had had nothing to eat since the previous night, and very little then, and he'd had no sleep at all. Also the Romans had done a terrible thing to mock him—they had fashioned a crown of thorns and placed it on his head. The three women wept at the sight, to see Yeshua thus humiliated. Some followers, as Yeshua had asked of them at Bethany, lined the street and called out words of hope to him as he passed, but many of the crowd—there for the Passover that evening—knew not who he was and merely watched in curiosity, then went on their way.

Along the way, Yeshua stumbled under the weight of the crossbeam and fell to his knees. The Romans kicked him and told him to get up. He tried to get to his feet but could not, falling back down. Then a man of black skin—not one of the followers—whom later we learned was named Simon of Cyrene, which is part of Libya—stepped forward to help Yeshua to his feet, for which the Romans struck him a blow, for he had not been asked. Simon was going back to his place, for his son was with him, when Yeshua stumbled and fell again. This time, the Romans themselves pulled Yeshua to his feet, and in their impatience, they grabbed Simon and made him to help Yeshua carry the beam to Golgotha. My aunt Salome saw Simon looking anxiously for his son, so she went and took the boy by the hand and led this child with her, so that he would not lose his father.

They exited the city by the *Sha'ar Yafo*, or Jaffa Gate, turned right, and began the climb to Golgotha, a place where stone was once quarried. The way is not actually long, but for someone who was in a condition such as Yeshua's, every step must have been agonizing. When they reached the top of the hill, where two men that had been crucified that morning were already hanging, the Romans dismissed Simon. But the three women saw that Yeshua said something to him. Simon touched Yeshua's shoulder, and the Romans hit him again, so that man departed, looking for his son.

My aunt Salome brought his son to him. Simon was winded from the climb under the weight of the crossbeam, and also from having his arm around Yeshua to help hold him up and steady him along the way. "Here is your son," she said to Simon.

"Thank you," Simon said, and he immediately turned his back to Golgotha, placing his son in front of him to shield his son's eyes from the scene that was unfolding on the hill.

"That man blessed me," he said. "Who is he? What crime did he commit?"

My aunt later said she had wanted to tell the man he was now holy in the eyes of God, for he had been blessed by his begotten Son, the Messiah, but she dared not even utter that word. So she just said, "He is my brother, Yeshua of Nazareth. A prophet. He has committed no crime."

Simon acknowledged this information and shook his head. "It is a terrible business."

And with that, he took his son and disappeared back into Jerusalem. My aunt hastened to catch up to the two Marys. Later on, this Simon of Cyrene, and his son Alexandros, were to become Followers of the Way.

The trees at Golgotha had been especially chosen by the Romans some time before, for they were olive trees, so they were short with many branches and they had already cut them back for the purpose of crucifixion. Those without a natural "saddle" had a seat already hammered on, just a short piece of wood, for the crucified man to sit on, although he was not fully seated, of course. It was just enough to help bear some of his weight so that he would die more slowly. The Romans had removed the crown of thorns from Yeshua's head, or perhaps, since no one actually remembers seeing them do this, the crown had fallen off. But they had stripped off his garment, which was also customary: for what is so humiliating as to hang, naked and dying, upon a tree, for all to see?

The time had come to nail Yeshua's arms to the crossbeam. The Romans did the one compassionate thing of this entire procedure: they offered to Yeshua the standard drug that would dull the pain: a cup of old wine, or vinegar, with the herb myrrh infused in it. Yeshua, peace be upon him for his bravery, refused it. Then the nails were driven through his wrists.

Next, with one soldier bearing the weight of Yeshua's legs so his hands would not be torn as they lifted him, the Romans placed the crossbeam across two branches of the tree, which formed a kind of Y shape, and secured it with rope. Yeshua's tree had a natural knot in the wood, which served as his seat. And then they twisted his legs to the left, bending them at the knee, and drove a long nail through both heels, to secure him to the tree. The *Kittim* did this whenever possible, to save themselves a nail. I have also seen crucified men with the heels nailed to either side of the tree. Finally, they nailed to the tree over his head his name with the charge of which he had been found guilty: "King of the Jews."

Now, I have written down this horrible thing in such great detail because I want to be sure you, who read this, or hear this read, understand completely the suffering Yeshua underwent, in his desire to take on the sins and the bad karma of the world, upon himself.

So, there he hanged upon the tree, wounded, the hot sun beating down upon his naked body, as onlookers gathered halfway down the hill (for none were allowed onto the hill itself, and indeed no one would have approached in any case) to be with him, as close as possible, in his suffering. The women wept on and off throughout the hours until their tears were spent and their voices hoarse. At some point Martha, Miriam, and Lazarus joined them, along with some other followers from Bethany, and together they prayed that the Lord might rescue him from the cross. Some members of the Sanhedrin came to observe for a time. Among them was Nicodemus, who was clearly upset that this thing had been allowed to happen.

Nicodemus came over to my grandmother and said, "Are you his mother?"

She nodded yes.

He said, "The entire Sanhedrin was not consulted after his capture. Only the twenty-three of the lesser Sanhedrin agreed to this."

She was confused.

He said, "The entire Sanhedrin of seventy-one, who meet in the Court of Hewn Stones in the Temple for those matters of great importance, did not agree to this. I wish you to know that had that whole court met, we, and surely not I, would have ever agreed to this atrocity."

And with that, he embraced Mary, and apologized, and said

he grieved and would pray for Yeshua, and he departed that place. So I write that Nicodemus was one of the righteous Pharisees.

Noon came, and passed, and Yeshua had been on the cross for three hours, suffering in silence—for to talk was to deprive oneself of air. There is a story that circulates that Yeshua had entire conversations with the two other men crucified with him, but that, of course, is also absurd. Only a person who has never witnessed a crucifixion could say such a thing. This assuredly never happened, else my grandmother would have said she saw them talking, and she never claimed any such thing.

Some tired of watching, giving up on the hope that an angel would come to rescue Yeshua and the End of Times would arrive, and they could no longer bear to watch him suffer.

More time passed. Then one of the Romans soaked a sponge in a liquid and lifted it on a reed of hyssop to Yeshua's lips so he could drink.

"Look," said someone in the crowd. "He thirsts."

What was given to him was very likely just the drink of the soldiers, called *posca*. It was made of sour wine, water, and eggs. Either this, or Yeshua finally accepted the vinegar and myrrh drink. Some refer to it as gall, for the myrrh is very bitter. In any case, the end was now approaching. It was almost three o'clock, at which time—since it was the day of the Passover—the crucified men would have to die and be taken down, for even the Romans knew not to leave a man, living or dead, on Golgotha during the Passover itself. It was enough deterrent to display the bodies beforehand; too much deterrent, and they might have a revolt on their hands for such a blasphemy on a Holy Day.

Then Yeshua cried out, *"Eli, Eli, lema sabachthani,"* which is Aramaic for, "My God, my God, why have you forsaken me?" He was, of course, quoting the twenty-second of the Psalms. And it was as if the Lord heard his cry, for my grandmother says he appeared to die shortly after this. From the distance they could not tell. But to the women it seemed he had, so they wept with a great wailing and lamentation. Martha cried out, "Where is God, that He did not save him?"

Also, and you may say it was a coincidence, because this land does shake often, but it was only a few minutes after this that the ground shook in all Jerusalem. This is a fact, and many took it as a sign from God. Of course, now this fact has taken on the proportions of the drama in a Greek play in one of the amphitheatres, and people say the veil covering the Holy of Holies in the Temple was rent in half or that the homes of the Sanhedrin were toppled over, and all such other things. It was a shake strong enough for us to feel in the house of Eleazar, though, for I remember being afraid.

At three, it was finally time to end the ghastly display on the hill. The centurion gave the soldiers the order to break the legs of the other two men since they still lived. Since Yeshua appeared dead, one lifted his spear to jab him in the side to ensure he was dead. Yeshua did not move, and the wound oozed only a little blood and water: so I write this down again: he was dead.

No one appeared to claim the bodies of the other two, so these men were quickly taken down and dragged off to be buried in a pit. But now Joseph of Arimathea appeared, with a few helpers who bore fresh linen and water and pitchers for washing. He called to him the centurion, saying he held a note from Pilate. The centurion came down, read it, then went back up and ordered the soldiers to take Yeshua down from the cross. At this point, the crowds had begun to disperse, for it was past time to be ready for the Passover. The soldiers came and dropped Yeshua's body at Joseph's feet, then the Romans departed the place. Joseph called to the women to come assist; they did so, asking how he had secured permission for the body, for my grandmother had been willing to claim it, although it would be impossible to get Yeshua to the family tomb before the Passover. She had been beginning to think she would have to ask the

Romans to bury him also in the pit.

"Pilate," Joseph said. "That man would sell his own mother for money. He wanted an entire talent." And that was all he said on the matter. "Now follow me. We must act in haste."

Therefore it became clear to them that all had been arranged, and Joseph's helpers carried the body while the women took the linen and other things.

Joseph led them to a freshly hewn tomb that seemed to belong to him, even though it was nowhere near his own family tomb: it was near to Golgotha, in a garden. There they washed Yeshua's body (there was no time for anointing as was customary), and they wrapped him in a clean linen shroud. Then the men placed Yeshua into the tomb and rolled the stone in front of it.

"Now," said Joseph to Mary, "get you back to Eleazar's, and tell James where the body rests." He embraced my grandmother. "I grieve your loss. I promise you, we will get Yeshua to the tomb of your family." While doing this, he slipped a note into her hand, and he whispered in her ear, "Give this to James."

So, all departed to their own places, even breaking into a run, for the sun was almost down, and the sound of the women singing the hymn could be heard in the evening air, and it was time for the Passover to begin.

Oh, I should add this. There is also a most strange story; I do not know if it holds any truth or not. But it is said after Yeshua's body had been removed to the nearby tomb, just before the sun set, Caiaphas himself was seen at the olive tree Yeshua had hanged on, picking the ankle nail up from the ground and secreting it in his cloak. (The Romans usually keep the forearm nails to reuse since they do not bend when driven into the crossbeam, but the nails in the trees do bend and become unusable.) Why Caiaphas would want such a souvenir is inconceivable to me. However, it is true that the superstitious believe that crucifixion nails are a talisman that wards off evil spirits and brings good luck. If this story is true, then that wicked man is wicked three-thousandfold to me. Stepping onto that unholy place, he would have had to sit for many days in his own elaborate *mikveh,* and even then I doubt the sin and uncleanness could be washed from his soul.

I am sorry for my vicious words, but I am only a man, and at times I cannot help my own feelings. Therefore I resolve to pray, for the sake of Caiaphas' soul, that this story of the nail is not true. But I will also say that it would not surprise me if it were.

Chapter Twenty-One

Yeshua was dead. He had *died.*

What did it mean?

All were aggrieved. Even I can remember plucking at my mother's sleeve and being sent to sit with my brothers and be quiet. I remember my father and uncles, the disciples, Mary of Magdala, my grandmother, everybody, weeping. I had never seen men cry before. It was so startling and frightening that I cried and knew not even why I cried. I don't know when it finally dawned on my understanding that my uncle Yeshua had been murdered. I am not even sure I really understood then the meaning of death.

A great storm cloud of despair cracked open in the room and later, when it dissipated, settled into a silent gloom.

It was decided that all the women and the children should go to Martha's home, for there was not enough room for so many to hide in one place, and the disciples wished to discuss matters. For once Mary of Magdala was not offended by being not included. Of course, the question of traveling on the Passover was brought up. Two miles far exceeded what was allowed.

But Yeshua would heal, or harvest grain to eat, on the Sabbath, if it was good to do so, they reasoned; and saving the women and children in case of trouble and further arrests was a good thing; and so we departed the city well after dark to go back to Bethany.

So the rest has been told to me by my father and uncle.

The disciples were sore afraid, and hid, therefore, over the next few days, in Eleazar's house. No one dared venture out lest he be seized by the Temple guards or some other betrayer, turned over to the Romans and put to death as well. Eleazar's wife would leave to buy food in one place, come back, go back out, and buy food in another place so as not to arouse suspicion that her husband was hiding almost a dozen men.

Only Simon Peter finally ventured the question that others

kept to themselves. "Was Yeshua not, then, the Messiah?"

"Not now," my uncle James said, his voice sharp. Had Yeshua simply given up on the world, and in misery let the Romans have him? Or had he truly believed his mission was to die? James was later to say Yeshua said to him in Gethsemane that the world did not yet seem ready for the Son of Man. So if he was to die, he would indeed make the best of it, as written in the Prophets, carrying on his shoulders atonement for the sins and karma of whoever would believe in his word. And that his life and death were to be an example for the possibilities of human beings if only they would believe and have faith. He took heart from his beloved Isaiah, who had written of the suffering servant of the Lord, the lamb led to the slaughter, of which Miriam had spoken.

Passover ended, and the Sabbath ended. Of course, the Festival of the Unleavened Bread goes on for an entire week, but most treat only the first and last days of the feast as true Sabbaths. But those that eat the Paschal lamb must have it entirely consumed by the end of the festival.

Much later on, I was to find out that my father and uncle stole out of the house well after dark the night the second Sabbath ended (Saturday), James having been given the note from Joseph of Arimathea and having been told by my grandmother exactly where the tomb was. Joseph met them there with two men. They rolled back the stone. Then they removed the linen from Yeshua's body, for it was foul, and wrapped him in fresh linen for carrying on a pallet. They covered all with a blanket and carried him the distance to the family tomb, the men taking turns as they tired. Of course Yeshua could not be allowed to stay in that tomb! As I have written, there is no law that says you may not move a body after it has been interred, even though touching the dead makes one unclean. Ritual cleanliness they could attend to when it was safe to do so. And Yeshua belonged in the family tomb, to be gathered to the bones of his father, Joseph.

It is what Yeshua would have wished.

They planned to tell the disciples of Yeshua's final resting place later on, back when they were in Galilee and safe. For now, they had wanted to keep their moving him in secret, lest one or more of the disciples be captured and tortured and forced to reveal the location of the family tomb. For themselves, they were committed to die rather than say.

The unfortunate thing was not telling Mary of Magdala or the women that the body had been moved. But how could they have in any case, since she was two miles away in Bethany at Martha's house with the other women, and the disciples were in hiding? But perhaps it is not unfortunate. For Mary, in wishing to keep with custom and anoint the body with oils and spices (and also to say a private goodbye, I suspect) went early in the morning, three full days after the crucifixion, which was therefore the first day of the week, with my grandmother and my aunt Salome, to the tomb where they had seen Yeshua laid—and there they found not the body. Unfortunate, because that very fact has led to much misunderstanding—but fortunate because they were the first to see Yeshua.

Mary described it thus: "At the beginning, I did not realize it was our Master. And he bade me stay back and not touch him. He appeared in the shape of a man but also as a great light. He said to me, 'Seek me not here, Mary, for here you will not find me.'"

She saw no spirit. She saw no fully embodied man, of flesh. She saw light, light shaped like a man.

Yeshua said, "Go, tell the others I live. And tell them I will see them in Galilee."

The women did not wish to arouse suspicion, and since my grandmother and aunt Salome were known as family of Yeshua, they had hurried back to Bethany and sent Mary of Magdala to deliver the message to the disciples.

She walked up one street and down another, to be sure she was not followed, and then cut through an alley and went to Eleazar's, whose wife let her in, where she broke the news.

At first the disciples thought Mary had imagined some vision of Yeshua in her grief, but my uncle and father were not so sure.

Simon Peter fairly snarled at her. "Women! Always hysterical and sobbing and concocting tales."

"I am not! I am telling you what we saw."

"Then you have lost your mind."

"His mother and sister saw him too."

James, who had been quiet until then, said: "Wait!"

They all stopped arguing and looked at him.

"The sign of Jonah!"

They still did not understand.

"Remember when the Pharisees twice asked the Master for a sign, and the Master said the only sign he would give to all would be the sign of Jonah?"

"Yes, yes." This they remembered. Of course they did, for no one had understood it.

"Well," said James, "Jonah was in the belly of the great fish for three days, and reason states he should have been dead and turned into food for the fish. But then he was spat out, living, onto the land."

The disciples marveled. Could this miracle be true? Could Yeshua truly be alive? He was in the belly of the earth for three days and then was risen?

"Peter, John," said James. "Do you not remember when the Master appeared to us, as a great light, with Moses and Elias?"

The men were silent.

"He said to me to tell you to return to Galilee, and he would appear to you there," Mary said. She was at the door, fighting back tears from Peter's stinging words, and turned to look at James. "Thank you, for being willing to believe my words."

She was still upset.

When she left, James said to the disciples, "We will stay here a few more days. Then we will leave by night and go back to Capernaum. I say to you now, I will not eat until I see the Master with my own eyes."

"Good," said Simon Peter. "I mean that we are going home. I need to rest my mind. I need something resembling that which is normal after all of . . . all that has passed. I want to see my house, sleep in my bed, sleep with my wife and not in a tent or on the ground."

The other disciples were agreed.

"And I would like to go fishing," Simon Peter added.

* * *

Now, you may wonder why James did not tell them the body was moved. As I have said, one reason was that if someone was caught, James did not wish the location of the tomb to be tortured out of him. Then, as word of Yeshua's Resurrection began being known, the secret was kept because some believed Yeshua had in some way reanimated his own physical body, much as he had done with Lazarus, although Lazarus went on to die like any man later on. Had the location of the tomb been revealed, James and the family feared the Annas family or others would find it, and desecrate it, and go about Jerusalem waving Yeshua's bones and saying, "See? Here he is. He was not raised." And then the disciples wound up being accused of moving the body anyway. The less people knew the better. It was much less confusing this way. Bodily Resurrection or spiritual Resurrection: did the difference matter?

But I write this down now in order to make it not confusing, and to make the matter of the Resurrection clear. Again, the whereabouts of Yeshua's physical body did not, and does not, matter. It is irrelevant. Can you understand this? And therefore I believe it is all right to write down these things now, although I will not reveal the location of the tomb. His Resurrection was not, as I just said, as if Yeshua had resurrected his material, physical body as he had resurrected Lazarus and the others. It was more as if Yeshua wanted to show to us his soul body, that his soul still lived and he could still move among us and communicate with us. So he was not some phantom or spirit of the dead. He was more than that.

I think back to Yeshua's last initiation in Egypt, in the Great Pyramid. Was this the great mystery about death he had discovered? For he told us he had learned there that death did not exist. But we already knew this, believing in reincarnation. But souls merely slept in *Sheol* until they entered human form again. But Yeshua was dead and slept not, yet had not retaken human form. What was this, some version of Ezekiel's vision of the dry bones come to life again? But he was not flesh. That story circulating that Thomas *Didymus,* my own father, doubted Yeshua was real and touched his body, placing his hand even into the wound in his side, is of certainty not a fact. That is a story made up by those who wish to believe Yeshua resurrected his own dead body. But in truth, physical matter that is without life cannot just appear where it was not before, nor can it walk on a road, nor can it blind others with a brilliant light—yet Yeshua did all these things after his crucifixion.

I do not know. The Egyptian *Therapeutae* used to tell a story of a Pharaoh named Amenemet the First. He was not even of a royal bloodline. He called himself "the Son of Man" because he was a commoner, not a born Horus god. But he claimed to be the true Pharaoh by prophecy (lest you laugh, remember that Alexander the Great was declared Pharaoh in much the same way, by traveling to the Siwa Oasis, where the oracle proclaimed him the Son of Osiris). Amenemet's capitol was in the Fayuum, yes, near Lake Moeris, which Yeshua visited as a child. Remember? This was where he healed the animals. Although I doubt Yeshua heard this story then, as a child, he no doubt heard it again in Heliopolis. And the Egyptians speak of the *ka* and the *ba,* the physical body's double (the *ka*) and then the soul body (the *ba*). Perhaps after death, Yeshua was able to merge his *ka* and his *ba* and this is how he appeared to us.

He has not appeared to me, but I imagine him as being in the form of one of the archangels, a shining celestial being.

I will also write even this: Yeshua did not appear to even Paul of Tarsus as a human being. No! Even Paul said that he appeared as a great blinding light, so intense that he was temporarily blinded until a believer in Yeshua restored to him his sight. Even Paul said he saw a spiritual being, not a literal man.

But then some wish to argue that this was so only because Yeshua's physical body had by then ascended to heaven.

I ask you, does it matter? Why this bickering over spirit or flesh? The point is that Yeshua lives, and he found a way to prove it. He found a way to prove it, to show us there is no death, that there is a Kingdom of Heaven, or a higher plane beyond this material world to which we may ascend. People may talk of these things, and have spoken of these things in numerous religious traditions from time immemorial, but no one had ever proven it. Yeshua proved it. *This* is the miracle of the spiritual Resurrection!

Well, I have digressed as I usually do, and I think I am waxing indignant. So, let me return to the story.

After another two days, James, who had kept to his word and not eaten any food, although he would take water, decided to risk travel to Qumran to speak with the Council of Elders. He did not wish to travel alone, however, for he was weakening; so he sent Eleazar into Jerusalem to the home of the brother of my grandfather Joseph. This uncle's name was Cleophas, who was glad to be of service, for he had also been grieving the death of his nephew Yeshua.

At Qumran they spent the night, and James still would eat no food. The Elders were not very helpful, for there were no further prophecies on the matter. But as the next eldest son in the family, they confirmed that James should now lead Yeshua's flock.

On the return from Qumran, James and Cleophas intended to travel westerly, past Jerusalem, then take the road to Emmaus, for it was a good and fast road, one the Romans had repaired after destroying that city some decades before, and also safer to travel, for no one would be looking for them there. From there they planned to turn southeast and sneak back into Jerusalem. From there, the next day we all would then go on to Galilee as Mary of Magdala had directed. This was also what the Council had advised. It was on the road to Emmaus that Yeshua made his second appearance, completely by surprise.

As James and Cleophas walked, a stranger approached them from the opposite direction on the road and greeted them as he drew abreast. "Peace be with you," he said.

"And with you," they told him.

The stranger reached into a bag slung over his shoulder. He drew forth a loaf of bread. This he handed to James and said, "Eat, brother, for I am alive and would not have you hunger for my sake."

In an instant, they realized the stranger was Yeshua in a different form; but upon their recognition of him, his form changed and became that of the one described by Mary of Magdala: a human shape appearing as a great light. The two immediately fell to the ground in front of him.

"Stand," said Yeshua. "I am no one to fear or worship. Such belongs only to God."

They stood, and although James wanted to embrace his brother with joy, he could now plainly see why Mary of Magdala could not. The Light that was Yeshua's form gestured to the bread, so James broke it, and blessed the bread, and began to eat, for he was indeed famished and, as I said, had been becoming weak. He broke off another piece for Cleophas, who was also hungry from the journey.

Yeshua said, "I am not here for long. But the disciples of little faith may heed you since they don't heed Mary. Tell them to gather in Galilee on the bank of the sea where we sometimes took rest."

With that, Yeshua vanished.

The two men ran and walked, ran and walked, making haste to Eleazar's house, a distance of about seven miles, reentering the city well after dark, where James delivered the news with Cleophas as witness.

The disciples marveled at this thing, for now no fewer than five people had seen Yeshua. And yet they still doubted. I suppose I can understand why, for it is a hard thing to believe. Reason dictates that it is impossible, and it is also true that grieving persons have been known to insist a dead loved one is not dead until they return to their senses, as Peter had accused of Mary. Yet I have never seen Yeshua, but I believe. He does at times come to me in my sleep, and these dreams are most vivid and real. But in them he appears as himself, as I remember him, and not as a light. So have I seen him? I do not really know since these are but dreams.

Anyway, the next day, the disciples and the family began the trip back to Galilee, departing before the sun rose so they would not be seen leaving the city.

* * *

And now I will digress again, to write down more fully the story of Lazarus, as I promised I would. Again, my attempt is to draw a distinction between Yeshua's spiritual Resurrection and the physical Resurrection of Lazarus. This story occurred years later, when I was visiting my family in Jerusalem during an absence from Qumran, and Lazarus was there at the church, visiting from Bethany. I found myself alone with him at one point and could not contain my curiosity. So I asked if I might ask him a question.

He smiled and said, "I know what you are going to ask, because everyone asks it of me, sooner or later. You wish to know what happened when I died."

"Yes!" I said, and since I was sitting on the floor, I scooted closer to him so as to not miss a word.

"It is hard to explain," he said. "I was in a place which had no time. For me, it felt as if I were there only a few moments, but when I came back into my body, I was told I had been dead for almost three days."

He paused, thinking, then continued. "It was like no place. I saw nothing. I felt nothing with my senses. My body seemed as if I floated upon water, but there was no water. All around me I sensed things; beings, perhaps, but mostly I just felt a warm sensation of love. And then I heard a voice, only I did not hear it with my ears; it was more like a thought was pushed into my head. 'You must go back; the Lord requires you,' and then, of a sudden, I could feel my body and hear Yeshua's voice calling me forth."

At my expression, he laughed. "You can see why I was confused. I don't think I even realized at first that I had been dead, until I could see that I was lying in a tomb and I was covered with a shroud."

"How did my uncle Yeshua explain this place to you? Was this *Sheol*?"

"He said there are many places those who die can go. He compared death to Jacob's ladder, a place of many levels. But he said I was not dead long enough to have been given a level."

Lazarus was right; I still do not understand fully his description.

"But Yeshua comforted me, and he told me that feeling surrounded by love was a very good sign indeed, and that the Divine Being feels nothing but love for all of his creatures, and that we are given an infinite number of chances to perfect our souls."

I nodded.

"I will tell you one more thing," Lazarus said, "that I also tell everyone. Death is nothing to fear, my son. It is only the end of the physical body. *You* remain very much alive."

And so you see, Lazarus had experienced a death, but he was resuscitated. As I have said, he went on later to die like any person, and was buried. Yeshua, on the other hand, died but came back, able to interact with others here before he left us, but not in his body, and this is what makes his Resurrection all the more remarkable and miraculous. Who knows, he may still make more appearances. But he did not—and I stress the word "not"—reanimate his own dead physical body. That body was gone, in the tomb, as I have written, and a year later, when the family returned to move his bones into an ossuary and pay him reverence, and we cried tears for him, the bones were just that: bones. No flesh. His body had decayed like that of any other dead person. And neither did he appear as a spirit or a phantom.

I am sorry to go on about this so much, but I feel I must do so to be clear, for there are many stories going about, some begun by Paul, or at least by his followers who may have misunderstood him.

Now I hope my words will put this confusion to rest.

* * *

In Galilee, word had already reached Joses and my aunt Mary that their brother had been crucified, and both were distressed but happy indeed to see the family and the disciples. James told them of the Resurrection, and as you would expect, Joses was skeptical. It wasn't until after all the disciples had seen Yeshua that Joses finally believed, and James and Peter took him down to the Sea of Galilee to be baptized.

Yeshua had not said when he would appear, only where: at a place they knew outside Capernaum, where grew a few trees for shade and where the breezes sometimes came off the water and cooled them on a hot day. Since the morrow would be the Sabbath, James said they would gather there on Sunday, to see if Yeshua would come.

In the meantime, all were relieved to be back safely, and Andrew and Thaddeus went to see their father, whom Joses' wife, Anna, said was doing much better.

During the period of rest was when the subject of Judas Iscariot first came up, for Joses asked after him, and right before the disciples had departed, Eleazar told them Judas had been found hanging outside Jerusalem. Now, the disciples discussed Judas Iscariot's betrayal of Yeshua many times but could never settle on his reason for handing Yeshua over. The obvious reason is the purported silver he received, but this motive made no sense to James and my father, nor to the other disciples, all of who knew him very well. Or so they had thought. But Judas handled the disciples' and followers' money, which was all pooled together. It would have been easier, if he just wanted money, for Judas to have simply stolen the purse and disappeared.

My uncles argued the point endlessly. James was of the view that Judas lost faith and became disillusioned. Yeshua kept promising the Kingdom of Heaven but it never came. He remembered Judas saying that Yeshua's triumphant ride into Jerusalem on a donkey, with a mere few hundred or so people waving palm fronds and shouting "Hosannas" was not the spectacle he had anticipated for the Messiah. And that Yeshua's rebellion of tipping over tables and freeing animals in the Temple was about as effective as the time it had taken for the sellers to recapture the animals and the moneychangers to set the tables aright. It changed nothing; the very next day those at the Temple were back at it. So, Judas had simply turned on Yeshua, no longer believing him to be the Messiah. But it could not have been for the money, for Judas had left the disciples' treasury with the others—which is how we came to know of the thirty pieces of silver, for there they were, in the purse: thirty silver shekels minted in Tyre.

My father would concede all this but say he suspected more.

Judas had been becoming more Zealot-like in his views as the time for Passover neared. He had been looking forward to a final showdown that had not come. So, my father theorized, perhaps Judas had handed him over to force Yeshua's hand. If directly asked if he were the Messiah, Yeshua would not lie. My father posed that Judas' hope had been that the people, when seeing Yeshua being sent through the streets of Jerusalem to be crucified, would rise up and fight. Or perhaps he thought that the Son of Man would arrive in the clouds just in time to save Yeshua and usher in the Kingdom.

When the people did not rise up, and no angel came, and Yeshua died, Judas hanged himself in his horrible guilt over what he had done. Much later, we all heard that since his body was not discovered for some days, it was bloated and rotting when he was found; and, when he was cut down, his remains burst open upon hitting the ground. Perhaps Judas Iscariot decided to follow the Torah and pass sentence upon himself: "an eye for an eye; a tooth for a tooth." He took his own life for having made Yeshua's be taken. My father reasoned that if disillusionment were the cause, Judas would not have felt guilty. He would have seen Yeshua's death as proof he was not the Messiah and gone on his way.

I lean more towards my father's view, but he was, after all, my father, and I am partial. But I still wonder. Yeshua had known Judas would hand him over. We have always assumed he knew because he possessed the power to read others' intentions. But perhaps there is no mystery in it. Perhaps Yeshua and Judas together conspired. Towards the end Yeshua had repeatedly said he would have to die to usher in the Kingdom, a thing no one understood. How was he to rule if he were dead? Maybe Yeshua sent Judas to betray him. He did say to Judas, at the last supper, "Go, do what you must do." And when he greeted him in Gethsemane, he greeted Judas as "Friend," and told him he had done what he had he do. Perhaps the other disciples did not realize this was intentional; it had been planned, and Yeshua had chosen Judas for this mission. If this is so, then Judas Iscariot has been most falsely accused of betrayal. He had simply done his Master's wishes.

Why, then, would Judas kill himself? Because the others would never understand or believe him and would call him Betrayer, and being blamed for the death of Yeshua was perhaps a thought too heavy for him to bear. He could not have known that Yeshua's spirit was to rise from death, so all that died was his human body.

I have prayed and fasted for the soul of Judas. In my heart, I have forgiven him, for my stomach tells me this would be Yeshua's wish. It is difficult to forget, however, as it should not be forgotten. There are many lessons to be learned from Judas Iscariot. Among forgiveness, these lessons are about faith and about never imposing your will upon another. But, we shall never know the motives of Judas Iscariot. Like him, we are but men and can only guess, until we reach the Kingdom and are finally able to discover the truth.

* * *

On Sunday morning, the disciples gathered at the place outside Capernaum and sat to wait for Yeshua. They had brought food with them, for they did not know if he would appear to them that day, or how long they would have to wait. But, my father said, all that was unnecessary, for it was as if he were watching them. Once they had all settled into places on the ground, some sitting, some reclining, Matthew even sprawled upon his back, Yeshua appeared to them.

He was as a great Light shaped in human form. My father said there is no other way to describe it. He said you could say his head was like unto a tight ball of lightning bolts, but that does not express it, for it sounds frightening. You could say his body was like he wore snow-white raiment, but that does not express it, for he was of a substance, yet was not of a substance. "Light" described him best.

Yeshua greeted them and said he could not stay long but he had instructions for them before he departed from this world. He also bade them to sit up, and to listen carefully to his words, and to not prostrate themselves upon the ground.

Simon Peter was the last to raise his head, and this was only at the prodding of his own brother Andrew, for Peter trembled.

Yeshua told them, "You must go out into the world and make disciples of all nations, baptizing them into new life, teaching them to obey everything that I have taught you."

James asked, "Is the Kingdom not to come, then?"

"It will, but as I have told you, the time is only for God to know. Therefore, act always in love and follow the Way of compassion; then the closer the Kingdom reaches to the individual, for the Kingdom is the purest Love of the Lord. If humankind has the wisdom to transform itself as a whole, then yes, the Kingdom will come even to this earth, and the Lord will again walk among you, as it was at the beginning.

"But if humankind hears not this message, and rejects it, and continues on its present path of acting from the willful heart, committing acts of self-destruction, being attached to material things, forming empires, lording it over others, enslaving them, desecrating Nature instead of acting as its steward, and committing other acts done in the absence of love, the path leads in another direction.

"God has said he will never again destroy the earth by flood; the next path prophesied by Daniel is that of fire, so expect an end to come by fire; and it will not be so much God bringing the fire as humankind setting the fire upon itself.

"So it is up to you, to bring the Word and the Way of the right path to all nations, so that humankind may learn to act always in love for one another and thereby avoid the destruction of the earth."

Simon Peter asked, "If the world is destroyed by fire, what happens to those who have acted in righteousness?"

"The righteous are always welcome in the Kingdom, and God sets them where they belong, according to the nature and number of their good works, and by how much more their hearts need to be purified. In this you must have faith.

"For indeed, I tell you, in the end, even the unrighteous do not die; they do not perish in everlasting flames, although it will seem so to them, for they never remember from one life to the next; they continue to live in the hells they create for themselves, trapped in their lower natures, until they do learn, in the many worlds of God's creation. So seek you always justice in this life; and the tempered reason of philosophers; and act without wrath; and call upon the Lord for assistance and guidance; follow the wisdom of your own hearts, which is that of your higher nature, and let love be the guiding principle of your lives. You will suffer on account of me; fear not, for your suffering is short and you will enter into the Kingdom. I tell you all, you must be even better than I am.

"And such has it always been, and such will it always be, for the Lord is infinite, and indeed the Lord your God never stops creating."

"Lord," said John the Beloved. "You must explain these things to us. I do not understand."

"I must depart," Yeshua said. "But where you are, you are to go to James the Just, for whom heaven and earth came into existence. Know also to look within, for the *ruach hakodesh,* or Holy Breath, the wisdom of the Living God. But remember also, I am with you always, to the end of the age."

The Light that was Yeshua dimmed and then vanished.

The disciples were left marveling over this thing, wondering over his words. There would be a destruction but not a destruction? Two paths for the world? Those who did evil would not burn in everlasting hell fire? If the world did end, where would the Kingdom be?

They found themselves debating. "The good to heaven, the evil to another world? Of yet more evil?" posed Thaddeus.

"There can't be more than one world," said Matthew, doubt in his voice.

Simon Peter said, "There is heaven, and the earth, and hell. At the End of Times, I thought heaven returned to the earth, where all the righteous would be, and this earth would be the Kingdom of God. And the wicked go to hell for everlasting damnation."

"The Master was telling us it is not that," said James.

"Then what is it?" Bartholomew asked.

James found himself laughing, and then my father joined in, then Mary, and before long all laughed together.

"It is a mystery!" James said.

"How like him, to leave us in the dark," said Nathanael, and they all returned to laughing again.

Finally they sobered, for they realized they had been sorely anxious for over a week, and then glad to see Yeshua, and glad that he was not dead, and glad that he was and would ever be their Lord and the Messiah—no matter what other people might say.

Mary of Magdala ventured, "I have an inkling of what the Lord meant."

"Tell us," said Simon Peter. And he must have felt bad over not believing her at the beginning, after she saw Yeshua at the empty tomb, for he added, "For it is true the Master loved you more than all other women."

"Heaven is a realm of ascended souls. We each may ascend of our own accord and virtue, if we but follow our higher natures. If enough of us do this on earth, then this world itself becomes like unto heaven. This is the first path."

"Go on," urged her brother, Philip.

"If enough of us do not, then the world follows the second

path, one in which we destroy ourselves. But either way, the righteous are always saved."

"So the first path is the Way of Yeshua," said James.

"Yes," said Mary.

Andrew was shaking his head. "Say what you will," he said to all, "but these teachings are strange ideas."

Simon Peter agreed with his brother. "Would the Savior reveal these things to her, a woman, and not to us? Are we to turn around and listen to her? Did he choose her over us?"

So much for Peter and his good intentions. His words stung, so Mary began to weep.

Matthew came to her defense. "Peter, you have always been a wrathful person. Now I see you contending against the woman like our adversaries. If Yeshua found her worthy, who are you then for your part to reject her?"

Philip agreed, and then James spoke.

"Brothers! It serves us not to squabble with one another. What Mary has said is like unto what Yeshua said and is a reasonable interpretation. We must all think upon his words."

"And he made James the leader of us, Peter, not Mary," my father pointed out. "It is not as if she was commanding you to believe her, like one of the Pharisees with their contorted versions of the Law."

James got to his feet. "Let us return to Peter's house. We will discuss these things. After a time, we will return to Jerusalem, and we shall establish our Church."

Hey: The Early Church

Chapter Twenty-Two

Therefore, following the words of Yeshua, James was made head, or Bishop, of the new Jerusalem Church, and he wore the very same *tzitzit* that Yeshua wore, and he began also wearing a white garment as had Yeshua. He set Simon Peter on his right hand and John the Beloved on his left, for these three were the witnesses to Yeshua's transfiguration. The remaining eight disciples became apostles, and the logical person to replace Judas Iscariot was Mary of Magdala, since she, better than anyone else, met the requirement of having been witness to Yeshua and with him the entire time. Even Simon Peter could not argue against this, so he did not make the attempt, and I think by now even his heart had softened towards her after Matthew's chastising of him. The task of the nine apostles was to leave Jerusalem as Yeshua had instructed and to go carry the Word and the message of the Way far and wide into all the world, even unto the Gentiles. James, Simon Peter, and John stayed in Jerusalem.

The original expectation had been that, as Yeshua had indicated when he had been alive on earth and preached, that the Kingdom of Heaven would arrive soon; no one, however, but God knew the exact time, as Yeshua had also said. So the followers were to preach to the Jews and to the Gentiles, and to show by example their righteousness through good works. We expected that, when Yeshua returned to establish the Kingdom, he (and perhaps a reincarnated John the Baptizer as well) would be the Messiahs of the Temple—yes, a new Temple of the Kingdom, which perhaps is what Yeshua had meant when he said the present Temple would be thrown down, and that even the Gentiles would flock to be a part of us, accepting the One God as no longer the God of only the Hebrews, but the God of All Humankind. It would be a time of peace and blessing, glory and joy, for the righteous for all eternity.

And was this not, after all, much the same vision as that of Pharaoh Akhenaton, who conceived of the sun disk as not just the god of Egypt, but God over All? In his famous Hymn to the Aten, he praised his one god as the God of all nations, shining His life-living light over all. Indeed, the words of that hymn sound so like unto our own Hebrew Psalm, the 104th, that the Essenes have always surmised this Psalm was inspired by Akhenaton's hymn.

Hence, the apostles departed, all going in different directions to spread the Word and the Way. Here is a summation of their doings:

Mary of Magdala and her brother Philip traveled to that faraway Roman territory known as Gaul. There Philip remained almost until the end of his days, choosing to stay and minister to those he had converted, even though he was given permission to return. Of his death I know nothing, but I have heard that he traveled to Turkey and died in that country. Mary returned to Jerusalem in old age, well before the destruction of the Temple. There, on Mount Zion, living with my family, she died peacefully. Since she had never married and had no family tomb, as I mentioned at the beginning of this narrative, it seemed good to us to lay Mary into our own tomb because she had been one of the apostles, after all, and much beloved to Yeshua. We left a small bottle of our tears next to her body. After a year, we returned and placed her bones into an ossuary and prayed for her and remembered. Afterwards, on impulse, I scratched onto the side of her ossuary: "Mariamene." This means: "Mary the Master." I am pleased that I did this thing. It made my heart in its grief feel better, for aside from my grandmother, I do believe Mary was the holiest woman I have ever met, yes—and I will say even this—and I hope Rachel forgives me for writing it—holier than even my own dear wife. Holier than I, of certainty.

Of course, knowing how the stories are already retold, and changed, and the many false accusations that have been made, and were made even when Yeshua lived on this earth, Mary of Magdala will no doubt be turned like my grandmother, Mary, into a harlot; or my grandmother will be turned into a virgin, despite having birthed seven children. How foolish is humankind; how foolishly we view women. They are either whores or virgins, when the truth is that most are neither.

James (Thaddeus), son of Zebedee, traveled to Iberia, which some call Hispania, and founded a church. He then returned to Judea from across the Great Sea and became the first of the martyrs among the twelve disciples. Agrippa, the new king who had been friend of the Emperor Caligula, had him put to death by the sword. Agrippa saw that this act pleased many of our Hebrew brethren, so he determined to do the same to Simon Peter, but Peter was saved by a miracle—a story that I shall write down later in this narrative. It is said that when the executioner witnessed James's courage and refusal to recant, he was convinced of Yeshua's Resurrection and was executed along with James. That seems a little far-fetched to me, but it does make for a good tale. I am sure Thaddeus sits with Yeshua in heaven.

My father, Jude (Thomas *Didymus*), and Bartholomew traveled to India. The territory was so large that the two departed each other and set off in different directions. There my father founded many churches and converted many souls. Each year he sent a letter to James, describing his many deeds. Every seven years he returned to visit the family, but he did also come back when my mother transitioned. James never changed my father's territory because it was so large; he even sent extra deacons with my father on two occasions. But my father met his end either by assassination or accident. It is said that a man was hunting and heard a rustle in the brush and threw his spear at the sound. The rustling noise turned out to be the footsteps of my father, as he was out for a walk along a small garden path, for he liked to think upon things while walking. This could very well be true. His bones remain in India, which is a matter of grief to me. However, my uncle Simon does have in his possession several letters that my father wrote. One in particular is of great interest, for he speaks of following the Way intended by Yeshua; and this was no doubt written in response to a letter from my uncle James telling him of the happenings in Jerusalem and the quarrels with Paul, who was called at Qumran another "wicked priest." But more on that later. We also, of course, have the scroll of Yeshua's sayings that my father wrote down.

Bartholomew's end came much more quickly. It is said he had traveled north, and it is possible he traveled even out of India. Because Bartholomew could not write, and therefore send letters, little is known. The story is that Bartholomew converted the brother of a prince, and the two together destroyed the idols of the gods in the town they were in. The prince was outraged and demanded that Bartholomew be brought to him, where he was scourged and then beheaded. May the Lord bless the soul of Bartholomew, the Jew who had been a former Roman slave.

Matthew traveled first to Parthia, where members of the Great Brotherhood greeted him with joy but wept bitterly over news of the death of Yeshua. Balthazar, of course, was no longer living, but the people of that land, as I have written, had long known of the prophecy of the Hebrew Messiah. The Parthians were a tolerant people and received the message of Yeshua with the openness that I would expect, although I do not think I can say they converted. To them, Yeshua was a great prophet whose teachings mingled well with their own teachings. Thus Matthew did not need to tarry in Parthia for long. On his way back to Jerusalem, he founded a church at Edessa, where there were already some Hebrews living, and he converted some of these.

Matthew was then sent by James to Ethiopia. There resided many Jews, dating from the time of Solomon and the Queen of Sheba. Most of these, however, resisted the Way and rejected Matthew. Still he founded a small church at Nadabah. But his proselytizing was viewed as an annoyance and eventually that city's ruler tired of him. It is said he was arrested and beheaded with a halberd. Of certainty Matthew has his place in the Kingdom of Heaven.

Andrew traveled to Greece and established a church in Patrae. For a time he sent letters, and then there was a period of silence. Finally word came to Simon, my uncle (my uncle James had been martyred the year prior) that the Emperor Nero had ordered Andrew crucified. It is said Andrew did not die quickly and hanged on the cross alive for more than a day and a night. Afterwards, no one was allowed to take down his body. More than this is unknown. Bless you, Andrew, for I know you are in the Kingdom.

Nathanael traveled to Phrygia in Anatolia, or Turkey, in the Roman Empire just east of the Mediterranean, to evangelize to the Jews and Gentiles of that land. He founded several churches, but the largest community was in Ephesus. However, the Jews of that land, finding him blasphemous, stoned him to death. Later on, John the Beloved was to travel to that land and continue the work of Nathanael, as did Paul. More on John and Paul will come as the narrative continues, but I wish to make clear that it was Nathanael who first brought the Word to that land. May God bless the soul of the humble Nathanael, our brother born of Nubian parents.

Finally, Simon the Zealot traveled to Egypt, Cyrene, and Libya. Because, like Bartholomew, he was unable to write or send letters unless he could find someone to translate Aramaic, not much is known of his travels, and nothing but rumor is known of his death. One story says he was sawed in half in Persia, but I doubt the veracity of this since Simon was in Africa, and no one in my family knows of his leaving that land. Another story says that he was martyred in Syria—but again, surely he would have stopped in Jerusalem before traveling there. So I am doubtful of this story as well. Perhaps Simon is another of the original twelve (the others would be John the Beloved, Philip, and Peter when he returned from Rome) who escaped martyrdom. As a former Sicarii, surely Simon could defend himself; would he have done so is the question I put to you. Regardless, the fruits of Simon's labor can be seen in the growing churches of Alexandria and Cyrene.

Again I say, may the Lord bless these ten departed souls, for they traveled far and wide as Yeshua had commissioned them to do; and they planted many seeds hither and thither, most of which appear to be growing and flourishing. May these seeds continue to grow, and may the persecutions of the Romans come to an end. The Kingdom of God? We still await.

Now I return the story to the early Jerusalem Church. After sending out the apostles, my uncle James also selected seventy to be deacons of the Church, which meant that they were blessed and received the Holy Spirit; for indeed the first time the apostles, before being sent out, met in the house of Eleazar, which became the first house-church, the Holy Spirit descended upon them when they took of the bread and wine in remembrance of Yeshua. There is, I must say, great joy upon being awakened to the True Reality. When one realizes there is no death and that we all return to God, and that the sufferings of this world are all brought about simply because of the selfish actions of mankind, the perspective restores balance to the soul. Worries fall away, and the experience of oneness with all things is intoxicating.

Alas, all too quickly, the cares of the days pile up and snatch away the feeling. But it returns, after meditation and prayer.

Now, some deacons stayed in Jerusalem while others traveled and preached much in the way of the apostles. Many did healings, and all of them ministered to the poor. The total number of Followers of the Way numbered, in Jerusalem alone, about two hundred, at the beginning. The names of the seventy deacons are too numerous to write down here, but some of the more famous deacons over the years of whom you may have heard were called Philip, who converted the Ethiopian eunuch and brought the word to the Samaritans; Stephan; Nicanor; Nicolaus of Antioch; Martha, Miriam, and Lazarus, whom as you know were friends of Yeshua; Barnabas, whom I have also written of before and who traveled both alone and for a time with Paul, until he returned, disgusted with that man; Sarah; Tabitha, whom Simon Peter raised from the dead; Zacchaeus; Clement of Rome; Mark, son of Simon Peter; Leah; Symeon, our cousin, the son of Cleophas—oh, this listing is fruitless, as there are too many worthy souls to name. For a time the seventy were kept as seventy in the land of Israel, as those among them who left were replaced by others, but eventually James dropped the restriction of seventy because the Church grew so far and wide; and James made anyone, in any land, who served a leadership role in a community of Yeshua followers, into a deacon, or missionary: one whose mission is to minister and serve.

As the Church continues to grow, however, it is my uncle Simon's thinking that we may need, at some time, if the Church survives and if the Day of the Lord has not yet arrived, to establish a further hierarchy of Bishops in each major city; with deacons beneath; then followers; but the Jerusalem Church and its leader, the Bishop of Bishops, remains the Mother Church. This is not so much to establish an order like that among hens that cluck and peck and squabble over which is to eat the choicest morsels first; no, those who lead are considered no better or holier than any other, but it is solely to establish a means of resolving disputes—which, as, you will see, became necessary with Paul.

To make the original full twenty and one hundred of the inner circle, counted also were, of course, Yeshua's mother and his extended family (including my uncle Joses since the Resurrection of Yeshua had finally convinced him his brother was truly the Messiah, as I have said; and also the families of Yeshua's two sisters, my aunts, Mary and Salome); the families of the disciples;

and those among the Essenes who accepted Yeshua as Messiah. The community at Qumran was largely with us, although some wished more aggressive measures to be taken (predictably, those Brethren who still held on to the belief in an apocalyptic End of Days, when the Sons of Light would be called upon to battle for the Lord). All of the twenty and one hundred were given the authority to preach in Yeshua's name. As a member of the twenty and one hundred, I also have this authority. So aside from Yeshua himself telling me that I would one day write down his story, I also have direct authorization from the Church to do so.

And thus was the organization of the early Church. Those who converted—Jew or Gentile—were simply called "Followers of the Way" or "Followers of Yeshua." Some referred to us also as Nazirites, which is incorrect; the Nazirites are those Jews who were like Samson, of the Scriptures; or Nazoraenes, or even Nazrenes. And in the Galilee, where the people remembered his miracles and his teachings, many indeed still loved Yeshua and lived in accordance with his teachings, believing in his name. However, as more pagan Gentiles and Gentile God-fearers (these were Gentiles who did not convert to Judaism but who loved the Hebrew God and worshiped him, and then who also came to love the Prophet Yeshua) joined the Church, and as the theology of the self-appointed apostle Paul took root, more and more the Jewish laws outside Palestine have fallen to the wayside, for in truth the Gentiles outnumber the Jews. Those of us followers of the Way who have remained Jews are now called the Ebionites, or the "poor men," for we keep only what we need and give the rest to those who are genuinely poor. We are mostly vegetarian and we did not make animal sacrifices in the Temple before its destruction. Other than that, we have continued the circumcision of male children, follow the dietary laws; and those in Jerusalem worshiped in the Temple in addition to attending the Church. And let me say this—the poor, the sick, the maimed, the blind: all were, and are, welcomed into the Church. And often the deacons of Jerusalem would leave the city and minister to the poor in the countryside.

And now to begin setting down what occurred in Jerusalem prior to the destruction of the second Temple, for there were quarrels and disagreements, as I have hinted at, and there are some untrue stories that grow as abundantly as one of Yeshua's mustard seeds, and these are often used against us. I will give one example. Those who converted and who wished to sell all their property and give it to the Church and join the Jerusalem community of followers did so. Modeled after the Essene community at Qumran, the Church pooled all this money and everyone was given from it what they needed. But unlike the Qumran community, it was not a rule to sell all and give it to the Church if one wished to be a follower of Yeshua. Many donated in the same way as tithes were given to the Temple. These were mostly the people who did not live in or near Jerusalem and did not wish to leave their homes. But there is a story about a man named Ananias and his wife, Sapphira, who told Simon Peter they would sell a piece of property and give the proceeds to him. Upon selling it, they decided instead to keep some of the money for themselves and gave the rest to Peter. The story goes that Peter was enraged, and chastised them, and that the Lord struck both of them dead.

That is a cruel lie! Simon Peter was certainly angry with them, for they had told him an untruth, but by now even you should know that such a thing would have made Peter angry. But that was the end of it. Simon Peter merely reminded them of what Yeshua had said: "Let your yes be yes and your no be no." Had they said at the beginning that they would sell their property and give only a certain amount of the proceeds to the Church, Peter would have accepted this generosity and been grateful.

So the story of Simon Peter's anger over a lie grew into God being angry, and then this grew into God smiting the couple down. I assure you, Ananias and Sapphira walked away from

Peter that day in full health. But the Gentiles and some of our own Hebrew brothers told this story to give the impression that Yeshua's followers' Church wanted only money, and that the Church tried to frighten people into giving all their money and property lest God strike them dead. They called us charlatans and thieves, from the very beginning.

Now, as head of the Church, my uncle James was in charge of organizing, and delegating, and occasionally traveling within Judea and the Galilee, and a little later even to Samaria, to visit the house-churches of followers of the Way. Therefore his right and left hands, Simon Peter and John, were originally the most vocal and visual presence in Jerusalem. For this reason, some think that Peter actually led the Church, for he was the loudest. And they say that James then replaced Peter when Peter departed Jerusalem for Rome. This is not so. If you have heard any of this man Paul's letters read aloud in a church, for I am hoping my narrative may reach the Gentiles who have been led astray by him, then you know he always lists James before Peter and any other Elders, so there is your proof. Also, to this day, some criticize James, saying he hid himself while Peter and John suffered the persecutions of the Sadducees. I ask you, what general stands at the front of the infantry to be taken by an arrow or cut down with a sword? Besides, when Simon Peter decided he wanted to leave Jerusalem and travel to Rome and other cities as an apostle, even though James appointed a new man to take his place, by then the organization and rituals of the Church had been well established. Then James often went into the streets and into the Temple to preach and to heal and to minister to the poor, just as the others. And for this, he, too, was made a martyr. Therefore my heart aches with grief every time I hear this just man—James—called a coward. And let me tell you, his death enraged many people, for he was a righteous Jew: the Sicarii, the various Zealot groups, the followers of the Way, the Qumran community, and even the righteous among the Pharisees—those who were not friends of the Herodians—were all so furious about this thing that complaints were made to the new Roman governor when he arrived. Indeed, one could say with fairness that the Sadducees of the Temple sealed their own fate when they killed James.

The church itself was in the Lower City on Mount Zion, not far from the Pool of Siloam, in what had been Eleazar's home, for he had donated it. Here, my grandmother lived until she transitioned to the next world; and here lived James and his wife Joanna, and Simon Peter with his wife, son Mark, and mother-in-law, until she went to sleep; and John. My brothers and I and my cousin Mattias were also there whenever we were not at the Essene school in Ein Kerem, or, later, at Qumran. And, of course, Eleazar stayed there with his wife until he died. We actually lived downstairs, in rooms off the courtyard, except for James and his wife, who took the small, drafty room upstairs since it could be very cold at night. The other room upstairs was the church itself, or the meeting room, for here was where Yeshua had the Last Supper with the disciples the night he was handed over.

And Yeshua had been quite right about persecution, and betrayals, and false witnesses and the suffering that would be done in his name. The first of all the martyrs was the deacon Stephan or Stephanos. Stephan was a Greek-speaking Jew with a gentle nature and an angelic countenance. He was one of seven deacons specifically appointed to serve the other Greek-speaking Jews, mostly the widows, who had been converted early to the Way. But he was said to have been full of the Holy Spirit, and also performed wonders and miracles and was so articulate in debate that the non-Aramaic speaking Jews of other synagogues, mostly those of the synagogues of the Libertines (or freed, non-enslaved Jews of other lands such as Italia, Egypt, and Syria) always lost to him whenever they challenged him on his beliefs about Yeshua. I never personally met Stephan because I was away at school when these events occurred, but I was told by my family that Stephan was no blasphemer. He had been born a Jew and had remained, like all of us, a Jew. So the manner of his death is rather remarkable.

These Libertine Jews visiting Jerusalem were so humiliated by his besting them in all dialogues that they plotted against him. They chose men among themselves, and paid a few others of the city unaffiliated with them, to bear false witness against Stephan to the High Priest, who was still Caiaphas, and the Sanhedrin. They accused him of blaspheming against Moses, the Law, and the Temple. So the Temple guards were sent to seize him, and they dragged him to be heard in front of the Sanhedrin, his accusers following along or already being gathered there.

It is said that, in defending himself, Stephan gave a long speech in which he laid out a history of the Hebrew people, starting with Abraham, proceeding to Joseph in Egypt, then to Moses, and so on, then to some of the great, later prophets. He pointed out that, all throughout Jewish history, some prophets had been persecuted by his own people, or at the very least, were not always believed or heeded. And that moreover, the fact that God moved about the lands with all the patriarchs was proof in itself that God was not confined to the Holy of Holies in the Temple. He also quoted Yeshua: "I desire mercy, not sacrifice."

He declared that Yeshua's presence on this earth had been prophesied in Scripture, yet still those prophecies went unheeded by them, and that indeed some of the people in front of him were those very same who had persecuted and killed Yeshua, the greatest of the prophets and the adopted Son of God. When he had finished his speech, his exact words are said to have been thus:

"You stiff-necked people, uncircumcised in heart and ears, you are forever opposing the Holy Breath, just as your ancestors used to do. You stood by as John the Baptist foretold the coming of the Righteous One, and did nothing when Herod killed him, and now you have become the betrayers and murderers of

Yeshua. You are the ones that received the Law as ordained by angels, and yet you have not kept it."

Now this is nothing but the truth, and I say this as a Jew! But, of course, the Sanhedrin did not like this at all, and became enraged. Some spat at Stephan's feet. But Stephan was full of the Holy Spirit after saying these things, and he looked up towards heaven and saw the glory of God and the heavenly host. "Look," he cried out in his ecstasy. "I see the heavens opened and the Son of Man standing at the right hand of God!"

This was blasphemy of a most serious nature to the Sanhedrin, for to them Stephan had just equated Yeshua, who had been executed not that long previously, with God himself; but "Son of Man" could have meant an angel and not Yeshua. Or even if it was, to set Yeshua at God's right hand is not to say Yeshua is God. Indeed, they did not understand the power of the Holy Spirit at all, and how, so often, it is impossible to articulate what one sees or hears. No, the Elders covered their ears so as to not listen to these things Stephan said, and Caiaphas rent his garment and wailed.

They then seized Stephan in their outrage, and they dragged him out of the Temple, outside the eastern gate, threw him into a pit for the proper elevation, and began to stone him without even administering to him the drug given to make him senseless, as was the custom. And this was also an illegal action in the eyes of the Romans; for under their rule, only they were to put people to death, as I have said previously. (And, indeed, for this crime, the Romans removed Caiaphas as High Priest and replaced him with yet another of the Annas family, Jonathan—who is not to be confused with the Jonathan who was slain by the Sicarii, for this was much later.) Others joined in with the stoning of Stephan, taking off their cloaks and laying them at the feet of a witness, a man named Saul. Pelted with stones, Stephan could only stand there and pray. "Lord Yeshua," he said, "receive my spirit." A heavy stone hit his head, and he fell to the ground, a shower of stones now being hurled at him. His last words were, "Lord, do not hold this sin against them."

Truly, Stephan was a man who well understood Yeshua's teachings.

There were also the persecutions of Simon Peter and John the Beloved, and I know not by what miracle they were not stoned to death either, so thirsty for blood were the Sadducees and the Romans in those days. For some time, as I have already written, the penalties for death as given in the Torah had been viewed merely as indicative of the severity of the sin, but rarely the punishment given was actually death. A Sanhedrin that gave a penalty of death more than once every handful of years was considered to be a destructive one, and the people would demand new appointments. Otherwise, and I tell you the truth, half of Israel would have been already dead, and not by the hands of the Romans, for who does not sin?

But back to John and Peter. The first incident took place before the stoning of Stephan. This started in the Temple, at Solomon's Portico in the court. There stood Peter and John, preaching the Way of Yeshua. And many of the people respected them, bringing them their sick to be healed (not in the Temple itself, but whenever they left the Temple. It is said that some even lined the street outside the Temple, along the way they would come, with their sick lying on mats, in the hope that Peter's shadow would fall on them as he passed by, and they would be healed. I think this might be a legend, but who am I to say? Yeshua proved to us the Holy Spirit, when working within a person, can do much. And there is faith, always faith).

The priests finally must have complained, because one day the High Priest came to them with others of the Sadducees and the Temple Guard. They arrested Peter and John and had them thrown, oddly, into the public prison where are put the debtors, their trial to be held the next day. Perhaps the High Priest, whom as I wrote was still Caiaphas at this time, did not wish the two to be seen being dragged to his house: that is how popular they were. Now, the story is that at night, an angel of the Lord came and freed the two from the prison, and told them to go back to teaching the Way in the Temple. Again, this is possible, for an angel really was to save Peter's life later, but I think it may be more likely that a prison guard was a follower of Yeshua, for there were many followers in secret, including even four among the Temple Guard, and some two or three among the Romans, and the guard simply let them out. Peter and John made up the story of the angel to protect the guard. The other was likely sleeping.

Oh, I can picture Simon Peter now, full of bluster and roaring with mischievous laughter, as he and John returned at daybreak to the Temple and began preaching again when they were supposed to be shut up in the prison.

The Sanhedrin was gathering together in the Hall of Hewn Stones, and the High Priest told the Temple guard to bring to them the accused. But when the guard went to the prison, naturally they did not find the two apostles there. They reported they had found the prison locked and guards at their posts at the doors, but when they entered, Peter and John were gone. The captain of the Temple Guard was angry and said this was not possible, but just then another elder entering announced, "Look, the men whom you put in prison are standing in the Temple and teaching the people!"

So the captain went himself, with a few men, and took away Peter and John, but not with any violence because it was clear the people listening supported them.

When they stood before the council, the High Priest asked them, "Did we not give you strict orders not to teach in the name of this criminal Yeshua? But here you have filled Jerusalem with your teaching, and you are determined to bring this man's blood on us. It is the Romans who hanged him on a tree."

Peter said, "We must obey God rather than any human

authority. The God of our ancestors raised up Yeshua, and this council conspired with the Romans to have him put to death. God exalted him as Leader and Savior that he might give repentance to Israel and restore the Kingdom of God. And we are witnesses to these things, and so is the Holy Spirit whom God has given to those who obey him."

They liked this not and indeed were threatening to stone them when one Pharisee got to his feet. His name was called Gamaliel, and he was among them a respected teacher of the Law. "Take these men out and let me address my brethren," he said, and so the guards took John and Peter outside the hall.

Gamaliel reasoned with the council. "Fellow Israelites," he said, "consider carefully what you propose to do to these men. For, some time ago, Theudas rose up, claiming to be somebody, and a number of men, about four hundred, joined him; but he was killed, and all who followed him were dispersed and disappeared. After him came Judas the Galilean, who rose up at the time of Caesar's census almost thirty years ago, and he got people to follow him; he also perished, and all who followed him were scattered.

"So in this present case, I tell you, keep away from these men and let them alone; because if this plan or this undertaking is of human origin, it will fail. They are like unto a splinter, which always falls out or disappears. But, if it is of God, you will not be able to overthrow them—in that case you may even be found fighting against God!"

The council heard these words, and that the words were wise, so they were convinced. They had the apostles brought in and ordered them to be flogged, as was the standard punishment. However, they did not wish them to be flogged in public as was the usual practice. No, they had the two flogged right there, against a pillar in the hall. Forty lashes minus one are the maximum allowed; the council called for five and twenty. After both had received their punishment, the council ordered Peter and John to never speak in the name of Yeshua again, and they let them go.

As the two departed, still able to stand but their backs stinging and marked, but not bloody—for Jewish floggings are not like Roman floggings, where they use instruments with hooks that tear off even the flesh or others with lead balls attached, whereas Hebrews use a paddle made of ox skin punctured with holes, with straps of donkey tail hair to provide extra sting—the two men rejoiced that they were considered worthy to suffer dishonor for Yeshua's sake. And every day in the Temple and at home, they did not cease to teach and proclaim Yeshua as the Messiah.

For a time, the priests left them alone, as Gamaliel had advised them. But when Stephan offended them, they could abide the followers of Yeshua no longer. So, there it was, Jew against Jew, a house divided against itself, all in a span of a few mere years.

And in events such as these and those I will write down shortly, Yeshua's prophecy to the twelve disciples came to pass. He'd told them, "Do not think I come to bring peace to the earth; I come not to bring peace, but a sword. For I have come to set a man against his father, and a daughter against her mother, and a daughter-in-law against her mother-in-law; and one's foes will be members of one's own household." And now they all understood what he had meant.

Thus, it was into this environment that came to us that great persecutor named Saul of Tarsus, a Pharisee who was friend to the Herodians and was a person we all feared. He was the same balding, thin young man who had witnessed the stoning of Stephan with approval, his pinched countenance wearing the permanent scowl for which he would become famous, as he watched over the cloaks of the men who had stoned Stephan to death so that their possessions would not be stolen by the poor.

Chapter Twenty-Three

Now, this Saul of Tarsus was nothing if not the most vindictive of men: as a Pharisee, with friends among the Herodians, and also as a citizen of Rome, he considered himself above most Jews and one of the privileged class. He hated the Followers of the Way, for he could not understand how anyone could call "Messiah" one who was clearly accursed of God, having been hung on a tree, as the Law of Moses itself indicates such a one is cursed. As to the Resurrection of Yeshua, he scoffed at this and, like so many others claimed the disciples lied. Else, he said, why did not this Yeshua appear to any other than to his own family and the disciples? (Indeed, this is likely why, later on, after his conversion, Saul spoke of many additional appearances of Yeshua, which I say to you did not occur; but—and this is not to defame the man, for I think, in the end, he meant well—but at times he was predisposed to invent anything to beat back people's doubt, as you will see.) He called us superstitious blasphemers and began a campaign of rounding us up and bringing us to the Sanhedrin to be charged and either held in the prison until a fine could be paid or to undergo a flogging.

For now, after Stephan, the Sanhedrin had had enough, and were bent on destroying us, so for a time we left Jerusalem and scattered into the countryside, some staying in Bethany, some staying in even smaller villages, others going elsewhere about the land and preaching, whereas James brought the family to Qumran for a few months until Saul, satisfied he had cleared the city of us, took his campaign of persecution elsewhere. When we returned to Jerusalem, we discovered Saul had indeed broken into our church-house and destroyed the altar. Therefore at this time James established several "houses of safety" within the city in various neighborhoods so that followers of Yeshua might always have a safe haven in which to hide if the need arose.

This trip to Qumran was, by the way, my first look at that community; I was seven, almost eight; and it seemed to me the place was filled with many Uncle Yeshuas, all dressed in garments of white linen, woven by an aged man whose nimble fingers I would sit and watch with fascination. I also was allowed to wander freely with my brothers, and we spent many hours exploring the land around the Salt Sea. Of course I did not see all of it then, only a part of the western side, but this is a strange body of water indeed. It is saltier, they say, than the vast oceans. The sea is a deep blue, yet so heavy from the salts that you can float upon the top and will not sink. The sea itself is fed by the River Jordan, but since there is no outlet, the entering water appears to vanish into the air rather than making the sea overflow its banks, instead leaving behind deposits of salts. The land here is also very low, so breathing is easier. There, I could sprint farther and faster than I ever had and imagined myself a powerful, untiring warrior, able to slay many Romans. Ah, the dreams of children!

Later in my life, I saw more of the Salt Sea and the many salt piles along the shore further south and the many white pillar-like formations, like phantoms twisting together in a dance, or like dozens of ghostly sentinels reminding us of the folly of Lot's wife. And there were bubbling up spots of pitch that I am told the Egyptians once harvested, many hundreds of years ago, to use in mummification. The salts themselves are also harvested, the copper-colored kind especially valued by some for use as fertilizer in the fields.

But, back to Qumran. There were stories of Saul that were told by the Brethren. "Saul," of course, is his Aramaic name; but being from Tarsus, which is in the Roman province of Cilicia, or the southern coast of Turkey, he often went by his Latin name, "Paul" or "Paulus." His parents were Jews originally from the land around Sepphoris; but after the uprising prior to the birth of Yeshua, which had led to the Romans leveling Sepphoris until

Herod Antipas rebuilt it, those Jews had been relocated, and Tarsus was where Saul's parents had been sent. It was said that at this point, his parents, who had not been a part of the uprising, felt inconvenienced by their Jewish heritage and became fully integrated into Greek and Roman culture. His father became a wealthy tent maker, selling tents of high quality to the Roman legions. In this way, as one who did a service to the Romans, he was able to purchase Roman citizenship for a hefty fee. And thus, when his son Paul was born, as the son of a Roman citizen, Paul was therefore also a legal Roman citizen. The story goes that Paul learned his father's trade and was not even raised as a Jew, and was uncircumcised. This last part I cannot vouch for the truth of, but it is what was said at Qumran.

But upon adulthood, Paul wished to expand his father's business, and since there was no one in Palestine making tents for the Roman legions here, Paul came to Judea. Since most speak Aramaic in this land, Paul became known as Saul. Here is where the story becomes interesting, although once again I cannot vouch for its truth: so please read this part with a skeptical eye, or hear it with a doubtful ear. Still, if it is true, it would explain much regarding Saul's later behavior. It is said that in Jerusalem, Saul became deeply infatuated with the daughter of a Temple priest, a Sadducee. It would not do, therefore, for Saul to not be a Jew. So, Saul "converted" even though his parents were Hebrews and he was Hebrew by birth, of the tribe of Benjamin. Therefore, as an adult, he had to undergo circumcision, and to show his worthiness to the priest, he became a Pharisee, and studied under the tutelage of that member of the Sanhedrin I have earlier mentioned, the wise Gamaliel. Now if this story is true, it would certainly explain why Saul later seemed to hate circumcision so very much. I imagine having his foreskin removed was excruciating, which is why Jewish boys have this done on the eighth day after birth—they tolerate it better, for it is just a tiny flap of skin then, and they also forget the experience.

Despite his enduring this pain, and despite Saul's embracing of the Pharisaic "two Torahs"—the written and the oral, and learning the Law backwards and forwards—the priest's daughter was said, after all of this, to have spurned him anyway. Therefore, it is difficult for me, in the end, to judge Paul too harshly, and even to forgive him and pray for his soul, for he was at times a man very filled with anger, and the bitterness of disappointment, which over the years he vented in every direction except upon himself. He did good things, too, and for this reason my uncle James counseled mercy towards him; the problem was that Paul also did some wicked things, as you will see.

But at the beginning, Saul persecuted the Followers of the Way in Jerusalem until he was satisfied that they were no more, and then he requested permission to travel north, through Galilee and into Syria and to Damascus, to scatter and destroy the Followers there, and to bring back the leaders to stand trial before the Sanhedrin.

With him gone, James and the family left Qumran and returned to Jerusalem. It was about this time that word reached us that my uncle Joses had drowned in an accident fishing on the Sea of Galilee. For Joses, though he had accepted Yeshua as Messiah, had preferred to stay in Capernaum and had turned the house of Simon Peter (with Peter's permission) into a church, and my two aunts and their families joined him in this. So it was outside Capernaum that Joses was first buried, with his head facing towards the Temple in Jerusalem, but after a year some returned to Capernaum to dig up his bones and bring them to the family tomb and place them into an ossuary there.

My uncle Simon had founded, likewise, a house-church in Cana. But Saul had mostly traveled along the coast of the Mediterranean, so those inland, closer to the Sea of Galilee, had avoided him.

Finally it reached our ears, though none of us was to see Saul until three years later, that an extraordinary thing had happened to Saul, yes, this same Pharisee from Tarsus, as he had traveled to Damascus. Among those he had set out to capture were some Jews who had known Yeshua when he was preaching in Galilee, and among them were two or three of the original seventy, all of one family, that Yeshua had sent out before his final trip to Jerusalem. So naturally we had sent word ahead of time that Saul was on his way there. At first the news we received back from them was hard to believe.

Paul had, on the way, experienced a divine revelation of some sort. We never were able to get a consistent account, but what happened was akin to this: on the road, he saw a great light that blinded him, which made him to fall off his horse, and he heard a voice that asked him, "Saul, why do you persecute me?"

Paul, greatly afraid, asked, "Who are you, Lord?"

And the voice told him he was Yeshua, and that Paul was to go into Damascus and find one Ananias, who would tell him what to do.

The men who were with Paul are said to have either seen the blinding light themselves and not been blinded, but had not heard the voice; or, they had not seen the blinding light but had heard the voice.

Now, some who heard this story joked that perhaps Paul knocked himself on the head upon his fall from the horse, and this is why he could not get his account straightened out. Others say the inconsistency is just the natural way that stories get mixed up in the retelling. Still others say the conflicting account is proof that Paul was simply making the whole thing up, especially since, upon his arrival in Damascus (his men had to lead him there since he was now blind), his men disappear from the account altogether as if they had never existed; but why Jews of like mind as Saul, sent with him to Damascus to persecute us, would not have continued in their mission without Saul remains an unanswered question.

But, I am inclined to believe that something happened on the road, for no one changes so drastically without a profound cause. And henceforth, Paul was so insistent that this thing had happened, and eventually became insistent that Yeshua directed his actions in all things and that he spoke with Yeshua frequently, that I will write here with confidence that Paul certainly believed he had seen and heard Yeshua. I do not believe he lied about this. Indeed, my uncle James accepted his account and directed the Church to also accept it. For, he saw in it the hand of Yeshua: who else would Yeshua choose to take the Word and the Way to the Gentiles, but the very man who was persecuting him, a man whose karma therefore would one day lead even to his own death for the very thing for which he had persecuted others? Also, the description of Yeshua as a great Light from which emitted his voice closely matched what James, the disciples, my great-uncle, Cleophas, and the women had seen.

James accepted this much, and he also agreed with Paul that the Gentiles should indeed be saved in addition to the Jews; for you must remember, all thought then that the End of Times was still going to happen within that generation, as Yeshua himself had said; but on other matters involving Paul, James differed; and the stubbornness of Paul, convinced that his beliefs and interpretations were the only correct ones, thereafter put the two men in conflict the remainder of their days, although James (and Peter) were more merciful to Paul than Paul seemed able to appreciate.

If I were challenged to sum up the nature of the conflict as simply as I could, I would write it thus: Paul thought the Gospel to the Gentiles was one thing, and he thought the Gospel to the Jews was a second thing, but that both groups were saved: the Jews by following the Law, the Gentiles by their faith. James disagreed and felt the Gentiles must act beyond simple faith and also do good works. "Good works" then became an argument over how both believed Yeshua would interpret the Law. Now, as the story unfolds, you will see how the conflict played out, for both good and for evil.

And . . . thinking back on it all now, I believe that perhaps both men have been greatly misunderstood. The Gentile followers of Yeshua dislike James; the Jewish followers of Yeshua dislike Paul. And then some Jews have come to dislike us, the Ebionites, for they believe we believe as the Gentiles following Paul; and those Gentiles called Xristos-followers, or Christians, dislike us, for they believe we, the Ebionites, are just irascible, old-fashioned Law-abiding Jews who blaspheme against Yeshua. It is, indeed, as great a mess and rubble as the present state of Jerusalem.

I believe the basic problem is that Paul tried to have things both ways, saying one thing to one group and sometimes another to another group, but I must say, I once heard him preach myself, in a synagogue, and it certainly sounded to me as if he was saying even to Jews that Yeshua, the Messiah, had fulfilled the Law and established a new covenant with all nations, thereby invalidating the old covenant, and he spoke of Yeshua as if he were God himself, and all that was required was faith in him to enter into the Kingdom of Heaven. And for this, he was dragged out of the synagogue and flogged for blasphemy, just as Peter and John were flogged.

So I am horribly torn, as my uncle James must have been torn, about what to do about Paul and his teachings: for on the one hand, he brought a message of hope to the Gentiles, but on the other hand, he did not teach precisely what Yeshua taught.

Writing this has made my head to ache; so I lay down this pen for now. I need to make more ink in any case. And I see Rachel looking at me, from the doorway, in concern, for it is also true that my skin takes on this pallor again.

But, tomorrow, I will go back to the story, now that I have laid this foundation.

* * *

I shall have to back up a little, for I see I have leaped far ahead of myself.

While this Paul, or Saul, was even traveling to Damascus and was converted and then proselytizing under his own authority until he was to finally meet with James, other things of note were happening.

Barnabas, a brave man indeed, volunteered to travel by ship to Rome and teach the Way to the Jews of that city. So, he went, but he was not well received, except by a young Gentile named Clement. This Clement then followed him, some weeks after Barnabas returned, landing in Caesarea where Peter and John were also for the time being (avoiding Paul), joining the Brethren in that city.

For, yes, Samaria had been converted by Philip (not to be confused with the brother of Mary of Magdala, who was in Gaul). This Philip had gone through Samaria preaching and healing and doing other miracles. Then Philip encountered a magician of Samaria, a man named Simon. Simon the Magician was himself so astounded by the wonders of Philip that even Simon converted, and was baptized. It was also about this time there was to be an incident with Simon the Magician about which much has been told—and, of course, about much which has been exaggerated. Indeed, one account has Peter holding Simon high in the heavens by the power of the Holy Spirit, then dropping him down to his death and other such madness.

It was nothing such as that. Simon, this magician, was merely misguided. He saw Peter and John laying their hands on the people of Samaria to symbolize their reception of the Holy Spirit. Simon, being a magician, thought there was some trick to this, so he offered money to Peter, asking that he might be given the same power to lay on his hands. All Peter did was to rebuke the magician, refusing his money, and telling him to repent of this wickedness in his heart. Simon fell to his knees and prayed for forgiveness.

That is all there is to tell of this incident. Clement, of Rome, was witness to this and was also much impressed, so he converted, staying with Peter, John, Philip, and Barnabas in Caesarea for a time. That is correct! They allowed a Gentile under their roof. But, he ate at a different table; and Clement did not mind, for he was not a Jew. This seemed to Peter and everyone else a fine and good thing; for Yeshua himself, though he had never entered the house of a Gentile while in his own country, had certainly eaten with them himself, with them in the same house, when he was in the home of the wealthy tax collector in Jericho. You will recall that the Pharisees rebuked Yeshua for this.

This was also why James allowed Gentiles into the church-house in Jerusalem, at least for a time, until their own church-house could be established. As I have written, they merely sat at a different table to take the community remembrance meal. At Qumran, the Elders cautioned James about not becoming a Seeker of Smooth Things by compromising the Law, but James reminded them of the precedent set by Yeshua, and they were satisfied. (Well, most were satisfied.)

After the incident with Simon the Magician, Philip then traveled south, past Jerusalem, towards Gaza, where another great conversion took place. This was of that of the Ethiopian eunuch, who was of the court of Candace, their queen, who was a Jew. (Indeed it was his conversion that made James later send Matthew to Ethiopia, thinking he may be well received, but I have already written of how that ended.) This eunuch had been sent to Jerusalem to make a sacrifice in the Temple for the queen, and he was traveling back along the road in his chariot. I record this because it is a humorous, and joyful, story.

As the eunuch was passing Philip on the road, Philip could see that the man was reading from a scroll, so Philip caught up to him and could hear him mouthing out the words of Isaiah. Philip said to him, "Do you understand what you are reading?"

The eunuch called to his charioteer to stop the horses, and he said to Philip, "How can I, unless someone interprets it for me?"

"I can do so," said Philip, so the eunuch moved over and asked Philip to join him in the chariot. Now, it turns out that the passage the eunuch was trying to make sense of was that portion about the suffering Messiah. So he asked of Philip, "Tell me, does this prophet speak of himself or of someone else?"

He gestured for the driver to continue on, so as they rode together in the chariot, Philip gave to this eunuch the good news about Yeshua. The eunuch, it turned out, was kind of heart and cried at the tale of Yeshua's crucifixion. But then he rejoiced when told of the Resurrection.

They were now passing by a creek bed, so the eunuch again called out for his driver to stop. "Look," he said to Philip, "here is water! What is to prevent me from being baptized?"

So Philip and the eunuch went down to the water, and Philip baptized this man, and together they rejoiced.

Now a version of this story has Philip vanishing into thin air at this point, so again you see how these stories change when passed about. Philip merely sent the man on his way, asking him to tell the story of Yeshua in his own land, and the man promised that he would. And Philip, having supposed that this eunuch was the reason he had felt compelled to travel this road in the first place, now felt that his mission was complete, so he turned around and went back to Caesarea.

* * *

Meanwhile, in Jerusalem, all had returned to normal with an end to the persecutions of Saul. Peter and John and others traveled about the land, saving souls and baptizing and doing miracles, while James ran the church-house in Jerusalem. There he taught the Way of Yeshua, although he continued going to the Temple daily as well, as did all the family and any in the community who were not Gentiles. For discussions he would sometimes go even to the synagogue, for many there often had questions about Yeshua. These were peaceful days. My brothers and I, and my cousin Mattias, attended the Essene school in Ein Kerem but frequently came back to visit the family. Ah, how those days were happy! For we did good things, and felt blessed, and among us were all kinds of Jews: Pharisees, Essenes, Nazirites, Zealots, everyday people who belonged to no particular group or party—all heard the Word and believed. We looked forward to the coming Kingdom of Heaven, knowing that we did our best to set as many as we could upon the path of righteousness, praying that enough were receiving the Way for all the world to avoid the second path, that of destruction.

* * *

It was about three years after the conversion of Paul that he finally came to Jerusalem to meet the pillars of the Church: James, Peter, and John. John, however, was away at the time, so Paul met only James and Peter. They did not really know what to expect. Paul was brought in front of James, who was seated in a chair in front of the very altar Paul had once smashed, and Peter stood on his right.

Paul greeted them humbly and prostrated himself upon the floor.

"Rise," James said. "I am but a man like yourself." I add that by this time, and throughout his remaining days, James was often treated like this and viewed with awe by many, for he was the Lord's brother. My uncle James said this kind of treatment made him to better appreciate Yeshua, for it is hard to be adored, and famous, and to fight off the puffed-up pride that comes from it.

James could not resist. "Do you remember striking me in the face on the Temple steps?" he asked Paul.

Paul's face first turned ashen, and then red began creeping up towards his cheeks until his face was florid. "I am sorry," he said. "I was angry and misguided in those days."

James smiled at him, to set him at ease. "It's just as well you did not know who I was," he said. "For you could've had the leader of the Church killed and brought us even more grief than you did."

"I atone for those evil things I have done," said Paul. "I am pleased to say I have converted many. I have been to Arabia, and north to Ephesus, and to Damascus and told many of the good news."

"How are you received?"

"The Jews in many places think I blaspheme," Paul said. "In truth, I am received better by the Gentiles."

James nodded but did not answer, for he was thinking.

"I think," Paul hastened to add during this pause, "It is because I am a citizen of Rome. Tarsus is no mean city. They perceive me as a Greek, not as—"

Peter finished his sentence for him with his usual burst of loud laughter. "Not as a crazy Jew from the tiny province of Judea!"

The three all laughed at this, and Paul inclined his head. "It is as you say."

"This seems to me a good thing," James said. "For although the apostles have been sent out to the Gentiles, and some of the deacons go as well, Greek is your native tongue, and I can see for myself you are a man of charisma."

James then got to his feet. "Spend time with Peter. He will tell you the story of Yeshua to fill in any gaps in knowledge that you may have. Aside from teaching the Way, our primary task is to feed, house, and clothe the poor, and minister to the sick. Therefore, remember you always the poor. Go, brother, with God."

And thus their first meeting, of three total, ended. It had seemed harmless enough, with Paul contrite, and willing. But you must note that James did not himself, nor did he ever, make Paul an apostle. That designation was only for the twelve. But later on, when Paul was to designate himself an apostle and declare that the only direction given him by James was to remember the poor—and that otherwise, all else he said and did Paul received directly as revelations from Yeshua and the Holy Spirit—well, this was to cause trouble.

It is true that often men of great charisma are also men of great self-will.

Paul spent about two weeks with Peter, who told him many things, and when Paul was to depart in his mission to the Gentiles, James sent Barnabas with him. This turned out to be wise. Then again, I am not sure I myself would ever completely trust a man who had once smitten me across the face.

* * *

More time passed peacefully; my brothers and I came of age, and they both married. I, however, was zealous for the Law and profoundly influenced by my uncle Yeshua. I set upon the path of chastity. For a time I traveled with some of the deacons, among them Peter's son Mark, even as far as Antioch, where, outside that city in a small settlement, as I have set down, I heard Paul preach at a synagogue there. It was as he had told my uncle James, and as happened, truly, to all of us at some time or other. The moment the word "Messiah" or "begotten Son of God" left your lips, someone would call out "blasphemy!" and you would find yourself thrown into the street, or, in the worst cases, flogged. I have my own scar upon my back as a testament, from a time when one of the donkey tails cut my skin.

But mostly Paul stuck to the Gentiles, and because I was a little concerned over how Paul phrased certain things, it was at this time that I sat down to speak with Barnabas, who asked me to bring a message to my uncle James when next I saw him.

Barnabas was quite concerned. He said that the Gentiles often misunderstood Paul when he called Yeshua the Son of God. This, of course, is the same misunderstanding the Jews often made when we spoke. So we hastened to explain "Messiah" meant only "anointed one," and that "Son of God" meant begotten Son, as in God's adopting Yeshua at his baptism, when he received the Holy Breath: that is to say, a chosen one of God. For this we were often chased out of towns anyway. But Paul, Barnabas said, had given up trying to explain to the Gentiles the difference and indeed, he had left it to Barnabas to discourage the misunderstanding, if any clearing up was to be done at all.

"Do you not understand these Gentiles?" Paul asked him. (I am setting down the conversation as Barnabas told it to me.) "They believe in many gods and believe these gods and goddesses hear their prayers and accept their sacrifices and do things for them. Why then would they shun their own gods and choose instead a man who is nothing more than a Jewish prophet?"

"Yeshua is more than a prophet!" Barnabas said. "But he is not a god, yet you do not discourage them from thinking this thing."

Paul believed it was nothing but a detail, unimportant, for the End of Times was nigh, so what difference did it make? "I bring them the good news, and the Word, and I give them faith in Christ Jesus, who died for their sins. It is sufficient, for it brings many to the Church. We must win them over."

Upon hearing this conversation, I was horrified. For Paul, perhaps, this was a trivial thing, a misunderstanding he let stand as necessary to convert the pagans, but the gulf between Prophet and God is wide indeed, and the Divine Presence is One, not two, nor three, nor a hundred. Also, what had concerned me was that I had heard Paul say that Yeshua had established a new covenant with God; when Yeshua never meant any such a thing. No, the Messiah was to renew the covenant with God, restoring God to the people. There is a difference.

"What is worse," Barnabas said, "is that I begin to think he believes it himself."

"I will inform my uncle," I said. In parting, I embraced Barnabas. "Continue cleaning up this man's sewage."

Well, I was young, and I was angry. In retrospect, I think it was incidents such as this, and tiring of traveling and being thrown out of synagogues and occasionally being lashed, that pushed me to go to Qumran. I needed a place where everything was clear, all was black and white, a confined place with an established hierarchy where disputes were settled easily. I had been considering it anyway, since, as I said, I was in my youthfulness trying to imitate Yeshua, and he had been at Qumran. And I felt my understanding of the Scriptures to be sketchy and incomplete.

In Jerusalem, my uncle James embraced me and kissed my cheek. "You are following in Yeshua's footsteps," he said. Then he teased me. "Will you next be going to India to join your father? Or perhaps to Egypt?" But he sent me off with his blessing. Of Paul, he said he would send a letter to him, to correct his errors.

And thus I tarried at Qumran, for about half a dozen years, until I was in my mid-to-late twenties.

But once again, I find I have leaped far ahead of myself, so I will now return the narrative to the next large event in the chronology, which is the imprisonment of Peter and Thaddeus, or James the son of Zebedee, who had returned from Hispania.

* * *

Herod Agrippa was our new false King of the Jews. One of the earliest things Agrippa did, in order to ingratiate himself to the Sadducees, who still opposed us, and to ingratiate himself to the usual crowd of collaborators with the *Kittim,* was to capture Thaddeus and hold him in his jail until he had him executed by cutting off his head, as I have already written.

Seeing that this action pleased the collaborators, Agrippa next set out to capture the "man of loud mouth," Peter, and uncannily as with Yeshua, this happened during the time of the Passover. Hearing from the priests that Peter had once before escaped the public prison, Herod had Peter placed into his own jail, with four squads of soldiers to guard him. He intended to bring Peter out for execution after the Passover.

As had happened during previous persecutions in Jerusalem, all had abandoned the church-house of Eleazar and dispersed into various houses of Followers of the Way, to pray for Peter in safety. They tried to form a plan to free him, but no one could see a way past all of the guards. Fervent prayer was all they could do.

Now, this next is from the mouth of Peter himself.

Peter was in the cell, bound with two chains, with a soldier sleeping on either side of him. There were guards outside the door, and more guards along the passageway, and then guards outside the jail itself. So Peter had resigned himself to his fate, and prayed to God that he would be allowed into the Kingdom of Heaven, and he repented of every sin he had committed that he could think of. Indeed, he had nodded off with heavy eyes in the middle of prayer when a light came into the cell, and an angel of the Lord appeared and tapped Peter on his side to waken him.

"Get up quickly," said the angel. The chains fell from Peter's wrists.

"Fasten your belt and put on your sandals," the angel commanded him, so Peter did so.

"Put on your cloak and follow me," the angel then said.

So, Peter followed the angel. The door to the cell opened by itself, and they passed by the guards, who all slept. They walked down the passageway, past those guards, who all slept. They left the building, past yet more guards, who all slept. Finally they reached the iron gate that led into Jerusalem from the palace itself, where, as by now you have gathered, these guards also all slept. The gate opened to Peter and the angel of its own accord.

Peter said he'd thought he was dreaming, and that none of this was real, until he was well past the iron gate and around a corner into another street, when the angel disappeared and he came to his senses, as if waking from a dream.

Realizing where he was, he ran as fast he could to the house of Mary, who was the mother of the deacon John Mark. It was the closest house of safety. He pounded upon the door, not knowing that many were within, praying for him.

A maid servant came to answer the door—and this part is humorous—and she recognized the voice of Peter calling out. She was so overjoyed that she ran back to the others and told them Peter was at the door; but she had forgotten to open the door!

This still makes me laugh. It serves Peter right for always making fun of women. And it also lends credence to what Yeshua once said, along the lines of, "If you think it is so, then it you make it so." For the girl had left Peter standing in the street.

Those within told the servant girl, "You are out of your mind!"

But she insisted it was true, so some said, "It is perhaps Peter's angel."

Meanwhile, all this time, Peter was still outside, banging on the door.

Finally they went and opened the door, and saw him there, and were astounded and let him in.

Peter, aware that his knocking and calling had perhaps alerted others, motioned for them to be silent. He told them the story of his escape as the women quickly packed together food for him to carry.

"I must leave before I endanger you all," he said. "I must flee from here. Tell this to James and to the others. I will send word of my whereabouts when it is safe."

And this is how Peter came to leave the right hand of James

and wound up in the city of Rome itself, hiding in plain sight, and converting more Jews of that city and leading the Church there for a time.

Chapter Twenty-Four

I was at Qumran, with the Community of the *Yahad,* when famine hit the land. Fortunately, the Brethren had some stores of grain, so they did not suffer as badly as many, and we were also accustomed to drought, living in the desert. Agrippa sent to Syria and to Egypt for assistance. But as usual, it was the poor who suffered most, for they could not afford the grain, and it certainly was not given to them for nothing. Many turned to the Church at this time, and James did not require of them conversion for help.

"Yeshua did not say to help only those who agree with you," was all he said, and he did what he could to feed the mouths of those in need.

It was also about this time that James stepped up his cries for justice for the poor, within the church, in the synagogues, and even at the Temple. "Come now, you rich people," he would call out. "Weep and wail for the miseries coming to you. You have laid up treasure for the last days. But listen! The wages of the laborers who mowed your fields, which you kept back by fraud, cry out, and the cries of the harvesters have reached the ears of the Lord of hosts." His words, of course, fell on many deaf ears.

Meanwhile, my sojourn at Qumran was coming to an end. In the Community of the *Yahad,* I had lived a peaceful existence, spending time weaving our robes when I was not working in the fields further south, for the old weaver had died; and at my leisure in the evenings I was able to read some of the scrolls, although as I have admitted, I have never been the most devoted student. It is impossible for any one man, no matter how devout and dedicated, to read them all, for as I have said, a great library was at Qumran, with writings of all kinds—even a Samaritan Torah! Certain scrolls were favored over others, and the ones that interested me the most were those having to do with the Messiah and Teachers of Righteousness (for there was more than one teacher; that title was given to the leader of the movement in any given generation, although the first Teacher was given great veneration); as likewise there were many Evil Priests, those who particularly opposed the movement in any way, either by collaborating with the *Kittim*, or, later, by opposing Yeshua and his successor, James. Therefore the self-designated Apostle Paul was sometimes referred to as an Evil Priest, for he opposed James in making up theology about Yeshua and in rejecting the Law, at least when he spoke to the Gentiles.

I remember reading also one scroll, said to have been handed down by a disciple of Moses, who wrote of the times of Moses' wandering in the wilderness after escaping those who had persecuted his teacher, Akhenaten. The people were still very much trapped in the thinking of the Egyptians and their many gods and had trouble conceptualizing of God as One. Indeed, throughout our early history in the land of Canaan, Jews were constantly giving to Yahweh a consort named Asherah, adding to God a feminine principle, for they were unable to conceive of a single Being as genderless, holding in itself both the male and the female. Moses would pray to God in despair, asking, "How do I unite this people?"

Poor Moses. The people are still not united. I do not think it was a failure of Moses, or of any judge or king, or of Yeshua, or of James; it is a failure of people in general, who listen not to their inner hearts and who do not feel their oneness with all things, and who believe that what they see with their eyes and hear with their ears is all that there is. So I came to appreciate more Simon Peter, who, despite his literal-mindedness, ultimately came to understand abstractions and the mysteries.

Others of the Sons of Light did not care for James, thinking he was too gentle in his tolerance of Paul and for counseling patience when it came to the Romans. These were the more zealous among the group, and tended to be the ones who treated even Gentile members of the Great Brotherhood who visited there as unclean people who must be avoided. I suppose there, at Qumran, I learned that every group has its hypocrites, or its people who are unreasonably rigid, judgmental, and unforgiving, and who think their path is the only path.

Thinking back on it now, perhaps this is the real reason Yeshua stayed at Qumran for only one year, for after a year one undergoes the first initiation, and Yeshua had far greater teachings that he was destined to learn. And perhaps being at Qumran for too long is what made the tongue of John the Baptizer more fierce and bitter, in comparison to Yeshua, whose tongue was, for the most part, gentle and sweet. The cup Yeshua offered was not harsh to drink.

For I knew better of my uncle James. After Peter had spent time in Rome, Peter returned to Jerusalem, having set as leaders two men to head that Church, and it was about this time that Clement returned home to Rome as well. With Peter back, James sent him and a delegation, including his son Mark, to find Paul, for his letters had apparently gone ignored by that man or were never delivered to him. James's instructions to Peter were clear: Paul was to be corrected in all loving kindness, and Paul was to travel to Jerusalem at his earliest convenience to speak with James himself. This question of how to handle the Gentile converts needed to be dealt with, for they were growing in number and Barnabas' letters had gotten increasingly indignant. Barnabas also wished to be free of Paul and the man's blasphemy.

Of course when a leader says, "come at your earliest convenience," everyone knows this is mere courtesy and means "come now." Not Paul. He waited almost two more years.

It was as if Paul knew he might have incurred the wrath of James as well, for he brought with him, when he finally came, a great collection of money to help with famine relief, although at this point the famine was mostly over. Still, my uncle was grateful for the money, and thanked him, and received Paul with hospitality, giving him a room in the house next to the church, for by then our neighbors, Judah and Sarai, had passed on and James had purchased the property, for now Eleazar's house was overfilled and there was a need to house some of the deacons.

There was a great meeting, with James, Peter, and John; Paul, and some other young man, a Gentile, whom Paul had brought with him, named Titus; and then many Elders from among the deacons. For James had had from Peter in full what had happened in Antioch when Peter's delegation caught up with Paul. I suppose the word I must write to describe the Antioch meeting is "ugly."

When Peter—quite rightly—refused to sit at the same table as the Gentile followers and eat with them, much less eat of their food, for there was swine meat at the table, which Paul ate with great relish—any semblance of accord between the two factions was gone. Paul felt Peter had deliberately set out to insult his Gentile converts by refusing to eat with them, and in his rage on their behalf, he got a hand's breadth from Peter's face and spat out venom, calling Peter a hypocrite and all else.

Peter later said it had taken all his strength of will to not lift a hand and club Paul with it. It is a good thing that he did not, for Simon Peter, of course, though aged by then, had always been a large man of much strength, and being struck by him would have likely knocked the senses from Paul, who was very thin and small of stature.

Instead, Peter calmed himself and said to Paul, "Brother, you have strayed from the path in your zeal to collect to yourself converts. But our brother James is in agreement that there must be a policy in place for how we might add to us the Gentile God-fearers, in such a way that it is not an affront to God."

He paused, and, seeing that Paul was calming down, delivered the message he had been sent to give. "James wishes to see you at your earliest convenience. You are welcome to come back to Jerusalem with us."

But, of course, Paul declined, for he was expected in another city, but he said he would come soon.

Peter said, "And look to your own soul, Saul. Don't forget that you are a Jew."

Paul said, "My soul is the business of God, and I do the bidding of the Holy Spirit."

Peter wished to not argue with the man, for it was like unto speaking with a boulder that would not be moved. He just said that James would settle the question. Then Peter gave his attention over to poor Barnabas, to whom Paul had also directed some of his ire, and Barnabas pleaded with Peter to take him back with him and away from this Paul. Peter reasoned it would be impossible to control Paul now, until James had given him direction, so he assented. The next morning, Peter and the delegation set out, therefore, with Barnabas, to return to Jerusalem.

It is said that Paul claimed in one of his letters to have "won this battle," but I will hold my tongue on this matter. The reader may make his or her own conclusions.

And so finally, two years later, was held the first conference of the Church in Jerusalem, and I am pleased to be able to write that I was there. Yes! For by now I had returned to the city, with the wife I have previously mentioned that I met at—of all places—Qumran. My beloved's name, the mother of my precious daughter, was Chana, or Hannah, indeed a woman of grace. Before I had come to Qumran, she had been the wife of one of the visiting Essenes, a good Jew, but he had taken ill and died. Having no father or brother's home to return to, Chana was one of the few women who stayed at Qumran, her house being one of the caves (as the caves served for many) in the nearby cliffs. The Brethren saw to it that Chana had plenty to eat and drink, and she assisted the cooks. I fell in love with her in the way that young men do—quickly, as if smitten with a mace, never able to keep her far from my thoughts. When I was ready to leave Qumran, I went to the Elders and asked if I might marry her. One of the astrologers cast a chart and said the match would be a good one.

Chana gave her consent, and I was the happiest man on the face of the earth, and she came with me back to Jerusalem, where I stayed until I fled here to Pella. I was a deacon; I earned some coins by weaving mats and garments, which I dyed, occasionally traveling to other cities to sell them in the forums if I was unable to sell them all in the Jerusalem marketplaces. When I was of thirty years, Rachel was born.

The birth was hard on Chana, however, and she was never fully healthy after that. When Rachel was a toddler, I lost my dear Chana. Of this I do not care to write, except that it took some time for my grief to ease, and I thank the Lord that many women in the Church helped me with Rachel. The thought of marrying again never came to me. Chana's bones lie in an ossuary that is unmarked, in the family tomb outside Jerusalem, for I could not think of any words that would suit to scratch onto the limestone box. She was so much more than "daughter of" or "wife of" or "niece of." I had also hoped, at that time, that one day my own bones would be added to the ossuary with hers. Then someone could write that we lay within together.

Why am I even writing this down at all? I am a foolish old man. This, too, I will need to strike out when I go back to re-copy.

Therefore, back to the conference. The theme of the council was the proper handling of Gentile converts. Jews—and this was a given, not even requiring discussion—would continue to follow the Law, just as Yeshua had done himself. The question regarding whether Jews and Gentile followers would sit at table together was therefore quickly settled. The Law is clear on this matter. Eventually, we supposed, they would have their own churches, and Jews would continue attending synagogues and the Temple, and the Gentiles would be treated just like the God-fearers, who had always been welcomed to listen to discussions inside the synagogue from outside the synagogue. Likewise, we assumed

Jewish Followers of the Way, who aren't allowed to enter the houses of Gentiles, would stand outside the house-churches of Gentiles if they so wished and listen to what happened within. There was no inequality implied, but I will repeat: Yeshua never, ever told us to reject the Law. On the contrary, he'd said that not one jot, nor one stroke of the pen, would be removed from the Law; he had not come to overthrow the Law but to fulfill it; not to replace the old covenant but to renew it.

Paul and Titus argued the question of circumcision. Titus was an impressive young man, eloquent in speech, and devoted to Yeshua. But he did not wish to undergo circumcision and become a Jew, which would set him apart from his Greco-Roman brothers and would make him an object of scorn. Paul argued that those who insisted that Gentiles become circumcised and be Jews before they could become Followers of the Way—or Christians; for at this point, outside of Palestine, this is what we were called—and I have lost my thought. Oh, Paul said that circumcision itself was discouraging Gentiles from converting. Moreover, the dietary laws were discouraging Gentiles from converting, for they saw no need to change their food. Had not Yeshua said that what goes into the body does not defile, but what comes out of the body, from the mouth in the form of words spoken from the heart, is what defiles? Could not the Way of Yeshua be accepted by Gentiles without adhering to the Jewish Law?

After hearing all the arguments, my uncle James rose and handed down his decision. I will point out that what he said was more or less from Jubilees, and precedent had already been set regarding the Gentile God-fearers, so James was inventing nothing new. He agreed with Paul: the Gentiles need not be circumcised to join the Church. (Paul's face gleamed triumph.) As far as food was concerned, they could eat as they liked, with three exceptions: they were to eat nothing that was strangled; they were not to consume blood, that is to say, meat that is rare;

and they were not to eat of any meat that had been sacrificed to another god (that is to say, no worshiping of other gods). To these he added a final restriction that is also from Jubilees: abstaining from the practice of fornication. This included sexual relations outside of marriage, adultery, polygamy, incestuous relations, and pagan temple fornication. Other matters of Jewish Law, such as not murdering, not stealing, and the like, were already the Law of other nations.

All in attendance—including Paul—agreed to these things.

James summed up by indicating that the prophets had even foretold the welcoming of Gentiles into the fold during the End Times, by quoting a mix of Scripture from Isaiah and Amos. "As it is written," James said:

"'After this I will return,
and I will rebuild the dwelling of David, which has fallen;
from its ruins I will rebuild it,
and I will set it up,
so that all other peoples may seek the Lord—
even all the Gentiles over whom my name has been called.
Thus says the Lord, who has been making these things
known from long ago.'"

Therefore, all in attendance were satisfied.

Even Paul made a bow, which was unnecessary, and he said to James: "You are indeed the brother of the Lord, and you are the just man that you are called."

We thought that was the end of it. We were wrong.

* * *

About a year or so after this time, the family suffered a series of losses. Many of us became sick with some illness, spoiled food, perhaps, or some other cause which to us is unknown. I did not get sick, but Rachel did; yet she recovered, for which I thank the Lord. However, my cousin, Mattias, the son of Joses, did not survive the sickness, and neither did my younger cousin Judah, the child of my aunt Salome, whom, as you will recall, had married Yeshua of Capernaum. They were visiting us at the time. Rather than take Judah all the way back to Capernaum to be buried in the ground, Yeshua assented to his wife's wish to lay the child in our family tomb. The last taken by this illness was my grandmother Mary. These were grievous weeks. My only consolation is that my grandmother, that most blessed of all women and the mother of the Master Yeshua, had lived to a good old age.

Then word reached us that the Gentiles had created a new community meal of remembrance for Yeshua, or the communion, in which we take the wine and the bread and sing a hymn: it is very like the synagogue, really, in which a teaching is first given, followed by the communion and a hymn, which the teacher chooses; and then there is a discussion of the teaching and any other matters afterwards. But the Gentiles had changed the communion. We assumed Paul was behind it. He had them saying, "Take, eat, this is my body that I gave to the Lord on account of you" and they would eat the bread, and then, "Take, drink, for this is my blood that I poured out for your sins" or something such as that. The ritual had to do with Paul's idea of a new covenant with God, ushered in by Yeshua, who had sacrificed himself so that no longer would animal sacrifices need to be made to God. For Paul, the act of Yeshua's Resurrection was proof that God had accepted Yeshua as a sacrifice to atone for human sin, so that by the grace of God all one needed to do was have faith in Yeshua, and he or she would be saved.

I am trying to be fair to this man Paul, although I confess it is hard. I imagine that it must have been impossible for Gentiles to come to Jerusalem for sacrifices, and as I have said many times, even the Essenes and Yeshua did not like sacrifices; and it was likely also impossible to sacrifice to Yahweh in their own pagan temples: and besides, there is only one Temple of Yahweh. So

Paul had turned the communion into a symbolic sacrifice of a kind. I follow this, but it is blasphemy, and offensive. Jews do not eat the blood of animals, much less symbolically drink the blood of a man! Was the man not thinking? Or did Paul no longer care?

And it got worse, blow after blow. Word next reached us that some of the Gentile churches did not follow even the few restrictions set down by James. And indeed why would they, if faith alone, as they were now being taught, is all that is required to be saved? Why not do as you please, if all you have to do is believe in Yeshua to enter into the Kingdom of Heaven? So these Gentiles reverted to their old behaviors, fornicating, worshiping pagan gods, drinking riotously, committing adultery, and all else. For them, Yeshua was just one more god, but he was worth worshiping, for he would give you immortality if you said you believed.

Poor Paul. I am told he did try to control his own damage, writing letters and returning to his churches to explain these behaviors were not what he had intended nor desired, but the Jews of Jerusalem heard these things right along with us, and heard that Yeshua was being worshiped as a god, and James was most distraught.

Finally, James had to send around delegates once again, with explicit instructions to all the churches to pay heed to no teacher of Yeshua who did not carry a letter of certification from James himself. Peter was sent back to Rome to deliver this message to Clement; John the Beloved was also among those who were sent out, and John traveled to Antioch. James also dispatched letters explaining that faith alone does not save a person. He stressed the importance of actions and good works. I quote from one of his letters, for Rachel repeats it often in our church: "What good is it, my brothers and sisters, if you say you have faith but do not have works? Can faith save you? If a brother or sister is naked and lacks daily food, and one of you says to them, 'Go in peace; keep warm and eat your fill,' and yet you do not supply their bodily needs, what is the good of that? So faith by itself, if it has no works, is dead." And again, "Be doers of the word, and not merely hearers who deceive themselves."

And then I believe my uncle James addressed the folly of Paul himself in writing, although with tact not naming him: "Who is wise and understanding among you? Show by your good life that your works are done with gentleness and born of wisdom. But if you have bitter envy and selfish ambition in your hearts, do not be boastful and false to the truth. Such wisdom does not come from above, but is earthly, unspiritual, and devilish. For where there is envy and selfish ambition, there will also be disorder and wickedness of every kind. But the wisdom from above is first pure, then peaceable, gentle, willing to yield, full of mercy and good fruits."

My own father, down in India, wrote a letter of his own along these lines, as I have mentioned before.

But it seemed clear, and was a matter of concern and grief to us, that our Christian brothers and sisters outside Judea were forming their own separate theology about Yeshua, instead of following the teachings of Yeshua himself. And this was already happening in the first generation.

"All else I can do is pray," said James. "All of us must pray. Let us pray for righteousness and the Day of the Lord."

* * *

Peter returned safely from Rome, for by ship it is about a two-week journey there, and then another two weeks back. But I am sorry to record that John, the Beloved one, never did return from Antioch. I must remind the reader of this narrative that they were all quite aged by now. We were informed that John simply died in his sleep. Bless him, Lord, for he died doing the bidding of God until the very end.

More time passed without additional incident, and all seemed well, but then, about a year later, Paul appeared—without announcement—in the Jerusalem church with two of his converts who wished to see the Holy City, and he brought an offering of money. This he laid at James's feet. "For the poor," Paul said. "As you have directed me."

James looked at the money, then looked at Paul. "Brother," he asked gently, "are there no poor in the lands outside Judea?"

"Well, of course," said Paul. "But we wanted to take up a collection for the Church."

"Thank you for your offering," said James. He thought for a moment about this thing. Finally he said, "It appears to be a considerable sum. But I must tell you, the Church fares well right now. I suggest you give this money to the poor outside our lands, for surely our need is no greater than theirs."

Now you must understand. James was not a Temple High Priest, who would take any money that was given and hold back a portion of it for himself. He led a Church of men and women who shared all they had and were deliberately poor. And, any trust he had in Paul had been destroyed by that man's actions. To be blunt, I think James saw Paul's money as an attempted bribe. For before, after James had accepted money during the famine, Paul was able to go out and say, "James the brother of the Lord has accepted my gift!" which gave to him some authority. Perhaps Paul thought if James accepted this gift, his heart would be softened, and James would give to him, also, a certificate. If Paul thought this thing, he was mistaken.

But in all honesty, I can only write that we did not know what Paul thought. As I wrote down earlier, it seemed to us he said to one group one thing, and to another group another thing.

Paul could not argue the needs of the poor in the other Roman provinces, so he picked up the collection and turned to go. He said to those he had brought with him, "We shall go see the Temple. It is wondrous to behold!"

James got to his feet. "Stop, Brother Paul."

Paul stopped and turned.

"You must not do this," James said. "You must understand, your reputation precedes you, and your reputation in this city is poor. If you set foot in the Temple, you will surely be put to death."

"The circumcision crowd," said Paul, and his tone was spiteful.

"No," said James. "Everyone: the Temple priests; the Pharisees; the Zealots; the Essenes; the Levites; the Nazirites; everyone, and yes," and here James sat back down, for his back continually ached, "yes, even the Followers of the Way."

"I care not," said Paul. "I do only the bidding of the Lord Jesus."

"Be that as it may," said James, "I perceive you see me as an obstacle." My uncle sighed. "All I can say to you is that I know the will of my own brother. I do not dispute that Yeshua speaks with you. He speaks to me! But, I am not convinced that you always interpret the words of the Master correctly."

Paul's eyes flashed with anger, so now my uncle softened his words.

"My son," he said. "I would not see you viciously killed. At the very least, I beg of you: undergo ritual cleanliness before all, so that they may see you do not flout the Law, before you set foot in the Temple."

"That is fine," Paul said. "I will go to the Bethzatha Baths and splash about loudly."

Until now, the two Gentiles with Paul had been silent, but at these words, they stifled laughter; for this pool was a double pool surrounded by four porticoes and one in the middle, and it was said to have healing powers. It was not a pool for recreation.

Even my uncle had to smile, for he was not without humor. But then he grew serious again. "I do not think that will be enough."

"What would you have me do?"

James thought a minute more, then said, "There are four men among us, Nazirites, who are under a vow. The Nazirites, as you know, are well known among the Jews for their piety. Join these men as their sponsor, and go through the purification rite with them for the seven days. Then all will know that you do not speak against the Law, but that you observe it; and they will conclude that the things they have heard, which I have also heard, are nothing but rumors."

Now this was clever advice, and you may think James was playing some kind of trick on Paul or testing him in some way; but, I deny this vehemently. My uncle was merely trying to save the man's life.

Therefore, even the obstinate Paul could see the wisdom in this, so he did as James bid him, each day going through the purification and then entering the Temple with the Nazirites, to make very public what he was doing. At the end of the seven days, a sacrifice would be made on the altar for each of the four men and for Paul, and had Paul not lost his patience, it is very possible that all would have been well.

None of us know what changed Paul's mind, but on the fifth day, Paul went into the Temple with the two Gentiles he had brought with him. I do not know: maybe these men had pressured Paul into taking them in, and he believed he had to, else lose credibility with them. In any case, Paul did the unthinkable. Not only did he bring the Gentiles into the main Temple Court of the Gentiles, he brought them up the steps, through the doorway, into the Court of Women and was almost to the Court of Israelites when he was recognized.

You must understand the great offense that was committed. Past the Court of Gentiles no Gentile may venture. Indeed, there was a sign that stated this in no uncertain terms: that the penalty to a Gentile entering the Temple was death.

Writing this now, I must wonder if Paul had not indeed lost his mind, or if it was a demon that spoke into his ear and not

Yeshua, or if he thought taking Gentiles into the Temple sanctuary would force the arrival of the End of Days. For, and I have alluded to it, one Messianic prophecy states that at the End of Times, even the Gentiles would come to Jerusalem, seeking the Lord in great humility and repentance, recognizing the greatness of God. And this makes me think of Judas Iscariot, who, perhaps, as I wrote down earlier, had handed over Yeshua in an attempt to force the End of Days to come.

This did not happen. No, Paul was recognized by a group of Jews from Asia, and at the sight of him with two Gentiles, they began screaming and tearing at their garments. Several of them seized Paul, shouting, "Fellow Israelites, help! This is the man who is teaching everyone everywhere against our people, our Law, and this place; more than that, he has actually brought Greeks into the temple and has defiled this holy place."

You can imagine the commotion. Paul and the two Gentiles were seized and dragged out of the Temple, and immediately the doors were shut. They were dragged across the Court of Gentiles, down the passageways, and into the street, people following and shouting. The Gentiles were struck repeatedly and then released. (For, it was sometimes true that some unwitting Gentile wandered by mistake into the Temple, and no one actually ever put one of these to death. Ignorance can be overlooked. They are severely chastised and sent on their way, knowing to never do that again. Sometimes they are fined, or made to pay for a sacrifice to be made on the altar. These two were fortunate, for the wrath of the people came down upon the head of Paul, who should have known better.)

They were beating Paul and beginning to take up stones to kill him, such was the people's rage at this offense, when some Roman soldiers, hearing the commotion, intervened and stopped them. Thinking Paul was some rebel or maker of trouble, they arrested him and took him off to the jail to be interrogated.

And that was the last we ever saw of Paul.

Later, we were to hear that Paul told them of his Roman citizenship, which entitled him to a trial, and after he was held in Caesarea in jail for a time, he was taken on board a Roman ship and sent to Rome.

* * *

Shortly after this incident, Simon Peter died of old age. There is, outside Jerusalem, a small graveyard of Followers of the Way, and this is where we buried Peter: or, Simon *bar* Jonah. This was his real name, and the name that was inscribed on his headstone. Many of the early deacons are also buried there. The first generation was now almost all gone, and still the Kingdom had not arrived. We all prayed that this was because the Lord was giving the world more time to repent, to be baptized, and to turn from the path of destruction; and we prayed that it was not too late, that we were not already on the path of destruction.

Meanwhile, James was worried. The Zealots and Sicarii were stepping up their activities in Jerusalem itself, so more Roman soldiers were sent to the Antonia Fortress, and that garrison was now filled to brimming. James told us all—he told anyone who would listen—to take stock of his or her soul, for bad things were soon going to come.

Then word reached us that a great fire had burned in Rome and that the Emperor Nero had blamed and put to death many Christians for this thing.

Chapter Twenty-Five

It seems necessary to now take a step back from the narrative and explain in some detail what had been going on in Rome since Yeshua's crucifixion and Resurrection.

At the outset, the Romans paid Followers of the Way no mind at all, seeing us as just another sect of Jews, which is what we are (or were, largely, until the number of Gentiles being converted outside the land began to exceed our own numbers in Palestine, and they started saying Yeshua was a god, or at the very least, God's literal Son). The first signs of trouble came under the Emperor Caligula, whom I have already mentioned, the successor to Tiberius and a man who, from all I ever heard of him, may not have entirely been in control of his senses or his mind, and his own followers murdered him. Caligula enraged Jews everywhere by wanting an idol of himself to be erected in the Temple. A coalition of Jewish leaders was sent to Rome to plead with him to not do this thing, but this rash young man seemed more interested in asking us why we did not eat pork and would not budge on the issue, for he saw himself as a god, and he threatened to kill us all if we did not also worship him in our Temple. Of certainty all Judea would have erupted into rebellion on the spot had Caligula's statue ever been erected, but he was murdered before this ever came to pass.

There was, however, one good thing that occurred under the reign of Caligula. A few years after the death of Yeshua, the Syrian legate removed Pontius Pilate from his office due to the continual complaints about his cruelty, theft of Temple funds, corruption, and the vast numbers of crucifixions he ordered. Thus, Pilate was returned in dishonor to Rome, where he was then exiled to Gaul. Indeed, we also saw some justice when Caiaphas, the High Priest, was finally removed from his office at this time, after his long appointment, for his collaborations with

Pilate. After Caiaphas, there was a series of High Priests, most giving us no trouble if we gave them no trouble. An uneasy peace reigned, largely due to the words and teachings of my uncle James, who taught that violence was never the Way; and since he was perceived as a righteous Jew, the people listened, and, as should be clear, he was popular among many of the various Jewish groups.

After Caligula, the Emperor Claudius came to the throne, who expanded Agrippa's territory and gave to us yet another "King of the Jews," whom, as I have already written, was the Herod who was friend to Caligula, or the first Agrippa, who was then succeeded by his son, Marcus Julius Agrippa. These Herods were not vicious in the way Pilate was vicious or the first Herod (the Great) and Herod Antipas were vicious, but Agrippa, as I have written, did slaughter James the son of Zebedee, called Thaddeus, and tried to do the same to Simon Peter. Also, there were still Roman prefects whose job it was to help them with tax collection and the keeping of the peace; so, very little changed. The only trouble the Emperor Claudius had with the Jews was in Rome, when he tired of the continual bickering between the Jewish Followers of Yeshua and those who were not. He temporarily expelled all Jews from Rome, but not from all Italia or the nearby provinces, so this expulsion was not to last for long.

Next Claudius' adopted son came to the throne, the man of great wickedness whose name I wrote down yesterday. Now this Claudius, after one wife had betrayed him in adultery, had married his niece, Caligula's sister, in the manner of these *Kittim* who were forever fornicating with one another. The offspring of this abomination, even though he was not Claudius' natural child, was a horror to humankind: the Emperor Nero. By this time, as I have said, the Romans were calling Followers of Yeshua "Christians" and were accusing us of all sorts of horrible behaviors, the reason for which can be laid squarely at the feet of Paul, in his teaching of Yeshua as both a god and a literal sacrifice made to god to appease for our sins (which I still do not fully understand, since God is only One, and I do not know how Paul got the Gentiles to understand this tangled-up theology); and, by turning the Last Supper ritual of remembrance into a symbolic eating and drinking of the blood and body of Yeshua. So the Romans thought we were cannibals who met in secret to eat children! About this time Paul himself was in Rome, to stand trial, as I have stated before. Nobody knows when he was actually put to death by Nero; but it is said Paul was beheaded and not crucified because he was a Roman citizen. I am of the impression Paul met his end, however, before the Great Persecution conducted by Nero after the burning of Rome. But I cannot say with certainty.

Nero blamed the fire on "the Christians," but I live in doubt that true Followers of the Way would have taken such an act. But always, always, there are these splinter groups of Zealot-like persons who wish to fight the Romans and bring on the End of Times, so who is to say some of these did not indeed set the fires? Others say Nero set the fires, or had his men do so, so that he would have reason to rebuild an even grander Palace for himself. There circulates a story of Nero playing his lyre and singing of the fall of Troy as all around him the buildings burned and toppled. In any account, the people of Rome were only too willing to blame the catastrophe on those they called the Christians, because even if they had not set the fires, the Christians did not worship their pagan gods, so they saw the fire as the wrath of their gods being visited upon them for tolerating the Christians. But I must stress that I cannot set these things down as facts since no one I know was actually there, except for perhaps Clement, but since he was not put to death, I assume he was not near Rome at the time and was shepherding a flock in some other province.

No, at this time we were much more concerned with what was happening in Jerusalem and throughout Palestine. It was during this time that my uncle James was killed in the horrible way with which I began this narrative. I wish to tear out my hair every time I think about it! All Jersualem, it seemed, groaned in anguish and madness.

Still, my brothers and I did our duty and returned in secret to the family tomb in a year to tenderly place the bones of James into his prepared ossuary. We wept many tears and prayed. As we began to depart the tomb, I had a sudden thought. I bade Zoker and James to wait, and I went back in. From the ossuaries of James, Mary of Magdala, and Yeshua, I removed the skulls. These I laid on the floor of the tomb such that, if a line were to be drawn to join them, a perfect triangle, or pyramid, would be formed, with Yeshua's skull at the point, or apex, which faced east. For me this symbolized the mastery of Yeshua, my beloved uncle, the Messiah and avatar of the Great Brotherhood, greeting the sun, with two of his greatest followers at the foundation corners.

I came out, and we rolled the stone back in front, and you will read shortly why it is we have not returned.

* * *

Now, as I have written, the execution of James upset all Jerusalem, for everyone knew the charge was false. Everyone knew of James's righteousness and his generosity towards the poor. The various Zealot factions were all outraged, for to them James had been a righteous Jew killed by the collaborators with the Herodians, who may as well have been Romans; many of the Pharisees were outraged, because even they knew the Law had not been followed in this matter, and the more liberal among them of the school of the Rabbi Hillel regarded James as a just man; the Qumran brothers were outraged, for James had been a Teacher of Righteousness; but the new prefect, Albinus, did nothing when he arrived, so the Pharisees complained to him about the incident. All Albinus did was refer the matter to Agrippa. King Agrippa's response was to wag his finger at the High Priest by removing him from office, and that was all. No real punishment, nor consequence of any seriousness, for killing a man of peace who had committed no crime. This could not stand.

By then, the Sicarii had also stepped up their movements in Jerusalem itself, at one point a few years earlier killing the High Priest Jonathan as a traitor to Israel. And then the Roman soldiers appeared to be taunting the Jews as well, as if daring us to rebel, on one occasion exposing their sexual parts in the Temple and on another even burning a Torah. The final blow was when yet another new prefect, Florus, stole a vast quantity of silver from the Temple for seemingly no purpose at all beyond that of greed (at least Pilate's excuse when doing the same had been to build an aqueduct). Hence the revolt that had been simmering in a pot over a fire for several generations reached a full boil, and the lid of the pot blew off. The people had suffered enough.

Beforehand, my uncle Simon, who had replaced James as Bishop of all Bishops and Head of the Jerusalem Church, could plainly see what was coming, for as I have written, James had even said before his death that a war seemed forthcoming. This was when Simon gathered the family, others of the community who would come, and those among the Qumran brethren who would come, and we fled here, to Pella and the surrounding area. I stress that we did this not because we feared death or a confrontation with Rome, but because we are not men of violence. That is never the Way, and it is not what Yeshua taught: those that take up the sword will die by the sword. Neither did we form an easily discernible community, for we arrived here in shifts, so to speak, over the course of about eight months. Simon and the Elders set up camp in the cave of John, where Yeshua had also taken refuge many years before. Artisans such as myself took up residence in the city of Pella. Others, who were farmers and laborers, worked for landowners in the countryside as tenant workers. Therefore we stayed near to Judea, in the Decapolis territory, praying for our brothers and sisters and for every Jew, and praying for peace, but we were also outside of Judea, Samaria, and the Galilee, which erupted, as Simon had anticipated, about half a year after we had relocated, into a horrible, horrible, protracted fight, and many were to die, and after some seven years of strife, it all ended with the Romans destroying everything, including Qumran, Jerusalem and the Temple, the final stronghold at Masada, and scattering many Jews to the four winds, taking many as slaves to serve in foreign lands, among them Followers of Yeshua as well.

At first, of certainty we thought that perhaps the End of Times had truly, finally come, except that the *Kittim* ultimately won the battle, and the angel of the Lord never appeared to help us.

Now I will go back in time and describe in more detail what happened, and if it is disjointed, I apologize, for it has all arrived to me in bits and pieces, being recent news. As I have written, bandits, Zealots, the Sicarii, and any other disgruntled Jew, it seemed, had taken to murdering Roman collaborators on almost a daily basis in Jerusalem. The prefect Florus demanded that the Elders hand over to him those guilty of these acts. Of course they could not, not knowing who the guilty were, so they begged his pardon for the sake of peace in the city. Florus, enraged, refused, and sent soldiers from the Antonia Fortress and from Caesarea into the city to murder people at whim, among them prominent Jews. Many died.

When the land erupted into full rebellion, young Jews joined the Zealot cause in swarms so that we at first outnumbered the Romans. In Jerusalem, the garrison at the Castle by the Temple was quickly wiped out. Then the Syrian legate sent in a larger force of soldiers to attack Jerusalem, and these were also destroyed. They had grossly underestimated the anger and numbers of the people, and this battle was a rout.

At first, then, it seemed the Jews had won the war, or at least had won Jerusalem. The Zealots held the Holy City, and it appeared the Romans had abandoned Palestine as a province. Jewish coins were struck to celebrate the retaking of the land and the expulsion of the Herodian collaborators from the Temple. Even in Pella, we celebrated, although Simon, reluctant to act prematurely, counseled patience. A letter had reached him from Clement, who had returned to Rome it appeared, informing him of what was happening in that city.

Therefore, I will write a quick summary to place all in perspective. The Jewish revolt had commenced towards the end of the reign of the Emperor Nero, but that wicked man, after forcing many of his friends—including his own mother!—and army commanders to commit suicide or be killed because he feared a plot against him, was finally declared a public enemy by his own Senate and forced to commit suicide himself. The madness of these *Kittim*! They had imploded on themselves! However, Nero had already appointed his proconsul in Africa, who had been exiled there for some absurd reason—I think it was for dozing off during one of the emperor's interminable readings of his own bad verses—to take back the province, shortly after the Jews had revolted; having also killed any other person of the Augustan dynasty as possible threats to his throne, Nero and his untimely death thus left a vacuum of power in Rome. There was a quick succession of three men who were made emperor, but they were toppled almost as quickly as they took the office.

Despite these conflicts, the Flavian general Vespasian, as he had been ordered, had commenced his quest to reconquer Palestine and Jerusalem, with his own son Titus helping to command the legions. These numbered some 60,000 men. They had destroyed their way through Galilee, killing or enslaving many, and cleared that area of rebels; they proceeded through

Samaria and other outer-lying regions, doing the same, wherever there were rebel strongholds; they reached Jericho and destroyed that city; they reached Qumran and burned it all down. I weep when I think of the Community of the *Yahad* that had not joined us, and I weep over the loss of the many scrolls, and I pray they were buried safely in some place. It was the practice to store some in a few nearby caves in the cliffs when the library was overflowing, so I pray the Romans did not bother to seek out rebels in those caves and burn all the holy writings.

Finally the Romans reached Jerusalem and laid siege to the city. But all came to a halt because the city itself could not be attacked without permission from the emperor.

Hence I record here now that Simon had been wise. I know he, my brothers, and I, and some of the Elders, had discussed returning to Jerusalem on several occasions. My uncle, however, reasoned that it may not be the End of Times, for the Son of Man, neither angel nor Yeshua, had yet arrived on the clouds in his glory. Indeed, had Yeshua not spoken of wars and strife that would precede the End of Times? So we would wait, and continue to pray for our Jewish brothers and sisters, and not return to Jerusalem in haste.

Then word came to Vespasian that many legions desired him to be made emperor; upon this news, he and his legions marched towards Rome, and after winning a great battle, he was officially made emperor. Rome quickly stabilized under this man. So the chaos that had been Rome lasted in actuality only for one year: this was how quickly events were taking place. Then Vespasian sent his son, Titus, to Egypt to secure the support of the legions there, and of the compliance of the people, to ensure the continued supply of food to Rome and its armies. Finally, Titus was sent to recommence his father's siege of Jerusalem, with Titus marching in to add yet another 20,000 more men from the Roman soldiers in Egypt to the legions already there.

So the original light that shone on us all turned out to be only that illusory calm which comes before a great storm.

Some few more had had the foresight to flee Jerusalem during this lull when they heard that the Romans were coming back, but most put their trust in God and stayed within the city, preparing to fight to the death if necessary. Also, rebels who had escaped from Galilee had fled into the city, so it swelled to almost bursting. But by this time, already the city had become divided against itself. Any leader who counseled moderation in the face of all the legions of Roman soldiers was put to death—not by the Romans, but by our own people. Two main factions of Zealots and Sicarii fought for control of the Temple, but I am told there were even others, controlling various sections of the city. Have mercy on their souls, dear God, for we Jews had now become just as foolish as the Romans had been! In anticipation of the siege, much grain had been stored up, with oil and wood, and it is said the siege could have lasted many years had it not been for two things: the Jews fighting amongst themselves and the Romans stripping the area of all surrounding trees to build an extra wall around the city to stop supplies from entering, and to build a siege tower with which to scale the last wall into the city. (The first two walls had fallen quickly.) Jerusalem may yet have stood half a chance fighting the Romans as they entered the city, however, if the warring factions within had not burned each other's food stores, in the belief that this would force everyone to stand and fight, rather than flee.

It is hard for me to write this down, but I believe our own infighting helped the Romans in their cause. As I have said, Jews within the city who wished to surrender or even counseled negotiation were put to death. The Zealots would not let anyone leave, and they guarded the gates. Any person who did not support their imprudence was treated as a traitor. So now they were all trapped within with no food.

Therefore all the Romans had to do was camp outside Jerusalem and wait for the city to starve and for the infighting to weaken the forces within. Agrippa (this was the second Agrippa) himself circled the wall, pleading for surrender, promising leniency would be given. They scoffed at him, for he fought against them, bringing his own troops to assist Titus. The traitor Josephus, who had abandoned his men in Galilee and now assisted the Romans, having had the audacity (or so I have been told) to call the Emperor Vespasian the Messiah, circled the wall, pleading with the Jews to surrender, also promising that leniency would be granted. No one believed him. And then it was too late. Anyone caught escaping the city, managing to get past the Zealots, even if just to gather weeds to eat, for they were starving, was crucified and placed in full view of those within the walls. Others were disemboweled by Roman soldiers in an attempt to find any jewels or coins that had been swallowed. Those within were trapped, starving and dying, and they knew it.

Why did God not intervene?

After allowing the people to go hungry for a time, the Romans finally broke through the last wall with ease, much as a giant swats at a fly and kills it instantly, even though he has not even used but a quarter of his strength. The Romans then streamed into the city, running through with their swords whomever they encountered, until, it is said, the streets ran red with blood. They entered each house, killing even the elderly, the women, the children, without discretion. As they left each house, it was torched. The screaming, the wailing, the blood, the fires—it was an unspeakable horror. Finally the Romans reached the Antonia Fortress to recapture it, and this they leveled so that they could breach the Temple walls with their siege weapons. Once they breached the Temple, they just as easily destroyed the very last of the Zealot hold-outs, and then the last Sicarii in the Sanctuary, who all fought them bravely, hand-to-hand, but they were vastly outnumbered. Once these were all dead and the Temple utterly defiled, stained with the blood of the Jews, corpses fallen around the altar, the Romans began their thievery. They stripped the

Temple of its gold. They raided the treasury. They stole the menorah, the altar, the golden trumpets and the table of the shewbread—anything of value. Then, at last, they set fire to the Temple and threw down the stones.

All that remains of it now is one western wall, not even of the Temple itself, but only the wall that retained the platform upon which the Temple was built.

And therefore the prophecy of Yeshua came to pass. Not a stone was left standing.

Finally Masada, the last stronghold, was destroyed. Masada fell just two years ago, after yet another protracted Roman siege. But it is said the men, women, and children there did not fall to the Romans. Rather than be killed by them or made into slaves, their last act of defiance was to take their own lives. May the Lord also show them His mercy.

And now I have come to the end. My uncle Simon is now tempted to rebuild a small church in Jerusalem with some of the stone of the thrown-down Temple, but he is also reluctant, for it may upset the Romans, as well as its seeming perhaps disrespectful to the memory of the Temple itself. So we shall wait and see. At the present, the Romans seem to be ignoring any Jew who has remained in Palestine, much like when the anger of a landowner who whips his slave is spent, and he sits, exhausted, unable to beat the slave any longer. I have heard that some rabbis have gone, or will be going, to Yavneh, to discuss ways to keep the Jewish traditions alive and to sort out how to worship God in the absence of the Temple. As for us, the Ebionites, we may be forced to travel farther east, or go into Egypt, or perhaps to Arabia. Meanwhile, a few tent encampments have gone up, one near the ruins of Jericho, and I am told some rebuilding has taken place in Jerusalem, but not much. It is too disheartening. One encampment of Followers of the Way has taken root in Ein Feshkha, where is located the spring and good land for growing some of the crops that fed Qumran. My little church here in Pella is expanding, although we remain cautious and ever vigilant, and we meet in secret. My daughter Rachel preaches most eloquently. I love to listen to her. Her voice—the voice of the next generation of Followers of the Way—gives me hope.

We welcome Gentiles into the fold, and, following James, we do not require of them circumcision. We do not forbid them to eat their own foods, to which they are accustomed. All we require is that they do not eat blood or the meat of strangled animals or of any animal that has been sacrificed to a pagan god, as James directed. And they also must not fornicate in the manner of the Romans: which means not marrying nieces or divorcing and marrying another and so on, as I have previously described. When we take the communal meal of remembrance, there are two tables: one for the Jewish followers, one for the Gentile. This does not mean one group is better than another. We call each other brother and sister and together do things to help the poor—for, as Yeshua once said, the poor are always with us.

Every now and then I am asked to preach, to clarify matters, because word from Gentile Christian theology—the teachings of Paul, to be truthful—in other lands reaches Pella, and people have questions and are confused, and I answer them with authority, but I feel inadequate doing so since my own voice is frail and trembles with age. I think I am like Moses, telling God that I do not speak well, and I require an Aaron! Thank the Lord for Rachel. Simon, who is older, fares better than I. Still, people listen respectfully and like for me to lay my hands on their heads and bless them, for I myself have been touched by Yeshua, and blessed by him, and I think it is a way for them to feel closer to him.

Well. We have survived, and with the blessing of the Lord we will continue to survive, until the End, or until the End of the Age. I do wonder who shall succeed Simon, for he is certainly to die soon. My grand-nephews are too young. The most likely candidate I would guess to be Symeon *ben* Symeon, the grandson of Cleophas.

And now I must stop, for I feel a profound sadness, and I will seek out privacy to shed tears for our scattered people and the loss of our Temple and the destruction of our land—even though I still hold hope. Always hope. And, I would not worry Rachel.

Epilogue

At the end of this long story, some things I can say for certain. My uncle Yeshua was a gifted man. He taught us, while he was tried and tested, many times. He loved humankind. He loved every living thing. He did his best to share what he believed. He suffered and died nailed to a beam of wood that was secured to a tree. He wished to show all that death is nothing to fear, and he demonstrated the true capacity of human beings through his works and his spiritual Resurrection. He wanted us to continue to spread his message of salvation through loving kindness and forgiveness and the good treatment of others. He would have rebuked most fiercely any man or woman who called him a god. He would have said there is only one God, but we are *all* the children of God.

For Yeshua, salvation was, or is, something all of us already have, within us the image of the Divinity who created us, a Divine Being with whom we are challenged to attune. We are all already immortal souls, yearning to fully reunite with God through the evolution of our spirits. Self-purity, good works, control of emotions springing from any well other than love, compassion, purging yourself of self-will or the folly of selfishness, and above all, deeply knowing your inner self, can lead you to the Divine. If you are truly a Master, the Holy Breath descends upon you, or perhaps more accurately, it awakens in you, to act out the Divine Will on the earth. Then you, too, may be an avatar—someone who evolves our very conception of God because you and God become like unto One. You are capable of miracles. I am capable of miracles. Each of us, using the Personal Trinity—body, the immortal soul, and the inner spirit that makes us each the person we are—is, in fact, an aspect of the Divine in its pure potentiality. Together, perhaps, all humanity when joined, are pieces of God becoming more knowledgeable of God.

Then there are things I cannot say for certain. Being an avatar or Master who has received the Holy Breath and who has developed his inner light into a great light that shines upon us all does not make you God, but with each retelling of Yeshua's story, he goes from rabbi to Messiah to literal Son of God, and now, finally, to God Himself among the Gentile believers. It is like unto a fisherman who catches a small fish and each time he tells the story of catching this fish, it gets larger and larger until it is a great monster of the sea. Yeshua, a very large fish to begin with, has become more immense than the great fish that swallowed Jonah. It is most strange to me to think of my uncle as a god. That seems to me much too Roman, with the Caesars always pronouncing themselves gods, or the Pharaohs of Egypt, calling themselves gods. When Yeshua taught the people how to pray, he did not pray to himself. He told us all to pray to "Our Father." And even then, he did not mean "Father" as a person but as a Divine Presence, the creative force of Love that brought all into being, mother and father. Perhaps the End of Times will come when all of us realize we are all avatars, and change ourselves and save ourselves, rather than making avatars into gods that will come back and save us.

For, another problem with calling Yeshua a god is that then we are not challenged to be like him. Instead, we give ourselves permission to *not* strive for the perfection he urged us to aim for in his sermons; after all, what mere human can be as good, as loving, as forgiving, or as selfless as someone we call a god?

And more questions linger. If one is an avatar and ascends past this earthly level as Yeshua has done, does one become an angel, one of the Sons of Men? When I look at the stars in the heavens, my thoughts begin to run wild. The heavens seem so vast, so infinite, and God is so vast He must have conceived of many creations. I cannot know, although it seems like vanity indeed to believe God has the capacity to create only this one place in all that vast sea of the heavens, when He is Infinite. It is just so far away we cannot see it. Or, rather, are the stars ascended beings like unto our angels, watching over us and guiding us, if only we will listen?

Why do we never listen?

Does Yeshua's death absolve us all of sin and guarantee us a place in the Kingdom of Heaven, if we do good works and follow the Way? Or is his Way just one Way, and other Ways are equally true, as long as one's heart and motives are pure? Must we all continue to suffer and judge and kill one another, and will karmic causation ultimately need to cleanse the world by fire, if we stay on this second path, the one of destruction? Will the exiled Jews return one day to Jerusalem, as we returned from Babylon, but only next time to fight with, perhaps, the followers of Yeshua, both groups laying claim to the holy ruins of the Second Temple? Or will we Jews always be persecuted and ruled by others? Or, the Gentiles now having made Yeshua into a god, will terrible things be done in his name, due to lack of right understanding?

Or, perhaps, the Romans will invent yet another new god of Jerusalem, or a new prophet will come, and then even more religions will fight over the same piece of holy ground. So many things I cannot know, but I tremble with fear when I think about the many hateful and vicious acts I have recorded in just this single narrative, which spans only the course of about seventy-five years. At other times my heart aches, and I worry and am full of doubts, thinking that perhaps I am all wrong and consider my uncle Yeshua a Master only because our family wanted him to be and because the Essenes and the Great Brotherhood had trained him to be, and that, perhaps in the end, he failed in his mission.

Yet, I cannot see him as a failure. He suffered so for us, and proved to us the Resurrection of the spirit, and has challenged us to reach the perfection that he had reached, and to reach even higher.

And . . . he spoke such simple truths. If he has indeed managed, though not of his own doing, to start a new religion, is that a failure? Is that, in the end, a bad thing? Symbolically he could be seen as the God of the Piscean Age, a man who started a new cycle of beliefs, a man whose teachings and suffering transforms lives. Is this not much like the Buddha, who did not intend to start a new religion but meant only to correct the problems arising in Hinduism, that of social castes and perpetual suffering? Then again, no one has called the Buddha a god. Did Moses even wish to start a new religion, when his original intention was merely to ensure the survival of the teaching of the One God, as given to him by the Pharaoh Akhenaten?

What I do know is that if we all followed Yeshua's teachings, to treat one another as we ourselves would wish to be treated, there would be no more wars, no more hate, no more greed, no more arrogance and self-righteousness, no more rich, no more poor, no more enslaved, no more suffering. There would just be love, peace on earth, and unity with the Divine. The Kingdom of Heaven would be here, now. As Yeshua said, "The Kingdom of God *has* come to you!" Surely he meant for us to act as if it has, to act always from that place of inner knowing, the sacred heart, the holy sun within us all. In this way, paradise can be restored, perhaps without an End of Days—the first path.

Yet even now, some of his followers do not practice his words. They preach, but they do not practice. I cannot even say I have always practiced his words. In my next life, if the End does not come, I must do better. I hope that my spirit is spared, for I yearn to join God, to return home to the Divine Being from which we all were first created, to lose myself in the glory that is God.

Yeshua told us he would be with us unto the end of this age. I suppose if we do not learn the lessons he gave us, it will remain for yet another avatar to come with the passing of this new Piscean Age into the next age in the precession of the equinoxes, the Aquarian. Perhaps by then the next great prophet will be a woman! Ah, only time and history will tell. Human beings seem to learn slowly. I await the day we are all able to set aside petty little differences, retaining the traditions and religions of our own cultures while respecting the cultures and religious rituals of others, but recognizing that we are all united under, all the children of, one single Cosmic Divinity, a Divine Presence who loves each and every one of us. Yes, all will be well. One day, all will be well.

And now I must go back to the very beginning, and recopy over this narrative, smoothing out my grammar and polishing my Greek, and striking out some of my many digressions. Rachel has procured for me a new stack of trimmed goat skins and some new reed pens for just this purpose. I have mixed more ink. I have read aloud to Rachel parts of what I have written. She says she is anxious to hear the whole thing, as one piece. I have been ill again lately; may God allow me to live long enough to finish this task I have set for myself.

May mercy, peace profound, and love be yours in abundance.

Joseph of Pella

Acknowledgments

This book is a tapestry woven together from numerous sources: First, the NRSV of the New Testament and some books of the Hebrew Bible; among the canonical gospels, I relied mostly on Matthew, a gospel said to be similar to one used by the Ebionites, minus the first two chapters, which they omitted because they rejected the virgin birth. I also relied on information kindly disseminated by the present-day Nazorean Church of the Essenes on Mt. Carmel.

Second, I drew freely on the observations, discoveries, and writings of Biblical scholars and archaeologists; I turned most often to Bart Ehrman, Elaine Pagels, Karen King, Jodi Magness, Dan Bahat, James Tabor, Amy-Jill Levine, Jeffrey Bütz, Luke Timothy Johnson, Cynthia Chapman, John Dominic Crossen, Simcha Jacobovici, Reza Aslan, Robert Eisenman, Gary Rendsburg, James Charlesworth, and various scholars too numerous to name who have published over the years in the *Biblical Archeological Review*.

Third, I used bits and pieces of the Dead Sea Scrolls and Nag Hammadi documents and other apocrypha/non-canonical texts; of these, I relied most heavily on The Didache, the Pseudo-Clementine literature, The Book of Enoch, Jubilees, The Temple Scroll, The War Scroll, The Damascus Document, The Community Rule, Rule of the Congregation/The Messianic Rule, The Infancy Gospel of Thomas, The Gospels of Mary, Thomas, Judas, Peter, and Philip; The Secret Gospel of Mark, The Gospel of Truth; The Acts of Philip, The Acts of Thomas; The Pistis Sophia; the First and Second Apocalypses of James; The Apocryphon of James; and the Protevangelium of James.

Fourth, I turned to streams from esoteric Christianity, some of which is channeled work and some of which is work done with past-life regressions. My beloved imperator Harvey Spenser

Lewis, founder of the Ancient Mystical Order of Rosae Crucis (AMORC), Edgar Cayce, Dolores Cannon, Tricia McCannon, the Aquarian Gospel of Jesus the Christ, The Gospel of the Holy Twelve, and even the Urantia Book all found their way in here and there.

A few friends and colleagues lent a hand in various ways, namely Kimberly Cates Escamilla, Maria Krasinski, Jennie Walters, Susan Elia Macneal, Evan Evans, and Roberta Reynolds.

Thanks also go to Dominic James, Denise Smith, and the entire crew at Roundfire Books.

Finally, I thank my wife, Chelle, for forgiving me those days I became a hermit and for forgiving me those nights I woke up, reached for my laptop, and began tapping furiously away at the keys, needing to get something down before it vanished into the ether. Without her . . .

At Roundfire we publish great stories. We lean towards the spiritual and thought-provoking. But whether it's literary or popular, a gentle tale or a pulsating thriller, the connecting theme in all Roundfire fiction titles is that once you pick them up you won't want to put them down.